#Long

Surreal

ଞୠୠୠ
Book Three
Of
The Divine Trilogy
ଞୠୠୠ

by
R.E. Hargrave

xoxo,
R.E.H

R.E. Hargrave

Praise for Surreal

Views from the Beta Reader:
So many times I have encountered authors who want to please the readers at the risk of the characters losing their voices in the story . . . but in the end I walked away feeling like this couple did the talking and was inspired by RE's loyalty and trust she put in them.

She infused it with wisdom, compassion and emotions that took me as a beta reader all over the map. With each draft she produced, the story just became better and better. I truly believe you will find, this last book in the trilogy is by far the best yet.

~Beyond the Valley of the Books

"RE Hargrave put her heart and soul into this book!"

"Written to perfection as always from RE Hargrave. Catherine and Jayden's story continues in The Divine Trilogy. It has its love, drama and emotions. This one had a considerable amount of emotional moments to the point I nearly cried...so keep them tissues handy ;) I can't express how amazing this book is, how amazing the whole trilogy is and am planning to read them all again in the future!"

"The perfect ending for this wonderful trilogy."

~ Goodreads Reviewers

R.E. Hargrave

WARNING:

This book is a work of BDSM erotic fiction. It does include instances of polygamy and same-gender pairings in addition to moments that could be troublesome for some readers with regards to the intensity of some situations.

R.E. Hargrave

Table of Contents

Acknowledgements

Four years have elapsed since I began creating the "Divine" world. In that time I've met so many wonderful people who have been there for me in one way or another. From hands-on help to the readers who've taken the time to reach out and share their stories with me, I have treasured every encounter. This feels like the end of an era that has been one hell of a rollercoaster ride. Thank you to everyone that has taken the ride with me.

SPECIAL MENTIONS, WITH MY HEARTFELT APPRECIATION:
To my Husband and children, I love you.

To my internal support system—Tammy, Mich, Mavvy, Lorenz, Tori, Lisa, and Massy—thank you for every time you wouldn't let me give up, and for being the best friends a gal could ask for.

To my crew—Tbird, Rae, Tammy, Massy, Dawn, Christina, Chris, and Lucii—you helped me make Surreal the best it could be, y'alls input and guidance have been priceless.

To J.C. Clarke—to work with you always has been and always will be divine. Pinky swear, babe.

To my Irish sunshine—Kris—thank you for being there to set my phrasing straight.

To the Grand Wordmaster, aka my editor—Elizabeth M. Lawrence—thank you for making my words shine and teaching me so much over the years.

To my street team, The Divine Darlins—y'all are superstars and rock my world with your unwavering enthusiasm of my craft.

To the Twilight Fandom, all the bloggers, and last, but certainly not least, the readers—The Divine Trilogy would be nothing without YOU.

All I can say is "Lucky me," to be so blessed with such amazing people in my life.

R.E. Hargrave

ೲಌ
CHAPTER ONE
ೲಌ

At the beginning of their evening, Master left her eyes uncovered. While he bound Catherine's legs to a spreader bar and her wrists to fur-lined cuffs that dangled from the ceiling, he explained that he wanted his slut to see everything tonight.

Eyes wide open, she watched him move around her while he brought her skin to sizzling life with the cat o' nine tails. Sir Jonathan had suggested it as an interim tool until the couple could begin their private whip lessons with him. Wielded much like a flogger, the cat delivered the stinging bite of a whip but on a less intense level, making it a perfect beginner tool for the submissive and her Master.

He'd turned the thermostat down so that the playroom was frigid—to Catherine, at least. The submissive didn't have a stitch of material covering her body, and her Master was playing mind games with her. Just the sight of him attired in tight, black leather had started the boiling heat within her. Combating that inner warmth was the chilled air, drawing her nipples into hardened buds and making Catherine quite aware of the metal that pierced them.

However, the coolness of the room was soon forgotten by the needy woman once Master began to flail her. Delivered with a steady, controlled hand, the leather *thwapping* against her skin warmed her until the cold air became welcome, keeping her balanced and comfortable. Master had not taken up the wheel until her whole body was striped pink and white, with the exception of her breasts—they'd been spared the flogger and ached because of it.

Bound and spread for her Master's pleasure, Catherine kept her eyelids lowered until he told her to do otherwise. When she raised her emerald eyes at his command, she'd found him mere inches away, his own gaze dark with desire. She didn't dream of resisting when he pressed his lips to hers, welcoming him in then crying out in surprise when he ran the spiked wheel over her nipple.

New age music reverberated around Catherine and her Master, blending with the submissive's soft echoing moans while Master teased her flesh with a Wartenberg wheel. The inconspicuous device, which her *maimeo* would have associated with transferring sewing patterns onto fabric, rolled over her tender skin and soon became maddening. Another twenty minutes passed, during which he teased her breasts with the spiked toy. She continued to assure him that she was "green," still eager and enjoying herself. Master was being cautious of her still-healing nipples, for which she was grateful although part of her wanted to ask him for more. Her nipples throbbed, desiring to be pulled and twisted despite the low, constant ache that had been with her since Sir

Landon had run the cold steel through them a few weeks before.

"There. I think you're prepared well enough now." Master's strong hands stroked her flesh with a tenderness that sent goose bumps up and down Catherine's body. Slipping his fingers inside her slick folds, he filled her, creating a firm pressure, and then stilled. "Always so wet and willing for my touch. You're a good little slut, aren't you?"

Catherine had enough wits about her to not fall for his trick. She'd not been given permission to speak. However, the submissive didn't fight the lustful moan that slipped from her lips when Master dragged his fingers from her heat with agonizing slowness, just to cram them back into her.

Bestowing a proud smile on Catherine, Master kissed her rough and quick. "Yes, you are, my *cailin maith*. As much as I would love to fill that cunt with my cock, we would both come too soon, and that would ruin my plans for later."

Her heart jumped at the new endearment he'd taken to using. She loved being his "good girl."

Catherine whimpered when her Master took his touch away, leaving her bereft and wanting. Every part of her felt alive with longing for any bit of friction she could get. The submissive fought the urge to plead for an orgasm, instead savoring his gentle attentions while he undid her cuffs and rubbed each of her wrists and ankles after the restraints came off.

"Your costume for the party is hanging in the en suite. You have twenty minutes to freshen up, dress, and meet me in the foyer. Do not touch that pussy. I assure you, Catherine, if you wash away the essence I worked so hard to get out of you, you will not enjoy the punishment. Do you understand? You may speak."

"Aye, Master."

Master beamed at her, and she straightened her posture. There wasn't much room to adjust, but Catherine prided herself on giving him the closest thing to perfection of which she was capable. After a searing kiss that left her lips puffy, he exited the room in a cloud of commanding confidence.

Catherine was slick and breathless upon his departure. She allowed herself a few moments to calm her breathing and center her focus before following him out of the playroom. Curiosity drew her toward the submissive's room. They'd discussed costumes for Dungeon & Dreams' Halloween bash just once. Catherine had told him that she trusted his decision and would wear anything he chose with pride.

Now she was giddy with anticipation, wondering what he might have selected. Would he have her in something cute and frilly, or would he be the stereotypical male who preferred the risqué? Naughty nurse, French maid, school girl—the possibilities were endless.

Arriving at the bedroom door, she paused, fingering the black diamond adorning her left hand. No matter what he'd chosen, she knew she could pull it off if Master believed she could. He would never humiliate her more than she was comfortable with. With that thought, Catherine turned the knob and walked into the room.

Waiting on the bed were two things, and both were made of metal.

A little bit nervous and a whole lot excited, Jayden paced the foyer. He couldn't wait to see Catherine on display for him. Any normal person might think it madness that he wanted to take his jewel out into a public setting in so little, but it was pride that drove the Dom, not insanity.

His close friends knew of Catherine's latest body modifications, but this would be the first time the couple had gone to the club since the changes had been made. What better way to show them off than to put her on display in a "cage" with himself as the "jailer"? Jayden had known the black leather outfit he'd chosen to wear would arouse his slut, which was the reason he'd worn it while preparing her.

The telltale clack of heels prompted him to move to the foot of the stairs. He looked up, fixing his stare on Catherine while she descended. *Perhaps the outfit was a bad idea after all*, he thought with meager amusement while taking her in. So seductive was she that Jayden wanted to ravage her right then and there. He had the sudden feeling that the night was going to be a long one.

Catherine's small feet were enclosed in black patent leather stilettos. When she reached the landing and spun for him, he could see the chain-work that ran up the back of the four-inch heel. He allowed his eyes to follow the curve of her strong calf and continue up her body. Held up by spaghetti straps, there wasn't much to the custom-made dress. Lightweight lengths of chain had been welded together, weaving the garment that now hung down to her mid-thigh. Two-inch spaces between each length of chain left nothing to the imagination. Her tattoo was on full display, as was her pretty, smooth cunt and the emerald J's in her nipples. When she twirled, the light from the overhead chandelier refracted off her black diamond.

"You look so amazing, my jewel. Please kneel."

Silent and obedient, Catherine took her place at his feet, her arms locking behind her back in perfect position. Jayden took a collar from his pocket and leaned forward. "Your servitude is surreal,

Catherine," he murmured while buckling her leather play collar around her neck. "You may speak."

"To serve you is divine, Master."

He smiled. "I expect that you will be on your best behavior tonight, slut. You will speak only when given permission, and I don't want you making eye contact with anyone but me unless otherwise directed. Do you understand?"

Jayden moved around her with slow, sure steps, waiting for her reply. It didn't come. "*Cailin maith*, you may answer me."

"Aye, Master. This girl knows her place for tonight and looks forward to making her Master proud." Her voice was breathy, and the Dom savored the knowledge that he had done that to her.

"That you do, my jewel. Rise, and show me the rest of your costume."

Catherine's breath caught at his words, but she did as requested. Standing before turning around, his submissive bent at the waist and grabbed her ankles with a muffled groan. Jayden's face broke out in a mischievous grin when he eyed the steel sunburst rays growing from the end of what he knew to be a rather large anal plug. The rays extended from the center, like hands, so that the custom accessory cupped her firm cheeks.

"Exquisite. Let's be on our way. I'll be driving tonight because Micah has requested the evening off. You have no objections to the Wraith, do you?" Jayden asked while snapping her leash into place on the collar then helping her into a dress coat.

The question was rhetorical. Jayden didn't expect an answer because it wasn't her decision to make. It was his.

ഇൗരു
CHAPTER TWO
ഇൗരു

Before even entering the club, Catherine could feel the electric vibe emanating from the establishment. So much had changed in her life since the first time she'd come to Dungeons & Dreams just over a year ago that, at times, it was hard to wrap her head around it all.

Warren greeted them at the door with a grin and a loud "Hulk smash," banging his fist against the bricks. Master laughed while the submissive kept her gaze down like she'd been instructed. However, curiosity got the better of her at the last moment. Catherine took a quick look over her shoulder when they passed to see that Warren had painted his muscular body green and was sporting a pair of ragged and torn brown pants. She stifled a giggle when he shot her a conspiratorial wink and brought his green index finger to his lips in the universal sign for silence.

Inside, Angelique Hendrix welcomed them and took their coats in her usual whimsical manner, whistling when she saw Catherine's outfit before crying with joy when she spotted the ring. The onyx-haired beauty looked much like she usually did, although she'd played up her looks a bit more to complete the persona of a Gypsy.

The submissive waited while her Master looked her over. She hoped everything was as it should be and to his satisfaction.

"Are you comfortable, jewel? Ready to do this? Please answer."

Catherine no longer held an ounce of shame about her body. Master had seen to that. Every scar, every imperfection, she wore them with pride now as part of who she was. Her Dominant had worked long and hard to help her get to a place in her mind where she accepted this as truth.

She couldn't wait to go through the interior doors and find their friends. "Aye, Master. This girl is ready to have some fun."

"Well then, by all means, let's have some fun." He pushed the door open, tugged on her leash, and passed through into the darkened club.

Eager, the submissive followed her Dom while he moved forward with caution, which allowed their eyes time to adjust. There was no doubt they were at a Halloween party. The speakers overhead belted out *Monster Mash*. Before lowering her eyes, she took in the spider webs that were draped across the human-sized bird cages, and skeletons made use of the manacles mounted to the cinder block walls. Bowls of candy, popcorn, and assorted nuts sat atop the tables amongst goblets of blood-red punch.

Catherine knew the punch was non-alcoholic. The safe and sane part of their Lifestyle wasn't possible when alcohol was involved. While Master shared a glass of wine with her on occasion, it was rare and never more than a single glass.

The submissive viewed what she could from beneath her downcast lids while they traversed the room. Her heel-clad feet were hidden in the swirl of fog creeping across the floor. She was pretty sure Master was walking her around the perimeter, taking his sweet time to show her off to all in attendance, and Catherine loved it. Her body ignited at the daring of it all.

Quiet words of appreciation for the art adorning her flesh were whispered, making her stand taller and prouder. The movement forced her breasts to press against the chain, and the admiring whisperers shifted the focus of their praise. Master paused in their journey to chat with some of the members, giving credit to Sirs Shawn and Landon for their contributions to her new look.

"Did I hear my name?"

Catherine smiled when she heard Sir Landon's familiar voice. That meant Paige couldn't be too far away.

"Landon, my friend. We were just making our way to the table," Master proclaimed.

Sir Landon's carefree chuckle rolled around them. "I noticed you were taking the long way."

"What can I say? If wanting to show off my beautiful woman is a crime, then I'm guilty. Lock me up and throw away the key."

Her insides warmed at his words, and she hummed with contentment when he pulled her leash taut, bringing her face near to his so he could claim her in front of their audience with a searing kiss. When he released her, leaving her dizzy, she was grateful he was still close. She might have fallen to the floor otherwise. As it was, Catherine had to rest her hand on his forearm for a moment to steady herself.

His brown eyes shot up in surprise at the contact, and then softened when he took in her flustered state. "Oh, my wanton little slut. If you swoon so easily at a kiss, I fear I may break you before the night ends." His smile was wicked.

Catherine's body clenched at the promise his words held, and she was unable to refrain from letting a small moan slip out. The plug sat heavy in her backside while her dress gripped her body with just enough pressure to help her hold herself together. However, the submissive was unsure how much longer she could stand to wait.

A lone finger met the underside of her chin, and with a gentle pressure, Master tipped her head up. Their noses touching and eyes fixed on one another, he murmured against her lips, "I love you."

The pure heat of the moment was too much, and her body shuddered, racked with the smallest of orgasms. Catherine's lips parted, and her eyes grew wide at the same time as Master's.

"Did you just—"

"This girl is so very sorry, Master. She's never done that before," she blurted out. The submissive felt shame at the lack of control of her body. *How could she have come with nothing but words and a look?*

"And now you are speaking out of turn. My my, Catherine. Whatever will I do with you?"

She kept her mouth closed and lowered her eyes back down out of respect.

"Aw, Jayden. Give her a break. It's a pretty special bond that can result in a hands-free freebie, ya know what I mean? Come on. Paige has been chomping at the bit all day for this. Best not keep her waiting anymore."

Master tapped beneath Catherine's chin and she peeked up, the movement reluctant. She'd made a newbie mistake and quite possibly ruined his plans for the evening because of it.

"Don't fret, sweet girl. Landon is correct, and I'll let you have that one. Besides, all that did was release the tiniest amount of pressure. You've got more, so much more, for me to draw from your willing body." His fingers had gripped her piercings, and while he drew out the words, he elongated her nipples.

Relief, adoration, and desire for her Master coursed through Catherine, his words washing away her worries. When he began walking once more, she fell into step behind him, the festive mood returning.

80CX

Jayden moved through the crowd, beaming each time he heard another compliment for his jewel.

He was grateful for the excuse to stop and chat so that he could discreetly shift his junk. His cock wasn't letting up. It kept demanding attention. The pressure was intense, but he welcomed the building need that pushed him deeper into his Dominant persona.

The club had a great turnout for the evening. Due to the tight press of bodies around them, keeping up with Landon proved a bit difficult while they moved around the edge of the dance floor. After few minutes, they reached a cordoned-off area with a large table surrounded by wide, comfortable looking chairs. As a board member, Jayden was entitled to a few club perks, and VIP seating during events was one of them.

Momentary *déjà vu* crept over him while he took in the assembled group. Six weeks ago, he'd called on his friends to assist with Catherine. Back then, his stomach had curled in on itself at the idea of what he had to propose. Now the sight of his friends brought nothing but delight, and even some enlightenment.

The first thing to catch his eye was his secretary, Samantha. Looking at her now, it was clear why they'd never been a suitable match.

27

She was dressed in white satin trimmed with pink lace, a baby doll nightie with matching ruffled . . . *knickers* was the word that popped into his head. Her blonde hair was divided into pigtails, and a cock-shaped pacifier hung about her neck from a pink ribbon. His secretary was a *little*—a submissive who acted like a little girl and who would please her Daddy in return for the loving guidance and discipline that only a Daddy Dom could give. Sitting on Ryan Bishop's lap while she nestled into the crook of his neck, Samantha looked content.

Jayden shared a nod with Ryan, smiled at Samantha, and then moved his attention to the next couple at the table. "Jonathan, so glad you could make it out tonight." He extended his hand, and Jon stood up from his seat to take it. There was a coiled whip hanging from his hip and a Stetson perched atop his head. Spurred boots and leather chaps completed the picture, although the loin cloth Jon sported in favor of jeans may have done the trick, too.

"So are we, Jayden. I didn't get a chance last time we were here, but I'd like to introduce you to my sub, Kelly."

Following his friend's line of sight, Jayden recognized the pretty blonde from the whipping demo, and he grinned at the leather enclosure on her neck. "You old dog! I didn't realize that you'd finally settled down and collared yourself a sub. She is collared, right?"

Tossing his head back to laugh, Jonathan's blue eyes sparkled under the dim lighting. "Yeah. Kelly has been amazing about keeping up with my travel schedule and always at the ready when I need her, so I decided to make it official. Teaching a whipping class is so much easier when you have a sub who trusts without question. The clubs never have a problem setting me up with a female willing to feel my sting, but it's just not the same, you know?"

Before responding, Jayden looked Kelly over. Her neck wasn't the only thing with leather on it. Her arms and legs were encased in a sleek black material, vinyl or latex, with metal horseshoes affixed over the palms and feet, and the bit that sat between her teeth was attached to reins draped over her shoulders. Around her midsection was a wide strap, suggesting a saddle. The piece de resistance, a long, luxurious, white tail, protruded from her backside.

Impressed, he turned back to Jonathan, "She's a fine specimen, that's for sure. May I?" Jayden nodded in Kelly's direction.

"Sure thing, Jay."

"It's lovely to meet you, Kelly. Welcome to Dallas, I hope you'll enjoy your time here." When she turned her wide, round, brown eyes up at him and neighed, it was slightly unnerving. He smiled and tugged at Catherine's leash, pulling her forward to make introductions. "Jonathan, you remember my Catherine?"

"Like I could forget your filly."

Catherine's breath caught when Jonathan fingered his whip and tipped his head at her with an eager gleam in his eye. *Jeez, he really couldn't wait to get lessons going.*

"How are you this evening, Catherine?" Jonathan asked.

"This girl is well. Thank you for asking, Sir," she replied after getting Master's approval to speak.

Jayden had just begun introducing Kelly to his jewel when a boisterous "Ahoy!" sounded from behind them. He turned around with a big grin plastered on his face. Shawn Carpenter, his favorite artist, was decked out like a rogue sea-captain, unruly black curls perfecting the pirate costume.

Standing next to Shawn, Micah was an exercise in humiliation. He looked like he'd just stepped out of the pages of *Treasure Island*. The pride glowing from Micah's facial expressions told Jayden he was enjoying every second of it, though. A too-small red and white striped shirt molded against Micah's lean torso and had holes cut out for his perky nipples. Fitted trousers left no question as to what a lush ass Jayden's chauffeur possessed—round, firm, and tight. The 'cabin boy' had his light-colored hair tied back with a black scarf, which allowed Jayden to spot the new gold hoops adorning Micah's ears.

"Love the costumes, Shawn. Glad to see you two hitting it off so well, and Micah, well, he looks the part to a tee."

Shawn let out a low whistle, his eyes raking over Jayden and his pet in response. "Not looking too bad yourselves, hot stuff."

An urge to clarify that Catherine was His washed over him, and Jayden pulled her in close, causing her to stumble in her heels. Her palm came up to caress his neck, and they looked at Shawn together.

"You two are a sexy sight for sore eyes. Damn fine, indeed. Come here, doll, and let me see how that ink healed."

Shawn's request drew the attention of their group, in addition to a few other club goers around them, so Jayden decided to have some fun. "Yes, slut, let everyone see your ink. Get up on the table and kneel." He unclipped the leash and gave her ass a firm swat, smiling at the clink of metal on metal when her dress pressed into the plug.

"Aye, Master." She wouldn't dream of hesitating. Pride swelled within him, among other things, while he watched her take her place.

He shook his head when she waved at Paige and mouthed "Hi." Jayden's attempt to narrow his eyes and glare at Paige went belly up when Landon started laughing at all of them.

Everyone took turns getting up close so they could admire the detail in Shawn's work. Once people's curiosity was satisfied, Jayden helped her back down, and they took their seats. Well, he took a seat. His slut stood beside him so that he could stroke her flesh whenever the mood struck while the evening progressed.

☙❧

CHAPTER THREE

☙❧

Catherine could smell herself and could feel the slipperiness of her thighs each time her stance shifted. If Master's occasional smirks were anything to go by, he could smell her, too, and that excited her further.

The evening had gone forward without incident. In sporadic bursts, people stopped by their table to exchange the usual "Hi, how are you?" but for the most part, their little group was left to themselves. They visited amongst each other, catching up on the goings on in their lives. Catherine remained by her Master. Paige knelt next to Sir Landon, Samantha sat in Sir Ryan's lap sucking her binky, and Kelly stood beside Sir Jonathan, pawing her hoof on the floor, tossing her blonde hair, and whinnying on occasion.

Micah had accompanied Sir Shawn, and he seemed awestruck. All the times he'd driven Master's car to this very club, yet he'd never been *inside* D&D. This was his first time, and remembering how much there was to take in, she knew it was pretty amazing.

"What do you think, slut? Shall we have a small play?"

The words, said strong and clear, pulled Catherine's attention back to her Master. She'd been letting her gaze wander the club to soak in the sights all around her. "Aye, Master, if you wish." Distracted, she didn't know what she had just agreed to, not that it mattered in particular. Master had said the magic word—play. After almost two hours of teasing touches and firm pinches, she was more than ready for some relief.

Catherine waited while the crowd at the table all stood and said their farewells. Sir Shawn and Micah were the first to depart, followed by Sir Jonathan and Kelly, after Master had confirmed their first session the following week. Soon four remained—Catherine and her Master, along with Sir Landon and Paige.

At the sound of a tiny excited whimper, Catherine darted her eyes over to Paige, who was grinning ear-to-ear. Sir Landon winked at her before turning to leave, and Catherine felt her heart rate spike when her leash was clipped into place.

Master led, and she followed. She'd follow him anywhere.

Making their way deeper into the darkened club, Catherine's curiosity built. The submissive's inner whore was plumping her boobs and pinching her ass to make it pretty and pink.

Though she'd been but a few feet away from Paige for the last few hours, Catherine hadn't been able to take in her friend's costume, or Sir Landon's for that matter. She'd been too distracted—no, too focused on Master's taunting strokes that sent fire coursing over her skin to settle in the simmering pit of her stomach—to notice the couple.

Ahead of her, Paige sashayed, her fluffy, sky-blue skirt sitting high on her creamy thighs. Her usual long, blonde waves were tucked neatly away in a white bonnet, leaving her tanned shoulders and upper back on display. She had a slender waist anyway, but tonight it was made tinier, cinched inside a white corset edged with sky-blue lace. The girl pulled off a not-so-innocent dairy maid with ease, in particular when her Master marched in front of her, his long, muscled limbs covered in nothing but a loose pair of coveralls and a straw hat perched on his wavy blond locks.

While they walked, Catherine's mind raced with the possibilities of what the men had planned for them. She and Paige had gotten together a few times in the weeks following the amazing proposal weekend Master had arranged. She and her new friend had done lunch, gone shopping, and even taken to getting their pussies waxed together. Since Paige worked at Silver Spurs, it was easy for her to squeeze

Erin in with her whenever she did a lunch waxing. The two girls had formed a fast friendship; one that went deeper than most, given the intimate circumstances of their meeting and their Lifestyle.

On more than one occasion, their conversations had drifted to the topic of a shared play session. With tact, Paige had answered any questions Catherine had regarding scenes she'd done with the men. In return for her friend's honesty, Catherine had fought down any jealousy. She knew her Master, her Jayden, had not been with anyone besides her since putting the black diamond on her finger. She couldn't hold him accountable for actions performed in his past before her.

Besides, the talks with Paige had a tendency to leave her rather horny, and she'd admitted as much in her journaling, which brought her to now—she knew *they* knew what the submissive and her friend had discussed.

When the small group reached a private room at the back of the club, Steven unlocked and opened the door, then passed the key to Sir Landon once the group had entered.

Catherine felt her pulse thundering in her head and in her tight nipples. The door closed, the lock clicked into place, and a throat cleared.

"I'd wager you girls have had your share of 'tricking' this evening?"

When she turned her head toward the sound of Sir Landon's voice, she found he had a dimpled grin and a cocked eyebrow in place. Cutting her eyes to Paige, who had turned toward his voice also, Catherine gasped.

The front of her friend's corset scooped down beneath her breasts, putting them on display. But what had drawn the sound from Catherine's lips was the sight of glass suction tubes attached to Paige's nipples—the short, clear cylinders half-filled with pink flesh.

Master spoke, "Yes, I do believe it's now time for some 'treating'."

Catherine and Paige's eyes met next, and they both grinned before replying in tandem: "If it pleases you." Shaking his head in an attempt to hide his mirth, Master unclipped Catherine's leash and gave her instructions to strip. At the same time she was being seen to, Sir Landon was freeing Paige from the tubes and undressing her.

Catherine's body buzzed with erratic energy while the submissive waited for what would come next. The plug sat heavy in her ass, and she wiggled against it, feeling the wetness in her center grow with her excitement.

"Slut, see to Paige's nipples. They need soothing." With Master's first command, the scene began.

She went to her friend, eager to suckle the elongated nipples being offered to her. Her tongue swirled around and gathered the pliable flesh before drawing it in between her lips and sucking. The aroused submissive was getting into a rhythm and giving herself an inner high-five at Paige's whimpers, when a breath whispered across the shell of her ear—hot and lusty.

"Is my pet enjoying herself?"

A tiny moan slipped out, and Catherine had to use her teeth to hold the flesh in her mouth while she mumbled around it. "Aye."

She shrieked, dropping the swollen bud in surprise when heat bloomed in her ass.

"Aye what, slut?" He grabbed her chin, forcing the submissive to look her Master in the eye.

"Aye, Master." The words were breathy, disjointed, because his free hand had sneaked around to start working the anal plug free of her body with slow tugs and gentle reinsertions.

"Show me, *cailin maith*."

Obediently, with the desire to please guiding her, she dropped her hand down to seek out the damp cleft where her legs connected to her torso. Off to the side, Catherine was aware of Sir Landon's voice, but his words were unrecognizable. She'd lost the ability to think with any clarity due to the incoming onslaught of sensations. Paige's soft lips were on her left breast, two of her own fingers were up inside her pussy, and then Master extracted the plug the exact moment he pressed his mouth to hers.

With a whimper, she drew her sticky fingers free of her body and brought them up to display, spreading them nice and slow so the evidence of her arousal stretched and glistened between the digits. A snapping lid echoed in the air, and Catherine wrenched herself away from her Dom to inhale a jagged breath when cold liquid began to coat her stretched rear passage.

Dark brown eyes stared back when she raised her face at Master's whispered request. He didn't blink or break their stare when he wrapped his lips around her fingers, compressed them with his tongue, and sucked. Her own eyes fluttered closed at the intensity, and once again, she was caught unaware when Sir Landon spoke near her neck—just before he applied firm pressure against the column of her throat with his teeth.

"I'm almost jealous that your Master will be fucking that pretty ass of yours. *Almost*, but it's going to be amazing feeling my yella rose coming on me while you feast on her little pussy."

And just like that, Catherine's body shuddered with her second unauthorized orgasm of the night. Although it was a tiny one, she still had not asked permission.

Everyone froze, and the submissive held her breath.

CHAPTER FOUR

꧁꧂

Had that really happened? Jayden couldn't believe she'd come again with no effort on his part. It was like she was on a hair trigger, and he loved it—his jewel's body got so responsive when she was worked up like this.

Letting her fingers slide from his mouth so he could take a step back, he watched Landon draw Catherine back against his chest, bare now that he'd shed the coveralls. His friend's knowledgeable hands kneaded her tits, tugging on her nipples the way she liked.

Jayden hurried to yank his shirt over his head, then worked his way out of the black leather that had been hugging his legs and ass all evening. The fresh air was a welcome relief on his hot, sweaty skin.

Because he'd wanted to thank Landon and Paige for their help with his and Catherine's anniversary plans, Jayden had been scheming with his friend to make tonight special. Both the girls had made mention, either in their journals or in casual conversation, that they wanted to have a couples' playdate. The plan had been to work them up to make sure they were good and horny, and then have some fun in one of the club's private rooms.

Using a club room would keep it on neutral ground. The two Doms had also agreed that Paige should get a bit more of the attention, seeing that Catherine had recently been pampered, so to speak.

Showing extreme patience, Paige awaited her instructions. Meanwhile, his jewel was emitting lewd noises under Landon's ministrations, which made

Jayden's cock ache. He took the swollen length in his fist and stroked it while moving toward where Paige stood.

"Kneel."

She complied and already had her mouth open when he reached her.

Without preamble, he rubbed the head of his cock over her lips, then pressed it between them. He waited till she'd closed her red lips around his tip, then he popped it out, groaned at the feeling and did it again. Reaching down, Jayden found her stretched nipples and flicked them with his fingers till she started panting, opening her mouth wider so he could slide in deeper.

Landon wanted his yella rose to get better at deep-throating, so he had agreed to let Jayden work with her. In Jayden's experience, he'd found that distracting a submissive by arousing them through pain and pleasure tended to help them focus less on the difficulty of swallowing a cock, and just do it.

There was a certain satisfaction in being right.

As expected, Paige's throat opened like a morning glory to Jayden, and he acted. While the Dom pleasured himself with her mouth, he maneuvered their bodies around so they could have a better view of Landon and Catherine.

His friend had stopped playing with Catherine's tits, and she was now on her knees before him. Watching her lips stretch around Landon's cock had Jayden thickening in Paige's mouth. Needing to back off and cool down a tad, he extracted himself and went to a tantric chair that sat in the corner. The two men had agreed that approaching the piece of furniture, which looked much like a lazy 'm' with the second hump higher than the first, would be the signal to move the scene along.

Landon groaned when he had to break the vacuum seal Catherine had on him, but he did and brought her to Jayden, stopping to collect Paige on the short journey across the room. The foursome gathered around the sensual piece of furniture. Dark red leather molded to the chair's curves and was finished with large brass tacks.

Jayden beckoned his pet with a snap of his fingers. She came to his side and waited while he got comfortable. He stood at the head of the sex chair, his crotch resting against the plush, upper curve.

The room was silent apart from their heady breaths while he assessed the set up. "Landon, do you mind if I make a couple of adjustments to our earlier plan? I think it might be a little precarious, and one of the girls could get hurt."

"Sure thing. Tell us where you want us." Amusement threaded Landon's voice.

Jayden was pleased that everyone seemed so relaxed. He'd hoped this would be fun for all of them, and so far, it was turning out that way.

"Okay. You're up first then, my man. Straddle the chair, then recline so that your head is down on the footrest. Your ass will be down here by the back." He patted the dip in the seat while Landon went into action. "Paige, you'll straddle your Master's lap next, facing him, but don't slide down that veiny cock until you're given permission."

She whimper-moaned but hurried to obey with a quiet, "Yes, Sir."

"Catherine, my divine little slut, get your pussy over Sir Landon's face." The widening of her emerald eyes spiked his heart rate. She was so beautiful that, at times, Jayden found the very air he depended on being whisked out of him. Corny though the coined phrase was, he was "twitterpated" where that woman was concerned. Giving his head a shake to dislodge the mushy emotion, he directed his attention back to the task at hand. They could be cuddly later, at home. Now was the time to let his dominant side get a deep drink of the illicit pleasure he craved.

"Aye, Master." Catherine's eyes twinkled, and the apples of her cheeks flushed. She turned to face him, then proceeded to back up into the position she'd been told to take, like the good girl she was.

While Jayden conducted their arrangement, he continued to stroke himself, almost without care, but with enough grip to keep his cock hard. Not that it was difficult to maintain an erection with all the bared flesh in his line of vision.

Jayden and Catherine now stood at either end of the chair, facing each other across the distance. Between them, Paige stood astride Landon waiting for her queue to lower her body.

Once everyone was in place, a single word slipped from Jayden's lips: "Now." The room filled with the lusty murmurs of appreciation when each of their groins received an erotic caress.

Catherine spread her stance to better offer her smooth cunt to Landon's eager tongue, a pleased sound escaping her when he made contact. Paige's head slammed back against the chair, a mangled cry breaking free the moment she impaled herself on Landon's cock.

That was Jayden's opening. It was nothing for him to pin Paige's shoulders against the high, curved back of the chair with his large palms when she arched back. He pushed his cock into her open mouth and a sense of power filled him when her eyes shot open in surprise at his unexpected action. Momentary panic skipped across her pretty blues, then they ignited into a dark fire within. He groaned with satisfaction and pressed his thighs tighter against the chair.

"That's it, Paige. Relax your throat, open for me . . ."

With short pulses, then long, and then back to shallow again, Jayden worked his length between her lips. He hadn't told Catherine what to do with herself, other than to sit on Landon's face, so when he managed to draw his eyes open and look over at her, the intense look she wore surprised him.

Catherine was fixated on the sight of his cock in Paige's mouth—she had to be. If he hadn't known any better, he'd have sworn what she was *seeing* was turning her on more than what she was *feeling*. Landon's dexterous tongue couldn't distract his jewel from ogling her Master's cock. Jayden shuddered in response, and Paige gagged below him. He pulled back to give her some air.

"Does his tongue feel good on you, Catherine? Do you like the way he flicks it across your clit?" The Dom loved to tease, to elicit begging and desperation from his pet.

Red hair billowed around her when she dropped her head forward, nodding. "Aye, Master. Sir Landon is good, but this girl still prefers your tongue."

While the answer pleased Jayden immensely, Landon must not have agreed, because Catherine let out a shriek then tried to stand up and pull away. Landon had been ready, though, and his hands snaked out to catch her around the thighs, allowing her to lift up but not step back.

"You'd rather feel the sting of my bite than the lap of my tongue, then?" Landon murmured from between her legs.

Jayden chuckled at his friend's response. Without a doubt, that little nip to her pussy had just brought her closer to orgasm than twenty minutes of sensual licking could ever do.

"No, aye . . . this girl does not know . . ." Catherine was babbling, and her words were scattered.

By the time he got her home tonight, she was going to be exhausted and ready to sleep like the dead. That didn't mean Jayden was prepared to go easy on her right then, though. Not even close. Instead, it was time to step up the intensity level.

"Jewel, I think you need some pussy of your own to enjoy. Get your mouth on Paige. Now." The Dom snapped his fingers then thrust into Paige's throat.

"As you wish, M-master . . ." she trailed off as Landon's tonguing resumed.

While Catherine leaned over the Dom's body, searching for Paige's smooth pussy where she was mounted on Landon, Jayden reached down to twist and pull on the blonde's hypersensitive nipples.

Between the three of them, Paige could only endure.

The poor girl was unable to even attempt to thrash about, given that she was skewered from both ends— much like a piece of meat roasting over an open pit. Catherine's tongue was the final straw, it seemed. Arched backward over the chair, Paige's small tits encased in Jayden's large hands, Landon's cock buried deep inside her from below, and now, Catherine lapping at her protruding clit, the submissive began to moan.

The sudden burst of arousal threatened to catch up with Jayden. In the urgency of riding out Paige's unauthorized orgasm, Jayden feared shooting his come down the girl's throat, and he had to pull out.

"Tsk, tsk, little girl. I don't think you asked permission for that," the Dom sneered with a wicked smile, stretching her nipples outward and away from her slim frame.

Paige groaned, and it was a tad surprising how guttural it sounded since her usual voice was very female, light and airy.

Releasing Paige's swollen buds, Jayden stepped out and around the head of the tantric chair, moving toward his jewel. The few moments it took him to shift around aided him in regaining his composure, and he was able to once again control his urge to come. As she had not been told otherwise, Catherine continued to slurp at Paige, the wet sounds hot and bothersome to Jayden.

In the best way possible.

The second he was close enough to reach her, Jayden placed an open hand on Catherine's shoulder. He trailed his fingers down her body, letting them press in a little harder, a little deeper, the farther down her body he went. When he reached her creamy ass, it afforded him the opportunity to bring his fingers in closer until he was gripping her rounded cheeks in each hand. Releasing her, he brought his right palm up to smack the plump under-edge of a cheek, and just as quickly, he turned his palm over to bring it back down on the top side of her ass. A loud set of cracks echoed in the room, and her flesh reddened.

Catherine cried out in surprise, but at least she knew he was moving into place behind her now.

Using both his hands, the Dom grabbed more of her juicy ass then leaned over to bite and nibble while pulling her open and closed, revealing her still-stretched passage. The lubricant Landon had drizzled on her when they'd first arrived in the room remained. Jayden slid a single, testing digit into her.

When there was no resistance, only a needy whimper for more from his pet, Jayden allowed a second and soon a third finger to penetrate her while he rotated his wrist, stretching her. Feeling Catherine's body accept him with such abandon and willingness stoked the fire in his loins, and he was soon lining himself up with her ass. Truth be told, he'd been excited about taking her like that since he'd first seen the plug in place earlier that evening.

Little by little, he inched forward, going slow to give her time to adjust despite having prepped her with the plug. Jayden was large, he knew, and to cram his cock up her ass could still be damaging. A few minutes spared at the beginning for proper stretching equaled unbridled thrusting once they got going.

And once that happened, the entire group lost themselves, without care for which bits dangled, bounced, or touched.

Landon and Paige slowed to a lackadaisical leisure fuck while Catherine continued lapping at her friend's pussy. Landon did the same between Catherine's thighs, Paige rolling and gyrating her hips to work her body above him.

Sliding into Catherine's constrictive channel was pure pleasure for Jayden so much so that he enjoyed taking his time building up a gradual, steady rhythm inside her ass.

The atmosphere had become near humid from their heavy breathing and perspiration, not to mention the release of other fluids. Erotic whispers and whimpers of longing escaped the women. Jayden and Landon added their own bass tones to the mix when they groaned.

Together as one unit they moved, a well-lubed machine with just the right amount of friction rubbing where each needed it. Breathy pleas met heady denials until the Doms knew there was no more holding back and they granted permission, at last. In a round of musical orgasms, the men and women took their turns peaking, then receding into a state of mush.

Tired but sated, the friends ended up saying their goodbyes for the night and going their separate ways after they'd collected their costume pieces. Catherine was asleep before Jayden's car pulled away from the curb.

ಬಂಞ
CHAPTER FIVE
ಬಂಞ

Jayden's eyes flew open before the alarm could wake him. Today was a big day—Erin was moving in with him at long last. Considering she'd accepted his proposal, it would've been ludicrous for her not to take this step. That didn't lessen the importance of the gesture to him, though.

At first, his girl had threatened to stay in her apartment until they were legally wed, which almost gave him a heart attack. It wasn't like they needed to protect her purity or some shit. He'd had her in every possible way imaginable, short of him growing a second dick.

He leaped out of bed and took a quick shower to rid himself of the last traces of sleepiness that pulled at him. Bypassing breakfast, Jayden made his way to Micah's apartment door. The coolness of the November morning tried to penetrate his bones, but he knew in another hour the temperature would be rising, right along with their heart rates and core temps while they worked.

"Morning, Sir." A weary-eyed Micah pulled the door open and leaned into it, dragging a hand down his face. Despite the covering of blond facial hair, his former submissive maintained a boyish appearance. Jayden smirked. "Late night?"

"Maybe . . ." Now Micah grinned, looking more alive.

"Come on. The others are going to meet us at Erin's. I thought we'd pick up some coffee and donuts on the way."

"Give me ten minutes, and I'll be ready."

Micah closed the door, and Jayden made his way to the garage. He cranked the truck's ignition and pulled around front to wait for his assistant. Forty-five minutes later, they were distributing hot drinks and pastries to Erin, Paige, Landon, and Shawn.

"Are you sure about this?" Erin fussed at his side, sipping her mocha. "It doesn't feel right leaving you guys to do all the work while I run off with Paige."

Landon's barking laugh broke the quiet morning. "Darlin', you haven't been immersed in a day of wedding planning with her yet. I dare say we'll be less tired than you by nightfall." He winked at her, and Paige huffed at him.

Jayden hugged Erin close. "And it won't be just be Paige," he confessed.

"What do you mean?" Erin asked. With her hair pushed back off her face and fixed in a braid, the emerald coloring of her eyes sparkled in the morning sun.

"I might have mentioned our plans for today to Mom—" A honking horn cut him off. "Speak of the devil." He laughed when a sleek black car pulled up next to the group.

"Jillian's here?" Erin's beauty was enhanced by the genuine happiness of her smile.

"You don't mind, do you, Erin?" Paige piped up. "Jayden said she offered to join us, and I thought it'd be fun."

"Are you kidding? Of course I don't mind." She turned to Jayden. "You always manage to surprise me. One of these days, I'm going to get you back, mister." He moved in for a kiss, then he whispered low against her lips in a seductive tone, "That's a promise I look forward to you keeping, *pet.*"

"Jayden, let that poor girl go and get over here to give your momma a hug!" Jillian Masterson stood next to the open car door with her hands on her hips and a huge smile plastered on her painted lips.

After a final squeeze, he released Erin from his embrace then closed the distance to his mother. They shared a long hug before she let him go to draw Erin in for a round of affection.

"You didn't drive up this morning, did you, Jillian? You would've had to be up awful early."

"No, dear." She tossed back her auburn hair, elongating her leathery, tanned neck to laugh. "I'm way past doing early mornings. Malcolm had business in town yesterday, so I came up with him. We're staying at the condo."

"Mom, ladies," Jayden tipped his head to each of them, "we can catch up tonight at dinner. Now let's get this show on the road, because the sooner the move is done, the closer this wonderful woman comes to being all mine." He lifted Erin's ringed hand to his lips, laying a possessive peck on her knuckles near the black gem.

"You heard the man, girls. We've got money to spend!" Jillian said.

They dispersed, Paige stopping to hug Landon and getting an ass smack for her efforts.

Erin handed her apartment keys over to Jayden, giving him a farewell kiss before she joined Jillian and Paige in the hired car. Jillian stuck her head out of the window and informed the boys they'd bring dinner back when they returned.

Landon stood next to Jayden, shaking his head and waving at the trio as they pulled away.

"Alright, boys, let's do this." Jayden clapped his hands and the quartet ascended the stairs to Erin's apartment.

ഔഇ

B efore the driver could pull the car out of the parking lot, Jillian was talking a mile a minute. Paige seemed to be following it all, but Erin felt lost while she watched them banter like a tennis match.

"Whoa, slow down. We've got all day and the only actual appointment is at the dress shop. Paige is meeting the seamstress who will be doing the custom work on her gown."

Paige and Jillian shared a look.

"What?" Erin was on alert at once.

"Erin, sweetie," Paige began.

"Oh, no. This isn't about me today, Paige. We're doing stuff for *your* wedding, not mine. Jayden and I haven't even set a date yet."

"And? Your point is?"

Jillian took over, "Because you two haven't pinned down a date is all the more reason to get busy straight away. There is so much to sort out and plan—"

"I don't know. In my mind, I kind of thought it would be small and quick."

Paige snorted at that, and Erin kicked her friend in the shin before she said something not suitable for Jillian's ears.

Jillian leaned toward Erin to lay a manicured hand on her knee. "I've waited almost forty years for my son to get married. This is one event that will not be downplayed if I have anything to say about it."

Erin felt her eyes begin to lower under the intensity of her future mother-in-law's stare. Paige nudged her knee, which reminded her that submitting to *one* Masterson was quite enough.

"Surely you've got some ideas, Erin? A general time frame and colors, for instance."

The young woman's thoughts went to the ink encircling her waist. It captured her heritage, the red and green braiding a permanent reminder of her Irish roots.

Paige clapped. "That dreamy look means yes!"

Across from her, Jillian relaxed into her seat with a smug grin, and Erin threw up her hands. "Fine. Bear in mind that I haven't discussed any of this with Jayden yet—and no decisions will be made without him."

"Yeah, yeah. Give us the goods, girl," Paige said with a snicker.

"Well, I don't want white." She glanced at Jillian and was relieved her preference didn't seem to be an issue. "I've always liked ivory—it's more down to earth. For accents, I was thinking red and green. Oh, and for flowers," she smiled at the secret she shared with her Dom, "I'm pretty sure Jayden will want orchids."

"Good, keep going." A notepad had materialized in Paige's hands, and she was scribbling at a furious pace.

Erin shook her head in amusement. "I like roses, too, so maybe we can combine them?" She continued to ponder aloud. "As for when, that will all depend on when Jayden can take time off from work—"

"My dear child, that boy would move mountains for you. If you have a special date you want, I assure you that business will not keep him from making it happen."

"July twenty-fourth."

"What was that?"

"It's the day my *maimeo* passed. July twenty-fourth. My whole life, I always thought that if I did get married, it would be on that day—to honor her memory."

Jillian's eyes softened. "My son found himself a rare treasure. Our family is so fortunate to have you joining it, Erin."

Erin reflected that the son's jewel had become the mother's treasure, and she beamed.

Paige continued taking notes. "July, huh? Well, that gives us nine months. Piece of cake, right?"

They laughed, and then Erin settled in to enjoy her girls' day out. Their first stop was the florist. No surprise, Paige and Landon—meaning Paige—had chosen to go with yellow roses for all the floral pieces for the ceremony and reception. Around the yellow would be dusky pinks and soft peaches, creating a sunset in bloom.

While her friend tried to bribe the florist into including out-of-season—and illegal—bluebonnets in her bridal bouquet, Erin was off to the side, admiring the orchid case. A particular plant with deep crimson blooms appealed to her and made her think of her lover.

"It matches your hair—I think it would be the perfect choice. Maybe some white rose buds tucked in around them?" Jillian whispered over Erin's shoulder.

The flowers *were* rather pretty, and she could easily picture them in a waterfall bouquet held in front of her while she walked down the aisle. Erin took out her phone and snapped a quick picture to show Jayden later. For good measure, she also took a close-up of the label with the orchid's information. *Cymbidium; Khan Flame Lucifer.* Kind of ironic that her chosen flower would have her dancing with the devil, so to speak.

Next up on Paige's to-do list was running by a local business, The Soap BARista. She was building her wedding around a beach theme since Landon had proposed at the beach, and she wanted to have custom soap and lotion sets done as thank-you gifts for the wedding party. After much deliberation and scent-sampling—which ended with all of them sneezing—Paige selected a hibiscus and coconut set for the ladies. A 'driftwood bonfire' set infused with coarse sea-salt for optimal exfoliation would go to the men. The ceremony details would be printed on the labels, which would be in complimentary sunset colors.

Before they left, Erin also ended up purchasing some soap that reminded her of Jayden. The natural ingredients made the finished bar look a bit earthy, like him—his amber eyes, the warm tone of his skin, and even how his hair shifted from brown to black like wood grain. However, it was the scent that won her over in the end. Infused with saffron and honey, the smell was simply . . . *Jayden*. She had to buy it.

By that point, the ladies had burned off their early morning coffee and pastries and were approaching starvation. They found a little hole-in-the-wall Tex-Mex diner and soon were gorging themselves on a family-style taco sampler. With chicken, beef, shrimp, and fish tacos to choose from, everybody was happy.

"It's a good thing we're not doing measurements today, just discussing the design elements, because I must've gained ten pounds in there," Paige said upon their exit from the restaurant.

Groaning and holding her stomach, Erin agreed. "Maybe I'll just nap in the car while you guys go into the dress shop." She was feeling nervous about that particular errand all of a sudden.

Jillian and Paige each hooked an arm through Erin's and all but dragged her back to the waiting car while she mumbled, "I'm guessing that's not an option?"

❧❧ CHAPTER SIX ❧❧

The girls chatted while the car made its way back across the Metroplex. Jillian relayed stories about her grandkids. Erin was excited to see everyone later that month for a big Thanksgiving feast at the Flying M Ranch. It sounded like the twins were growing up way too fast.

Their conversation drifted through various topics—Erin's work, how her Da had settled in as part of the crew at the Ranch, and Landon and Paige's honeymoon plans in Jamaica.

The last had Erin fighting not to laugh. She knew the couple were booked into a BDSM retreat on the island. However, Jillian did not, and Paige's answers were as vague as possible.

In spite of a midday traffic jam on the George Bush Tollway, they managed to arrive at Tailored by Tanner with ten minutes to spare.

Diane, the dressmaker's assistant, welcomed them with a broad smile that displayed chemically whitened teeth. After collecting their drink requests—sweet tea all around—she disappeared into the back.

To pass the time, Erin strolled around the compact sales floor, browsing.

London Tanner made one-of-a-kind dresses. When a wedding gown was custom, the price tended to fall into two categories—"a lot" or "If you have to ask, you can't afford it."

Paige wanted a pirate-wench gown done in peach and white seashell colors. Erin had sat in on their initial consultation and had *not* asked about the cost afterward. The thought of that much money being spent on a costume that would be worn for just a few hours was ludicrous.

London's business was steady enough that she was able to spend her days consulting and designing. The physical production of the dresses was left to her crew of skillful seamstresses. This left her time to create about one gown each month to go on the rack at a lower price. The catch for the reduced price gowns was that London designed each piece with a certain body type in mind. If a bride loved a dress and it wasn't in her size, too bad.

Erin froze, her eyes landing on an ivory strapless gown mounted on a dress form in the corner. Though it wasn't quite finished, it had an understated simplicity, and she was drawn to it. A moment later, she was fingering the draped material of the lower skirt. *Chiffon, and it feels so luxurious.* The thought pulled a tiny giggle from her. She couldn't believe she was getting excited over a dress. It was so . . . girly. *How could she resist the gown, though?* It made her think of a Greek goddess but with a modern edge— the sharp points of the bodice's edge and the angular ruching over the torso gave it a corseted look. When she stepped back to take it in, it dawned on her that the gown looked about her size.

A bustle of activity erupted behind her.

"Hello, hello, hello." London made a grand entrance. "I'll be with you momentarily, my darlings. Let me put my things down and grab the designs—"

"I have them here, Miss. Let me take your bag." Diane stood by, ready to swap with London.

"Ah, wonderful. Remind me to give you a raise, Diane. Paige, Erin, lovely to see you again. And who is this?" London turned her attention to Jillian.

"This is my fiancé's mother, Jillian Masterson. She's up visiting from Sweetwater. Jillian, this is London Tanner." Erin watched the women size one another up and rolled her eyes. She'd never understand high society. "I love the dress you're working on in the corner, London. Is it for a customer?" Maybe a distraction would move this along.

London tossed her head back and laughed. "Aren't you an observant little thing? In fact, it is, but we'll talk more about that later. First, I've got some amazing ideas for your wedding ensemble, Paige."

London's voice faded into the background. The knowledge that the dress was spoken for hit Erin with an unexpected sadness and disappointment. Even so, she turned her head to look at it again and sighed. The longer she looked, the more convinced she became that it would fit her. If only she'd known what she wanted when she'd come with Paige last time, Erin could've put a bid in with London. Now some other bride would be wearing *her* perfect dress.

"Oh, what a great idea, and I love the color. What do you think, Erin?"

Paige's excited twang brought Erin out of her thoughts. "I'm sorry, my head drifted for a minute. What did you say?" Out of her peripheral vision, Erin noticed that Jillian was observing her with a curious look on her face.

With a frown, Paige reached out to touch Erin's forehead. "Are you feeling okay, sweetie?"

"I'm fine, silly. Show me."

They spent the next half hour perusing sketches of Paige's gown and her bridesmaid's dresses from multiple angles. London had nailed Paige's vision for her dress and had delighted her with a wrap-style bridesmaid gown design that would be fun but formal. Done in deep coral, the dresses would fall to mid-thigh and were designed to look like bathing suit cover-ups, except with fancy pleating and jeweled twist work at the neck.

"You're pleased, then?" London asked.

"Absolutely. What you've come up with, London," Paige clasped her hands and beamed, "has captured my vision and then some. Thank you so much. I can't wait to see them finished."

Relaxing, the designer let out a breath. "Well, that will be the next challenge. February isn't much time, Missy."

Paige blushed and shrugged her shoulders. "I'm sorry! I didn't know what I wanted, not until Landon suggested we echo our beach trip. Once he said that, I couldn't get the idea out of my head, and I came straight to you."

"No worries, dear. I have every confidence my girls will get your order ready with no mishaps. Now, I'm going to let Diane take you to the desk and sort out your payment and fitting schedules while I have a little chat with Erin."

Erin's eyes snapped over to the woman. *Had she done something wrong?*

London had a soft smile playing at the edge of her mouth. "Jillian, would you be a doll and join us?"

Jillian agreed at once. Erin fell into step behind the two women and soon found herself back in front of the ivory gown. "As I was saying earlier, Erin, you are observant. I think you know that I take on side projects when inspiration strikes?"

She nodded, her heart catching in her throat.

"Well, I was inspired when you came in last month with Ms. Halston."

Now Erin's mouth popped open while the pieces began to fall into place. "Oh? How's that?" She brushed an errant red tendril from her forehead, trying to keep her encroaching excitement tamped down.

London turned to the dress and waved her hand over it. "This."

Happy tears began to prick at the corner of Erin's eyes, and she felt the smile spreading on her face.

"You were so subdued and patient while I talked with her. After you left, I envisioned this beauty. I sketched it at once, along with some ideas for bridesmaids and flower girl dresses. Those are still on paper, but I wanted to have the gown ready today to surprise you. Of course, the price will be reduced since I was taking liberties."

Next to Erin, Jillian scoffed. "Money really isn't an issue for my son."

"Regardless," Erin coughed, a bit embarrassed, "I'm gobsmacked at the gesture, London. Thank you. I've not been able to take my eyes off the thing since I noticed it. Even at full price, I'd buy it. It's just what I wanted without knowing it."

London squealed, and it was odd seeing the usually composed woman let her hair down.

"Wonderful! Let's have you try it on so I can see how close I was on your size, and then we'll see about setting a time to go over the rest of the sketches."

Blinking, Erin found herself in a whirlwind of activity when Jillian ushered her into the changing room. Behind them, London followed with the dress.

"Everything off but your panties," the designer ordered, drawing the curtain closed across the opening. "Given the bodice design, you won't be wearing any brassiere with it, so I need to ensure we don't leave it too snug or too loose."

Eager to see the dress on, Erin yanked her shirt off and unclasped the front of her bra without thinking. She tossed her bra to the side then moved to step into the gown.

"Good God, Erin! What are those?" Jillian had one hand over her mouth in apparent shock while a shaky finger pointed at Erin's chest—where her son's initials dangled.

Oops. At least she'd worn high-waist panties today—her tattoo hadn't been revealed. Wouldn't that have been awkward? Her mind was looking for an explanation but coming up blank. She knew their Lifestyle wasn't an open topic between Jayden and his parents. *Shit, shit, shit.*

"Oh, Jillian, you know how the young kids are these days. Ink and metal all over their bodies. Though, I have seen some beautiful artwork," London said, taking the lead.

Erin exhaled, blowing the curls back from her face. More locks had come loose when she removed her shirt.

"But why an initi—"

"I did it for Jayden," Erin blurted out, cutting over Jillian, whose eyebrows rose with her sharp intake of breath.

"What do you mean?"

"Well, um, like London said, it's a . . . thing. Anyways, I did it as a surprise for Jayden, to, um, well, show him that I belong to him . . ."

Jillian blanched, and Erin could've kicked herself. *Jesus, she was fucking this up.*

"Suck in, and puff those girls out," London ordered while slipping the dress up over Erin's hips and torso, covering the offending jewels.

Easy enough, she thought and inhaled a jagged breath. The bodice cinched against her like a corset. Though snug, for the first time since this ordeal started, Erin relaxed, and her mind cleared. She felt safer when bound.

The silence was broken when Paige sauntered into the crowded changing room and her mouth dropped open. "Jayden's going to bust a nut when he sees you in that!"

It was so crass, and so Paige-like, that Erin burst out laughing, and the others joined in. Catching her breath, Erin caught her friend's eye across the small space. Paige winked. *Sneaky girl.* Erin owed her one.

The distraction seemed to do the trick, and once everyone had convinced Erin she had to get married in London's design, they finished up and piled back into the car. For the moment, the incident seemed forgotten. After stopping at the spa to get mani/pedis done, they picked up some curbside dinner from a nearby restaurant and were soon on their way back to the Villa.

ॐॐ
CHAPTER SEVEN
ॐॐ

"Please, Erin, it's been a busy day for you. You should be enjoying the first night in your new home and putting up your feet. Let Jayden and me do the cleanup."

"Oh, you don't have to do that," Erin tried to argue, but Jillian wasn't having it.

"I insist, dear. Go on upstairs and relax. It'll give my son and me a chance to catch up with each other." Jayden's mother moved behind his chair and brought her hands up to rest on his shoulders.

Erin's eyes sought his, probably hoping to see that he had some idea of what Jillian was up to. He didn't, so he shrugged in response. The last thing he expected was Erin mumbling "I'm sorry" against his lips when she came over to kiss him before leaving the dining room.

She knew something after all—and had left him to face it alone. Jayden blinked at the spot where Erin had been, then turned to face his mother.

"Hop to it, son. I'll wash, you dry."

Fifteen minutes later they were almost done, but Jillian hadn't said a word. It was bugging the hell out of him. His mother had always been excellent at the game of 'let the subconscious guilt build until you cave and confess all.' *Dammit, she was going to win this round, too.* Except, he had no idea what he needed to confess.

"I thought you wanted to catch up, Mom? An actual exchange of words would be a good way to facilitate that," he prodded while trying to keep his tone light.

"M'hm." She rinsed a glass and handed it to him.

Jayden tried again. "Did you girls have fun today?"

"Mostly."

"Mostly?" *Uh-oh, here it comes*, he thought.

"Yes, Jayden. Mostly. The day had been delightful, and then I was helping Erin try on a wedding gown—"

"Mom! You weren't supposed to hijack her today."

"Hush your tone with me, young man. You should've seen how she was eyeballing that thing. Besides, London insisted she try it on. It was the one by the way—she's stunning in it."

Jayden groaned.

"Anyway, the cut of the dress doesn't allow for a bra . . ."

This wasn't going to be good. He swallowed, bracing himself.

"I saw—well, that is to say, I think I saw—"

"Just spit it out, Mom."

Jillian sucked in a breath. "Why does Erin have your initial hanging from her," she lowered her voice to a whisper, "breasts?" His mom stood there blinking at him.

He erupted with laughter, which carried on full and hearty for several minutes, while he watched his mother's emotions warp and change from awkward defiance, to shock, and then concern.

It was the last which sobered him, and he stepped forward to take her hand. "Mom, you and I agreed several years ago that my personal . . . preferences were not open for discussion so long as I was happy and not hurting anyone."

"Jayden Matthew Masterson," she gasped his name.

He could see her gears turning and knew he had seconds before it clicked.

"Are you telling me you tie up and beat that precious girl?"

A slight nod was all the answer he was allowed to give before her hands started flailing around her head and she began to pace, murmuring incoherently.

"Mom, enough." It still wasn't her business, and at almost forty years old, he would not allow himself to be scolded like a child.

Jillian's mouth opened then closed.

"Everything between Erin and me is consensual. I don't do anything to—or with—her or her body that she doesn't want. And I'm happy." Jayden wasn't sure where he'd gotten the balls to be this blunt with his mother, but she had to understand. He wouldn't let her think, for one minute, that what he had with Erin was anything but right.

Her eyes shot up to his, studying him. "You are."

He started nodding, a goofy grin reshaping his mouth. "Yeah, I really am."

Though never one for touchy-feely moments growing up, Jayden had always had a soft spot for his momma's hugs, and this time was no different. As soon as she wrapped him in her arms, a silent understanding passed between them.

With a final squeeze, his mother stepped back. "She's a special girl, Jayden. And you're special, too, son. I can see it when you're apart, and it's unmistakable when you're together."

"What's that, Mom?"

"How much you two love each other." She smiled and hung up the hand towel she'd been folding and re-folding while they talked. "I'm going to have the driver take me back to the condo now. Your father should be getting back from his meeting soon. You keep loving Erin with all that you are, Jayden. Pour your heart, mind, and body into it, and you'll survive anything life throws at you. Remember that."

Obediently, he nodded.

"See you in a couple of weeks at the Ranch. I can't wait to have all of my kids under one roof again." She kissed his cheek and walked out, tossing a wave back over her shoulder.

Jayden took a few minutes to consider the gravity of her words, not moving from his spot until he heard the front door close. His mother had said to love Erin with all of his being. Considering he'd been away from her most of the day, it was past time to show her just how much he loved her.

Starting with a spanking—for pleasure, of course.

෩൙

"Catherine O'Chancey, you have some explaining to do, little girl!"

She heard him shout from the hallway right before the bedroom door flew open. He'd lost his tee, and his jeans were undone, the fly hanging open. With the way his hands were perched on his hips and how his dark, hooded eyes looked at her, he appeared intimidating—and delicious. Erin squealed and ducked under the covers to the echo of his laughter.

"Oh, I don't think so." His voice was near—he'd come closer.

The bedding disappeared, and her body tightened all over. Excitement prickled her flesh, drawing her nipples into hard rocks and sending signals to her groin to prepare for her lover.

"Fuck, Erin. Where are your clothes?" he rasped out.

"Pesky things would just get in the way ... *Master.*" Aroused and wanting to be ravaged, she reclined back on her elbows and opened her legs, offering herself.

Large, powerful hands wrapped around her thighs, and then she was being dragged across the expensive cotton sheets. Seconds later, Erin discovered the rest of his clothes were now gone. In one swift move, he filled her with his cock, drawing a hiss from her at the force of the impact deep inside her.

With the next beat of her heart, he was gone and her body was being flipped over. Her hips were yanked upward, and his warm palm met the small of her back. Erin squirmed under the pressure of his hand while he slid it down her spine toward her head, where he gripped her neck then drove her face into the mattress.

She turned her head to the side, and a loud grunt escaped her when Jayden smacked her ass, which was sticking up in the air. This position allowed the strength of his strike to sink in and vibrate through her. Another pop echoed around the room, and white-hot heat danced across her bottom. Her body was responding, swelling and becoming slick—preparing to accept anything He offered.

Fingers slid into her wetness, making her choke on the air she'd been sucking in. Just as unexpectedly, they were taken back like his cock had been minutes before, leaving her open and empty. Yet another smack, chased by a flutter of gentle kisses upon her stinging backside, dragged a lusty sound from her lips.

"Are you a cock slut, Catherine?" He pushed a digit back in then teased it out of her. "I can see your welcoming hole. I'm watching those shiny pussy muscles of yours clench at the air in desperation."

Again he teased her, running his fingers over her swollen lips but not penetrating this time ... Back and forth he rubbed, coaxing her natural juices from within and heightening her need. At last, he pulled back to give her a succession of quick, sharp spanks, and then shoved his fingers back inside.

Grinding back against his hand, she huffed out a thank you to her Master. Resuming the slow, taunting rhythm, he worked in and out of her until she was begging for him to give her more, go faster—do something to get her *there*.

Then he stopped.

Again.

God, how she wanted to scream out in frustration. The whole of her body felt alive, like hundreds of pins were pricking her. Tingling all over, she didn't have to wait long for his next move. This time it wasn't his hand smacking her bottom. It was something heavier and wider, and it drew a loud satisfied groan from the submissive upon contact.

A peek over her shoulder revealed a martial arts target pad in his hand. With a loud *wallop*, the pad connected with her ass again. Catherine freed her mind to Him with a body-wracking shudder.

Master laid into her with the implement. Her lucidity faded fast with the rising levels of sexual need. One strike blended into the next until her bottom and the back of her thighs were nothing but a buzzing zone of warmth. The good feeling radiated outward from her core, and Catherine's breaths leveled to a controlled in-and-out. She was dropping, each spank taking her deeper into subspace.

Everything became fuzzy—a melding, warping blob of sensation and euphoria during which He allowed her to come several times before satisfying himself with her body.

∞

Erin woke a few hours later, needing a drink and to use the bathroom. She found a full glass of water on the nightstand, along with some ibuprofen, which she took gratefully once she scooted to the edge of the bed and discovered how tender her ass was. *He'd had fun with her.* The thought made her smile, and a warm feeling spread through her.

Coming back from the bathroom, she perched on the edge of the bed to watch Jayden sleep. A gap in the curtain allowed in enough moonlight for her to make out her man's features. In repose, the lines of his face were less intense, and she imagined his younger self used to appear like that all of the time before life and adulthood sank in their claws. Funny what time could do, how it could shatter dreams—or make them come true—in the blink of an eye.

Thoughts formed in her head. What if she'd met Him first, instead of Spencer? Would they still be the perfect match they were? Did the what-ifs really matter at that point? This was her life now, and she was content.

She maneuvered herself under the covers and tucked in next to him, smiling when he wrapped an arm around her without waking. Sleep overtook her with a final, distressing thought.

R.E. Hargrave

Did content mean happy?

ೞೲೲ

CHAPTER EIGHT

ೞೲೲ

With a languorous stretch, Erin shifted in the warmth of their bed. Despite the earliness of the hour, she felt energetic. It was time for them to start their holiday vacation. In a few hours, she and Jayden would be getting into the packed Wraith and heading south to Corpus Christi, where Jayden's sister and her partner were hosting the holiday festivities. They were both looking forward to spending time with the whole family.

Though only a month had passed since the family's Thanksgiving gathering, they'd had such a good time seeing her Da and Jayden's relatives that she was eager to do it again.

After the Mastersons had hosted the family at the ranch in Sweetwater, they'd all agreed Benny and Joon's first Christmas should be in their own home, meaning Stephanie and Veronica were up next on the hosting roster. Everyone was excited for the chance to dote on Steph and Ronnie's twins and give them a grand first Christmas.

The previous weekend, while shopping for his niece and nephew, Jayden had pretended to grouse at Erin's exuberance as she picked out toys and cute, tiny outfits. However, more than once she'd caught the sparkle of joy in his ocher eyes. That joyful glimmer had been paired with an easygoing grin, and there'd been no doubt to her that he'd enjoyed the outing as much as her.

Not all the shopping had been for the babies. Erin had convinced her lover he needed to give Steph and Ronnie more than a restaurant gift card—his apparent gift of choice, she'd learned. At her insistence, they'd ducked into a lingerie store, where Erin had been able to select a few tasteful but sensuous pieces for her future sisters-in-law. Now the whole lot, including the gifts for their parents, was tucked into the Wraith's trunk, covered in festive wrap and ribbons that the adults would appreciate *on* the boxes while the babies would have fun once it was *off* them.

It was easy to reflect on how her life had turned around for the better at Jayden's side. Erin snuggled closer, and he sighed, the hand tossed above his head coming down to scratch himself through the covers. She suppressed a giggle and moved her head closer to rest on his chest. For several minutes, Erin enjoyed the rhythmic rise and fall while he breathed at a steady, sleepy pace. Drawing her knee upward over his thigh, she slowed when nearing his crotch, then stopped altogether. A slight bulge had blocked her progress.

Erin slipped from beneath the covers and scurried across the darkened room to the en suite, the soles of her feet luxuriating in the plush carpet. After relieving the pressure on her bladder, she washed up and brushed her teeth.

Free from all potential distractions, Erin traversed the space and crawled back into the bed. She ducked beneath the covers to settle between her fiancé's legs. While she looked on, his semi-erect cock twitched and shifted against his toned stomach. She could imagine it saying in a teasing lilt: "Hi, how are ya? Fancy a play?"

It was definitely one of the times when she was thankful he insisted they sleep in the nude.

Licking her lips, Erin stretched her neck so she could reach his pretty cock with her mouth. After nuzzling his soft balls with her nose, she feathered kisses upward along his shaft—some with sealed lips, others with mouth parted so her warm breath caressed him.

No longer did Jayden sport a semi. He'd swollen to full size, the flesh was tight, and she longed to taste. Opening her mouth wide and drawing her lips against her teeth to prevent an accident, she moved over him. To Erin's surprise, she was able to complete three full tight-suctioned passes before a large hand wove into her hair. Seconds later he bucked up, ramming his cock against the back of her throat while preventing her head from moving. Her physical response was immediate, and her inner thighs became slick.

Fresh air rushed over her hot skin when the covers disappeared. Jayden tightened his grip on her red locks and pulled. Reluctant to let go of her treat, Erin had to allow his girth to fall from her mouth so she could be guided up the length of his body.

The surrounding darkness did not deter the couple. The moment she was close enough, their lips found the each other. Erin stretched her body atop his, and though she was small, she was cocooned in a sense of security. It didn't matter what position they tried. She never failed to fit against him like they had been made for each other.

Jayden's hand relaxed in her tresses while their bodies softened and molded into one another. Wide and warm, she felt his hand move down her back with a gentle kneading pressure on its descent. He reached her waist, and the air whooshed out of her when their bodies twisted—he'd rolled them in an unexpected move.

A contented sigh escaped Erin when the weight of him settled against her and he nudged her thighs apart. Their tender kisses continued on, Jayden driving forward, burying himself deep, and filling her with his love.

With the barest movement, the two lovers ground against each other, just enough sensation burning in their loins to keep them on a honed edge. The whole time their eyes were locked in a gaze that spoke of everything each felt for the other, even when Erin reached the moment when her body burst into a flurry of tingles and the desperate need to come smashed into her.

Jayden didn't want her asking permission when they were together like this, but Erin was still working on that. Her mouth didn't form the word, but her eyes did. *Please . . .*

Always attentive to what she needed, he pressed his hips tighter against her and pushed up on his arms, breaking their kiss so that he could thrust with ease. Erin lifted her knees toward her chest then let them fall outward. With Jayden's increasing tempo, she could feel her clit swell. Her hands moved to his chest, where his muscles undulated beneath her fingertips while he worked his length within her.

"I'm almost there, sweet girl. Please . . . join me." Though spoken with control, she sensed his need in the husky depth of his voice, so she let go with a loud cry that was matched by his own a few minutes later.

☿☿

"You're sure we have everything we need? We are going to be gone for a whole two weeks, after all. Wouldn't want you to run out of anything in the back forty of Corpus Christi," he teased after putting her last-minute bags into the back seat of the car—all three of them.

"Oh, shut it. I'm still adjusting to normal living with people who have money, Jayden. I get nervous over what to wear and change my mind . . . a lot."

For a moment, Jayden was surprised by her admission. He'd had no idea she was intimidated by his wealth, considering the topic had never come up. He helped her into the car, choosing to wait till they were moving before he said anything. The Wraith purred to life, and after making sure the gate was secure behind them, they said goodbye to the Villa.

"Does my money bother you?" He shot her a glance before the light changed at the end of the street. "Because in a few months, it's going to be your money, too."

Erin flashed him a beautiful grin, but he had to return his attention to the road. At least the emerald sparkle of her eyes was burned afresh into his retinas. She was happy. This pleased him.

"I don't think it's so much that I'm bothered by it, just that I'm still learning, if that makes sense. I grew up where sweatpants and old tees, comfy and grungy clothes, were fine for informal get-togethers. Your family tends to do things on a little bigger scale than that, and I'm still trying to find my happy medium."

"You don't have to change anything on my account, or theirs. You're perfect just the way you are." Jayden let go of the steering wheel to grasp Erin's hand and pulled it over to rest on his thigh, their fingers laced.

"I love you," his girl said, then she giggled.

Since they were at another light, Jayden reached out and grabbed her knee. Erin squealed as expected and begged him not to tickle.

"Tell me what's funny or I will," he negotiated.

Her cry of, "Okay!" was breathless.

Satisfied with his victory, his hand went back to the wheel, and he accelerated with the green light.

"To be honest, I'm more worried about how I'm going to not lose my mind in the next two weeks."

"How so?" He flipped on his blinker then pulled into a parking lot.

"That's a long time to go without playing. I can't promise *Catherine* won't turn bratty after being hidden away like that." She giggled again, which he found enchanting.

Jayden gasped in mock-disbelief, playing along with her. "Is my pet threatening me?" The deepening timbre of his voice was automatic, and he felt a stirring in his crotch when her breath caught in reaction to him.

With a slow movement to the left, right, then left again, Erin shook her head while whispering, "No, Sir."

"You have to trust me, Erin. They know about my choices, and we've agreed to disagree on our views. What matters to them is that I'm happy. Is it too much to show respect for their beliefs by not flaunting my sexual tendencies in their face? I think not. And rest assured, my jewel, I will make it up to you."

A shiver racked her body at his declaration. *If they hurried, perhaps there would be time for a quickie inside.*

It wasn't until he was opening his door that Erin noticed where they were. "Now this is just cruel, Jayden," she whined, and he laughed.

"The club is closed right now, sweet girl. We have a recognition ceremony coming up, so all the board members need to review the applicant portfolios. Angelique was going to leave my packet in the conference room for easy pick up on our way out of—"

His words trailed off when they came around the corner of the building. There were two cars parked in the back lot, which was supposed to be employees only.

"Something wrong?"

Erin's gentle voice kick-started his mouth again. "Um, no, I don't think so, anyway. If I'm not mistaken, that red car is Natalie's."

"She's the bartender, right?"

"Yeah. Don't recognize the other car, though. Maybe Natty is using the lot as a meeting point for a group activity or something over the holiday." He shrugged and held the backdoor open after he'd unlocked it.

The club was quiet save the hum of the heater. When they reached the stairs that led to the upper floors where the business offices were located, Erin told him to go on ahead so she could use the bathroom. To her left was the Hall of Play, the back section of the club where the private play rooms were located. Every few rooms were separated by a bathroom.

"I'll be back in just a couple of minutes. Meet you here." Jayden kissed her nose, then mounted the stairs.

꧁☙CHAPTER NINE☙꧂

CHAPTER NINE

Erin spared a few seconds to watch him ascend the steps, or to be more exact, to watch his ass ascend. His jeans hugged him with precision, making for a rather luscious bowl of eye candy. On impulse, she gave a wolf-whistle, laughing when he shimmied his ass for her before he disappeared around the corner at the top.

A long-missed sense of normalcy, and dare she say peacefulness, warmed her while she stepped into the first toilet in the long hallway. Afterward, she returned to the base of the stairs to wait for Jayden. She recalled that her phone had chirped a text notification while she was occupied, so she pulled it out to check.

Sorry~ Samantha called with a small emergency. Give me fifteen to make some calls. Help yourself to a juice or water behind the bar. Xo ~J

Not fussed, though not particularly thirsty, Erin sauntered over to the bar anyway. She was a little curious. This was the first time she'd been inside the club without being in the mind frame for play. Erin could lift her eyes and really look around the place right then, without risk of repercussions.

She found it amusing that under the silence and fluorescent lights, the sensual gothic feeling she loved about the club had dissolved. Looking around, it was nothing more than a large room made of wood, concrete, and metal. It was amazing what the right lighting and music could do. Of course, the absence of life played a large part in the current atmosphere. Any space could become a den of sin when filled with aroused, consenting adults giving into their darkest desires.

Ducking behind the bar, she found the small fridge that housed the juices and grabbed a grape-raspberry. Her hand was slipping from the handle, having just closed the fridge, when she noticed a board of keys tucked at the back of the shelf, under the bar.

This reminded her that spare room keys were kept there, and her curious nature flared up. Master always used room three when they played here. She wondered if the other rooms were similar in design and decor, or if they had varying themes.

Checking the time on her phone, she saw she had at least five more minutes, but knowing Jayden and business, it would be more like another fifteen before he'd return. She snatched a random key off the board and made her way back to the Hall of Play.

Heart racing and adrenaline coursing through her, Erin looked at the number on the key tag. Seven. Down the hall she went, wondering what she would find . . . *four, five, six*, there it was. Slipping the key into the lock, she turned it.

The door was swinging open when Erin heard a muffled scream. Spinning on her heel, she tried to zero in on which direction it had come from. A few seconds later it came again, to her right. Backing up to room six, Erin put her ear to the door.

A whistling sound, followed by a resounding crack, made her heart freeze. She'd recognize that noise anywhere. The bottle of juice slipped from her fingers and hit the carpeted floor, rolling a couple of feet before stopping.

Her hand braced against the door, and she leaned forward to listen better. The club was supposed to be closed and locked up. There should be no one inside at all, let alone there being a scene taking place without any dungeon masters on the premises. It didn't take a genius to see this violated the safe ambience that the club prided itself on providing.

Under the slight pressure of her weight, the wood inched forward, opening—much to Erin's surprise. Another whistle, crack, and scream—not muted this time—met her ears when the barrier swung away.

The scream faded into a whimper while Erin looked on.

Fear-drenched sweat gathered at her pulse points before seeping from all of her pores and tainting the air around her. A ringing started up in her ears. Erin was pretty sure the bound naked woman, whose backside was on display, was Natalie, the bartender. The springy, brown curls were unmistakable.

Movement on the periphery drew her gaze up and to the left, where a blue-haired young man stood, a manic gleam in his eye. In his hand was a bamboo cane.

With horror, she recalled bumping into this same man, Dominick Poles, her first night at the club—and how the bartender had swooned over him. *Oh, god— how long had this been going on?*

"H-hello, is someone there? Please, help me . . ."

"Shut up!" Another sickening whack and a fleshy *thwap*.

The desperation in Natalie's voice, coupled with the atrociousness of what she'd stumbled upon, tore at Erin's heart. Drawing upon the reserves of strength that Jayden had so patiently helped her to rebuild, Erin spoke out. "It's okay, Natalie. Jayden and I are here. You are going to be fine." To hear the resolve in her words shocked her. Her body was frozen.

A low cackle began, growing into a dark laugh that made Erin's spine hurt with the malice it contained.

"You stupid whore. Who do you think you are, barging in here uninvited?" His eyes moved up and down her body, lingering on her fitted sweater. "Though I could be convinced to mount you up as well. That could be . . . fun." Dominick sneered the last word, and the images his suggestion conjured sent a wave of nausea through her.

In the back of her head, a tiny voice was begging Erin to run, insisting that this wasn't her battle, yet she did not retreat. She couldn't. Instead, she stepped into the room, and defiance stiffened her body while she crossed her arms over her chest and planted her feet in place. Raising her eyes, she met his stare head on, determined not to crumble—for Natalie, and for herself.

Dominick's arm moved faster than she could see. The whoosh of air being displaced was the single warning she got before the cane connected with Natalie's ass. Blood appeared, then trickled down her rump in a crooked, thin line.

Casting her eyes over Natalie, seeing the scabs and contusions threatening to burst with even the lightest touch, Erin came to a conclusion. This was her battle. Erin had survived an abusive situation and was now recovering because she'd had help. People had cared about her. She wouldn't leave Natalie to try and understand alone.

Again Dominick laughed and raised his arm. Since it was obvious that her words were no longer keeping his attention from the bound girl, Erin leapt in of front of him, her arms raised to absorb the inevitable impact, and declared "Red!" at the top her lungs.

∞⟆

It figured. Jayden wanted to get this trip underway, so of course there were last minute problems with the holiday orders.

If it isn't one thing, it's another, Jayden thought while closing the door behind him for the second time. He'd been halfway down the stairs when he'd realized the applicant packet was still in the board room, so he'd had to go back.

Packet now in hand, he descended but was not alarmed when he didn't see Erin straight away. However, concern bloomed when he reached the bottom of the staircase and still didn't see her.

Ice flooded his veins when her emphatic cry carried from the Hall of Play. The memory of the cars in the lot outside flashed in his head. Dropping everything, Jayden let his long legs carry him forward in a sprint. He soon found an open door and in mere moments had assessed the situation.

A blue-haired man, who had to be Dominick Poles, stood with his arm raised, back to the door. Cowering before him was Erin.

Except she wasn't cowering. When Jayden's eyes raked over the grouping, pride bloomed with the realization that his sweet girl was in a defensive stance, protecting the woman behind her. Seeing Erin in such control kept his anger in check . . . for the moment.

"If you finish that swing, I will take that stick and use it on you myself." His voice did not waiver, the fury boiling inside him evident in his emotionless tone. "It's been much too long since I've had the pleasure."

Poles jerked around in surprise. "Oh. Hi, Mr. Masterson. I was just—"

"Listen, Poles, I don't know what the hell you're doing inside this building right now, since the club is not open," his eyes cut over to Natalie and back, "but this stops now." Looking to Erin to check her for damage and finding none, he calmed a fraction more. Though her creamy skin was paler than usual, it appeared she was no more than shaken. He returned his attention to the bartender.

Natalie was a different story. Her wrists were suspended above her head in cuffs with a basic buckle on them, so no key was needed. Jayden heard her whimpering sobs and looked closer. The more marks he saw on Natalie's body—both aged and fresh—the more his admiration of Erin increased, right along with his ire. How she'd put herself in the way of Dominick's attack, he'd never know.

113

Was it strange that the more assured he was that his precious jewel was safe, the angrier he became? He pursed his lips in a tight line to avoid screaming and then attacking the idiot. Erin had never seen him angry, and he did not want her to. She didn't need to worry that he was capable of such dark thoughts. Besides, the last thing Natalie needed right then was another male venting his anger in her proximity.

The poor thing was already terrified, as was proven by the acrid scent of urine in the air and the puddle at her feet.

It saddened him to realize their vacation had just been shortened. Indiscretions the likes of which had happened here could not be swept to the side. Swift action was necessary for all parties involved.

In the blink of an eye, Jayden transformed into the man-in-charge. Staring down the room's occupants, he challenged them to say anything while he retrieved his phone and hit the speed dial for Samantha's private line.

"Jayden, I told you I had it covered—"

"Samantha," he barked, his voice gruff and no-nonsense, "I need you to call my mother and tell her we won't be arriving tonight. I'll call her later to explain. You're a doll. Gotta go. Bye." His mother wasn't the only one he owed an explanation after that. He'd hung up on his secretary before she could get a word in.

Erin's eyes widened, her confusion and surprise evident.

In the name of efficiency, Jayden needed her full cooperation, without question or hesitation. A little warning bell was sounding in his head that she might not be as calm and collected as she appeared, and that worried him. Even if they made it through the next few hours without any incident, Erin would need to deal with what she'd walked in on—whether she wanted to or not. He had no intention of taking her on vacation without being positive she was okay.

"Catherine, get Natalie down and take her to the bathroom. Help clean her up. Understand?"

"Aye, Master." Her gaze shifted down. *God, she was so perfect for him.*

He hated to put the girl on the spot in her fragile condition, but Jayden needed to know what had transpired before he could proceed. "Natalie, can you tell me what happened?" he asked from behind her in a gentle but firm tone, and she began to shake.

"Master?"

"Yes, Catherine?"

"May this girl suggest she get Natalie sorted and covered before you question her? She is in a vulnerable state."

Of course, I should've thought of that. "By all means. One more question, though, and a simple nod or shake of your head will suffice. Natalie, did you let this man into the building?"

She shook her head.

Bastard! "Thank you." He moved to stand in front of her but stopped about a foot back, not wanting to crowd her. Bending at the knees and dipping down to her eye level, he took her chin in his hand and encouraged her to look up at him. "Erin is going to take care of you now. You are safe, Natalie."

Gratitude flooded her brown eyes along with the tears that now brimmed over.

At the feel of Erin's small hand on his forearm, he looked over to see the same look of gratitude in her eyes, too. He must have done something right.

"Love you," she mouthed.

Jayden mustered a smile. "Lucky me," he mouthed back.

Their moment of sweet levity over, the Dom turned to deal with Dominick. With long strides, Jayden closed the distance between them, experiencing more joy than he should have when the man flinched back with fear in his beady, blue eyes.

"Give me that." It was nothing to yank the cane from Poles' sweaty grasp. Jayden then pinched Dominick's ear and began dragging him from the room. Again, he was secretly pleased when the man squealed like a small child.

At the sound of whispering when they neared the threshold, Jayden paused and looked back. Erin had released Natalie's wrists and was kneeling to do her ankles.

"I'm so sorry, miss—"

"Shh, none of that, lass. Come now, let's get you freshened up. And call me Erin." Erin stood tall and took the girl's trembling hand to lead her past the men and into the hall.

"But why? I asked for this; I—I deserve what he did," Natalie whimpered, cringing when they neared Dominick.

Erin's back stiffened.

"Dunna ever think that. No matter what. I'm going to tell you the story of a girl I once knew who wasn't too unlike you, Natalie. My story . . ."

Jayden stood there immobile while her accented words faded as they walked away. If Erin was ready to share her horror with a near stranger, she had come much farther than he'd hoped.

Next to him, Poles shifted on his feet and let out a discontented grunt, so in a partial daze, Jayden got them moving again.

Ascending the stairs for the second time that morning, he felt . . . conflicted? He was beyond furious with the whole situation. Unauthorized access to the building, club rules being blatantly disregarded during a scene—or whatever the fuck it was he'd walked in on—the nerve of this idiot to in any way threaten his beloved. All of it made him want to yell, scream, and break things.

Yet in a moment of sublime restraint, his jewel had been more composed than he, the man who'd spent his life perfecting the art of control. His submissive had shown bravery and compassion enough to shame him. If he'd entered that room first, well, Jayden couldn't say for sure what might have transpired.

One thing was certain—it would not have been a scene that either Erin or Natalie should witness.

ಶಃಡ೮ಽ
CHAPTER TEN
ಶಃಡ೮ಽ

W hen the girls had disappeared from sight, Poles began putting on airs. He made snotty comments behind Jayden's back while being dragged through the club back to the meeting room. Vile things, like boasting how Natalie had been begging him to do this, and more, to her for months.

Somebody needed to teach him a lesson.

Once they'd entered the room and he'd ordered the man to sit, Jayden called Angelique. She would have all the board members' phone numbers at hand and be the most proficient at organizing an impromptu assembly. This was going to be dealt with right the fuck now.

A small click echoed from his phone when he ended the call. Satisfied that Angelique would handle the task he'd set for her, Jayden turned to face his problem head on. The expensive soles of his leather shoes marked the Dom's approach with distinct taps, and the closer Jayden came to the blue-haired trespasser, the more rank the air became.

Fear.

Inhaling deep, Jayden absorbed the emotion, almost getting high off it while his palm pulsed. He still held the length of bamboo. God, did he want to use it in that moment. It had been too long since he'd enjoyed the sensation of landing this particular tool across willing flesh. Micah had been the last, months ago.

The unexpected desire alarmed Jayden. He'd only ever swung a cane to cause pleasure, never as a tool for punishment. To do so now could ruin any future chances he had of Catherine accepting the cane. He had to get himself under control, and he began by breaking the length of wood across his knee in a rather abrupt move.

Poles yelped and started shaking.

Even after the jagged crack of the bamboo breaking, the pieces hitting the floor sounded harsh when he threw them to the side. Jayden began pacing with concise movements. Three strides to the left, stop and sharp pivot, then three to the right, and repeat. Dominick's eyes followed him, his dilated pupils revealing that fright wasn't the sole thing coursing through his veins.

When Jayden did begin speaking, Dominick flinched at the sound of his voice and he chuckled, a thought occurring to him. He came to a resting place in front of the seated man, his left hand hooked in his pants pocket, a casual gesture, while he scratched his chin with his right—the picture of calm and collected.

"I've done no harm to you, yet you sit there, cowering like a beaten puppy. Why?"

Poles blinked, the stare in his eyes vapid, refusing to connect.

"Could it be your guilty conscience whispering in your ear? Bringing to light what a sleaze you are?"

The accused attempted to swallow. Dominick's leg began bouncing, while he drummed his fingertips on his thighs.

Jayden pressed on. "Or are you high out of your fucking mind right now, asshole? In what respectable world do you think it is okay to accept a submissive's gift while you're under the influence of any substance?" he hissed, inches from Dominick's face, having rushed forward to spit the words at him.

"Gift?" Dominick made it clear the concept was foreign to him.

The Dom wanted to roar at the stupidity he was seeing. Instead, he seethed through clamped teeth. After a few controlled breaths to get himself collected again, he was able to resume. Jayden straightened then backed away.

"You've been lingering around my club and my Lifestyle for too long, Poles. Except," he paused for dramatic effect, "this isn't just my club. I'm a member of the board—the board you've applied to for membership and backing into the community and Lifestyle." Sue him for gloating.

"So what? You're gonna tell them I was a bad boy and can't be in your stupid little club?"

The arrogance and defiance dripping from the words pulled another chuckle from Jayden, and he grinned. "Not at all, Mr. Poles. In fact, I've just had your interview moved up."

Understanding dawned in the man's eyes, and he gulped.

"Everyone will be here and ready to begin within an hour. Best be preparing your intro speech, sir." No respect was delivered with the title.

"But I'm not ready," Dominick spluttered, the dry spittle at the corners of his mouth disgusting Jayden even more. "I'm not dressed right and haven't had time to plan a scene or prepare a slave—"

Slave? He'd heard enough. "Oh, but sir, you have a *submissive* in the other room, remember? And she happens to bear the evidence of how you conduct a scene. As for your attire, well, let's just say it suits you." With disdain, Jayden dragged his gaze over the man's grease-stained, unbuttoned jeans.

Uncertainty flashed in Dominick's eyes when Jayden's came to meet them. *Good*. Yes, it was good that he was worried.

Silence fell over the two men while the clock on the wall ticked off the seconds.

ॐ

Catherine guided Natalie to the nearest bathroom and then helped her get into the shower. She kept her voice low and soft, speaking in calming tones while collecting a washcloth, towel, and robe from the closet. Body wash and shampoo were housed in wall dispensers mounted inside all of the club's showers.

Sometimes Natalie would ask a question, but mostly Catherine talked and she listened. To Catherine's surprise, sharing her story about Spencer, starting with Andrew, and of course, ending with Jayden, was easier than she'd thought it would be. It was of paramount importance to her that she stress to Natalie the differences between each man's approach. However, when quiet sobs started up behind the curtain, she knew it was time to give the girl some space.

"Natty, there's a towel and robe on the counter for you. I'll be out in the hall. If you need me, just shout and I'll hear you, okay?"

The door was almost closed when Natalie's red and swollen eyes peeked around the curtain. "Erin?"

"Yeah . . ." Catherine looked at the girl, trying to impart with body language that she was a friend and could be trusted. Soft voice, gentle smile, no fast movements . . . all precautions that one would take with a wild animal.

Natalie blinked, and there was the faint hint of a smile on her saddened face. "Thank you."

Catherine's throat constricted. She knew the roller coaster that Natalie was on right now all too well. The external physical marks would heal and become just a blip on the radar, but the deeper wounds were lodged in her mind and heart and might not ever go away.

Unlike Catherine's long-term abuse by Spencer, Dominick's had just begun. Therefore, it could be more easily recovered from. At least, that's what

Catherine hoped for Natalie's sake. Even with all the love and support she'd gotten from Jayden, Catherine still had her momentary lapses.

She had so many questions for Natalie, but they'd have to wait. "You don't have to thank me, lass. Try to relax and enjoy your shower. You're safe, Natalie. Jayden won't let Dominick bother you again." With that, she pulled the door shut and then slumped against it as a dry sob choked her.

No, we can't do this right now, Erin. Clothes—the girl is going to need more than a robe.

Grateful to have something to busy her, Catherine went back to the room where she'd found the pair. Discarded in the corner were Natty's belongings—a pastel pink jogging suit, white cotton undies, and a back pack. Not an outfit for seduction, that was for sure.

A tri-folded piece of paper was sticking up out of the front pocket of the pack. While Erin hadn't intended to snoop, the bold red letters stamped across the sheet were hard to miss. It was a disconnect notice from the electric company.

Was that why Natalie had been there at the club? For a warm place to stay? *Fuck.*

Knowing she shouldn't but unable to stop, Erin pulled out the letter to see the date. Maybe her power hadn't been turned off yet and Jayden would be able to pay the bill. It was Christmas, after all. They couldn't leave the girl without a warm place to stay. When the notice came loose, another piece of paper fluttered to the floor.

There was one thing Erin would likely never have but deep down wanted more than anything else, and for her, the kind of news printed on the paper would have been good. For the young bartender, it had to have been devastating. Dated from the day previous, the Dallas Pregnancy Resource Center letterhead revealed shocking news—Natalie was pregnant.

Double fuck.

Erin became nauseous, a cold, clammy sweat seeping from her pores. Moving with haste, she stuffed the papers into the backpack, grabbed everything, and went to wait for Natalie.

To tell Jayden or not—it was a hell of a question.

Thirty minutes later, Natalie was dressed in her pink outfit and they were sitting in the common area of the club. Jayden and Poles were still upstairs. Natalie was nursing a bottle of juice, and all Erin could think was how young and innocent the girl looked. Naïve. What was crazy, though, was that she had to be close to Erin's age. Being a bartender put her over twenty-one, at least. How, at just shy of twenty-five, did Erin feel so much older and more experienced than this woman?

Maybe because you've already survived two lifetimes worth of terror and pain.

"Hello?"

"We're over here, Holly," Erin answered, relieved that reinforcements had arrived to give her help with Natalie and a chance to get her out of her own head.

After Natalie had dressed, Erin had fessed up about what she'd seen in the girl's bag and had convinced her to allow a call to Dr. Holly Ellison on her behalf. Erin kept the number programmed in her cell phone. When Holly answered the phone, she indicated that she'd already been on her way thanks to a call from

Angelique—at Jayden's request. Erin hadn't seen him again since they'd parted ways, so she had no idea what he was up to. The strong urge was there to go find him and get some answers, but a hunch told her she needed to give him his space and focus her energy on Natalie.

Instead of the usual sharp clack of heels on the concrete, tennis shoes whispered over the floor when Holly crossed the room.

"Sorry to bother you on the weekend like this. You remember Natalie?" Erin greeted the older, well-put-together woman with due respect when she reached them.

Holly nodded and smiled in a non-threatening manner. "No bother at all. I'd just been on my way out for a run when Angelique called."

Even dressed for exercising, the Domme was beautiful. No makeup caked her mocha skin. She was an exercise in simple elegance.

"How are you feeling, Natalie?" Holly asked, getting down to business and turning her attention to the person who needed it. Someone besides Erin this time.

Natalie scoffed. "I've been better, Doc."

"Well, let's see what we can do about getting you back to better. What do you say?" Her hand extended to help the trembling girl up from her perch on the edge of the armchair. "Erin, can you duck behind the bar and get the key for room twelve, please?"

Surprise hit her—she hadn't thought the keys were such common knowledge. Curiosity soon overtook the surprise as she wondered why the doctor wanted that specific room. "Aye, Miss."

She grabbed the requested key, and the three of them traveled back down the Hall of Play. In the distance, Erin thought she heard voices. While unlocking the door, she inquired, "Were you the only one Angelique called, Holly?"

The woman's dark eyes sparked at the question, darting from Natalie back to Erin. "No, I wasn't. Everyone on the board was contacted, I believe. But you don't need to concern yourself with that just yet."

Erin gasped when she opened the door and stepped inside. Her earlier question about theme rooms was now answered. This room was quite

131

clearly for those with a medical kink fetish. She could even smell the antiseptic odor that permeated hospitals. *To each their own.*

Once they'd entered, Holly went to the cupboards, seeming to know just what she needed and where it was. Then she sighed. "I keep asking Angelique about setting up an official triage room here for emergencies. Maybe now she'll listen to me. Guess I'll have to make do with this in the meantime." She shook her head then planted a smile on her face. "Natalie, I understand that today has been difficult for you. Do you want Erin to stay or go while I look you over?"

Timid and nervous, Natalie looked in Erin's direction. "Do you mind staying? I—I don't really have any friends, and I'm scared." Her eyes were beginning to well with tears again.

Erin rushed over to the girl's side. "Of course I don't mind, Natty. I'll stay as long as you want me to—on one condition."

"Okay . . ."

"Please tell us what happened."

೫ುೀౕ
CHAPTER ELEVEN
೫ುೀౕ

The entire time the men waited neither one spoke. For that, Jayden was grateful. If he'd had to listen to any more vitriol ooze from Dominick's lips, he might have done something regrettable. Something physical and damaging.

He'd always had a soft spot for those less fortunate. He could see that now, but there was more than that. Jayden did what he could by donating to local organizations, and even encouraged his employees to donate their time at soup kitchens, orphanages, or any other charitable programs in the Metroplex. One of the many perks of working for Masterson Metalworks was being granted up to five days off each year, with pay, for volunteering.

Yet as Jayden stood there reflecting, it became clear to him that he also had a knack for getting involved with souls who needed more than basic material care. In opening his heart to love, he'd also allowed his sights to widen. With a jolt of acute clarity, he realized he'd never been the cold, emotionless bastard he'd once thought he was. The powerful Jayden Masterson was a mere man. *Go figure.*

With Micah, he'd helped transition him from the boys' home. Catherine had been on her way to healing, and he'd just made it a smoother trip. Now there was Natalie. They all shared a commonality. A part of them was, or had been, broken inside. And Jayden had wanted to fix them all, feeling responsible for them in one way or another. Even Samantha had become part of his unique flock, not because she'd had some deep-seated issue or tragic past, but because he'd grown to care for her in his time with her.

Unlike the others, though, Natalie had never flashed on his radar as being the submissive type, so this whole scenario confounded him.

The first time he'd seen her had been outside Dungeons & Dreams. It had been a scorcher of an afternoon, and she'd been hiding under the awning by the front door, out of the sun. Not expecting anyone when he'd exited after a board meeting, he'd almost tripped over her where she sat with her back against the wall. She'd been thin—too thin—and her eyes dull. Seeing her cracked lips, Jayden had insisted she come inside for some water and air-conditioning.

Once Natalie had a chance to rehydrate, the obvious widening of her eyes while she looked around had disclosed how unaware of the Lifestyle she was. An innocent.

Angelique had been there, too, and in chatting with the young woman, they'd learned she was on her own and trying to make ends meet. He'd felt bad there were no internships he could offer her with his company. If she'd graduated high school, then he could have pulled some strings. However, without a diploma, she didn't meet the basic requirements for any of the positions.

That had been when Angelique stepped in. It was rare that she flaunted her ownership of the club, but she did that day, insisting she'd been about to place an ad for a bartender. If Natalie was willing to work hard, both at the club and on getting her GED, Angelique would let her have the job. Satisfied, Jayden had not found it necessary to include the girl in his small herd, and had moved on.

But now, almost two years later, he had to take that responsibility back, because this was all his fault. Intentional or not, he had been the one to bring Natalie into his world. Her path had crossed Dominick's thanks to him. *Just once, would it have killed him to not be the nice guy?* Before his thoughts could veer off into a full-blown self-berating, there was a knock at the door.

Jayden followed Dominick's beady eyes and looked over at the door when it opened. In marched five of the people who made up the seven-member board of directors—Landon Michaels, Shawn Carpenter, Warren Smith, Angelique Hendrix, and their newest member, Sheila McCray.

Sheila was a stunning brunette with green eyes rivaled by none but Erin's—in his book, anyway. She could've been a doppleganger for that actress in *Grease 2* and *Catwoman*. The Domme had moved to the States from England a few months back to take over Events and Promotions for the club. She wasn't new to D&D, though. Sheila had visited the club with regularity over the years whenever she happened to be stateside.

Greetings were exchanged while inquisitive glances lingered on Poles. Holly Ellison hadn't arrived yet, and Jayden was anxious to begin. He wasn't alone, judging by the rising level of voices in the room. Everyone wanted to know why they'd been summoned and what was going on.

"Bloody hell, would you lot shut the fuck up." Sheila's commanding tone silenced the room.

All eyes turned to Jayden then, full of expectation and impatience. His polo and sport coat felt too warm all of a sudden.

"That's one way to call the meeting to order," he joked. "Once Holly arrives, we can start. You were able to reach her, weren't you, Angelique?"

"She was the first one I called. I'm surprised she's not here yet, to be honest."

Because Dominick had drawn blood, even if just a little, Jayden wasn't comfortable proceeding without his friend's input—as a doctor and a Domme.

"Thank you all for coming so fast and with no questions asked. If you'll bear with me, I'll explain all of this soon." He pulled out his phone and dialed Holly.

₧◐◑

"Alright, sweetie. That's all I can do here. I want you to come see me next week to get a blood panel and start your OB file—"

"I can't. I don't have any insurance, ma'am," Natalie cut in, and Holly's face pulled tight with disapproval.

Erin gave Natalie's hand a gentle squeeze and rubbed her back. Holly'd had the girl change back into a robe to facilitate the exam, and now Natalie held it closed, clutching it in a tight fist against her chest.

"We'll sort out the logistics later. Your health— your *baby's* health—are more important. Right now, I need to get upstairs and join the rest of the board. I'm going out on a limb and saying that Jayden called this meeting over you. I'm going to need to share with them what you've told me. Are you okay with that?"

For a few seconds Natalie just stared back, then her head moved up and down.

"You need to think about whether you want to press charges. The tissue damage around your anus alone is enough to bring Dominick up on rape."

A single tear slipped free, moving across Natalie's cheek in a slow, jerky path. If the situation hadn't been so tense, Erin would've laughed when Holly's phone came to life with Depeche Mode's *Master & Servant*. The busted look on the woman's face while she ran to her discarded purse was comical.

"Hello, Jay. No . . . Yes, I'm here in the building . . . room twelve. Jayden, I think you need to come down here before I head up. We need to talk. Okay, see you in a minute."

Erin stared at Holly in shock. "What's going on?"

Holly came closer and took Erin's hand in hers. "Things are about to get really crazy around here, Erin. Can you do me a favor?"

She nodded.

"Until Jayden tells you otherwise, I need Catherine here. Keep your mouth shut, and let Jayden and me do the talking. You keeping your emotions in check is imperative right now."

This time it was Natalie squeezing her hand in comfort when Erin's body tensed at Holly's words. Erin looked down and the younger woman smiled back up at her.

"Together?"

Erin smiled. "Yes, Natalie. We'll face this together."

"Hello, ladies. How is everyone doing?"

At the sound of his voice, Erin's heart leapt in her chest, and she spun around to hurry over to him. His arms enfolded her, drawing her in close while she inhaled his spicy scent. At once she calmed, all her muscles relaxing. She'd not realized how tight her body had been wound. With a hint of satisfaction, she noticed it wasn't just her who relaxed when they embraced. His lips were warm on her forehead, but they had to keep it brief, so he soon moved back.

"Holly," Jayden greeted her with a nod. "Why are you down here? Everybody's waiting upstairs."

Dr. Ellison tucked a strand of her jet-black hair behind her ear and crossed her arms. "I came here first because Catherine called me. We have a situation—"

Erin shrank back a tad when his eyes cut over to her.

"No shit, Holly. You think I'm not aware of that? Erin and I were on our way out of town for Christ's sake, and instead we're here having to deal with this clusterfuck."

"Jayden!" Erin snapped. There was no reason for him to yell at Holly, and it made her uncomfortable to the point of reacting. Even so, the moment it was out of her mouth, she felt awful.

Both Jayden and Holly had requested she keep herself in check by letting her submissive side take the reins, and she hadn't. She'd barked at her Master, and that was uncalled for. Catherine dropped to her knees and bowed her head. "Please forgive your girl, Master. Emotions are high, and she overstepped herself."

Her lover knelt down, squatting in front of her. His hand was warm on her cheek when he cupped it, signaling for her to look up at him.

"Do you have whiplash yet, sweet girl?"

Did she ever, and wasn't it just like him to pick up on that. "Aye."

He took her hand and stood, drawing her upward. "Nothing about today is any kind of normal, so I'm going to let that slide. This time. However, Catherine, if you ever raise your voice to me like that in a defined setting, you will find yourself on my whipping bench. Do I make myself clear?"

"Crystal, Master. This girl would never . . ." She trailed off, horrified at the thought of acting out in such a way again.

"I know." After gracing her lips with a brush of his own, Jayden addressed the three ladies: "Now, who wants to talk?"

"I will. All of this is happening because of me. It's only right, I guess."

Jayden nodded. "I'm listening, Natalie." He grabbed a chair from the corner of the room and placed it near where she sat. With a snap of his fingers, Catherine was instructed to kneel beside him.

Holly took his girl's spot next to Natalie while Catherine came and positioned herself at his right, laying her head on his thigh.

ॐ

CHAPTER TWELVE

ॐ

P etting his jewel's soft hair was like a balm for his frazzled nerves while Natalie's nervous voice filled the room. Jayden sat there in disbelief, attempting to wrap his head around everything the bartender had shared. He couldn't continue to sit there saying nothing, so he decided to start where he was most comfortable. "Do you want to be a submissive, Natalie?"

"I don't think so, sir. Not, well, not if this is what's involved." She waved her hand around to indicate the atmosphere in general.

A small part of him died inside, knowing that what she was taking away from this situation was the impression that his beloved Lifestyle was violent, instead of seeing its beauty. It was an awful shame, but he couldn't force her to accept it, either. He supposed it was one thing for her to have watched from a distance, behind the safety of the bar, and a whole other to be taken into one of the rooms to be shackled and beaten. In particular, by someone as careless and slimy as Dominick.

What made this whole thing such a mindfuck for him was the pregnancy. Poles had wooed the girl, hiding his real intentions so that he could get her to let down her guard, which she had done in her desperation to be loved by someone, anyone.

He shook his head and sighed. "To be honest, Natalie, this isn't what's involved. Dominick took advantage of you, and I am so sorry."

"But don't think it's your fault, sweetie," Holly interjected. "This is all on him, and he will be dealt with accordingly."

"I just wanted to tell him about the baby. I thought he would be happy and want to help . . ."

"So you did call him here, then?" Jayden hedged, his head shooting up at her comment.

"Yes," Natalie whispered. "But just because he hasn't been to my place. I didn't want him to see how small it was, how little I have. We've always met here and then gone back to his apartment in his car."

"Ouch, Master." Next to him, Catherine whimpered.

Looking down, he realized his hand had gone from petting her head to closing over a fistful of her crimson hair. "Shit. Sorry, Catherine." Not wanting to hurt her by accident again, Jayden stood and moved away. "We need to get this show underway. Holly, do you agree that the board needs to deal with Poles now, today?"

She nodded.

"What I'm not getting," he paused, tipping his head to the side in an inquisitive fashion, "is how you were able to get inside. The door was locked when we arrived, and only board members have keys."

"Shit." While Natalie attempted to keep her voice down, they all heard her.

"What aren't you telling us, Natalie?"

"I'm sorry—I promised . . . I can't tell . . ."

Was she kidding him with this? The one thing that kept him from slamming his fist against the nearest flat surface was the voice of reason—in the form of Holly.

"Upstairs first. Everyone is here, giving up their Saturday without complaint, so have the decency to move this to a central location. Let everyone get the facts at the same time, so a plan of action can be shaped."

"Fine. Ladies, let's go upstairs."

Holly led the trek to the conference room, followed by Natalie, while Jayden clutched Erin's hand in his bringing up the rear. Needing to assess how his jewel was holding up, he hoped for a fast resolution so that he could get her somewhere alone.

Moments later, all hell broke loose.

"Thank you all for coming," Holly greeted the room when their small group entered.

"Whatever she's told you is a fucking lie!"

Jayden yanked Erin behind him when Dominick started yelling, and Sheila jumped into action. In the blink of an eye, she'd crossed the room and had his chin and jaw in her tight grip so that he resembled a surprised fish.

"I'll not be having any more of that bollocks passing your lips, boy," the Domme hissed.

"Ow, hat urts . . ."

"I don't give a flying fuck, quite frankly. Several pieces of this mystery just lined up, and you, my dear boy, I'd bet are at the center."

"Fk o, ch!" Poles began thrashing in an attempt to free his face from Sheila's hand, but it was no good. She had him, and it was obvious to everyone in the room that she was getting off on it.

"Excuse me?"

"I think," Jayden offered, "what Mr. Eloquence is attempting to say is along the lines of 'Fuck you, bitch,' which would be a shame. Such rudeness is not attractive."

The full swell of Sheila's bosom, exposed by the low-cut sweater dress she wore, flushed with color. To put it simply, her look when she stared down at Dominick was one of hunger.

Mistress Sheila was known to have a thing for putting arrogant little boys in their place. Dominick would be right up her alley on a normal day, but what about today?

"No, no, it's not attractive at all. However, it is intriguing."

Her words, followed by a resounding slap, pulled Jayden's focus back. Poles was staring at Sheila with a shocked look. Nausea, triggered by disgust, rolled Jayden's stomach at the sight of Dominick thrusting his hips up toward Sheila. The man was an idiot.

And a pig.

"That can wait for now, though. By the time this meeting is over, I want information until I know the ins and outs of a duck's arsehole," declared Sheila, ignoring the boy's perverted antics.

Next to Jayden, Catherine giggled. He had to squeeze her hand to shush her, and himself. *It was an interesting choice of words*, he thought while suppressing a smile.

Much to Jayden's surprise, the next hour was quite smooth. Sheila stayed near Dominick and pinched or smacked him anytime he got rude or mouthy. It only took a couple of times before he adopted a petulant pout. However, he stopped being a pest and let everyone speak in their turn.

Jayden began by explaining how and why he and Catherine had come to the club. Catherine took up the tale from there, detailing what she'd heard and then seen when entering the room.

Sheila had questioned Catherine's loyalty as a submissive at that point, wanting to know what kind of sub would walk into any kind of scene uninvited. It had been unnecessary to react, though, since every other board member ended up speaking over each other in support of his jewel. He hoped his girl was hearing their words, but more importantly, understanding what they meant—that she was respected. With the Domme's apology, they'd moved on.

The next part was the hardest. Natalie, with Holly and Catherine's help, disclosed her situation. When the bartender stood and dropped her robe, there was a collective gasp at the sight of the fresh wounds.

"To be clear," Sheila's nails were digging into Dominick's shoulder while she spoke, "this girl is not a part of our Lifestyle, just an employee of the club?"

Natalie was nodding but silent, so Catherine verbalized. "Aye, Miss."

Landon spoke up next. "Is the pregnancy confirmed?"

"With a physical by me and a blood test from the clinic she went to, yes," Holly responded and laid the letter on the table for them to see.

When the matter of the baby came up, Poles became non-compliant once again. "She's a slut," he blurted out, rising from his chair faster than Sheila had been prepared for. "The lying whore can't prove if the thing is mine or one of the other fuck buddies she has."

Natalie's head snapped up, and though tears ran down her face and her body was visibly shaking, her voice was loud and clear. "I don't sleep around, Nick. There has been one other man in my life, and that was two years ago. This baby is yours."

Shawn stood and pushed his seat back. Moving with confidence, he put himself between Dominick and Natalie to help corral the man back to his chair with Sheila's help.

"Get your fag hand off me," Poles growled when Shawn's palm touched his shoulder.

Shawn laughed him off and kept urging him back.

Landon, ever the mediator, also jumped in after sharing a look with Jayden. They were both concerned about Dominick's stability with the women in the room. "Why don't you sit back down and keep your opinions to yourself, Mr. Poles. Let's take this down a notch."

Jayden stood back while the fact-finding continued, waiting to see how long it took before they were left with the same conclusion he'd reached. *How had Natalie gotten into the building?* One-by-one, the questions were asked and answered. After a while, Jayden realized that Warren wasn't saying anything. He stood silent in the shadows behind Dominick's chair, almost in an attempt to disappear. For a man his size, that wasn't an easy feat. *Curious.*

The more Jayden concentrated on Warren, the more he noticed how odd the bouncer was acting— eyes darting over the room, the continual wiping of his brow with the back of his sleeve, general fidgeting.

"Why are we all here, again, Jayden?" Shawn asked.

"I can answer that one, Shawn." Angelique held a manila packet in her hand, which Jayden recognized. It was the same as the one that had brought Erin and him there that morning. "One Dominick Poles, having reached his maximum allowable guest vouchers, has applied for official membership within Dungeons & Dreams. Further, he wants the full package—to be deemed a suitable Dominant and introduced into the local community as such."

Shawn's barking laughter echoed around the room before he quieted down. "You aren't kidding?"

Angelique's lips were pursed tight. "No, Mr. Carpenter. I'm not kidding."

"Oh."

"Jayden, you requested that we go ahead and do his review now, today, correct?" She'd turned her attention to the meeting's organizer. "Because I don't know about anyone else, but right now I have a bigger concern than whether this boy has the right to act as a Dom. Like who the fuck let him into *my* club after hours, for instance, and what are we going to do for Natalie."

Jayden smiled and pivoted to stare straight at Warren. "I've been wondering the same thing, Angelique."

"Damn it all to hell, it was me," Warren announced while throwing his meaty arms up in the air. "Natalie had mentioned she was a bit tight on money this month and wasn't sure she could pay her electric bill on time. I didn't have the cash to loan her, but I thought if her power did get shut off, then she needed some place with heating to go, and I gave her a spare key."

"Goddammit, Warren! What were you thinking? I could lose my business license over this if the girl wants to push the issue. She was raped on my property, for crying out loud." Angelique was gathering steam.

"Oh, ma'am, I wouldn't do that to you, not ever. You've been so good to me. I can't say enough how sorry I am for all of this—"

"Shut your mouth, child. Yes, part of the blame is on you for associating with and inviting this man into your life, but I won't let you take all the credit for this mess. It was lax of me not to educate you better about the environment you were working in."

"I do believe you've just hit the nail on the head, Angelique." Sheila drew all eyes to her once again.

"What do ya mean?" Landon appeared the calmest in the room, reclining in his chair and crossing his long legs in front of him while he took notes of the proceedings. Dr. Michaels was in his element.

"I mean this, Landon. Dominick, what education or training have you had in BDSM?" In a move that was disconcerting to Jayden, Sheila slithered behind the boy and pressed her breasts against the back of his head while teasing her nails through Poles' unnaturally colored hair.

"Um . . . enough. I have Internet."

Catherine spluttered next to Jayden, and Sheila began laughing. It started as a slow, amused chuckle that built while the older woman tossed her wavy hair back to allow the laughter to rumble out of her unimpeded.

Sheila's green eyes were full of mischief. Her fingers curled into a fist, and she yanked his head back to look down on him. "Oh, my dear boy. Won't you be fun?"

Jayden's curiosity was piqued. "What are you thinking, Sheila?"

Turning a brilliant smile on him, she crooned, "What's the foundation of training for some of the best Dominants, my friend?"

He felt like a right dunce. Something tickled in the back of his head. He knew he should understand where she was going with this, but it eluded him until Catherine coughed and nudged him with her elbow. When it clicked, he started grinning like a Cheshire cat.

"Are you sure you've got the time this one will take?" Checking in his peripheral vision, Jayden was pleased to see Dominick's eyes following their dialogue, sweat beading on his brow.

"I'm confident I can make it work. My other boy is ready to graduate to having a playmate. Once we take care of this blue fuzz, Nicki here will do quite fine." Sheila leaned in and licked Dominick's cheek, long and slow.

Dominick jerked away from her touch, eyes wide and, perhaps, scared. "Get off! The fuck you going on about, lady?" Forgetting his hair was in her grip, all he accomplished was getting it pulled—and putting a bigger smile on the Domme's face.

Jayden had to admit that he was enjoying the show.

"Wait a minute." Holly held up her hand. "Sheila, back off for a sec. Have you forgotten that we've had a girl forced into anal sex here, as in without her consent? Don't go off half-cocked making dungeon plans just yet. Natalie has the right to press charges."

A frustrated sigh huffed out of Sheila. "You're right, of course. Go on, then."

"The fuck?" Dominick quipped again.

What do you know? Something finally has Poles's attention, Jayden reflected. Or maybe sufficient time had passed since his last fix that the young man's head was clearing enough to comprehend what was happening around him.

Scoffing, the boy added, "I told you, she's just a slut that wanted me to fuck her, so why would she press charges?"

Sheila's reprimand for the crass outburst came in the form of her pristine nails darting out, cobra-like, to clutch Dominick's most prized possessions. Even Jayden flinched in surprise at her reaction time.

"Listen here, Nicki. If you have any love for your wedding tackle, you'd best be considering some better manners. Don't worry, though, pet . . . one way or t'other, you'll be taught." She squeezed and Dominick's Adam's apple bobbed along his throat. "I can be a very good Domme and show you unfathomed amounts of pleasure . . . or I can be a bitch. The way you're heading, you're one step away from seeing how much of a bitch I can be. Do you fancy finding my fingernails embedded in your bollocks so deep you'll need a pair of pliers to yank 'em out?"

He gulped and shook his head while Sheila chuckled. "There's a good boy."

Jayden toggled his attention back and forth between Holly, Angelique, and Sheila. They were a trio to be wary of, and each one wanted Dominick dealt with for different reasons.

"So where does this leave us?" Landon took the lead.

Eyes on Dominick, Shawn piped up. "Warren, Dominick, and Natalie all need to be addressed. On the first, I'm going to say right now that I don't think Warren should be punished with too much severity. We all know he's a good guy, with a good heart, and he just made a bad choice here." Assenting murmurs rose up.

"Fine, you aren't fired, Warren. But I'll be docking your pay or something as probation." Angelique's face softened, and her voice quieted. "Don't ever do this again. You're the perfect dungeon master here because of your conscience, I get that. Next time you feel the need to play martyr, come see me and we'll figure it out together."

"Yes, Miss. Thank you, and I'm sorry." Warren looked properly abashed.

"Hmph." Angelique tried to keep the smile off her face but couldn't when Warren turned his puppy dog eyes on her. She turned to their offender. "My initial reaction is to tear up your application and have a restraining order filed against you with regards to these premises. I could have you arrested for trespassing . . ." her words tapered off while she pondered.

Sheila took up the discussion. "Natalie doesn't want to press charges, and I think she's been through enough. We shouldn't try to force her. So what to do with Nicki is our issue. The boy is not ready to be a Dominant yet, as we can all see, but I see potential in him with proper training. So what I propose is this," her voice carried to all in the room, but her focus was on Dominick, "I will take responsibility for you, boy. You will learn to serve at my feet so that you can understand what it means to be on the receiving end of such a treasure. In time, either your hidden submissive will come forth, or you'll transform, through knowledge and experience, into a respectable Dominant. One who has earned the right to have a submissive kneel at his side."

"Go on," Dominick mumbled.

Jayden about fell out of his seat when Dominick showed interest. That was the last reaction he'd expected. Catherine's strengthening grasp on his palm told him she was surprised, too.

"As it stands now, you're not fit to be a Dom. First, you need to decide if you can become the kind of man that the Dom you think you are needs to be. Be warned, boy, you're going to work for it. You're going to prove it beyond a shadow of a doubt by submitting to me, and if at the end I think you're good enough, the first thing you'll be doing is getting on your knees and begging Natalie's forgiveness."

"Fuck you, psycho. I'm man enough already. Why don't you stop being a tease? Let me bend you over and prove it."

Jayden closed his eyes and shook his head. *Stupid, foolish man.* Things had been taking a turn for the better, and then the kid had to go and open his mouth.

"You'll submit to me, or you'll go to jail." All playfulness had evaporated from Sheila's voice. She was dead serious, and every person in that room knew it.

"You aren't touching my asshole."

Sheila threw her head back and laughed. "Oh, pet. You are going to be so much fun. We have to do some paperwork, checklists and the like, before I touch any part of you. But I'll wager you'll be begging me to touch your nasty arsehole before you know it."

An hour later, following the completion of a contract and a limits checklist, Sheila escorted Nicki from the building.

He didn't look back or offer any parting words to Natalie, but Jayden didn't miss how her eyes lost some of their vibrancy when she watched him walk out of her life.

ଃୠଓଔ
CHAPTER THIRTEEN
ଃୠଓଔ

Erin waited until their exhausted guest had drifted to sleep before making her way out of the room. When she found Jayden waiting outside the door, it didn't surprise her. His back to the wall, he sat with knees drawn up to his chest to support his head.

She took the spot on his right and leaned against him.

"How is she?" Though whispered, his words were loud in the dark hallway and sounded tired.

At Erin's suggestion, they'd invited Natalie to come back to the house with them. The girl couldn't stay at the club, and she had no place else to go.

"Finally asleep, but worn out. Thank goodness we found out now. Sp—" She dragged in a breath and tried again. "Spencer took months to work up to the point where Dominick was." *Damn her trembling hands.* "If he's this bad now . . ."

"Shh, *A rúnsearc*, it's okay." Jayden's arms engulfed her, and she was being lifted, carried away.

When had the tears slipped from her eyes? With each step he took, her head thumped against his chest, each little rise of her skull allowing enough air in to chill the damp spot on his shirt.

"Where do you want to go, sweet girl?"

His words didn't make sense. She was where she wanted to be, safe in his arms. Jayden—her Master, her lover, her life. There was no place better. "You," she mumbled into his pectoral muscles.

The answering rumble from within his chest brought a soft grin to her lips. After pressing a warm kiss to her forehead, he elaborated.

"I want us to talk about how you're doing. *Before* we go to bed tonight."

She swallowed before choking out, "Aye, okay."

"I just want . . . I need to be sure that you're okay, Erin. The calmness, I guess is the best way to describe it, with which you handled today was impressive."

Erin looked at him with a lazy blink. *Had she been calm?* Funny, she could've sworn she'd been functioning in a fog most of the day.

In the past, Landon had likened her instinct for going on autopilot whenever faced with a difficult situation to setting up a triage unit. It was easier for her to deal with the most pressing matter while her brain blocked the rest, saving it to be handled later.

This morning, that pressing matter had been making sure Natalie didn't get hit again. Once that was handled, she'd then been able to cast her senses out further. Taking a bit more in, a little at a time; baby steps.

Goddammit, why did a dead man still have power over her? How was it fair that he could still devastate her from the grave like that? Thanks to Spencer, she was afraid of a damn stick, and it pissed her off. To hand over control willingly was freeing, for her mind and body, and she longed for it. However, there was no pleasure in it for her when that control had been taken by force.

"Please take your girl to the playroom, Master." Jayden's step faltered, his body going rigid at her request.

She didn't regret it. He'd asked where she wanted to go, and she knew what she needed. To escape. For her, that meant a session with her Dom. After a pregnant pause, their movement resumed, and they descended to the lower floor—to her sanctuary.

Even when they crossed into the room, he kept Catherine in his arms, cradling her close to his body. She loved the warmth of him, the familiar scent of his musky cologne, but she didn't want to be coddled right then. Wriggling from his grasp, she fixed her gaze on the floor and disrobed before going to kneel in her usual spot.

At once, her chest felt lighter.

Breathing in through her nose, Catherine held for a count of five, then exhaled for another five. Each time she repeated the technique, another section of her body relaxed until her mind reached a state of peaceful blankness. The submissive welcomed the cocooning comfort of her mental destination.

೫০౪

While caught off guard by her request, Jayden understood it. It also proved his hunch that she was frazzled. What he had to figure out now was what she needed from him.

She moved with an eerie meticulousness and presented herself to his worried gaze. With some restraint, the Dom refrained from pacing. His jewel didn't need to worry what his actions might be.

Witnessing her seeking, and then finding, that safe place she went to inside never failed to mesmerize him. The process was beautiful to watch, the tension fading from her body before his eyes.

Did she realize, or would she be embarrassed to know, that he always knew when to begin with her because she'd make an adorable noise of contentment in her throat? Probably not. That was his little secret, because Jayden was pretty damn sure no other man had ever drawn that from her. No one else had ever loved her like him, so it wasn't possible.

What to do? he wondered, looking from her passive form over to the wall that housed his assorted impact toys and bindings. His eyes settled on the cane section.

Over the last year, Jayden had been able to return his various rods back to their places of honor on the wall. He added one back every couple of months, and it wasn't touched again once hung. The hope had been for Catherine to adjust to having them in her sight so they'd become commonplace. Then, and only then, would he begin taking them down and moving the toys closer to her.

Catherine's creamy skin had taken on the slightest glow in her time with him. Much like the palest honey, it was sun-kissed from her use of the pool. When she colored beneath his toys, it was art. How he longed to complete the picture by adding carefully placed red stripes after a thorough flogging.

He shook his head. They were in this whole mess because of a cane. Why would he even be considering it? Her soft sigh brought his attention back to her.

She wasn't ready.

Not even close.

In a rapid shift of his body, Jayden pulled off his t-shirt then removed the belt from his pants, dropping both to the floor. Catherine's puckering nipples were the lone indication that she'd heard the loud clatter of the buckle on the hardwood. Otherwise, she didn't flinch.

The bare soles of his feet padded across the floor while he closed the distance between them and moved behind her. Tempted by her hair, he reached out and wrapped his hand until it disappeared in the strands of soft, crimson silk, and he sighed.

He tugged, and she emitted a gentle moan.

"You are so lush, my pet." Guiding her head back to rest on his thigh, Jayden slid his free hand down over her shoulder, across her heaving chest, and up to cup her throat and jaw as he released the grip on her hair. "So brave and strong." He leaned over his submissive to take possession of her mouth. Firm and demanding, he pressed into her, teasing the cavern of her mouth with his tongue.

A shudder ripped through his body at the thought of replacing his tongue with his hardening cock. Yet he resisted, catching her lower lip between his teeth and tugging with a gentle bite instead. Jayden paired the bite with an unexpected pinch to her nipple.

With her surprised sharp intake of air, her breast pressed into his hovering hand, and he squeezed rougher than first intended. Her responding moan was more guttural. She *wanted* to be manhandled, to endure endorphin-creating pain.

"Please . . ." She whispered the plea so low he almost missed it and would have if he hadn't still been leaning over her.

"For you, *cailin maith*, anything." Bringing both of his large hands to her breasts, he began kneading and squeezing with harsh motions. The hours he'd spent gaining intimate knowledge of Catherine's body had trained him. Jayden knew just how to manipulate her body for maximum pleasure and was soon including her reactive peaks in the enthusiastic massage.

His back was beginning to ache from leaning over her, so Jayden sat down and pulled her back to his chest. He moved the attentions of his mouth to her neck and clavicle, laving and marking her while the breast massage continued.

The change in position made his erection obvious to both of them, and he ground his crotch against the small of her back. Her squirming increased while the minutes ticked by. Unable to resist expanding the scope of his touch any longer, Jayden pulled his jewel up onto his lap, spreading her legs across his thighs to give him access to the heated space that awaited.

She was gooey to the touch and he wanted to taste, but he would wait. There was a twinge in his back because there was nothing supporting their weight but him. Despite this, Jayden focused on sliding his fingers over her slick labia. His abdominal muscles began to burn.

The Dom was thankful he still worked out every morning. Without it, his aging body wouldn't have been able to maintain the precarious position they were in. Jayden was determined they weren't going to move from that spot until she'd coated his digits with her come—muscle cramps be damned. Her orgasm, when he granted it with very little begging from his pet, was glorious.

"Thank you, Master," she panted out, then added. "Please, may this girl have more?"

Horny little thing, he thought with amusement, but then a warning flag fluttered in the back of his head. *He hadn't come yet and she was asking for more?* That wasn't like her, at all.

"More what, Catherine?"

Her body began to shake in his lap, and alarm bloomed. The noises she was making were unclear. Was she crying? Laughing?

All at once, she was out of his lap and pacing the room. The old saying of 'hell hath no fury like a woman scorned' came to him at the sight of her. Her back was ramrod straight, her nipples were puffy and erect, and her short legs somehow looked longer due to the distance her steps were carrying her, but her hair took the cake. Fiery and wild, it cascaded behind her, swishing and moving with her manic motions while she mumbled to herself, shaking her head.

"Catherine?"

The desperation in her eyes scared him when she paused and looked to him. "Master?"

Then she did the last thing he expected, leaving him speechless and in the dark as to how to proceed. Shoulders back, his submissive marched over to the wall, and in one fell swoop managed to pull all of his canes down into her arms.

"It's time, Jayden. I won't be controlled by them any longer." Pieces of Lexan, bamboo, rattan, and other materials clunked and rattled against the floor when she dropped the whole lot.

"Jesus, Erin!" He was on his feet in a heartbeat. "Have you lost your mind?"

Maybe it wasn't the best reaction he could've had, but hell, what was he supposed to do with that? He wanted to call Landon for help, but this needed to be settled between the two of them, alone. Low self-esteem, sexual timidity, tears, and sorrow—he'd helped her through them all. Jayden had never witnessed her angry over what had happened to her, though.

So, is this a good thing? he wondered. *Why can't things be plain and simple anymore?*

Before Catherine, before Erin, his life had been black and white . . . routine, easy. Jayden let out a defeated sigh while admitting to himself it has also been boring. Erin had brought color and vibrancy to his dull existence. Being challenged by his jewel was exciting. Engaging with her, no matter what role they were in, was intoxicating.

Should he encourage her venting or put a stop to it? Per their contract, her current outburst warranted him putting her over his bench or on his table post haste to go at her ass with his aerated paddle. *Fuck.*

Rattan was being pressed into his hands, but Jayden still hadn't shown a visible reaction to her tirade.

"Show me, Jayden." His beautiful girl was openly weeping in front of him now. "You promised me all those months ago that you would help me not to fear. I don't want to live like this anymore . . ." She shoved at him once again, pressing the cane against his torso, her voice cracking with the force of her wail, and with it, his trance broke. "You . . . promised."

"I know, sweet girl." He twisted his upper body away from her to lay the cane on the table behind him. Then he had her in his arms, holding her close while memories of their first night together hit him hard.

Erin had come so far since then, yet she was still so fragile. He realized now that she might not ever get over what that bastard had done to her, nor should she be expected to. Awful as the experience had been, it had strengthened and shaped her into the woman she was now, the exquisite creature who owned his heart.

"Please . . . please . . ." Erin repeated the words, mumbling into his chest. "Make it go away."

"I will, Erin, I promise. But not tonight, not like this, *A rúnsearc.*"

Her will seemed to evaporate from her body altogether when he lifted Erin into his arms and took her back to their room. No words were spoken—they weren't needed. What the lovers did need was to just be.

Jayden managed to fall asleep about two a.m., according to the bedside clock. Erin had cried herself to sleep within minutes of getting settled on the bed. In his arms, she'd rested, safe, while he plotted.

By the time he let sleep take him, he'd come up with a plan, as long as Landon was game to help.

☙❧

Jayden woke up alone, cold, and stiff—and not in *that* way. Though morning wood had returned around the same time Erin had become part of his life, he was usually safe from the problem if she weren't right next to him.

Since they'd fallen asleep on top of the covers, the bed didn't need more than a quick straightening, and he was soon hurrying through a shower. Opting to pull on a pair of heavy black sweats and an old hoodie from his alma mater, Rice University, he appraised himself in the mirror. Jillian would have to deal with him showing up casual, and he was going to insist Erin do the same. The next two weeks were going to be stress-free and all about comfort, if he had anything to say about it.

Arriving in the kitchen, he spotted the girls out on the back patio. Though they each held a coffee cup, there was no evidence breakfast had been prepared. Jayden poured himself a cup of rich, brown coffee, and seeing it was the last in the pot, flipped the machine off. The kettle on the stove top surprised him—he hadn't known he even owned one. On the counter near the tea pot sat a container of some over-priced gourmet cocoa mix—another thing he hadn't realized they had on hand. On a whim, he decided to add a scoop to his coffee.

Enjoying his first taste, he pondered the pair outside. They appeared deep in conversation, and with Natalie's condition, Jayden knew food was in order. Dried and canned goods were all they had left in the house, since they'd made sure to clean out the perishables before leaving on their trip. Scribbling a quick note, he left it leaning against the coffee pot in case Erin came back inside before his return.

While he drove to the nearest bakery, Jayden's mind ran about a mile a minute. When they'd invited Natalie back to the house, it had been his intention to let her stay at the Villa in their absence. Micah could do a grocery run to make sure she had supplies, and she'd have him nearby if she needed anything. Yet he couldn't get the image of the two girls on the patio out of his head.

Erin and Natty had hit it off rather well. Was it right to leave the girl there alone after her ordeal, and over the holidays no less? *Not really.*

Once he parked the car in the bakery lot, he called his sister. "Hey, Ronnie, do you mind if we bring a friend?"

After giving his sister the basics of Natalie's situation, Ronnie demanded the girl come along. Considering they only had one spare room, Jayden made arrangements for him and Erin to stay at a hotel so Natty could use the room at the house. Both Ronnie and Jayden agreed she needed to be around loving, supportive people. He didn't mind the new plans—he and Erin would be able to make good use of the privacy a hotel room granted.

Feeling confident the girls would be pleased with his arrangements, he strolled into the bakery. His nose was assaulted by butter, sugar, and other sweet smells, and Jayden's appetite roared to life. He stepped up to the counter to order.

"Morning, sir. What can I getcha today?"

"Good morning." He flashed her a smile. "I'm on vacation and think some splurging is in order." Fifteen minutes later, he returned to the car with two dozen assorted sinful delights in his possession. Before starting the car, he helped himself to an apple fritter—his favorite.

An hour after that, the trio was well on their way to Corpus Christi. Erin and Natalie were sharing the back seat, where a box of donuts sat between them. Their happy chatter was soothing background noise while he drove.

ℬℭ
CHAPTER FOURTEEN
ℬℭ

"Oh my god, I'm so full." Erin flopped back on the bed, her knees bent over the edge, and toed off her heels. She and Jayden had just gotten back to their hotel after a 'date night' with Ronnie and Steph. Natty had stayed with the babies.

"You will be," he promised, nudging her legs open with his knee.

She felt the heat of his body between her thighs, and then the mattress compressed at either side of her head. He was leaning over her; so close she could taste the sweet musk of his scent on her tongue. Erin puckered her lips and lifted her head, looking to be kissed.

Her lover granted her a brief reprieve, pressing his mouth to hers hard and fast, but then he straightened up and backed away.

Erin groaned and propped herself up on her elbows so she could see him. She exhaled, blowing away the loose wisps of red hair near her face. Her mouth went dry under his heated stare while he untucked his shirt from his slacks and began unbuttoning it.

The look he was giving her clearly stated: "I'm going to fuck you, and you will enjoy every second of it." However, Jayden went on talking like he wasn't contemplating doing naughty, dirty, wonderful things to her while he stared her down. "Ronnie mentioned having some concern about Natalie."

All the man was doing was disrobing in front of her, but her sense of propriety was evaporating in favor of greedy lust. His continuing conversational tone flummoxed her, but she played along.

"Something does seem off, but I've chalked it up to everything that happened before we came down here. And we can't forget that she's in a house full of people she's never met, so it could be a case of shyness."

"Maybe. I can't let go of the fact that I never should've taken her through the club doors. Natalie doesn't belong in our world. She's too sweet and innocent."

He worked the shirt off his shoulders and let it fall to the floor. Her eyes zeroed in on the flexing of his pectorals. A lecherous grin pulled at his lips, and he unhooked the button on his trousers.

"However, you, my jewel, are anything but innocent in this dress, though I'm sure you taste quite sweet."

Erin's chest tightened at the sight of him dropping to his knees. He scooted up to the end of the bed and her legs were forced further apart. Her already short skirt inched higher.

"You can't blame yourself, Jayden. You didn't know this would happen."

"Open your legs, Catherine." The roughness in his voice did things to her, muddied her thinking, and got her heart racing.

"Um, I take it we're done talking about Natalie?" she whispered.

He braced his hands on her knees and pushed. "Open."

The skirt material dug into her thighs when it bunched and rolled up to her hips, exposing her center. She wore a poor excuse for panties. The tiny scrap of lace barely hid her—until he hooked a finger in the crotch and twisted the material. With a sharp yank that jerked her whole body, the flimsy fabric gave way, making any further resistance futile.

She bucked when his adept tongue was buried in her pussy. "Mm, thank you, Master."

The occupant of the room next door could be heard moving about. Knowing their upcoming activities might be overheard sent a spike of excitement through Catherine and a pleading noise escaped her throat.

Master chuckled against her pussy lips seconds before she felt cooler—all over. The zipper which ran the length of the front of her dress was being opened, the metal teeth retracting to expose her fair skin. At the bottom, he freed the zipper from the track, then threw back the sides of her dress.

"Damn, woman. You're fucking exquisite." He delivered the words while touching her pussy with lazy back and forth strokes.

Spread like she was made his attentions feel more possessive, and her core throbbed because of it. Catherine thrilled at being His slut. A pleased smile took over her face while she absorbed his compliment.

"There's my jewel. You have such a beautiful smile." He slipped two fingers into her, curling them forward to tease the spongy flesh inside of her. It took mere moments for pressure to start building, taking over her lower abdomen and making her writhe against his hand, seeking release. "I'd do anything to get you to share it with me."

She tried to smile at the sweetness in the sentiment, but he pressed a hand to her belly and began thrusting those fingers in and out of her with the perfect roughness, which soon had her begging: "Please, Master, may this girl come?"

He ignored her plea, but slowed down his movements. The change in speed let her compose herself—for a few moments, at least.

"Master, please—"

He cut her off with what she thought was a rather random inquiry. "Why do you wear those pearls, Catherine?"

Giving the question consideration distracted the submissive from her need to orgasm. She rode the edge of it, of course, but her mind was busy seeking the answer. Touching the smooth stones around her neck, it came to her: "Because serving you is divine, Master."

One last thing escaped him before he could no longer speak, his mouth returning his mouth to her pussy. "You may come when ready, pet."

Ready turned out to be the third lap of his tongue, and all worries over Natalie evaporated for the duration of the night while the couple lost themselves in the steamy, passionate meeting of flesh.

❧

The day of Christmas Eve dawned, and Woody O'Chancey arrived first thing that morning. He'd be staying for a couple of days before he had to get back to the ranch. While the rest of the group would remain in Corpus Christi through New Year's Eve, Jayden was glad Erin would at least get Christmas with him—it had been too long since they'd celebrated the holiday together.

About mid-morning, Jayden got up to stretch his legs from the couch where he was watching the game with Woody and his dad. He noticed Natalie shuffling down the hall, her shoulders hunched forward. The rest of the ladies were in the kitchen, baking, cooking, and laughing way more than was probably safe for the men in the house. Curious, he followed her to her room to check on her.

She tried to blame her hormones when he asked her if everything was okay.

"I'll buy that to a point, Natalie, but you haven't been yourself since we got here. Is there anything Erin or I can do?"

"You're a kind man, Mr. Masterson, but my burden is not yours to bear."

"I'm touched you think so, Natalie. But I'm also a man of means, and you are far from being a burden to me, little one. Erin and I just want to help. A new baby should be about happiness, right?" His voice lowered with his thoughts drifting to Erin. "Not everyone can have one, though. They're a true gift."

Natalie burst into tears, and Jayden reached for her but then shrank back, tucking his hands into his pockets. She wasn't his submissive or family, and he had no place touching her. He just didn't know what else to do for the girl while she continued to break down in front of him. *Fuck it*, he thought. Jayden gathered her up in a hug, and she latched onto him, soon soaking the front of his shirt with her tears.

"Hey, Natty, Jillian's about to teach us her secret fudge recipe—" Erin pulled up short when she poked her head around the door and saw them.

He glanced down at the top of Natalie's head, then over to his love with a look that he hoped conveyed "Help me."

"Oh. Hi, Jayden. Everything alright?" She stepped into the room and pushed the door closed behind her to maintain some privacy.

Natalie sniffled against him, then pulled away, wiping her nose on her sleeve. "Oh, jeez. I'm sorry, Erin. This must look awful, but it was nothing, I promise."

Erin laughed. "No worries, lass. I hug him every chance I get, too. He smells awful good."

A small smile snuck onto Natalie's face.

"What's up, guys? Why do we have tears at Christmas?" she asked, and Jayden shrugged, still unsure what had set Natalie off.

She fed Erin the same line about hormones that she'd given him. Seeing a hint of longing flash in Erin's eyes in response, he let it drop for the moment. Jayden had every intention of revisiting the issue with Natalie at a later time. And now, it seemed he also needed to get Erin to share how she felt about the girl's pregnancy, or more specifically, how she *really* felt about having kids with him. *Damn.*

Plastering a smile on her face, Natalie hooked arms with his girl. "I've always wanted to learn how to make fudge. Mine comes out grainy every time."
With a laugh, Erin blew him a kiss then let Natty lead her from the room. He watched them go, lingering behind for a few minutes.

ଛଔଓଷ

Christmas morning turned out to be an exercise in controlled chaos in the small house. Pushing nine months, Benny and Joon were crawling everywhere and beginning to pull up and walk with the aid of furniture. In other words, they were mobile, and into everything. It was hilarious to watch, yet Erin noticed Natalie stayed withdrawn, observing from a quiet corner while the rest of the family laughed and stuck bows on Joon's head. Drooling, Benny would grab the shiny decorations and stick them on his own wispy locks with a cheesy grin and a gurgling noise.

When Erin tried to catch Jayden's eye, she couldn't. It seemed his attention was on Natalie, too. Thinking the girl might be fighting a bout of morning sickness, Erin slipped away to the kitchen to prepare a cup of ginger tea. Her effort was rewarded with a thank you and Natalie re-engaging with the group. The morning went on, and while the kids ripped through their packages with glee, the adults took turns passing gifts to each other.

Erin got teary-eyed when she unwrapped the small gift from her da. It was her *maimeo's* handwritten recipe book—he'd kept it and taken care of it. Erin had given up ever seeing the collection again when she'd run from California, so to have that treasured piece of her grandma returned meant more than she could put into words. Instead of trying to vocalize her gratitude, Erin crawled into his lap for a hug while they shared a silent moment in Caroline's memory.

From Jayden's parents, she got a 'paid' receipt from Tailored by Tanner. They'd bought the custom gown for her. Likewise, they gave Jayden a similar receipt for the florist, showing that all of the orchids and roses for the ceremony had been taken care of.

Grateful for their generosity, both objected that Malcolm and Jillian had done too much, but Malcolm spoke up, telling Jayden he needed to save his pennies to take his woman somewhere classy for the honeymoon. Which, of course, led to the discussion of destinations.

"Have you been to Ireland, Mr. Masterson?" Natalie posed the simple question, and it was like a light bulb went on.

Erin's breath caught, an involuntary smile creeping onto her face at the very idea of going back. Over two decades had elapsed since she'd last walked on Irish soil. She'd been ten, and her da had taken her to Bunratty in County Clare for Caroline's funeral.

"Could we?" The two words were whispered low but were filled with hope.

"Anything for you, sweet girl. If that's what you'd like, then that's where we'll go."

"Aye, I think I'd like that very much." Her mind began spinning, a building enthusiasm threatening to burst the more she dwelled on seeing the emerald landscape again.

Benny chose that moment to plaster a metallic green bow on Erin's nose. The room dissolved into laughter, and the next set of packages were plunked down in front of the twins. After all the boxes and envelopes had been pillaged, they gorged themselves on dinner. Being a ranch family, the traditional ham and turkey were overlooked in favor of a slow-smoked brisket with all the trimmings.

In front of the family, Jayden gave Erin a voucher for a year's worth of couple's massages at Silver Spurs. However, back at the hotel that night once they were alone, he had one more surprise. Her Master presented Catherine with a certificate issuing her a registered submissive number and a silver anklet, from which a charm engraved with the digits hung. He'd taken the time to have his ownership of her recorded in the public Lifestyle annals, which left her speechless for the second time that day.

It was the wee hours of the morning before she finished showing her appreciation for the official declaration.

ॐ
CHAPTER FIFTEEN
ॐ

A few days after they'd gotten back from Corpus Christi, Natalie had ended up revealing to Erin that she had an older sister. It turned out that Nina had been away at college when things had gone sour between Natalie and her parents, which had led to her being kicked out. It took Jayden and Erin several days to convince Natalie that she needed to reach out to her sister. Nina had been beside herself to hear from her baby sister at last, explaining that by the time she'd found out what their parents had done, Natalie was nowhere to be found. Nina was now married and living in Denver.

Natalie's withdrawn behavior over the holiday had continued to disturb Jayden, so when he'd learned of Nina, he'd insisted on buying a plane ticket for Natalie as a belated Christmas gift. He hoped a few days free from worrying about the reality of her situation would be good for her. Who knew? Maybe Nina would be in a position to help Natalie. The girl needed family. Dr. Ellison also encouraged the excursion before she got much farther into the pregnancy and it became risky for health reasons—in addition to going before Natty's increasing size made travel miserable. So, for the first time in what seemed like months, Jayden and Erin had the house to themselves.

Surprise over how fast Natalie's body was changing had Jayden's thoughts wandering more frequently to having that talk with Erin about whether they should pursue having children of their own someday. There were so many factors to be considered. First and foremost, he needed to ascertain his jewel's readiness to take on the topic.

Should he get her hopes up? What if she wanted to be a mom with all of her heart and it couldn't happen? Was he too old to be a dad? If she was able to give him children, would they be able to maintain both sides of their Lifestyle?

Upon their return from their Christmas vacation, the dental office Erin had been temping for hired her full-time. No longer able to have her swing by the office for a quickie, he wasn't seeing her as often.

A baby would just add to that distance, wouldn't it?

He would've preferred that she go back to school and finish her degree rather than work, but Jayden couldn't deny she was happy. That's what mattered. She had agreed to enroll in one online course per term so that some progress toward her diploma would be made, since Spencer had prevented her from getting it the first time around.

Again, how would a baby fit into her, their, burgeoning plans?

Her main concession to him had been allowing Micah to drive her to and from work, not that he'd given her much choice. Caveman-like, Jayden had played the Dom card by reminding her of his responsibility for her comfort and safety. To him, that safety meant knowing she wasn't using public transportation alone since she didn't want to get her driver's license. Because they rode together, there was a small bonus of a few precious extra minutes on the morning commute. However, his workday ended later than hers, so he was always the last one home.

Home.

He had never considered the surrounding brick and mortar as anything more than just that—building materials. Erin's permanent presence had changed his outlook. Her arrival had breathed life and hopeful expectations for the future into the place. Even Natalie was beginning to make her mark.

Arriving at the Villa, weary after a long day at work, Jayden parked the Wraith. Due to a late meeting, he'd driven himself that morning. At least it'd been a successful day. He'd finalized the details for Erin's birthday surprise next month while handling some overseas business. Now all he wanted to do was get some food in his stomach and his girl in his arms.

Entering the foyer, he paused at the absolute quiet of the house. There was no music from the sound system, accompanied by absent-minded singing in the kitchen while dinner was prepared. No sounds came from upstairs to indicate she might've opted for a quick shower, either. Concern bubbled in his chest, tightening it.

Why wasn't she home yet?

Jayden dropped his briefcase under the hall table, tossed his keys in the collection plate, and strode toward the garage while digging his cell phone out. If the Towne Car wasn't there, he was calling her, but it was, so Micah had to have brought her home. Spinning around, he retraced his steps back to the kitchen.

Everything was neat and tidy, and the dishwasher running. *So where was Erin?* Pivoting, he noticed a piece of paper on the refrigerator and moved closer to read it. Jayden grinned at what he saw—Erin's pretty handwriting inviting him to join her in the hot tub.

The woman was amazing, never failing to know just what he needed. Wanting to show her what she meant to him, he rushed upstairs to get out of his suit. Jayden found her in the hot tub, naked, just like he'd hoped. Her head was against the edge, red tresses a deep scarlet where the tips had caught in the whirlpool of the tub, and eyes closed while she rocked her head to the music playing in her ears. Her pierced nipples floated on the water with the buoyancy of her breasts. Exquisite, and so delicious looking.

He'd been able to get in the water and to halfway close the distance between them before he bumped her foot and her eyes flew open. Bright emeralds flashed at him while her lips turned up in a pleased smile.

"Jayden," she crooned, yanking the buds from her ears and lifting herself out of the water to get to him faster. The water sluiced down her tits, and he licked his lips, bringing a delightful giggle from her. "Did you have a hard day, baby?"

At his nod, she moved into his arms and pressed her hot body against his cool one. Unlike her, he hadn't been simmering in the steaming water. Their lips found each other, seeking out a re-acquaintance like they hadn't been entwined just nine hours earlier.

It didn't take long for their hands to join in, moving and sliding across each other's flesh. The moment Jayden confirmed that she was slick and ready for him, he lifted her up, then lowered her body onto his cock. Moaning at the sensation, their mouths ripped apart for air, and he began to move deep within her.

Together they rocked, working toward the common goal of their release, yet not caring if they achieved it. To be locked together that way was more than enough for the couple. As one, they reconnected, and their love strengthened. Their final moment of blissful release came after changing positions. Jayden sat on the wraparound bench while Erin mounted him, reverse cowgirl style. *So what if the surrounding deck was soaked from all the water they'd splashed out?*

Sated and drowsy, Erin leaned back against his chest while the bubbles frothed and popped around them. His softening cock was still buried inside her, and he was content to let it stay while they recovered from their impromptu ravaging of each other.

"We should probably think about getting out, Erin. You're going to get all pruney." His finger sought her side and poked her, making her squeal and wiggle so that his cock slipped out of her.

With a groan, she rolled off his lap, sloshing more water out of the tub. Turning, she darted in to peck his lips, then climbed out with Jayden right behind her. She started shivering. The water had been hot, but the early January temperature outside, not so much.

Laughing and scrambling to dry off, the lovers rushed back inside. Upstairs, they elected to pull on some comfy pajamas and have a movie night on the couch.

Jayden put in a call to Micah to see if he'd run up the road to the deli café and pick up some dinner for them, but the phone went unanswered. Then he remembered it was now Micah's official day off, along with weekends. Sharing his personal assistant with Shawn was taking some getting used to.

"It's Tuesday, Jayden," Erin scolded, catching on to what he was trying to do when she came into the room. "Let the poor boy have some space to get acquainted with his Dom." She laughed, the sound warming his insides.

"But I'm hungry and we just got our PJs on—"

"So," she cut him off, "doesn't change the day. You go get the movie going, and I'll whip up something for us to eat." After a kiss on his pouty lips, she disappeared into the other room, and Jayden began looking over the selection of Blu-rays.

❧◊☙
CHAPTER SIXTEEN
❧◊☙

E rin didn't have to think too hard to come up with a meal plan. She'd taken on the task of the shopping and cooking, and therefore knew what was in her cupboards. *My cupboards*, she thought. The idea was still new enough that she felt giddy anytime she let herself dwell on it.

Happiness saturated her whole being while she moved about the kitchen, throwing together some chicken quesadillas and a mixture of salsa, sour cream, and cheese for a dip. When the food was ready, she loaded it, along with some sodas, onto a carrying tray and went to the den.

"What are we watching?" She set the tray on the coffee table.

Jayden held up the case for *Zombieland*. "That smells fantastic, whatever it is."

She let out a playful groan. "Again? Don't you have it memorized yet?"

Jayden gave her a smile, and it went all the way up to his deep brown eyes. "I have, yes, but you haven't," he teased then pressed play.

They dug into the cheesy-chicken goodness, Jayden first complimenting the way she'd gotten the tortillas to crisp to a golden brown color, then giving porn stars a run for their money with the sounds he made after tasting it slathered in dip. Taking turns, they recited the movie lines, cuddled and shared sweet kisses, and laughed about rules and Twinkies. All around, it was a fun evening.

It wasn't until later, while rinsing up the few dishes she'd dirtied making their dinner that something dawned on Erin. While she'd learned a fair bit about her fiancé since first meeting him, even a lot about his childhood thanks to chats with Jillian, Erin didn't know how he'd gotten into the Lifestyle. *How could she not know such a vital piece of who he was, when she would be taking such a major step as marriage with him?*

Erin and Jayden made their way through the house in silence, checking locks, setting the alarm, and turning off the lights. With no awkwardness, they shared the large bathroom while they got ready for bed. The whole time, Erin's brain was working to figure out a way to ask him about his past. In the end, she waited to broach the subject until they'd crawled into bed and were shrouded in darkness with her firmly tucked against Jayden's side.

"*A rúnsearc?*" she began in a low voice, her accent flaring when her mouth shaped around the endearment.

"Yes, sweet girl, what is it?"

She could hear the exhaustion in his voice and almost let it go. Would have, if he hadn't chosen that moment to seek out her hand and thread his fingers through hers.

"I was curious . . ."

Jayden's chuckle jarred his torso where her head rested. "When aren't you curious, Erin?" he teased, then brushed his lips against her forehead.

With a light slap to his abdomen, she settled back against him and began running her fingertip in figure eights over his bare chest. "How did you know?"

"Know what?" His voice had deepened, and his nipple hardened when she traced it.

"That this life was for you. How does a guy who was raised on a ranch, in the middle of nowhere, learn about BDSM, let alone decide to pursue it?" The words rushed out, and she held her breath, waiting for his answer.

Jayden had been on his back, an arm around Erin's shoulders and crossing over her body to lock fingers with her. His other hand, which had been behind his head, he now brought down to cradle her face. "You want my story, huh?"

Erin nodded, letting out a little of the breath she was holding. He seemed calm enough—that was good.

"It's nothing sordid or macabre, if that's what you're thinking."

Her shoulders moved up and down with a shrug at his joking response. She didn't have any preconceived notions about his answer, considering the question was more of an afterthought than anything else.

He went on. "I didn't have a sexy nanny who was into spanking—"

Erin's braying laughter cut him off. Her head filling with the image of a young Jayden in a suit and a full grown woman offering her ass to him for a paddling was too much. It didn't help when he ignored her antics, adding more fuel to the fire instead.

"Nor was there some illicit relationship in my college years." His hand had moved from her face, down her side, and now he tickled her waist until she was breathless and begging him to stop between gasps of air. When he let up and she'd regained her composure, she turned on him.

"Hey, now! Nothing inappropriate ever happened with Andrew while I was a student. He was very adamant those lines never be crossed. You know that, you bully." She stuck her tongue out and got a bright smile from her lover. Calming down, she crawled back into his arms. He'd moved into a sitting position, so she nestled her naked back against his warm chest and hummed in contentment when he hugged her.

"You know, I think it'd be nice to meet this Andrew guy someday. He seems like a good fellow," Jayden mused, his fingertips trailing along her neck and shoulder, then down her arm.

With a small snort, she suggested they invite Mr. Brenner to the wedding, which, to her surprise, Jayden got rather enthusiastic about.

"I'll see what I can do about finding his address, if you're serious."

His chin bounced on the top of her head while he nodded. "I am."

"Fine. Enough about Andrew, though. I want to hear about you."

�❧

The moment she'd surprised him with the question about his past, Jayden's mind had begun scrambling. *How much should he tell her?* Erin knew he and Landon had a Lifestyle past, but would she be okay if she learned how the pieces had come together?

Distracting her with light-hearted teasing bought him a few minutes. She was just being inquisitive, and he couldn't fault her for that. It was silly of him to be hesitant about this. After the personal history she'd shared with him and the experiences they'd actualized together thus far, there was no fear of Erin running from this information. Besides, she was going to be learning it first hand in a few months, once he and his friend sorted out the logistics for the weekend they were planning.

Suck it up man, and spill for the lady.

"It starts with Landon . . . and the Marquis de Sade." He stopped there to gauge her reaction.

She shifted after a minute, swiveling her neck to look back and up at him. "Interesting. Go on, then."

Jayden exhaled roughly, and Erin chuckled in his arms. Of course she was going to be okay with this. He started talking.

"I met Landon at Rice. He was in the graduate program, zeroing in on his PhD in psychology, while I was working on my Masters through the Jones School of Business."

"Wait, but that means Landon is *older* than you?" The disbelief in her voice amused him.

"Yes, by a couple of years."

"But Paige is so young looking . . ."

"Our age gap isn't exactly insignificant either, Erin. Does the idea bother you?"

He thought he could see her nose crinkling before she settled back against him with a harrumph. "Not when you put it like that."

Long hair spread over his chest and ribs, and the scent of her cherry-bamboo shampoo wafted up his nose. When he breathed in, his body reacted to the sweet odor.

"Oh, no, mister. We're not fooling around right now. I'm tired, and you're talking." She clapped her hands. "Chop, chop."

The playful response drew more laughter from him, and he opted to taunt her further while pressing his hips up into her. "Yes, Madame, as you wish." Her body went rigid then ever so slowly relaxed while he resumed stroking his fingers up and down her arms.

"Anyway, we ended up in the same English class, a Humanities course focused on the grotesque in literature. While it was a degree requirement for Landon, I was there for fun. I'd chosen it as an elective to shake up the monotony of my math and business courses."

Erin wriggled from his grasp and turned her body so that she could straddle his thighs. "Sounds reasonable. Out of curiosity, now that you mention your courses, how did you end up in the metalworking business?"

"Easy. The horses." It was clear that didn't answer her question by the 'what the fuck' look on her face, and he laughed. "I always found it fascinating to go down to the stables and watch the smiths and farriers work on the horseshoes. Seeing the metal heat up, become red hot, and then get bent and shaped under the smith's hand . . ."

She'd started shaking her head while laughter bubbled out of her. "Sounds kinky."

He squeezed her bottom, and she shrieked.

"I still can't believe he's older than you."

"You're cute." She sighed when he kissed her nose. Reaching out to the side, Jayden switched on the table lamp so he could gauge her emotions while the conversation progressed. Her emerald eyes shone with curiosity, nothing more. "We were polite to each other in passing for the first half of the class term. Then came the 'Defend or Refute' team project. The professor went through the roster and divided the class into two groups for pro and con representatives. From there, we were allowed to find a partner and select a book."

"So let me guess." Erin shifted on his lap, and he groaned at the increased pressure. "You dragged your feet and got stuck with de Sade?"

Shaking his head with amusement, he went on explaining. "Not quite. Landon approached me right after the professor finished outlining the assignment and had released us to pair up. From what I'd seen of him, he seemed like a decent guy, and I didn't know anyone else in the class, so I said sure. He rushed us down to the book selection so fast, I didn't really know what was happening." A small chuckle escaped Jayden when he recalled that afternoon.

"Somehow Landon guided me toward *120 Days of Sodom* and let me think I was choosing it. I know better now, of course."

Fine wrinkles appeared on Erin's brow, a sure indicator she was working something out in her head. "You have a question, sweet girl?"

Some of her silky red hair slipped down over her bare shoulder when she shook her head. "I've heard of de Sade, but haven't ever read his works, so I'm not familiar with the specifics of his titles."

This surprised Jayden. "Oh, really? A pain slut such as yourself . . ." he snaked his hands up to her tits and grabbed them roughly, drawing an elongated sigh from her, ". . . hasn't read the infamous Marquis? The horror!" Releasing her, Jayden brought a hand to cover his open mouth in feigned shock.

At her pout, he pulled her in for a kiss then promised to task her with reading assignments in the future. It would be perfect for the next time he had to be gone on business. With Erin gainfully employed, he couldn't take her away with him at the drop of a hat. Though for her to accept the job, Jayden had stipulated she was granted the last two weeks of February off. They had plans that started in Harlingen for Paige and Landon's wedding but ended in another country for his girl's birthday.

"If it would please you," she purred against his lips, "but until then, how about the Cliff Notes version?" With a giggle, she bounced back on his lap, forcing a mangled grunt from him.

"Well, some feel that it is de Sade's most depraved work, and it crosses extreme limits. Rather controversial, you can imagine. *Sodom* relays the story of a group of rich men who think themselves above the rest of society. Out of boredom, they bring in both willing whores and not-so-willing captives, then proceed to act out any and all fantasies they can conjure in their perverted minds. The scenes quickly move from morbid curiosity to darker themes, and eventually to snuff levels. All stages of the book include some degree of torture to them."

"Oh." The word slipped from her lips on a hushed murmur.

"Yeah. My task was to find the redeeming quality in the book and use that to defend it. You've met my parents, Erin. 'Wholesome' best describes my upbringing. I was taught to be respectful to all, people and animals alike. Above all, Mom and Dad drilled it into me to respect women and to never take for granted what a miraculous creation they are."

His jewel's arms slithered around him, and she laid her head upon his chest. "Your heart is racing just talking about it," she whispered.

"Yeah, so anyway, Landon told me he'd heard it was a great book and said we should definitely do it. That the piece would be 'challenging.' I agreed, and by the third night of reading it, I was realizing just how challenging it was going to be." Jayden paused to pull in a breath.

It was truth time.

"In reading it, I started having physical reactions, and all kinds of conflicting thoughts began cropping up in my head."

"Oh?" She tilted her head to the side.

He hugged her, soaking in the warmth of her body on his. "Suppose I should clarify that at that point in my life, I'd had sex a grand total of three times."

"No way." Erin sat up in surprise.

"All with the same girl, and in the most vanilla fashion you can imagine, too." He chuckled.

"Wow. Okay, then. Go on."

"That's the gist of it, really . . ."

"I don't think so, mister. All you've told me is that reading about some whippings got your cock hard. Knowing you now, that doesn't surprise me in the slightest. I wanna know how the leap was made to go from *that* to getting you into a playroom with the whip in your hand."

"Jeez, woman, all right." Jayden laughed at her feistiness. "Landon picked up on my issues at our first study session. We'd agreed to meet twice a week until we'd finished the book, to discuss our thoughts and findings, and from there we would determine what was needed to do our presentation. He had a small loft apartment just outside of the campus and had invited me there so we could 'talk freely,' as he put it.

Long story short, it turned out that Landon was a Dominant in training."

Erin's face startled at the revelation.

"What can I say? It was the start of a beautiful friendship." The right side of his mouth quirked up in a half smile. "With his help, I finished the book, we got the project out of the way, and then we delved into the true nature of my reaction to *Sodom*. Landon and his mentor—Tommy Sharpe, Sir Tom—helped me understand what made me tick. But the most important thing I walked away with after my time with them was that it was okay, and I wasn't a freak."

"So when you've mentioned in the past that you've subbed for Sir Landon . . ." Erin put the question out there unfinished.

"I meant it. I've also submitted beside him, but only to Sir Tom, and there was no penetration. It was mental training more than anything." There was no point in holding any of the details back from her.

"I thought Paige told me he used to work on a ranch, though."

"He did, the Flying M." Jayden burst out laughing when her mouth fell open again.

"Are you sure you two aren't brothers? I mean, how many areas of your past overlap, for crying out loud?" Erin queried with a shake of her head.

"After that class, and with our newfound friendship, Landon and I ended up rooming together the rest of his time at Rice. During the summer months, he'd come home with me and earn some extra pocket change working for my dad. Once he graduated, he headed up here to Dallas, and it seemed natural to follow him when my time came. While Landon used the summers as downtime to educate his soul and body with 'Good hard labor and pore-cleansing hot sun,' I was using my time outlining my business portfolio and working on contacts, all of it in preparation for launching Masterson Metalworks."

"It really is a small world, isn't it?" Erin said with a sigh before rolling off his lap. She flopped onto her back, her arms opened wide, and Jayden couldn't help noticing how her tits jiggled.

"Yeah, I guess it is, isn't it? It's been second nature, having him around all the time, so I never thought about it before." On impulse, he reached over to draw his fingertips over her soft belly.

"You're right. It's a cool story, but it does seem a bit anticlimactic," she teased. "Though it is proof that we can't help who we are—even before we know what it is we need. We both got lucky that we stumbled across someone able to shed some light on our dark cravings for us."

"And I was the luckiest of all, when I happened upon you in that line all those months ago, sweet girl."

ℛℐℛ

CHAPTER SEVENTEEN

ℛℐℛ

While Erin was busy with work, helping Paige and Landon with their final preparations, and ensuring Natalie was taking care of herself and keeping her appointments with Holly, January turned into February in the blink of an eye. Before she knew it, the time for their friends' Valentine's Day wedding down in Harlingen had arrived.

Using the Masterson Metalworks private jet, they were going to fly down with Natalie, Paige, and

Landon in tow. After the ceremony, the newlyweds would travel on to the Caribbean for their honeymoon using the jet. Erin and Jayden would fly out of Valley International on a commercial line to get them overseas. However, while Erin knew Jayden had made plans to continue on after the weekend for an extended 'birthday vacation,' she still had no idea of their final destination. He'd been sure to keep that information under tight wraps.

The ceremony was being kept comfortable and small. Jayden's parents would be in South Padre for the wedding since they considered Landon a son, but they wouldn't be able to stay the whole weekend. They'd be there Friday for the event itself, and then Natalie would return to the Flying M with them so she wasn't on her own at the Villa while Jayden and Erin were gone.

Paige was originally from the Harlingen area, so the Halston clan would be there in force, making up the majority of the guest list. Other than that, Landon's brother Liam had said he wouldn't miss the wedding for the world. With the exception of the Mastersons, Liam was the only family Landon had.

The Michaels brothers had lost their mother a few years earlier to ovarian cancer, and their dad was in a special facility that catered to Alzheimer's patients. Mr. Michaels no longer knew who his boys were, but they seemed to have made peace with that.

While the ceremony was set for Friday at sunset, they were flying down Wednesday night. Thursday would be spent on the rehearsal and handling any last minute tasks, then Friday morning the wedding party would meet at the spa owned by Paige's aunt to get made up for that evening. Erin had assumed they were going down the night before so that they could hit the ground running on Thursday, and so she was surprised when they arrived and Jayden directed *Catherine* to freshen up and get ready for dinner.

"No disrespect, Sir, but should we do this with Natalie present?"

"She won't be. I invited her to take advantage of room service and Pay-Per-View. She knows we will be out and is content to hang out upstairs for the evening. Now, don't dally, my jewel. Landon and Paige are expecting us for a special evening."

Oh. "Aye, Master." With no further hesitation, Erin went to the bedroom and got ready.

Catherine emerged ten minutes later dressed in a simple but striking black and white sundress that showed off the inky pearls around her neck. Her Master waited by the open patio door, which opened onto the beach. When he turned to greet her, she eyed him hungrily, feeling her body begin to heat.

He still wore the loose fitting jeans he'd traveled in, but he had changed into a clean shirt. It was unbuttoned all the way down, and his bronze abdomen looked amazing framed by the moss green linen. Without a word, he crossed the room to take her chin in his large hand. Tilting it up, he leaned down and drove his tongue into her mouth, staking his claim.

"You are beguiling as ever, Catherine. Come, we're going to be late." Master turned on his heel and passed through the patio doors out onto the sand.

She paused at the door to slip off her heels and carry them—there was no way she'd be able to maneuver the beach terrain in them—then fell into step, behind him and to the left. A few minutes later, they arrived at a condo down the beach. Sir Landon appeared at the door and invited them in.

Straight away, she recognized the scent of burning candles and noticed Paige standing in a corner. Her friend wore a simple white shift, through which her dark nipples were visible. In her hands she held a white rosebud that had just begun to unfurl. While uncertain what was happening, Catherine could feel the importance of the moment hanging heavy in the room.

Master reached for her hand and escorted her to a nearby chair. "Please kneel, jewel." He perched on the edge of the chair then directed his attention to Sir Landon.

What she witnessed in the next twenty minutes had her weeping quiet tears. They slipped down her cheeks at the beauty unfolding in front of her. It was a part of the Lifestyle she'd never known existed. Catherine witnessed her first Ceremony of the Roses, and her respect for their way of life deepened.

With thorns, flames, a little blood, and a chain, Sir Landon and Paige exchanged private vows, committing to their Lifestyle roles for eternity. Master assisted with parts of the ceremony, acting as an extra pair of hands when needed. The symbolism and raw emotion of the deed rocked Catherine down to her core, and she hoped one day Master would invite her to partake in the Ceremony with Him.

Paige changed into a public-appropriate outfit afterward, and the foursome made their way down the beach to Blackbeard's Restaurant. Getting a table out on the sand, they enjoyed a relaxing night. The men reminisced about their Rice days, while the ladies laughed at the stories and even managed to share some of their own. Once everyone's bellies were filled with fresh seafood and virgin daiquiris, the tab was settled, and the group strolled back to the Bahia Mar. Saying goodnight, Master got her back to their rental in record time. The way he ravaged her, she had to assume the night had been special for him, too. The magnitude of the occasion must have made him as desperate to connect with her as she had been to connect with him.

Catherine slept better that night than she had in weeks. With the sound of the waves, her lover's hand laid possessively around her waist, and her freshly-spanked bottom nestled against his spent cock, it was a given.

୧୨

Erin fought hard not to cry at the beauty of the wedding ceremony Paige had orchestrated. In the end, a few tears had escaped anyway. The weather was balmy and mild, with the gentlest of salt-tinged breezes shifting the air around the small assembly. Flowers, décor, and wardrobe all blended without effort into the setting sun in the background. It could've been a Norman Rockwell painting in the perfect way everything came together.

Standing to the side, she couldn't get the images from the rose ceremony out of her head. Now they flashed faster and in sharper focus, overlapping Paige and Landon's exchange of vanilla vows and driving home the commitment her friends were making to each other. It was the same pact she couldn't wait to seal with Jayden in a few short months.

Following a good, old-fashioned crab boil reception on the beach, Jayden and Erin made the rounds, saying goodnight and goodbye. They were on the first flight out at dawn.

ॐॐ
CHAPTER EIGHTEEN
ॐॐ

Half-asleep and near comatose, Erin let Jayden guide her through Valley International Airport. She dozed her way through check-in and security, leaning against him in a sleepy daze whenever they came to a standstill. Just because they'd left the reception the night before at a reasonable hour didn't mean they'd gone to sleep at early.

Without toys or bindings of any sort, the lovers had embraced the raw emotions of the evening and used nothing but their bodies to express the depths of their passion to one another. Last night might have been measured and sensual, but it had also been every bit as intense as their evening of kinky abandon the first evening they'd arrived—and she was worn out.

It wasn't until they were standing in line for coffee that her head caught up to what her ears had been hearing over the airport PA system. They were taking an international flight.

"Jayden?"

"Yes, sweet girl?" His eyes were fixed on the menu ahead of them, scanning the selections.

"Where are you taking me?" On her right, a gate showed a flight to Tokyo, while the gate next to it was for London. To her left, there were gates for assorted destinations in Germany and Mexico. Most of them were American Airlines gates, so that didn't help her make any deductions.

He looked down at her with a grin then answered in cryptic fashion. "I have an old friend I want you to meet. What do you want to drink?"

"Quad venti white mocha with soy, no whip. Where are we going?"

"I think you're frequenting this chain too often if you can spout off that tongue twister, when you can't even keep your eyes open."

"Jayden."

"That's my name, Erin."

He was being a stubborn ass, and she loved it. Her pulse picked up with their banter. "Arg–" His mouth crashed into hers, catching her offguard and melting her so that she whimpered under the onslaught while getting lost in his taste.

The barista cleared his throat. They were up next.

With a snicker, Jayden pulled away, leaving her mouth moving against empty air. He placed the order for their drinks and two muffins, then took her to the corner, where they nestled down in one of the community couches.

"So . . ." Erin let the word dangle, not ready to release the proverbial bone.

Jayden took the lid off his coffee and blew on it, the fragrant steam curling and vanishing as it wafted away. Her eyes followed his fingers to the pastry, where he pinched off a small portion with a berry in it and brought it to her lips. "Open for me, sweet girl," he murmured low.

So innocent.

Said with such simplicity.

Yet the request sent a lightning strike through her core, zinging to the tips of her toes and fingers and forcing her nipples to draw tight around their embedded metal.

"Anytime." Erin let the encroaching lust reflect in her eyes and wrapped her lips around the morsel, along with the tips of his fingers. After taking her sweet time accepting the treat, she daintily wiped at the corners of her mouth then sat back, sipping her own coffee.

He shook his head at her antics and smiled. "Think you're cute, do you?"

"I know I am." She flashed him a tooth-filled grin. Jayden laughed. "Good."

"All joking aside, though, can't you tell me where we're going now? The cat's gonna be out of the bag once we board anyway." She batted her eyelashes for good measure.

"This is true, but I think I'll make you wait a little while longer. Just because I can. Now, be a good girl and finish your muffin." He took another sip of coffee to hide his smirk when she grunted in frustration.

"Fine, will you tell me about your friend, at least?" Erin was excited about the trip. Other than going to Ireland for her grandmother's funeral when she was younger, she'd never traveled outside the US. "Is he kinky, like us?" she added with a teasing snicker.

"Patience, my jewel."

Yeah, right. Patience.

⇝⇞

Jayden was having more fun with this than he could've imagined; Erin made it so easy to tease. Though he knew he *shouldn't* be encouraging her pouting, the morning was relaxed, and it felt comfortable being with her like this. He chuckled to himself. If she only knew just how kinky Haro Okamoto was, she might not have posed the question with such nonchalance. *Oh, yes.* Okamoto was a man who could open her eyes to things that Jayden only dreamed of dabbling with at the edgiest of times.

She would learn, though. His old friend and Shibari mentor had agreed to some private demonstrations and lessons with the couple. Jayden couldn't wait to see what Catherine thought of his surprise. He was pretty certain she was going to love it. He hoped.

Sparing no expense in the name of comfort, Jayden had booked first class tickets for the fourteen-hour flight to Tokyo. Once she knew *where* he was taking her, his jewel deserved the *why* of it—beside the obvious reason of her birthday—and he planned to enlighten her once they were seated. He could've taken Erin anywhere in the world for her birthday, but this trip had been planned with an ulterior motive, and as such, they had some things to discuss.

The Michaels' rose ceremony had confirmed for Jayden that he'd overlooked Erin's lack of knowledge in their chosen way of life. She had the gist of their Lifestyle down, that was true, and without question she was a natural submissive. Yet, for all practical purposes, the love of his life was still a newbie. In his opinion, he couldn't have arranged this experience for her at a better moment. The timing was fortuitous.

Andrew Brenner had opened the door for her, awakening Catherine's tendencies and teaching her the basics. Spencer Talbert had nearly destroyed her. Neither man had endeavored to share the traditions and history in which the lifestyle was steeped, however. Jayden had about two decades of this life under his belt to her handful of years. His 'upbringing' had also been more ceremonial, thanks to the opportunities that had been presented to him.

Like a summer in Tokyo with Landon. It had been a present from his parents, following his *magna cum laude* graduation from Rice. Sir Tom happened to be free and had joined them, introducing the pair to *Kinbakushi* Okamoto soon after their arrival. Though they'd landed in Japan with an itinerary of everything they wanted to do and see, after three days with the rope master, all those plans were forgotten in favor of a new one. It became a summer of erotic training, with a heavy focus on finding the mental center before the physical pleasure could be appreciated.

Just thinking about that long ago time made his skin tingle with the memories of the *asanawa* biting hard into his skin, ensuring that when the natural fiber rope was removed, the marks would remain for hours. A low moan escaped him, and Erin's hand found his. He looked over to find confusion in her eyes. "Once we get in the air, I'll explain everything."

CR80

Forty-five minutes later they were settled in their plush seats. Erin was now wide-awake and looking at everything. Oh, and touching all the knobs and levers, as well.

"One would assume you'd never been on a plane before by the way you're acting."

"I haven't. Well, not first class." She grinned and bounced in her seat.

Did she have to be so adorable and irresistible?

"Welcome aboard, Mr. Masterson. Can I get you a beverage before take-off, sir?"

Despite the flight attendant's offer, Jayden's attention stayed on Erin. "Water, my jewel?" He'd added the pet name in warning. He was asking for appearances but didn't approve of anything else right then. She had caffeine and sugar in her system already, and with the upcoming altitude changes, he wanted her hydrated, not drunk.

"Aye, thank you."

When her eyes dropped in silent acknowledgement of his request, he warmed inside. Pushing her chin up with his finger, he pressed his lips to her warm ones. Upon directing his attention to the flight attendant, Jayden pulled back, seeing her eyes shoot daggers toward Erin.

Somebody needs a good fuck, he thought with amusement, then turned on the charm. He'd kill her with kindness, and if she did anything to demean his sweet girl, then he'd make sure the woman was relocated to a position with less customer interaction. She managed to get the hint, however. Their waters were served with a subdued smile, and then she moved on to the next passenger, leaving them to talk.

Jayden opened the topic for discussion before taking a drink. "His name is Haro Okamoto."

"Who?"

"My . . . friend, who will be hosting us while we are in Japan." Okamoto was much more than a simple friend, but that identifier would work for now.

"I'm still in shock that we're going to Tokyo. This is so cool." Her cheeks looked fit to burst, stretched as they were to contain her smile.

"Glad you think so, sweet girl. Landon and I had the honor of spending a summer under Okamoto's tutelage. It was . . ." he trailed off, trying to find the words he needed, "Intense."

꧁
CHAPTER NINETEEN
꧂

E rin's temperature was rising. Though he was speaking low, a shift was happening within him. She could detect it in the cadence of his words, the deepening of his breath. Whatever thought was playing out in his head had grabbed tight and wasn't letting him go. Funny how his internal reactions beckoned her in the cramped space, encouraging her to follow his lead.

Over the next hour, Jayden regaled her with tales of that summer with Landon, Sir Tom, and Okamoto the rope master. She'd known her Master carried a fondness for the art of rope bondage. He reserved it for special occasions because it could be so time consuming. As a result, they'd not engaged in it more than a handful of times. Catherine had loved every moment when they had. Having him spend an hour stroking and touching her naked body while he bound her in silky ropes was nothing short of pure sensuality. He'd put it into perspective for her by explaining that often, in erotic binding, the benefits of the experience came from the process, not the final creation.

Listening to him go on, she realized this was her Master's way of making up for the hectic schedule over the past months. This was a chance to recharge before forging ahead. A mere five and a half months remained until Natalie's baby was due and Erin would be marrying her prince. There was still so much to be done in preparation for both events.

"I want this experience to challenge you, Erin. With all the things that keep popping up, I've decided there might not be a better time to let you have a taste of a 24/7 arrangement. When we get off this plane, you will be my slut for the duration of our time on Japanese soil. Is this okay with you?"

Two weeks completely immersed in her submissive half? She thrilled at the idea. So many outcomes were possible, and both mental and physical exhaustion were almost guaranteed. *Freedom . . . from decisions and responsibility. Nothing mattering but pleasing Jayden and seeing to His needs.*

"Oh, aye, 'tis quite alright, Sir."

"I should warn you before we arrive, Okamoto runs a slave household."

Uncertain as to why, Erin's gut clenched at the admission, and her pulse took up a pounding in her temples. She knew relationships with a true slave dynamic existed in their Lifestyle, and most were not forced like she had been. What alarmed her now was Jayden's need to forewarn her. *How severe was this man she was being taken to?*

"Hey."

Erin lifted her eyes to meet his. In the dark brown orbs, she found both concern and undiluted love.

"I don't say that to frighten you, sweet girl. Simply to give you an idea of what to expect, and to try and keep you off his radar." He sighed. "Though I imagine that is going to be damn hard to do. Unless his tastes have changed, all of his girls are matching dolls—tiny and waif-like, with black silk hair and onyx stares. Your red hair and vibrant eyes will be alarming in contrast, and therefore make you desirable as a rarity."

Jayden paused and undid his lap belt. In one fluid motion that drew her eyes to his torso, he stood and moved to the aisle. Reaching into the storage bin overhead, his crotch came level to her face.

On impulse, she leaned forward to blatantly kiss the bulge pressing at his zipper.

He stiffened then bent down, a blanket now in his hand. Jaden hovered his mouth near hers, and Erin could feel the warmth of his breath when he whispered, "Put the armrest up, spread the blanket over your lap, and remove your bra."

Her eyes widened, and she threw a panicked look around the cabin. Two other passengers sat in the front area, ears covered and attention otherwise engaged by something in their laps.

"I want your panties, while you're at it. Have it done by the time I return." He moved in as if to kiss her, but at the last second, shifted the direction of his mouth, catching the edge of her jaw with a bite, which he eased away with soft kisses. Jayden stood up, tossed her the blanket, and then left her befuddled and trying to catch up.

The redhead blinked, his words taking a moment to digest while her lover disappeared into the bathroom. After a moment, she shook off her daze and hurried to follow his instructions, thankful that she'd chosen a skirt that morning. Her almost see-through blouse was a small concern—her pierced nipples would be apparent behind the gauzy thinness of the cotton—but she let the fear go. This was an adventure. She didn't know any of these people, so what they thought didn't matter as long as she and Master didn't break any laws.

The plane lurched on a pocket of turbulence while she was tucking her lingerie into her purse, sending her nipples dragging against the inside of her pink top. It felt good—so good that Erin dared to slip her hand under her shirt to give her nips a small pinch while she leaned back into her seat and arranged the blanket over her lap.

"Are you touching what is mine?"

She jumped at the deep baritone. Her lips parted with a gasp, and she nodded, not hiding her naughtiness while she pulled her hand out from beneath her top.

Jayden folded his long frame back into his seat, lifting the blanket and sliding beneath it with her. His movements seemed stilted, not displaying his usual feline grace. "And what did you find, Catherine?"

There it was. Playtime had officially begun.

"Aching breasts, Master," she breathed the words out, needing desperately to run her palms over them, wanting pressure compressing the flesh. *Jesus, the man tilted her axis whenever he was near.*

"Good to know. Spread your legs so your thighs don't touch."

The air in the cabin thickened, making it harder to breathe while she complied.

"Where was I?" he mused as hot fingertips touched her bare thigh. "Oh, yes. Okamoto. But first, lift your shirt until the hem sits above your perky nipples. Be careful, though; keep the blanket over you."

If she hesitated to consider what He wanted, she might chicken out, so she didn't allow herself to pause. Catherine had to choke back a tiny sound of surprise when the coarse blanket wool met her tender peaks. With a test wiggle that scratched her nipples like a fine grade sandpaper, she grinned.

The flight attendant came back through checking on everyone. Master requested another water, along with a cup of ice. Catherine watched him pop some of the frozen cubes into his mouth then lean toward her. With a degree of stealth, he managed to tug down a portion of the blanket and coax one of her nipples into his ice-filled mouth.

She drew in a breath with a hiss then swallowed a groan. Keeping quiet became a difficult task when his fingers inched toward her waiting pussy and the cold suckle grew urgent, pleasantly painful. Catherine's eyes rolled back, and her eyelids fluttered closed. His sucking grew more intense, taking in more of her nipple with each pull, and she wanted to cry out. For all she cared at that moment, anyone could witness the way Master worshiped her, and they should count themselves lucky to see such devoted passion. Her mouth dropped open, and her throaty whimper began to gain volume.

"Quiet yourself, jewel."

Her nipple burned where he'd dragged his teeth along it before releasing it to shush her. Clamping her lips closed and peeking through heavy lids, she found Him grinning at her while he brought the blanket up to cover her.

He turned his hips toward her, positioning his back toward the aisle while spreading his legs. Beneath the cover of the blanket his hand sought hers and brought it to his zipper. "Reach in and stroke me while I talk."

Good lord. Catherine dragged some of the canned air into her lungs and carried out her order. His earlier stiffness was explained when her palm enclosed his cock and she discovered it sheathed in latex.

He clearly expected her to jack him off where he sat.

𝔰𝔬𝔠𝔰

J ayden was depraved for doing this. *Wasn't he?* Upon returning to his seat, he'd noted the cabin was empty for the most part, the few passengers spread out. Unless he allowed Catherine to get loud, no one would be the wiser about their activities. A surprise moan caught him when she squeezed and twisted her palm around his length just right, however.

While Catherine found an angle with which she could keep up a constant, shallow stroke, he gathered his thoughts. Drawing on his inner reserves of control, Jayden was able to let the building sensations from her adept hand job sit on the edges of his awareness while he resumed his explanation. When he'd started talking, it had dawned on him to add an element of daring on the off chance the talk of slaves managed to be a trigger for Catherine. The kinkiness would help distract her.

"I'd forgotten Andrea until I was telling you about Okamoto's doll girls earlier." He bit his lip to stifle another moan. The minx had dug her nails into his heavy balls, the pressure just this side of making his stomach churn. A plea for her to back off bubbled up in his throat, coming out as a sigh of relief when her nails retracted on their own and she gripped his solid length once again.

His crimson haired vixen's shoulders shook while she let out a quiet laugh.

"Okamoto brought her into his home the last week we were there." Jayden pushed his hips up on Catherine's down stroke and slammed his head back into the seat. The move had sent fire licking up his spine and down his cock. If he'd been bare—not stuffed into the constrictive rubber—the man might've sent come spraying with geyser-like force.

He sought her face with his eyes. Though her chin rested on her chest, he could see the corners of her smug grin—*and wasn't seeing her pleased with herself sexy as hell*? Her breath caught, a tiny hitch of air, and he hoped it was in reaction to his thickening cock in her hand.

"You're a beautiful creature, Catherine." She dipped her head and murmured a thank you, never losing the exquisite rhythm of her stroke. The sincerity of her tone and actions was surreal, lulling him into a sleepy trance.

"What happened?"

"Hmm?" With some effort he opened his eyes, though he couldn't recall closing them, and leveled his stare at her.

"In that last week. What happened with Andrea that has you so spooked now, Master?" Catherine's voice lowered to a whisper at the end.

A lump formed in his throat. "Okamoto liked his girls all matched. The one difference they were granted was in their rope bindings, which varied in style and, occasionally, rope material. Andrea already stood out from the others with her voluptuous figure and icy blue eyes, so he indulged in more . . . extreme games with her."

The color drained from Catherine's face, and he hurried to clarify, "As hardcore as his treatment of her was, she *wanted* it that way. Andrea got off on being edged. Activities like breath control and knife play were some of her favorites." He halted the story, giving Catherine a few minutes to process it.

Over the low thrum of the airplane's engines, he almost didn't hear her unsure, "Did you help?"

"What? No! God, no." Jayden softened his voice then. "But I did watch. Okamoto was our host, and to refuse his entertainment would've been disrespectful."

She scoffed, followed by an adorable little snort sound. "I suppose you got your cock plenty wet, too, then? Did he send you a new girl every night?" Her grip tightened with her words.

Oh. She's mad about something. Jayden replayed their conversation, looking for what he'd said wrong, where he'd messed up. But all his head told him was that she was being a bratty submissive. *Catherine messed up, not you. She owes you respect in lieu of the snotty attitude.*

Then his thoughts drifted again. He'd just sprung the shift in their dynamic on her, outside of their regular routine. His heart was telling him this was one of those give-and-take moments, where he had to be flexible and consider not just his submissive's feelings, but Erin's feelings—as an individual—too. Jayden took a moment to examine it from *her* side.

The week had already been hectic with all the activity surrounding Paige and Landon's wedding. On top of that, she'd been told to prepare for another two weeks somewhere, but she was not given the specifics, which had left her in limbo. Now he was finally giving her information about where they were going, but it was with the added extra of learning that she was being taken into a hardcore slave house where she was expected to be in subservient mode at all times. *Okay, he could see where maybe he'd gone too far.*

"Erin, please tell me what's going through your head."

❧❧❧

CHAPTER TWENTY

❧❧❧

*H*ello, whiplash.

First, Erin boarded the plane, then Catherine was told to jack his cock, and now, Erin was up again, being asked her opinion. She took a deep breath and moved her hand back to her own lap. After a second thought, she also tugged her shirt back into place, letting the blanket slip down.

Jayden didn't stop her.

"If I'm being honest?"

He nodded.

"I'm jealous." His mouth popped open, and she rolled her eyes. "I know. It's ridiculous. But hearing about you having a full blown 'summer of love' orgy thing is just rubbing me the wrong way right now. I can't explain it." She looked up at him then, hesitant at his reaction. Instead of finding him scowling at her silliness, his smile had to be even goofier than she felt.

"I think I like this," he teased. "Not the attitude, mind you, but seeing you all possessive of me has its merits."

"So glad you can love a crazy person," she managed to get out between giggles.

Jayden's arm snuck behind her back then, and he pulled her into his side. "Not crazy, just adorable, sweet girl."

His nonchalance over the whole thing made her feel like even more of a ninny for letting something that had happened the past, when she had still been in diapers no less, bother her.

"Look, Erin. I won't lie and say it's not going to be a severe change from what you're used to seeing and being a part of. But I can and *will* promise that all of your limits and safe words will be protected and honored by me—along with anyone we encounter. You are my priority. I won't let your well-being be sacrificed to appease our host."

She could feel the sincerity and weight of his words and snuggled deeper into him. The play he'd initiated was forgotten while he welcomed her close, and for the next few hours, they held each other in quiet contentment while the plane droned on, carrying them to Japan.

CR80

Disembarking from the plane allowed Catherine a much-needed stretch. Aye, they'd been in first class seats, but still, one could only sit for so long before the muscles began complaining. Hers were definitely making their presence known, and a hot shower and some food didn't sound too bad, either. That point was emphasized when her stomach rumbled, and Jayden laughed, promising to feed her soon.

Under normal circumstances, the submissive would've dropped behind Him and to the left, but he'd had her go ahead of him when they got off the plane, then kept her ahead by guiding her with his hand on the small of her back. The airport was huge and bustling with activity, making his touch a soothing balm against her rising panic about the unknown. Catherine was also acutely aware of her nipples reacting to the cooler air of the airport by poking through the thin cotton of her shirt, which then led to a problem between her legs. With no panties to absorb the increasing dampness, her thighs soon began slipping against each other with every step she took.

Reaching baggage claim, his palm gripped her waist, stopping her. Master pulled her against him, lowering his mouth to her ear to inquire how she'd fared on the walk through the airport. *Sneaky fecker! He'd known just what was happening to her.*

Catherine closed her eyes and made a purring noise while she tried to be discreet and rub her backside against him. His hand slipped from her waist to her ass, where he squeezed hard enough to make her swallow down a yelp that would've drawn attention to the pair.

"Behave, slut." Low, filled with warning, his words were but a hot breath against her ear. All of a sudden, Catherine was questioning the sanity of agreeing to serve his every whim for two whole weeks.

"Aye, Master. Your girl apologizes," she murmured just loud enough for him to hear then ceased her wiggling.

"Because it's late and Okamoto lives about an hour outside the city, we'll be staying at a hotel tonight. He is sending a car for us in the morning. Once we've got our bags, we'll get settled, and then there's a noodle house I want to take you to for dinner. If you're a good girl, we'll have some fun."

The playful glint in his eye told Catherine that his dinner plans included more than food.

ᏣᏧᏒ

Catherine stood next to her Master, looking up at the hand-painted '69-n-Roll One' sign with mild curiosity. It was a good thing he knew what to do, because the little bit of Tokyo she'd seen thus far had been enough to make her decide that, had she been alone, Catherine would've been beyond lost. Deferring to Him during this trip was looking better—and easier—the more she encountered. A prime example was how they had to pay for their meal before even entering the restaurant. Yen went in, and a token—or chip—came out, which would be handed to the chef when they got inside.

"Ready, jewel?" The remote-controlled egg he'd tucked into her pussy after their quick cleansing but unsatisfying shower at the hotel began vibrating, making her jump.

When her low whimper started, Master shook his head with a smile. "No sounds, Catherine. The chef here insists on quiet in his establishment—with the exception of slurping." He paused to chuckle when her jaw dropped open. "Noodles, pet. Slurping the noodles."

For the next hour, Catherine was suspended between a state of near-satisfaction and an odd sort of exquisite torture. The restaurant was busy enough that, once they made it inside, they each had to take their seats as one became available—another of the chef's rules. She ended up sitting two seats down from her Master, the elderly man between them oblivious to the debauchery unfolding on either side of him.

Given that Master had insisted she be seated first, Catherine was able to enjoy a few delectable bites of her ramen before the toying began. She was mid-slurp into a bite of noodles when the low vibrations inside her pussy intensified, and she squeaked.

The chef, despite his severe rules, was decked out like Elvis to match the rock-n-roll décor. His hand slammed the counter in front of her bowl, and she shrunk back, lowering her eyes under the intense warning of his glare.

From her left came a stifled cough. Peeking to the side, she could see the look of amusement dancing across Master's face. Holding her attention with his gaze, his hand slipped into his pocket where the remote hid, and she barely suppressed the groan when he cranked the egg up again.

The brief spike of intense thrumming sent tingles up and down her body and had her dropping her

chopsticks to clutch the counter edge. Then it
receded, the vibrations dimming to an almost
unnoticeable buzz inside her while He resumed
eating like nothing had happened. Catherine did the
same.

Their dinner continued to play out in the same
fashion—teasing, retracting, arousing. Master added
his glancing caresses to the torture in the cab ride
back to the hotel. However, He made everything she'd
endured over the course of the afternoon and evening
since getting off the plane worth it within moments
of getting into their room.

"Lift your arms." Over the soft *click* of the door, he
came at her in a rush, pulling her dress off with rough
yanks that made her stumble even as her nipples
hardened. "Goddammit, Catherine," he nipped at her
lips, "you've got my cock harder than steel. You did so
well tonight, my hot little slut. Fuck me, but I'm a
lucky man."

She cried out when her breast was gripped tight in
conjunction with his fingers delving into her pussy,

seeking her clitoris once they were coated in her own sticky fluids.

"Come, Catherine. Hard. Fast. I don't care. Just come!" The egg zinged to full power while he rubbed harder, circling her swollen clit so that it almost hurt. *Almost.* When he lowered his mouth to chew on her nipple, she exploded with a colorful collection of expletives and platitudes. The tingly current-like sensation, which had kept her attentive and on the edge, dissipated. In its absence, Catherine went numb and cold, a serene peace cocooning her.

₧₧

Jayden sipped his coffee while staring down at her. Against the stark white of the hotel linens, Catherine looked like an angel—and a sin. He needed to wake her since their ride would be there soon, but she looked so peaceful.

She'd given him a mild scare the night before with how fast, and how hard, she'd dropped into subspace when she came. Jayden would go so far as to say she'd *crashed*, since her knees had buckled during her orgasm.

He'd caught her, of course, then carried her to the bed where he wrapped her in his arms and held her. In protective mode, he whispered soft words and cooed near her ear until the change in her breathing had told him she'd fallen asleep. After covering her and ensuring the blankets and pillows were pressed tight to her body to give the illusion of being held, he ducked into the bathroom to knock out his own release. She wasn't the only one who'd been worked into a right state the evening before.

Just recalling their activities from the night prior had Jayden's cock swelling against his thigh. He took another sip of his coffee, set the mug down, and then stepped closer to the bed, cock in hand. Jayden knelt on the mattress, and she shifted. When she licked her lips, it pulled a needy moan from him.

The corner of her mouth twitched minutely, but he caught it. She was playing with him. He darted his hand out to snatch back the covers, sending a cold blast of air over her naked torso. When her eyes and mouth popped open in surprise, he was ready to slide

259

his cock in. Her initial protest morphed into the appreciative sounds of wet, eager sucking.

Catherine reached for him, but he wanted to fuck her mouth, not get a hand job. It was simple to catch both her wrists in his large hand, and once he had them, he pushed them upward, stretching her arms above her head so those plump tits of hers taunted his senses. Jayden stared, fixated, while her breasts jiggled each time he thrust into her mouth. When he took hold of her gold hoops and pulled so that her nipples stretched, her teeth scraped his flesh, drawing a hiss from him. In order to tug on her jewelry, he had to release her wrists, but she kept her arms raised, not moving them from the spot where he'd left them. For Jayden, seeing her voluntarily restraining herself could be so much more intoxicating than real binding at times.

Getting head from his girl was always an experience in extreme pleasure, and this time was no different—proven by how fast he came, which was almost shameful. But he didn't give a fuck, and let his roar of satisfaction echo off the walls. The proud grin on Catherine's face when he was able to open his eyes and look at her was more than enough justification for his actions.

"Alright, beautiful. Let's get a shower and get out of here. Okamoto's driver will be here soon."

Glorious in her nudity, he watched her with a piercing gaze as she rose from the bed and stretched, then strolled toward the bathroom. When she drew abreast of him, a slight pivot spun her around so that she backed away from him the remaining distance. Upon reaching the threshold, she dropped to her knees and placed her hands, palms up, on her thighs.

His submissive waited.

ଇଉଓଃ

Though Master had tried to warn her, Catherine still felt a sense of overwhelming awe when they reached Sir Okamoto's estate. From the outside, the house looked like a traditional Japanese dwelling, unassuming but ornate. When they breached the interior, the house was proved to be anything but. A better description for what waited inside would've included statements such as 'feast of flesh' or 'house of perversion.'

She found it odd, even a bit rude, but didn't question it when they spent the first hour waiting for their host. *So much for being expected.* They were shown to a sitting area where Master got comfortable and gave her the signal to kneel next to him.

The young woman who'd escorted them in offered tea in a soft voice, but Master politely declined while Catherine tried not to stare.

He had been spot-on in his description of the rope master's girls. Dolls. They were living, breathing erotic dolls. Everywhere she looked, or was able to look from her lowered position, were women . . . naked, bound, and on display.

Some stood still as statues, spotlighted by sharp, white lights. These girls were decorations. Vibrant-colored ropes entwined their bodies, squeezing their breasts into taut purple mounds from which jutted their tiny brown nipples—some clamped, some circled by long pins or needles standing from the flesh like quills. It was acupuncture of the kink variety.

The other women Catherine had noticed, like the tea girl, wore dresses fashioned with lengths of natural looking rope, skimpy but nothing that could be misconstrued as vulgar. Never knew who might be at the door, after all.

Realizing Sir Okamoto took into consideration the sensitivities of potential unknowing bystanders gave Catherine a degree of assurance. The master was clearly intense in his practices and philosophies, but he was a long way from insane. Her mood darkened for a moment, becoming sad at the thought of how so many viewed their Lifestyle as something less— something sick or broken.

"Catherine."

She looked up to find Master had stood, and next to him an older man—short and heavy set— appraised her. If she had to guess, she would've placed the man at about sixty or sixty-five years of age. The look on his face was a mix of distaste and fascination. Catherine averted her eyes.

"Aye, Master?"

"Rise, pet. Allow me to introduce you to *Kinbakushi* Hari Okamoto, my mentor and friend, and our host."

Keeping her eyes down, she dipped her knees in a curtsy. "Tis a pleasure, Sir. Thank you for your generous hospitality to Master and this girl." The last thing the submissive expected was the bark of delighted glee bursting from Okamoto moments later. After the initial shock wore off, she smiled.

"Very good, Jayden-san. I approve. You have done well, young man."

Master scoffed. "I'm not so young anymore."

Okamoto looked at Catherine and winked. "This is true for all of us, my friend, but when surrounded by youthful beauty such as this," he gestured to her direction, "age is, how do you say? Just a number. Yes?"

Master laughed, and the sound tickled her low, where she was nude beneath her skirt. The urge to squirm was strong, but she held herself still.

"I welcome you both to my home. Allow me to give you the grand tour, and then I'll leave you to get settled into your room. Dinner is served at six each evening, and lessons begin at six each morning. Come."

As the tour progressed, Catherine found the house to be much larger than she'd first thought. Sinking back into the surrounding flora, the main house and gardens covered several thousand square feet. It was exquisite, especially the gardens. She hoped there would be some free time during their visit to enjoy the peaceful serenity promised by the babbling streams and precision-groomed landscapes.

ଞଠଔ
CHAPTER TWENTY-ONE
ଞଠଔ

Blinking, then stretching, Catherine bolted upright and jumped out of bed in a panic. There was too much sunlight. It was late.

She was late.

Each day had begun in darkness, then carried forward into the afternoon while following the routine established by Sir Okamoto. Catherine had never been more tired, or endured such an overall body ache, as she had in the last two weeks. Not willingly, anyway. The abuse she'd suffered under Spencer hadn't brought her any of the deep gratification that came from her voluntary service to Master. Learning from him and with him under Okamoto's tutelage had been eye-opening and she knew had brought them closer as a couple, in all senses of the word.

The gardens had indeed ended up being a place of reflection. Every morning, after their five a.m. dip in the heated baths, they assembled adjacent to the Zen garden for a workout of mind and body. Catherine had found the controlled, fluid-like movements awkward at first, but after a few days, she'd limbered up and gotten the hang of it. That was the point when Sir Okamoto allowed the binding lessons to begin.

As each Shibari session became longer and more elaborate, Catherine welcomed their morning *Tai chi*—yearned for it, even. Going through the non-stressful forms eased her muscles and loosened them for the upcoming paces her Master would be putting her through. Okamoto had stressed how the combination of the Tai chi with the rope lessons was achieving the optimum level of *kokoro*, the Eastern philosophy of bringing the heart, spirit, and mind together as one.

Following the morning ritual, they broke for a simple lunch—usually a hearty bowl of ramen with seafood—and then the submissive and her Master were left to their own devices until dinner time. Sometimes they napped, other times they scened, but whatever they did was Master's choice. She was finding that the more time she spent in a full submissive mindset, the easier Catherine was letting go and trusting her well-being to Him. It was rather refreshing to be able to do so.

Thinking back, Catherine realized the only discontent she'd felt the entire visit had come in the hours after the evening meal, when the household split up. Master and Sir Okamoto, along with any guests who'd joined them, retired for some "male bonding." She didn't know where they went or what they did, and therein lay her upset. Catherine hated being apart from her Master.

Ironically, she also cherished this time, because while the men vanished into the bowels of the house, Catherine went to class. Along with the newest members of Okamoto's harem, she was being taught the *why* of Shibari—properly known as *Kinbaku*. Getting to learn the history and ceremony behind the ancient Japanese rope bondage was proving to enhance the experience. She figured it was just a matter of time before she found herself in 'rope-space,' a trance-like state similar to sub-space, except brought on by the pleasure of being lovingly and artistically bound. Every inch of the *asanawa* touching her, cinching her flesh in hemp, bound her deeper to Master and cemented the certainty that there was no other for her. Knowing the symbolism of everything, from the materials used to bind, to the variety and placement of the knots, made her feel beautiful.

These thoughts drove Catherine through a rushed stop in the bathroom to splash water on her face, brush her teeth, and empty her bladder. Glancing about for her outfit, since Master had laid one out for her each morning thus far, she found nothing. She donned the silk kimono that had been her allowed covering within their room—*washitshu* she whispered, practicing from her lessons—then slid back the . . . *fusuma* and stepped into the hallway. Looking left then right and seeing no one, Catherine opted to head for the usual workout area.

When she arrived a few minutes later, the sight of Master and Sir Okamoto and no one else sitting at a low table sharing tea brought her up short. Steadying her resolve, she took a few more steps to get within Master's peripheral vision, then knelt to wait for His acknowledgement. The longer she was ignored, the wetter she became. Something big was going to happen. The calculated routine had changed, and her body was awakening with naughty desire.

�

"Jayden-san, I must insist you enjoy the pleasures of nuru on your last night here."

Catherine knelt at her Master's side, still 'floaty' from that morning's session. She'd been correct in her hunch that today would be different from any other during their visit to Tokyo. At Master's insistence, the submissive had been nude for their session, which had begun when he slipped the kimono from her shoulders after finishing his tea. Until today, he'd allowed her to wear a bodysuit or leotard to enforce the educational aspect of their instruction over the sexual. Today's session could be likened to a final exam, and Master had wanted her to get the full experience of erotic binding amongst the lush gardens. Without a doubt, he'd followed through on his promise of heightening the session for her once they didn't have an audience. Okamoto had observed, but from a distance, letting the couple get lost in their connection.

"Open for me." Master brought a bite of udon and shark to her lips.

She didn't feel like eating but had recovered enough of her senses to know she needed the caloric infusion of the fatty fish and noodles and accepted the food. Closing her eyes, Catherine rested her head on his thigh and chewed.

"That is kind of you, *Bakushi*. However, I'm afraid I must decline again tonight."

"Your girl is welcome to participate this time."

Hearing herself mentioned caused Catherine's ears to perk up in mild curiosity. *Was this where Master had gone each evening?* Her stomach clenched. She racked her brain trying to put a definition to the term 'noo Roo,' but came up blank. It didn't help that she was still shaking off the blissful cobwebs of their earlier activities.

"Well, that may change things, then."

Catherine felt his hand stroking her head. When he tapped her lips, she left her eyes closed and parted them to take another bite. While the food settled in her stomach and her blood sugar levels evened out, their conversation became clearer, and she peeked through her heavy lids to observe the two men.

❧☙

Jayden could tell she was coming around, regaining her senses. Her frame didn't lean so heavy against his side, her breathing was taking on a more regular rhythm, and she was eating at last. She'd slept through lunch and most of the afternoon. For the evening meal, he'd had to practically carry her to the table, but he wasn't letting her wait anymore. Catherine needed to get some food in her system.

He needed her alert.

While it troubled him to admit, Jayden sensed their welcome had run its course and was glad they were departing in the morning. His old friend was losing sight of the fact that he and Catherine were guests, *not* part of his harem.

That morning, Jayden had gotten so involved in binding his jewel, stretching her limbs to their limits, then locking her in position with the ropes, that he'd forgotten Okamoto was observing. Nothing and no one else existed while Jayden watched Catherine's emerald eyes glaze over and become unfocused. She was his everything when he took up the multi-tailed bull whip they'd recently graduated to under Jonathan's teaching.

Knowing Catherine was in the early stages of a drop, he pulled his arm back and snapped it forward to take her closer to the edge. A hissing whistle crackled through the air seconds before the thin, knotted tails connected with her puffy breast and sent a few strands of her scarlet hair fluttering around her face from the displacement of air.

Her scream of pleasure incensed his desire almost as much as watching her nipple swell in conjunction with the red welts rising from her flesh. Again he withdrew his arm to unleash a lash upon her opposite breast; again she screamed, her tight bindings keeping her upright when her body began to slump.

The Dom had taken care to tie her so that she was spread-eagle with a large knot rubbing against her clit and her tits wrapped at their base, to ensure they were full and distended. For a fun bonus, he'd wedged a fresh-carved finger of ginger into her ass, preparing her to beg for his cock later. His slutty girl always loved a deep, thorough fucking to try and combat the burn of the fragrant root.

Over and over, he cracked the whip against her exposed flesh, speaking—*taunting*—while he moved about. Gentle words and crass alike, all delivered with the same praising tone that let her know her Master was there and she was safe to let go and fly. Sensing when she needed more, he dropped the leather then followed the whip to the ground. Kneeling in front of her put him at the perfect height to lean in and lap at the copious amounts of sticky wetness that coated her sex and had darkened the ropes around her cunt.

It wasn't until Catherine was begging with muted whimpers for permission to come that Jayden remembered their audience of one, because a new sound reached his ears. When he turned away from his jewel to find the source, he was quite surprised to see Okamoto tending his own flesh—a phenomenon Jayden had never seen.

The rope master, to the best of Jayden's knowledge, always found his release through one of his girls. Self-gratification was below the great man. So it wasn't a big surprise that the sight had been shocking enough to yank Jayden from the lust haze he'd gotten lost in with his pet, and he'd ended the scene immediately.

Now he wanted Jayden's pet to be present for a nude massage? Yeah, fuck that. A strong need to protect what was his surged through him at Okamoto's invitation to the slippery beds. "First, I need to clarify if you mean to have Catherine in service for the massage or if you're just inviting her to observe."

Jayden's tone didn't hide his clear reservation when he openly challenged the man's intentions, and a displeased scowl drew Okamoto's brows together. "This morning, you showed me what a slut she is, Jayden-san. Would you not have such a *yorokobi* . . . such a delight . . . in service?"

While it was a reasonable enough question, the words raised Jayden's hackles something fierce. After two weeks of keeping Okamoto's personal interest off Catherine, he'd let the wall down too far. In blocking out everything but his jewel during their morning scene, Jayden had revealed her true magnificence to the leering observer.

A tense silence crept over the room, and Catherine stiffened by his side. "Master?" She was still drowsy.

Okamoto was crazy if he thought Jayden was going to press Catherine any further that day. The girl was still half out of it and needing aftercare, not another kinky session. A massage *would* be good for her, though. If he took care choosing his words, she'd be able to enjoy the experience, and he wouldn't have to lose his shit in a jealous rage. That was always a good thing.

Fixing a non-threatening smile on his face, Jayden looked over to his old teacher. "We'd be honored to partake of the nuru tonight, *Bakushi*. May I make a few requests? My slut is not used to such strenuous activities as she partook of today, and I'd like to use the time for an aftercare session. You understand this is a personal thing between a Master and his pet, of course."

Jayden held his breath while he waited for Okamoto to respond.

ᘓᘔ

Entering the natural stone room felt different this time. A true excitement for the sensual ordeal about to unfold coursed through Jayden, even as he absorbed the warmth radiating from Catherine's bare back—they'd disrobed outside. He led her around the perimeter toward the open shower in the far corner. She sighed and melted against him under the rush of hot water that doused their bodies. He turned her in his arms and pulled her close, breathing deep when the steam heightened the scent of her . . . her lotion, her sweat, and that sweet underlying odor that was simply Catherine.

Jayden's pulse slowed, and his muscles relaxed under the onslaught of rich pheromones. Dipping his head, he caught her lips with his own. While the flowing water rinsed them, the two kissed without care for the passing minutes. He danced his fingers across her back then down to cup her lush derriere. Her responding moan when he rubbed at the residual rope indentations in her silky flesh went straight to his gut, then eased lower—one heartbeat at a time.

The growing need to lift Catherine and pin her against the shower wall with his cock was hard to resist, so he didn't. She was limp and heavy in his arms. Her whimper when he filled her was audible ecstasy. Jayden allowed himself a single, deep thrust then pulled out and set her back on the ground.

"Come, pet. You're going to love this." He guided her to the large mattress in the center of the space.

The bed was more of a low-lying mat, so they had to bend down before crawling onto it. Two of Okamoto's girls knelt at opposite corners, waiting to begin. Every other time he'd come here as a polite observer, the girls had been nude. Tonight, at his request, they wore bathing suits.

Jayden laid Catherine down on the vinyl surface and then spun himself around after affirming she was comfortable. They were resting hip-to-hip, head-to-feet. At his nod the girls rose, wooden bowls of the odorless and tasteless nori gel in hand, and approached.

Cool and viscous, the gel drizzled over his damp skin, which was still warm from the shower. Catherine's fingers found his, threading them together while the full-body contact massage began. With every pass of the girls' busy hands over his limbs, his body grew slick and slippery. Meanwhile, his jewel's sighs of enjoyment hardened his cock. When he was sure enough time had elapsed to satisfy Okamoto's requirement for his girls being in service, Jayden sat up and stilled their strong hands. "I can take it from here, ladies. Thank you."

Their tone became frantic, the hushed words they were whispering too rushed for Jayden to follow with his rusty Japanese.

"*Ochitsuku*." He was going for 'Calm down,' and then took a stab at adding "*Anata ga iku*." 'You may go.' Their high-pitched chirps quieted, and while uncertainty still showed in their expressions, Jayden nodded at the doorway, saying again "*Anata go iku*."

"You are . . . sure, Sir?" Though the young woman's English was broken, he appreciated her effort and granted her a large smile.

"Yes, *hai*." He looked at Catherine before adding a dismissive, "Very sure. Now go."

"*Hai*, Sir." Nodding and bowing, the two girls set their bowls on the edge of the table then retreated, leaving Jayden to worship his jewel in the way she deserved.

He straddled her thighs and picked up one of the bowls to splash the entirety of its contents over Catherine's torso and breasts, then tossed it to the side. The vessel clattered on the stone floor moments before Jayden leaned forward to cover her body with his own. Slick and aroused, he moved along her form, dragging his chest against hers. Her hard nipples dug into him, and he repaid the favor by pressing his erection against her slippery cunt. Jayden pushed up on his arms and began a worm-like motion, gyrating in a slow wave that had him arching back then coming forward. Catherine's moans grew louder while her legs dropped open, and on his next pass, he drove his cock into her then stopped so they could gasp and catch their breath.

Her green eyes shot open, her gaze landing on him in a silent plea for more.

Jayden nodded once, caressed her lips with his, and then began to move. Rolling his hips with deliberate restraint, he took them away from everything that surrounded them, ensuring that once again there was nothing but Jayden and Catherine.

No, Jayden and Erin.

The force of the unexpected orgasm crashing into him knocked the air from his lungs, and he collapsed on top of her, murmuring her name over and over. "Erin. Erin. Erin . . ."

It was time to go home, if not for her, then for him. For the first time in his life, Jayden wanted to just curl up with his girl and not worry about anything even remotely kinky.

ℰℭ
CHAPTER TWENTY-TWO
ℰℭ

"Hiya, Mr. Masterson. Welcome back. Did you have a good trip?" Natalie looked up from the bowl of cereal she was eating while standing in front of the open refrigerator. She'd gotten back to the Villa a couple of days before they had.

"We did, thank you. What about you? How was your time at the Ranch?"

"It was good." She turned away, shutting the fridge and moving to the counter.

Something in her body language was raising Jayden's flags.

"Coffee? I put some on, knowing you guys were home."

He wondered what she was holding back from him. "Yes, please."

"Should I fix Erin one, too?" Natalie offered while reaching for the mugs. Her shirt pulled tight across her belly and Jayden noted she'd grown larger in the two weeks since he'd last seen her.

"Not right now. Thanks, though. I'm letting her rest this morning, considering we got in so late last night." Natalie nodded and went back to fixing his coffee. When she brought it to him, she lingered next to the island, her belly a few inches from his hand. The sudden urge to touch overcame him, and he reached out, stopping when he realized what he was doing.

"May I?" His palm hovered over her while the whispered words slipped out.

"Oh, sure, I guess."

Jayden lowered his hand slowly, unsure what to expect. Spanning the swollen curve, he was taken aback by how firm her stomach was. *Is that normal?*

He thought baby things were supposed to be all soft and sweet. "It's so rigid," he mused with a chuckle. "That's kind of weird." At that moment, her flesh shifted . . . softened and undulated, and he jerked his hand back with a shocked, "Shit, what was that?"

His exclamation sent Natalie into a laughing fit.

"What happened?" he asked again.

She giggled. "That was the baby. He must like the sound of your voice, because that's the most I've felt him move since he started a couple of days ago." Jayden was in awe. "He?"

Looking sheepish, Natalie shrugged. "I don't know for sure. Just a feeling. Dr. Ellison said we'll do a scan this month and I might be able to find out then."

"Oh, I see." He returned his hand to her belly, but the stony rigidity was back. "So you think he can hear us?"

Tipping her head to the side, she gave him a quizzical look. "You don't know much about babies, do you?"

It was his turn to look sheepish. "Not really, no. I have to be honest, Natalie. As much as I love my family, I've never seen myself as being 'family man' material." He made air quotes around the term to stress his point. "Not with the business and my lifestyle choices."

"Fair enough. But then you met Erin." For the first time in months, he saw a sparkle in the girl's lonely brown eyes.

"Yes. Then I met Erin."

Natalie placed a tentative hand on top of his, where it still rested on her small bump. "And now?"

"Now I'm rethinking that. I want to give her everything, including a family of our own if she wants it. And I think she does."

"You think? Have the two of you not talked about it?"

He took his hand back to lift his coffee mug to his lips. "Not recently." With a thick swallow, he lowered his voice and continued. "There was a brief mention of it when Holly, Dr. Ellison, informed us Erin probably wouldn't be able to carry a baby full term— if she could get pregnant in the first place."

"I—I don't know what to say. Erin has told me about Spencer and what he did, but I didn't know she might not be able to be a mom because of it. That's awful."

He scoffed. "That bastard did a number on her, that's for sure. Please don't think I blame her for any of it or love her any less for the scars she bears because of him. What I hate is that I can see the desire in her eyes when we visit Ronnie, Steph, and their twins. I can feel the longing radiating off of her when she fills me in on what you two have done, your classes, and doctor's visits and such. Yet she hasn't voiced the desire out loud. Because of that, I don't know if she's simply written off the possibility altogether, or if she wants to try, but because of my earlier stance, she's held back from telling me." The words tumbled out of him, gaining momentum and becoming more of a ramble than coherent thoughts the longer he went on.

"No offense, Mr. Masterson. I know I don't know much about how you live, but I think I've learned here in recent months that communication is key. Why keep beating yourself up over this? Just talk to her.

287

My guess is that if you're battling this much inner turmoil over the issue, then Erin probably is, too."

"Thank you, Natty. You may be right, and I might be overthinking this. I need to quit psyching myself up to talk to her about it and just do it." He gave a firm nod, and she laughed. "Can I ask you a question?" Jayden became serious.

"Go on."

"You're clearly a smart girl. What are you going to do with your life? Do you have any plans for raising your baby?" He could see the figurative wall come down between them. Her eyes dulled, and her shoulders slumped.

"I'm still trying to figure that one out, Mr. Masterson. I thought about asking Nina if I could move in with her, but she has a newborn of her own. And while it was great to see her, I didn't feel like her husband really cared for me." She rinsed her cereal bowl and made to leave without another word, but Jayden stopped her.

"If we can do anything, Natalie—"

"Thank you. I know. You keep offering."

"It's not an empty offer. Anything we can do. You name it."

Her soft curls bounced when she started to shake her head, but then she stopped and looked directly at him. "What's your middle name?"

The question perplexed him. "Matthew. Why?"

"No reason, just curious. I'm going to go lie down for a bit. Talk to her, Mr. Masterson." She gave a smile, a weak attempt at one anyway, and wandered off.

Jayden had a hell of a lot to think about.

ঙ৩জ

"Do you want kids?"

Erin almost dropped the wooden spoon she was using to push their eggs around the hot pan when she spun around to see Jayden leaning casually against the doorframe. *Did she?* Maybe, as a young girl with grand visions of what her future would entail, she had. However, since Dr. Ellison had confirmed the damage to Erin's insides, she hadn't allowed herself to think about that possible future. It was too painful.

Composing herself, she placed the spoon on the little bell pepper-shaped plate meant for such things, and turned back to him. "Where's that coming from?" While Erin watched, Jayden's face reddened, and he looked away.

"I've been doing some thinking since seeing everyone at Landon's wedding. Also, with Natalie around, it's kind of hard not to think about it. You're always so good with Ronnie and Steph's twins. A natural. It makes you glow in a way I can't."

Swoon. Desire bloomed within her, a bright flash of heat that settled to a low simmer while his words sank in. *Was he saying he might want kids?* But she couldn't give him that.

Holly said "Possibility," not a definite "No," she reminded herself. "What are you saying, *A rúnsearc?*"

When his deep brown eyes met hers again, they were filled with determination. "Honestly, I've been thinking about the possibility much longer than that. Since Natalie took up living here with us, it's been a constant in my mind. I want to be the one to put that kind of serene look on your face, Erin. More than that, though. I want to know what it is to experience that kind of happiness and contentment—with you."

Was he kidding her with this? He was asking for something beyond her physical capability. *Sure, Erin, and you didn't think you'd live to survive Spencer, either. Look at you now.*

"Breathe, sweet girl. I've got you."

She'd started gasping for air and hadn't realized it. Now Jayden's arms were wrapped around her, applying just enough pressure to make her feel safe but not trapped.

"I'm not saying we have to do this. I know we have obstacles to deal with, lots of them, if we decide to try, and I imagine there will be several visits with Holly along the way. I guess what I'm trying to say is—well, I just wanted you to know . . . If you want kids, then I do, too. We can figure the rest out."

୫୬୯୬

CHAPTER TWENTY-THREE

୫୬୯୬

Friday evening found the submissive seated at the table with her Master, enjoying a light dinner of shrimp cocktails and Caesar salad. The meal would be enough to nourish their bodies without weighing them down or making them groggy later in the playroom, where their weekend playtime was slated to begin in thirty minutes.

Having trouble sitting still, Catherine's eyes continued to dart over to the clock. She'd been restless the past week, more so than usual since their return from Japan over a month ago. *Perhaps the stress of wedding planning was getting to her?* Knowing Jayden wanted to try something new that weekend might have had something to do with it, too. Hell, there was a good chance it was a combination of both.

At the close of their playtime the weekend before, he'd mentioned something new was in the works for them. She'd tried to get hints out of him all week, but to no avail. Catherine knew she'd gotten a little pushy and pouty since they'd taken their relationship to this new romantic level. *What was he going to do, punish her?* She looked forward to it!

Her incessant nagging had gotten to him last night, though, and he'd snapped at her. Remembering how Jayden had reverted to his no-nonsense Dom voice to put Catherine in her place helped to stifle her fidgeting.

"Catherine, you will stop this childish behavior right now. I expect patience. Do not forget that while we have designated playtimes, I am your Master at all times. If you bug me about this again before six o'clock

tomorrow evening, I will cancel my plans, and you will spend the weekend on my whipping bench. Are we clear?"

She'd managed to squeak out, "Aye, Master," before he'd left the room and gone to his office, closing the door behind him. Considering he'd disappeared into his office every night that week and closed that damn door, he must've had a difficult week, too. Whatever the reason, they both seemed on edge, and Catherine was hopeful the weekend would be therapeutic for them both.

"Catherine." His voice was loud, and she jumped, pulling her eyes from the clock. A mere twelve minutes had passed.

"Aye?"

He looked amused. "I've been trying to get your attention for a couple minutes, sweet girl."

"Oh? Guess I'm a little distracted. I'm sorry."

"That's obvious. Come here, please." Jayden shifted so that his lap faced Erin and then opened his arms to her.

She moved into them, sitting atop his thighs. Jayden pulled her in close, and she laid her head on his shoulder, smiling when his warm lips brushed over her forehead with light kisses.

"Relax, Erin. I need you to focus on the right mindset so that neither of us will get hurt tonight. Can you do that for me, *A rúnsearc*?" he asked while rubbing her back.

His familiar scent was all around her, and it did wonders for Erin's erratic feelings. Her body and mind calmed in reaction to his spicy smell, soft touches, and the soothing cadence of his words.

"M'hm," she mumbled into his shoulder while nodding her head.

"That's my good girl. Alrighty, Ms. Ants-in-your-Pants," he teased while tickling her side with a light touch and drawing a giggle out of her, "it's ten of six. Close enough, I think. Why don't you go take a shower? I'll lay out what you need on your bed and meet you in the playroom when you're ready."

Jayden stood then helped Erin settle on her feet. Gathering their dinner dishes, he headed for the kitchen. He stopped at the doorway and turned back to her. "Don't keep me waiting too long, sweet girl." With a wink, her fiancé was gone.

Eager and excited, Erin spun on her heel and ran upstairs, past their bedroom, and into the submissive's room. After accepting his proposal, Jayden had wanted her to move everything into his, now *their*, room. After some discussion, Erin convinced him she needed the routine of using the submissive room during their playtime. That routine helped her separate the two halves of their relationships in her mind. They compromised by agreeing Master would still have the right to order Catherine to sleep in 'His' bed if she were tethered to it in some way.

She started the water so it could warm while stripping off her clothes and pinning her red hair up off her neck. There wasn't time to dry it if it got wet.

It wasn't until she was rubbing scented suds into her body that Master's choice of words clicked in Catherine's brain. He hadn't given her a time limit to present herself. Master had said, "When you're ready." That couldn't have been a slip on his part. He was so meticulous about everything that the chance of it having been an error was minuscule.

Catherine finished washing her body then shaved her under arms and legs. She'd stopped at Silver Spurs after work, so her pussy was already silky smooth. Hopping out, she dried off then spared a minute to appraise her naked form. Satisfied everything was clean, she unpinned her hair, ran a brush through it, and pulled it up into a high and tight ponytail. A quick application of light makeup, and she was ready.

Moving from the en suite, the submissive was curious to see what had been laid out for her to wear. His announcement that there would be an outfit had surprised her, since it was so rare that he had her wear anything to the playroom. What she saw stopped her in her tracks.

Neatly laid out on the bed was a black vinyl cat suit. On the floor next to the bed were a pair of red leather, thigh-high, lace-up boots with a four inch heel.

Looking closer, Catherine noticed cutouts in the bodysuit where her breasts and pussy would be—her sexy bits would be accessible. Lifting one of the legs, she peered at the backside to see that the ass area was open, too. In shifting the garment, she found the sides were open, with red leather ties crisscrossing from the ankle, all the way up the body, and then down the underside of the arm. Next to it sat a bottle of baby powder and an envelope addressed to MADAME ERIN in Jayden's perfect penmanship. *Huh?*

With a trembling hand, she removed the note from inside the envelope and began reading.

MADAME ERIN,

I HAVE JOKED WITH YOU ABOUT THE IDEA OF US SWITCHING. EVERY TIME I HAVE, I'VE GOTTEN SO FUCKING TURNED ON THAT I DECIDED IT WAS NOT POSSIBLE TO WAIT ANY LONGER

I WAS NEVER JOKING.

THIS WEEKEND, YOU WILL BE DOMINATING ME. I TRUST YOU. I LOVE YOU. THIS IS WHAT I WANT FOR MY BIRTHDAY. YOUR BOY . . .

She paused to take a deep breath. Her hand had gone from trembling to full-blown shaking. The uncertainty over whether she could pull this off was overwhelming.

. . . HAS PLACED ENOUGH COSTUMES FOR THE WEEKEND INSIDE YOUR CLOSET AT THE FRONT. IF IT PLEASES YOU, MADAME, YOUR BOY TOOK IT UPON HIMSELF TO SELECT ONE FOR THIS EVENING. DUSTING YOUR BODY WITH THE BABY POWDER WILL MAKE IT EASIER TO GET ON.

Her green eyes darted over to the cat suit, and she saw it in a new light. Yes, parts of her would be exposed, but the vinyl would also wrap around her and help hold her together to feel safe. Catherine's body warmed with the acceptance creeping into her mind, so she resumed scanning the words before her.

IN THE PLAYROOM, YOU WILL FIND A TRAY WITH ALL THE INSTRUMENTS YOUR BOY IS COMFORTABLE HAVING USED ON HIS BODY. PLEASE DO NOT HESITATE TO UTILIZE ANY THAT WOULD AMUSE YOU. YOU KNOW MY HARD LIMITS. YOU KNOW MY DESIRES. YOU KNOW ME. ARRANGEMENTS HAVE BEEN MADE FOR SIR LANDON TO COME OVER TOMORROW EVENING AT FIVE O'CLOCK FOR DINNER, FOLLOWED BY A SUPERVISED SESSION. HE WILL ANSWER ANY QUESTIONS YOU MAY HAVE AND CAN DEMONSTRATE ANY OF THE TOOLS YOU ARE UNSURE ABOUT. IF YOU ALLOW HIM TO ASSIST YOU, HE WILL BE ABLE TO HELP YOU FOCUS. SIR HAS EVEN AGREED TO

SUBMIT TO YOU, SHOULD YOU DESIRE TO HAVE US

BOTH—— WITH PAIGE'S BLESSING, OF COURSE.

The idea caused Erin to ponder a moment. Could she handle Sir Landon submitting to her? *No, I don't think so*. It was going to be daunting enough taking control of Ma–*Jayden*. Maybe in the future, if they ever did this again, she'd consider it. However, she also knew how things could sometimes get carried away as passions built, so she wouldn't rule it out just yet. Knowing Paige was okay with Landon being involved was a great relief.

Her excitement building, she finished reading the note.

YOUR BOY IS AWARE THIS IS A SURPRISE AND THAT

YOU'VE BEEN GIVEN NO TIME TO PREPARE. TAKE AS

LONG AS YOU NEED. YOUR BOY IS WAITING FOR YOU

WHENEVER YOU ARE READY.

TO SERVE YOU THIS WEEKEND WILL BE DIVINE,

MADAME.

LOVE, J.

Erin had to reread the letter to be sure her mind wasn't playing tricks on her. When she was satisfied that this was real, not some test or joke, she let out a little squeal and jumped up and down. She considered running to the closet to look at the other outfits but decided that could be done later. Her lover was waiting downstairs for her, and she was anxious to get to him.

Applying the baby powder like Jayden had suggested, she was soon in the cat suit. Next, she pulled on the boots and went to stand in front of the full length mirror on the closet door. While *Madame Erin*—thinking the title made her giggle—took in her appearance, a slow grin spread across her face. She looked hot—and in control. And just like that, she knew what her first task for Jayden was going to be.

With a confident stride, she crossed the room to where the intercom panel sat on the wall next to the door. Pressing the button that opened the speakers to the playroom, she gave her first official order as Madame.

"Jayden, blindfold yourself and assume an inspection position. I will be with you shortly."

∞∞

Dismissing Erin to get ready for the evening, Jayden hurried into the kitchen to wash up the dinner dishes. He couldn't be sure she'd noticed that he hadn't stated a time limit in which meet him in the playroom. Remembering how fidgety she'd been while they ate caused him to snicker. It had been a long week for both of them, and they needed this.

Kitchen tidied, he ran down to the playroom to load up the rolling tray with an assortment—lube, anal plugs, vibrators, nipple clamps, a candle and a box of matches, a riding crop, the rabbit fur flogger, the leather paddle, and his newest purchases, a cock ring and cock cage. His heart skipped a beat when he lifted a cane down from the wall.

He had no fear of her using the tool on him, but he did have some concern over how she was going to react to seeing it. After her meltdown following the Dominick and Natalie ordeal, this plan had formed. Several conversations with Landon to hammer out the specifics had brought them to now.

Jayden's hope was that if Erin had the opportunity to wield it first, then her fear of the toy would lessen. Neither he nor Landon expected she'd use it tonight. They were guessing that if she did decide to push herself, it would be tomorrow when Landon joined them. Nonetheless, he added it to the tray so she could at least begin contemplating it. Satisfied with the playroom set-up, he grabbed the new dominatrix outfits he'd hidden, then ran upstairs to lay everything out for her.

While Erin finished her preparations, Jayden took care of his own by showering and returning to the playroom to take his place on the pillow, where he kneeled and waited in the nude.

The crackle of the intercom made him jump, and his erect cock bounced, in turn causing the liquid that had been gathering at the tip to drip down to the floor. Her strong, calm voice issuing the command to blindfold himself and assume an inspection position went straight to his cock. *Fuck me, I may be in trouble.*

Not wanting to disappoint his Madame, Jayden was up and over to the storage drawers in an instant. He retrieved a sleek blindfold and, as a last minute addition, decided to add a ball gag and some ropes to the tray for her consideration.

Returning to the waiting mat, the eager man lowered himself to his knees and spread them until they were more than shoulder width apart. Sliding the blindfold into place, he checked to make sure it was snug and then positioned his hands behind his back, grasping the opposite elbows. The position pulled his chest taut, forcing him to thrust the toned muscles forward while his ass rested on his heels.

It was time to clear his mind, level out his breathing, drop his chin to the floor, and wait patiently for his Madame.

The heartbeat in his cock was his lone company . . . for the time being.

꙲ꙮꙨ
CHAPTER TWENTY-FOUR
ꙮꙨꙡ

Being extra careful in the deathtrap boots, Erin made her way downstairs. Every step brought her closer to the love of her life. To the man who was kneeling to offer himself to her in every way. Her heart felt like it would burst, and while her mouth was dry from the nerves, her pussy was so very wet. And they hadn't even started yet.

Pausing outside the door to their room of consensual sin, Erin took a moment for herself, then pushed the door open. The sight awaiting her was incredible. A blindfolded Jayden waited, kneeling, while his cock—his luscious, thick cock—was fully erect and standing up toward his tight stomach. Erin could see, and appreciated, the sinewy lines of every muscle in his body. The surreal presentation made her heart hurt. He was so damn beautiful, so . . . magnificent.

Her heels tapped on the wood, warning him of her approach, yet he didn't move. When she reached him, Erin circled her man while appreciating every tantalizing inch of him on display—for her. She dragged her manicured nails over his shoulder, across the back of his neck to the other shoulder, then came back to stand in front of him. By stepping in close and putting her sex inches from his face, she knew he'd be able to smell her arousal.

"Hello, *peata* . . . my pet." Erin stopped to see if he would respond. Not surprisingly, he was perfection and remained still, save the rise and fall of his chest while he breathed. "Good lad," she praised in a whisper then ran her fingers through his hair, scratching his scalp.

He shivered at her touch, the movement traveling up her arm from her fingertips and settling in her already hardened nipples.

"Oh, whatever shall I do to you tonight, my *peata*? Let's take a look and see what you've laid out." Madame Erin began her perusal, surprised by how many things he'd selected. Shock might have been a better word to describe her first impression, not that she wasn't pleased by the variety.

"My my. It seems somebody *really* wants to play." Erin wasn't expecting an answer, considering she hadn't given him permission to speak, but it was fun to be the one doing the teasing this time.

Her gaze stopped at the lube and plugs. She held up a plug that was rather large for a beginner. It had a soft point on the tip that flared outward before curving back in and forming three balls spaced a half inch apart. Looking closer, she noticed there were metal beads *inside* the ball sections. On the tray near where the plug had been lying was a remote control, and when she pushed the on switch, the metal beads began rotating. *This could be fun*, she thought while playing with the controls to get a feel for the toy.

"Are you sure you're ready for me to use these toys?" She walked toward him with a heavy step, letting him hear her footsteps. "While I'll be the first to admit that an assfucking feels fabulous now, in the beginning it can be a little much when you aren't ready for it. You may speak." Erin stopped behind him so that her vinyl-covered skin pressed into his back, except for her exposed pussy—that was flesh on flesh, and she loved how warm he felt against her.

He started to speak but stopped to clear his throat when she ground her heated core against his back. "Your boy has been preparing, Madame."

At his words, and hearing him call her Madame for the first time, her heart stuttered. "What do you mean?"

"Each night this week your boy has gone to his office and used the butt plugs to stretch himself for your pleasure. Your boy is confident that he can take anything that is laid out."

Well, fuck me.

"Um . . ." Erin found herself speechless while she tried to figure out how to respond to his admission. "Okay, then."

Smooth, Erin, real smooth.

Thrown for a loop, the Madame went to review the items again. She looked everything over with a closer eye, developing a plan, when she noticed the cane and reached over to pick it up. Feeling the rattan weight in her hand, Erin braced for the panic attack to start but found that she was calm. Still, she returned the toy to its spot. *Maybe later, but not now.*

Instead of dwelling on it, Erin collected the things she wanted for her first scene with Jayden, then set the items on the padded table near him and returned to his side.

"Lift your head, *peata*." Erin placed a wide play collar around his neck and fastened the buckle, followed by a leash.

His breathing picked up noticeably while her hands worked, and when she glanced down at his cock, which was taking on an interesting purple hue from how swollen he was, she grinned at the copious amount of precome leaking out. On an impulsive whim, she reached down to wipe away the viscous fluid with her fingertip, drawing a surprised hiss from him at the contact.

"Open," she commanded. Erin pushed the come-coated finger into his mouth when he parted his lips. "Taste yourself, Jayden," she whispered, uncertain whether this was too much. To her astonishment, his lips closed around her finger and he sucked with fervor, moaning while he did. "G-good lad," Erin stuttered, caught off guard by his reaction. However, she was encouraged by it, too, and wrapped her hand around the leash to pull his head toward her tingling sex. "Now, taste me." That time, she managed to get her words out louder.

Though he was blindfolded, Jayden had no trouble locating her clit, which he began sucking on with as much vigor as he'd applied to her finger. She became so lost in the sensation that she didn't realize she was pumping her hips against his face until he released the sensitive nub and buried his tongue between her folds.

Enjoying the tonguing, she threaded her fingers into his lush, dark hair and pulled him closer. To make it easier, Erin raised her left foot and placed it on his thigh, opening herself to his ministrations. She could feel her orgasm building under his tenacious tongue and wondered if she wanted to come so soon. *It feels so good, it would be so easy to let go.*

You are in control here, Erin. This is your chance to demand as many orgasms as you want without reprimand. I say, go for it!

"Fuck, Jayden!" Erin yelled while his efforts increased. "That's right, my *peata*, eat my pussy. Make your Madame come." She ground against his face with enthusiasm while guiding his head by his hair. The whole time Jayden ate her out, he moaned into her, his sounds proving he was enjoying this as much, if not more than, she was.

The rush of tingles erupting throughout her body told Erin she was moments from exploding. "Suck my clit," she insisted, getting into the scene, and he obeyed without hesitation. "Aye! Oh, shit, I'm coming! Fuck, ah god, shit . . . feck . . . damn!" Erin was unable to control the screeching profanities emitting from her mouth while her demanded orgasm crashed over her.

The thrill of power was alluring.

"Pleased with yourself, are you, lad?" Madame inquired of her boy when she was able to open her eyes and take in his glazed face.

Jayden nodded and gave her a lazy smile, but he remained silent.

"Well, let's see what we can do to wipe that grin off your face," she snapped, a tad surprised by this forceful side of herself. "Come." Erin tugged on the leash, and he fell forward onto his hands then crawled after her while she led him over to their padded leather table. The surface was about knee level, making it perfect for fucking—and other things. "Up you go, *peata*."

His hands came out in front of him to feel around and get his bearings before he crawled up onto the table. She resisted reaching out to pop his ass with her palm.

"Kneel, hands behind your head." Erin's tone was clipped, and she was still shaky from her earlier orgasm. Once he was positioned like she wanted, she began licking and pinching his nipples, encouraging them to harden. "Take a deep breath, lad." The second he inhaled, she hurried to put a set of clamps into place and then told Jayden to exhale.

He whimpered, but to his credit, he refrained from using words.

"I want to hear you today, Jayden. You have permission to speak as needed. Mind your attitude, however." Though Erin attempted to sound stern, her amused giggle threaded its way into her words, and her lover's lips curled in a quick grin. She did want to take this seriously, but it was all so odd to be on the 'top' side of things.

She coughed. "What color are we, *peata*?"

"Most assuredly green, Madame," he purred.

"Excellent. Now, bend over and show me that ass," Erin coaxed, giving him a gentle shove against his back.

He leaned forward onto his elbows and lifted his gorgeous rump in the air. Madame retrieved a bottle of warming lube and squirted a generous amount onto her fingers before drizzling some over his puckered hole for good measure.

When she slid one finger into him, he moaned and arched his back. Pulling back, she added a second finger next to the first and pushed into him again. With the third stroke, Erin added a third finger, and began pumping in and out of him with cautious tenderness until he opened to her. After a bit, she was able to add a fourth digit. Though her hands were tiny, she was still impressed that Jayden was taking this with no sign of discomfort.

She continued to work her fingers in and out. "Do you like that? Are you ready for more?"

"Fuck, yes. Please, Madame, give your boy more!"

"Good lad." Pleased, and with her desire growing, Erin patted his ass then picked up the remote controlled plug, lubed it thoroughly and placed it against his hole. Applying steady but gentle pressure, she worked the toy into his passage.

A loud groan erupted from Jayden once she got the plug seated all the way inside him and turned the remote onto a pulse setting. The beads rotated every ten seconds, giving him little bursts of sensation. The first time it happened, Jayden choked out a low, "Oh, God," pleasing her and making her a little bit jealous.

After cleaning her hand on a towel, she collected his leash again and gave her next set of instructions. "Move forward and come down off the table on the other side. We are going to the hook." Erin palmed the rope she'd chosen from the table with her free hand. Jayden crawled along next to her, all power and graceful lines. Each time the beads rotated, he would stumble a bit.

The hook was in the far corner of the playroom. There was a padded mat beneath it that aided in comfort for whomever was being mounted to the hook, but it also made for easy clean-up of any fluids that happened to leak out onto it. Catherine had spent her fair share of time hanging in the spot, and without question, she had done her fair share of leaking onto the mat, as well.

Once he was kneeling on the mat, she removed the leash. "Lift your hands above your head and lock your fingers together." Now Erin had to take a step back for a moment. It was one thing to tease him and probe his backside while he had a leash and blindfold on. It was another to attempt mounting him while bound— she didn't want to end up hurting him out of carelessness or just plain old lack of know-how.

"Madame?" Unexpected in the silence surrounding them, his voice surprised her.

"Aye?"

"Is everything okay? Can your boy be of assistance in any way?"

"Well . . ." Her answer trailed off while reassessing the hook and her plan, because she wasn't sure. It dawned on her that she wasn't quite tall enough to reach the hook, even in the heeled boots, which meant that he'd raised it in anticipation of her putting him on it. *Here's hoping that he can get himself fastened without much help from me, she thought with some agitation.*

It wasn't easy admitting she didn't know what she was doing, but as he'd told Erin so many times, communication was key, and there was no harm in playing it safe. She swallowed her pride. "I want to tie your hands so I can put you on the hook. I'm just not sure how to go about it."

His plump lips curved up into a smile. "Your boy thought you might. With your permission, may your boy walk you through the process?" he offered.

The would-be Domme let out a sigh of relief. "Aye, please."

"Do you have the bondage rope from the tray?"

"Aye."

"Okay, this is what you need to do . . ."

For the next few minutes, Jayden patiently guided her through how to wrap the cord around his wrists several times, linking them together and ensuring there was enough rope to slide over the hook without rubbing against his skin. Once he felt comfortable with the tightness, he let her know he was good, and she resumed control.

It took a couple of tries with Erin holding his waist to steady him, but at last the rope was over the hook and Jayden's arms stretched tight above him, elongating his torso and heightening her desire while she looked him over.

A tap from her to the inside of his thighs told him to spread his legs, and then she retrieved the flogger. The rabbit fur threads of this particular flogger were her favorite for pleasure, and she wondered if that's why he'd included it. On many occasions Erin had come from this toy alone, with Master's permission of course. Now it was time to see if he'd like the toy as much.

With the flogger in her left hand, she stepped in close and wrapped her right around his throbbing erection. Slow and teasing, she stroked it. "I'm going to flog you now, my *peata*. You are not allowed to come without my permission."

"Yes, Madame. Thank you."

When she connected the fur to his ribs, a guttural sound rumbled out of him. Erin circled her lad, boots rapping on the floor, and brought the flogger against his thighs, ass, upper back, and his clamped nipples. She avoided his cock on purpose, saving that for when he was closer, needier.

About five minutes into the flogging, she changed the plug from the sporadic pulse to a low constant setting, then continued working him over. Every pant, whimper, and groan that escaped him sent a tingling sensation to her pussy.

Ten minutes later, she increased the plug setting to medium and switched out the fur implement for a flogger with suede fronds.

"Feels so good, Madame. Thank you." He was panting, and his skin was turning a light pink all over. It was intoxicating to look at.

After landing several more passes of the suede upon his skin, she upped the setting again to high and then brought the flogger down on Jayden's engorged and leaking cock.

"Fuck!" With absolute wantonness, the male submissive began thrusting his hips against the air. Without words, he was begging her to make contact with his cock again, which she did.

"Oh, shit! I'm going to . . . Fuck . . . I need . . . oh, God, please!" he cried.

"*You* need?" she teased. "What does my *peata* need?" Her aching arm rested at her side, the fronds sweeping against her leg while she stroked his sweaty brown hair.

"Please, Madame, may your boy come? He needs to so bad. I–um, *he* can't hold back much longer." The plea was whimpered out through trembling lips, which he had to wet more than once.

A surge of power coursed through Erin's body, setting everything on fire. Her nipples tightened and the fire settled between her thighs in a pool at the desperate longing in his voice. Like a lightning strike from above it hit her, and all at once she understood what he got from their relationship. How it was a sexual thrill for him in the same way it was for her.

"Not yet." Embracing her role of Domme, she denied him, then lashed the flogger against his cock again. Her reward was a deep growl from within his chest while he fought, at her command, the urge to explode.

In a split second decision, she reached out and removed the blindfold. Erin was used to seeing his dark eyes heavy with lust. She wasn't prepared for what she saw when he blinked, adjusting to the light, and took in her appearance for the first time since she'd donned the cat suit.

His eyes were smoldering, and his apparent need burned into her while they stared at each other, their chests heaving.

ΩΟ3
CHAPTER TWENTY-FIVE
ΩΟℜ

H *oly shit!*

Jayden had suspected his jewel had a dominant streak in her and that they could have some fun if they traded places, but this was turning out better than anything he could've imagined. She was astounding him with how well she'd taken to the switch.

Erin wasn't holding back and was in full Domme mode. If he hadn't known better, he'd have sworn she'd been through intensive training. She was a natural, and fuck him if she weren't the most beautiful and erotic thing he'd ever seen. Jayden chuckled on the inside. He'd long since learned to expect the unexpected with Catherine, and as usual, she didn't disappoint.

When his eyes adjusted to the lighting, he was able to see how close the picture in his mind had been to reality when he'd looked at the cat suit on the hanger. The reality was a hundred times better than any vision he'd concocted over the last week while working with the anal plugs in his office each night. By forcing them in and then jerking off to memories and visions of his Erin, he had been attempting to train his body to associate the intrusion with pleasure.

Prior to the blindfold coming off, Jayden had thought he needed to come, but now he knew that had been nothing more than a mere want. Seeing her body wrapped tight in the black vinyl, with her creamy tits and smooth cunt on display, not to mention the boots . . . *Fuck!* Now it was an undeniable *need*. Those red boots had been the perfect choice, for sure, and whether he wanted or needed to come was fast approaching a moot point. The man's body was going to mutiny on him and do whatever the hell it wanted.

Jayden's rebellious lips choked out a "Please," then she was on her knees before him in a flash. Fixing him with a direct stare, Madame Erin gave the order to come moments before her mouth descended over his cock.

Delicious, delirious nirvana . . . That vacuuming warmth was all it took for him to begin flooding her throat with his seed, which she swallowed down without spilling a drop. Jayden gasped and moaned. Hell, he even cried.

His tears fell thanks to her efforts to tease and work the release out of him. He simpered at the bite of pain in his still-clamped nipples. The warm, stinging sensation that covered his body, compliments of the flogger, had his nerve endings on high alert. Most of all, Jayden realized, he cried at the chance to just let go, to not have to make the decisions or be in control. It was freeing and one of the most gratifying sensations he'd ever felt.

When had he last come with such abandon?

Without the rope and the hook he dangled from, Jayden would've collapsed to his knees. His legs were shaky, and his head fell forward while his cock twitched in her fantastic mouth.

In her mouth.

It took the bound man a minute, but he noticed she hadn't released his shaft. She was still sucking him, keeping Jayden's cock hard despite one of the most forceful orgasms of his life—and it felt fucking fantastic. The stirring of another orgasm starting to build low in his stomach wrenched a moan of disbelief from him. *He was too old to come back-to-back, wasn't he?* His eyes rolled back, his head soon following.

When his Madame was satisfied, he assumed, that he wasn't going to lose his erection, she withdrew down his length, sucking with vigor, then finished with a kiss to the head. She stood up and took a step back, and he lifted his heavy head to focus on her.

Jayden's breath caught in his throat. *Goddamn, she was beautiful.*

"Are you steady enough to unhook yourself?" she asked, her voice soft. The green of her eyes had a different intensity from what he was used to. The fire he knew so well was there, but somehow they also seemed softer . . . soothing.

"I think so. Spot your boy, please, Madame," he replied while drawing his legs together, then rising up on his toes. When his weight pulled him into a sway, her hand was immediately against him, steadying him while he freed himself. Muscles screaming with relief, he brought his arms down in front of him to await her next instruction.

"I need you, Jayden. I need to feel your cock inside me." Her tone had lost some of its previous forcefulness and now had an edge of pleading to it. It appeared her natural submissiveness was surfacing to reclaim its rightful place.

Jayden wasn't ready for her to let go of her control yet. He was going to need to guide her through the rest of the scene, without taking over. "Anything for you, Madame. Where do you want your boy?" Maintaining and reminding her of his current role, he tried to be subtle in handing the proverbial reins back to Erin.

She blinked at him, her brow drawn up with uncertainty, but once he nodded his okay, she looked around the playroom. Jayden knew when she was ready, because her back straightened and her head dipped with a light nod, a look of determination settling across her face.

"To the cross, *peata*. On your back."

He didn't need to be told twice and hurried over to recline against the cross and wait for her. She was right behind him, it turned out.

Gathering Jayden's still-roped hands in a gentle grip, she lifted them above his head and looped the rope through the O-ring fastened to the top of the cross. Once she'd secured him, her fingertips stayed in contact with his skin, trailing first down his arms, then his sides, until reaching his hips. Bringing her hands in, she wrapped both around the base of his cock and pulled them up, pushing his shaft into his stomach.

Jayden whimpered when her hands slipped over the head of his cock and moved up his stomach toward his nipples.

"I think you've had these on long enough," she taunted and flicked the clamps.

The minx giggled when he hissed at the sharp zing traveling across his chest.

"Okay, you need to take a deep breath and hold it until I get them off. You won't feel anything at first. But I'm not going to lie, Jayden, as the blood returns it's gonna hurt like a son of a bitch for about a minute." Her laugh was short and apologetic. "Ready?"

He wasn't, but he nodded his head and took a deep breath. She released the clamps, and he let out the breath nice and easy. *That's not so—* "Shit!" he screamed out when his nipples erupted in flames and severed his thoughts.

Distracted by the inferno that was his nipples, he didn't notice her positioning herself above him. All at once his cock was engulfed in hot, wet tightness.

"Ah fuck, Erin!" Jayden was too blown away by the heat sliding up and down his cock to care about the words pouring from his mouth.

His Domme leaned forward while moving her soft hands up his arms until she pinned his elbows. All the while, her hips rolled against his groin, slow, erotic, and almost to the point of pain. The shift in her position placed her tits in front of his face.

He'd never wanted his hands more than he did in that moment. Jayden longed to knead her tits and pull them to his mouth so he could devour her. Instead, he was bound and helpless while she took her pleasure from him—and it was fucking great!

"Suck them."

Her whispered command floated through the air moments before his mouth filled with a knot of hard flesh. Not ashamed to be greedy, Jayden closed his lips around it and sucked on her with the desperation of a newborn baby.

A vision of Erin, her belly swollen with a growing child, assaulted Jayden. The thought of her breasts firm and enlarged while her body prepared to nourish *their* baby weaved its way into his mind.

Imagining suckling her afterward, being able to feed from her; the idea of being able to drink her warm, sweet milk was enticing.

But the idea of seeing a tiny person created from their love cradled at Erin's breast was mind-numbing.

Jayden shook off the rambling thoughts. Now wasn't the time for them. He gave himself over, becoming lost in an ocean of sensation. The plug still hummed in his ass. While the fire in his chest was abating, every time she dipped against him, the warmth flared again. His lips and tongue laved at her nipples each time she offered them. Writhing above him while her face displayed her concentration, Erin lifted and lowered herself on him. She was magnificent.

For all he knew, days passed while she rode him. At some point, she impaled her pussy until she was all the way down. This took her breasts away from his mouth, but she'd soon replaced them with her own mouth. Erin's tongue tortured his mouth while he thrust upward, meeting each of her downward thrusts until they were both panting with the desperate need to release.

"I'm so close."

"Me too, Erin, me too. Can you . . . will you release my hands?" His request was breathy, but respectful.

She paused before reaching up, placing a nipple within reach of his mouth again. Jayden flicked his tongue out while she tugged on the rope and sat up, bringing his hands with her so she could untie him.

The moment his hands were free, he was standing up, his palms open under her ass while he kept himself buried in her, and he walked them over to the king-sized bed. Once he'd laid her down, he proceeded to give the final thrusts they both needed. Erin's orgasm grew in intensity, and when he could fight the constriction of her inner walls no longer, he joined her. Almost in sync, they fell over the edge. Profanities laced with the words of devotion fell from their lips while Jayden collapsed on top of her.

Later, as their breathing became less ragged, Jayden stared into her eyes. Every bit of the love and adoration he felt for this amazing creature was reflected back at him.

He was spent, in the physical and mental sense, and he was pretty sure that his jewel was in the same condition, meaning the scene was over for the night. However, his backside was quite aware that a part of the scene was still taking place. He lifted her up and off of him.

"Um, *Madame*," he smirked at her, "think we can lose the plug now? It is getting a bit uncomfortable."

She sat up, her mouth in an adorable 'o'. "Oh, my god, I'm sorry!" Erin hopped off the bed and scurried behind him. "Okay, spread your legs and bend over for me please."

Once he'd complied, she was able to remove the plug. Jayden felt empty, but a certain amount of relief accompanied the action. She dropped it on the table with the other toys she'd used and looked around.

Catching on, Jayden decided to help her out. "Why don't you go on up and start a bath for us? I'll clean up down here real quick and then join you."

Her eyes were always so expressive, and now they shone with gratitude. "That would be wonderful.

Thank you, peata." She grinned, then winked at him before heading out of the room.

Jayden might have been ogling her ass while she walked away.

CHAPTER TWENTY-SIX

While the bathtub filled, Erin stared off, zoning out. She was used to having her body feel like a puddle of goo after a scene, but not her mind. Well, not like this. If tonight had taught her anything, it was that there was a lot more involved in taking control than she'd ever realized. Where submitting always took her to a blank place, one where she didn't have to think or decide but just *do*, being the one in control had her mind going a mile a minute. There was so much to be conscious of at all times.

She peeled out of the cat suit, her muscles aching all over and her body coated in sweat. It was easy to understand why Jayden's body was so muscular and toned, his morning workouts notwithstanding. Until she'd done it, Erin hadn't dreamed how hard swinging a flogger or doing most of the work during sex could be on a person.

The inviting bath called to her, and she stepped into the hot water, sinking down to lay her head back against the side. Closing her eyes, she let the heat seep into her. The aches began to fade, as did Erin.

∽∾

She woke up alone in their bed, his half untouched and still made. Disoriented, Erin looked around for Jayden. In a rush, the memories from last night came back to her.

Good job, Erin, on managing to screw up your first time as a Domme. You left a vibrating plug in his ass, probably left the nipple clamps on too long, and then you passed out in the bathtub without making sure he received his proper aftercare. You suck.

Burying her face in her hands, Erin groaned. How could this switch thing have been a good idea? Would she be able to get through the day—or tonight, with Sir Landon? *That will be just what I need, someone to bear witness to my failure*, she thought with a shred of sarcasm.

A light knock at the door pulled the confused woman from her inner turmoil. Glancing down revealed she'd been dressed in one of Jayden's soft, black cotton T-shirts that she loved so much. Considering herself decent, she called out a tentative "Come in." When the door opened, she had to lower her eyes to discover the identity of her guest.

Jayden was on his knees, head bowed, with a serving tray held out in front of him. His torso was bare. She was unsure about the rest of him, though, considering she couldn't see his lower half from her current position.

"May your boy present you with breakfast in bed, Madame?" The softness of his voice tickled along her skin.

"Yeah, sure. Jesus." The words were hard to form, and she stumbled over them, willing herself back into a Domme frame of mind since Jayden obviously wanted to pursue this crazy game of his. "I mean, yes, please, and thank you, my *peata*."

Erin didn't miss the grin Jayden flashed her right before dropping his chin down and approaching her on his knees, going slow so as not to jostle the tray. When he reached the bedside, he slid the tray onto her lap and then dropped back into a waiting position.

He was naked. Completely bare-assed naked and serving her breakfast in bed.

I love this man!

The strong smell of coffee hit Erin's nose, so she reached for the steaming mug to start. Sipping on the hot liquid, she could feel the first hints of caffeine beginning to wind their way through her, waking her up. Her appetite awoke as well while she looked over the assortment on the tray. Warm coffee cake muffins, a fruit salad, and a plate of fluffy scrambled eggs with a large side of bacon sat there tempting the suddenly ravenous female.

"This looks delicious! Have you eaten already?" Erin asked while plucking a raspberry from the fruit salad and popping it into her mouth. *Sweet.*

"No, Madame, your boy wanted to see to your needs first."

Well, shit, even as a sub he is taking better care of me than I did of him last night. She sighed. "Uh, Red, or whatever ..." Fluttering her hand around in the air, the words were spoken in hushed tones.

Jayden relaxed his form and placed his hand on her calf. "What's wrong, Erin?"

With a halfhearted smile, she tried to put her thoughts together. "It's just that, I can't believe you want to keep doing this after all my mess-ups last night," Erin explained with more than a little dejection in her tone.

"What on earth are you talking about, sweet girl?" Now he was the one sporting a confused look.

"Jayden. Please. I screwed up, and we both know it."
He looked at her, waiting for her to continue, and she
sighed, then held up her hand to start counting her
errors off on her fingers. "I'm sure I left you in the
clamps longer than I should, and I forgot about the
toy altogether . . . you never do anything like that to
me. To top it off, then I crashed in the tub without
seeing to you. I failed you last night, *A rúnsearc*."
Shame tainted her whispered confession.

Without a word, he pulled the tray off her lap,
moving it to the nightstand before crawling onto the
bed behind her. Pulling Erin into his strong arms, he
kissed the top of her head, and she leaned into his
chest.

"Oh, Erin. Trust me, last night was beyond
amazing, even with the minor mishaps." He turned
her around so she was straddling his lap and cupped
her face in his warm palms. "Jewel, you've not had any
formal training. I wasn't expecting perfection from
you. You did better than what I hoped, to be honest."

"Really?" Erin was beside herself with shock.

"Yes, you silly woman." Jayden's nose nuzzled
against hers, and she swooned a bit when he tenderly

kissed her, their lips and tongues teasing. "Our scene was splendid. I was so turned on the whole time, and I promise you didn't hurt me. As for falling asleep in the tub," he shrugged his shoulders, "your body has been trained to let go and crash after a scene. You did what was natural for you, sweet girl. I was fine with getting you out and tucking you into bed. Promise."

"But I should have taken care of *you* afterwards, not the other way around," she argued.

"Catherine, listen to me."

"Aye, Master."

"This isn't permanent. Think of it as a weekend of role-playing. I'm still Master here, which means ultimately, I am responsible for you. I was, and still am, prepared to play both parts as needed while we progress through the weekend. Please, sweet girl. You've done nothing wrong, nor do you have any reason to feel ashamed or worry you've disappointed me."

"Are you sure, Jayden?" He smirked at her then, arrogant and promising, it went to parts low in her belly.

"Yes, Madame, your boy is sure. Nothing would please him greater than for your domination to continue. Please let this boy pamper you, at your command. Anything you desire, your boy will do for you." With his words came a wicked grin, and Erin could feel his erection swelling beneath her.

Her natural instinct was to wriggle against him, followed by a carefree laugh when he grunted and rolled his eyes back. She could do this. Jayden wanted her to let go and have fun with this experience, so that's what she was going to do.

"In that case, *peata*, I want you to feed me and help me eat all this food you brought!"

"Your wish, my command." His arm darted out to grab a muffin, and soon the air was flavored by the escaping steam when he broke the treat open. He offered her a bite, then took one for himself. They continued in that fashion until most of the food was gone, stealing kisses from one another in between nibbles.

When Erin couldn't eat another bite, she stilled his hand then shifted her body to slide down onto his hardness. They made love while she held his arms above his head, unhurried, and with sweet abandon.

Afterward, Madame Erin instructed her lad to join her in the shower, where she guided him through washing her. In reward for his good behavior, the satiated woman got on her knees and worked another orgasm free of his tiring body with her skilled mouth.

Upon exiting the en suite, Erin donned a lightweight robe, deciding that was all she wanted to wear today. However, she instructed Jayden to remain naked. His shocked look had made her giggle before she 'threatened' him with the whipping bench if he gave her any attitude over her request. He'd bowed his head with a "Yes, Madame," before heading back to the kitchen to clean up breakfast.

While he took care of the kitchen, Erin got comfortable on the couch, reading the morning paper and enjoying more coffee. When Jayden came back into the room, he dropped to his knees then crawled to her.

"Does Madame desire anything?"

She considered his offer for a moment. "Aye, I want you to play with your cock and balls while I read. You're not allowed to come." He gulped, and she grinned.

The next hour was spent with Erin *not* reading the paper, although she pretended to. Each time his breathing got ragged, indicating he was getting close, she ordered him to stop for ten minutes and then resume. Not once did Jayden complain, although each time Erin looked at him, his eyes were getting darker, more lust-crazed. *Perfect.*

Enough time had elapsed that Erin was ready to play some more, so she folded up the paper. Standing, she crooked a finger at him and told him to follow her down to the playroom. Once inside, the Domme instructed Jayden to stand by the bed while she went to the cupboards and fetched the cinnamon oil.

Letting her robe drop from her shoulders into a puddle on the floor, Erin climbed up onto the bed and got comfortable, lying on her stomach. "I want a thorough massage, *peata.*"

"It would be your boy's pleasure, Madame."

After squeezing a generous amount of the oil into his hand, Jayden grasped her feet and begin kneading. With a gradual progression, he massaged her legs, over her ass, and along her back to her shoulders. From there, his magical hands worked down her arms to her hands, which were tingling by that point, and at last, each individual finger before he paused.

"Roll over please, Madame."

His voice was distant to Erin, who was floating along in a state of total relaxation. With his help, she rolled over then waited for him to resume once he applied more oil to his palm. Again, Jayden started at her feet and worked his way up. He kneaded her pussy without any penetration, drawing a needy moan from her. She'd been on the verge of ordering him to finger-fuck her when he moved on, continuing up over her stomach to her breasts.

Moisture continued to gather between her thighs under the onslaught of both hands on her breasts, working the flesh from the base to the tip. The cinnamon extract in the oil was hot on her nipples and felt splendid, especially when he gave her piercings a tug.

By the time he brought the massage to a close, working over her collarbone, around her neck, and into her scalp, her nipples were erect and ached. Erin was limp and teetering on the edge of an orgasm. Moving like a rag doll, she dragged her knees up into a bent position then gestured toward her pussy. "Make me come."

Indulging in a heavy blink, she looked down the length of her glistening torso to see his cock, thick and tight, hovering near her sex. It would've been clear to anyone that saw him that the man had enjoyed touching his Domme.

He backed up and maneuvered between her legs, lowering his mouth to her hypersensitive clit. It didn't take long for her to explode on his tongue and then beg to be fucked until he came.

Wiped out, Erin crawled off the bed, took Jayden's hand in hers, and led him back upstairs to the submissive room. After drawing the covers back, they crawled into the cool sheets. Content, she drifted off into a peaceful sleep cradled against her love's chest while he stroked her sweaty hair.

CHAPTER TWENTY-SEVEN

Jayden's backside was cold when he woke up. However, his chest was hot and sweaty from the beauty bundled in his arms. A light, buzzing snore came through her parted lips, drawing a dopey smile from him. Though he longed to lower his lips to hers to wake her in a slow, teasing fashion before taking her, Jayden knew she needed to sleep. If she was going to survive their evening with Landon, his jewel would require the extra rest.

The Dom's thoughts turned to his careful planning with Landon. This weekend had been in the works since their run-in with Dominick and Erin's subsequent meltdown back in December.

After asking his friend to assist her, he'd given Landon a list of the items he'd be making available to Erin for the weekend. Jayden wanted her pushed through a more hardcore scene than what he thought she'd attempt on her own. Of course, extra emphasis was placed on the cane situation in their discussions. Bottom line, that was the impetus for this session.

In the end, they concluded Erin should use a cane on Jayden first. The hope was once she'd wielded the power and control of the tool, she'd realize it was nothing to fear. If they could cross that hurdle, then he'd be able to reciprocate and show her what a sensual addition to their play the cane could be.

With some effort, he peeled his body away then tucked a pillow in his place. Erin's face scrunched up for a few seconds but soon relaxed while she nuzzled into his replacement. Satisfied that she would sleep a little longer, he slipped from the submissive room and went down to their room for a quick shower. Pulling on a pair of lounge pants, Jayden headed down to the kitchen to start on dinner.

It took him about an hour to prep the vegetables and assorted seafood he'd be using to recreate his mom's spicy seafood stew. A bottle of white wine from a local vineyard was chilling in the fridge. The last thing to do before he started cooking was slice the artisanal bread and lather on the garlic spread he'd made, then set the baking sheet aside until they were almost ready to eat.

He was bent over, digging around in the lower cupboard looking for the large stew pot, when Madame Erin made her presence known.

"Now that, my *peata*, is a luscious sight after a refreshing nap."

Just the sound of her voice caused Jayden's skin to erupt in goosebumps and his cock to pulsate. Grabbing the pan, he stood then turned to face her. Dressed in a pair of cotton shorts and one of his wife beaters, sans bra, Jayden spotted her hard nipples poking through the shirt. He couldn't decide what enticed him more—that, or the visible side swells of tit flesh, compliments of the low-cut armholes.

"Your boy is glad Madame enjoyed her rest. Do you want some juice or a light snack? Dinner's still a couple of hours away, but we slept through lunch."

His Domme sauntered across the kitchen, her tits bouncing with each step, to look over the food prep area on the counter. "Juice sounds good. Bring it to me in the playroom," she ordered then strutted away with an unexpected abruptness.

Jayden stood there, staring and wondering where his quiet, reserved girl had gone. With a shake of his head, he looked over at the clock. Unsure what she was up to, he was concerned about starting a scene when the food was still raw. All he had to do at that point was toss the lot into the pan, along with the lobster stock, and set it to simmer. He decided to risk the few minutes it would take and got the stew going quick as he could move.

He set the burner on low, then grabbed a berry smoothie from the fridge, and poured a glass. While he was returning the bottle, he noticed a carton of fresh strawberries on the shelf and snagged a few, rinsing them to take, too.

Upon entering the playroom Jayden found his Madame standing by the waiting mat. Her arms were crossed over her chest, and she was tapping her foot.

Oh, shit. "Sorry to take so long, your boy just wanted—"

"I didn't give you permission to speak. And I certainly didn't ask what you wanted," she snapped.

Ah hell, she was pissed, but fuck him if it wasn't one of the sexiest things he'd seen.

"Put the stuff down over there." Her arm extended, pointing to the table near the door. "Then lose the pants and get your ass on the mat!" For the next several minutes, she didn't speak.

Jayden heard her getting her juice, her small moan of appreciation not going unnoticed by his reactive body. While he waited, he closed his eyes to try relaxing into the submissive mode. There was no doubt that he was having fun switching roles this weekend, but it was starting to take its toll on his mental state. So used to being in complete control and in motion, the Dom was finding it hard to just stop and let go.

A whiff of candle smoke tickled his nose, but he kept his eyes closed. *Odd.* His patience paid off, and soon her soft footsteps approached, stilling when she knelt behind him. Her tiny hands came around his torso, grazing his skin with her fingertips, swirling over the planes of his stomach up toward his hard nipples.

Setting her nails against his flesh, she dragged them down while speaking. "Unfortunately, we don't have time for me to punish you *and* get what I wanted to do done. So, your punishment will wait for tonight, when Landon can assist me." With both hands, she grabbed his cock and gave it a few fast and rough pumps.

Jayden couldn't hold in the grunt or the "Shit" that slipped past his lips.

"M'hm," she crooned in his ear, "seems my *peata* is still having trouble keeping his mouth closed. We'll have to fix that." Jayden's cock grew cold when she removed her hands. "Look at me."

Jayden lifted his head in obedience. In her hands was a ball gag.

"Open." After he lowered his jaw she pushed the ball between his teeth, then fastened the strap. "Since you won't be able to speak now, if you need me to stop, I want you to snap your fingers or slap your hand against, well, whatever surface I have you on." He stretched his neck side-to-side, maneuvering to get the ball to sit comfortably in his mouth, or as comfortable as was possible with a gag.

"I asked you down here so that I could get you dressed for dinner and our company. . ." Her words tapered off while she turned her back on him. Returning, she fastened a collar around his neck, then snapped a leash into place before stepping back to squat down in front of him at eye level. "Are you game for a quick scene, Jayden?"

In total agreement, he nodded. Madame stroked his cheek, and he leaned into her palm, hoping to show her the love he felt for her. Her resulting smile stole his breath. *Did she feel this rush when he caressed her the same way? When he bestowed his own pleasure on her?*

"Good lad." Jayden dropped to his hands and knees then crawled behind her while she guided him to the St. Andrew's cross by the leash. "Up you go. On your back, hands up in the cuffs." She gave the directive with a quick pat to the wood.

While buckling the cuffs around his wrists, Madame explained what she wanted to do to him. Jayden's cock liked what she was saying, and he grew hard listening to her erotic lilt.

"I want to be able to show you off tonight, Jayden, and to brag about your incredible stamina. You understand I can't have you coming right away, now can I?"

He nodded his head, holding his breath.

"So I decided to help you with that—by emptying those heavy balls of yours now, to allow you more time to fill them up before you're begging me to let you come again." Hot fingers trailed over his cock, surprising him when she gave his balls a hard squeeze. His hips thrust upward in an involuntary response.

"Mm, your cock is thick, *peata* . . . so hard, and crying for my touch." With an evil giggle, she bent over to lick away the wetness seeping from the head. Again, his hips rocked up, pushing his cock between her lips. "Naughty lad. Be still!" she ordered after retracting and slapping the top of his thighs.

His eyes must've looked wild when she lifted her tank top and freed those awesome tits of hers, if the knowing smirk on her face was anything to go by. In a deliberate tease, she fingered her nipples, tugging on the J's dangling from them, and he began to pant— while she groaned.

The minx was torturing him.

His torment continued when she turned her back on him and slid her shorts down her toned legs. The sight almost made him come. Spreading her legs made him whimper, and then she bent from the waist, giving him a clear view of the puffy pink wetness waiting for him. Air whistled out of Jayden when she righted herself with a sexy toss of her hair, sending it cascading down the pale skin of her back in red waves.

Looking over her shoulder at him, Madame blew him a kiss and mouthed: "I love you."

With a slight nod of his head, Jayden's lips tugged upward of their own accord, his happiness seeping out of him. He was surprised by how very aroused her adeptness with topping was making him.

She was going back to the padded table to collect her prepared selection from earlier, and he was curious. Jayden sucked in his breath at the sight of her returning with a lit candle and a riding crop.

"Would you like me to blindfold you so you're forced to just feel?"

As enticing as that sounded to Jayden, after taking a moment to consider her offer he decided that, no, he needed to be able to see her to gauge her actions and reactions. She'd experienced being candled, but this would be her first time doing the candling. The Master in him had to be present—just in case. He shook his head.

Raising the crop, she took up a light tapping pattern, moving it up the inside of his left leg. "Very well, lad. The choice is yours."

৪৩৫৪

CHAPTER TWENTY-EIGHT

৪৩৫৪

Under his Domme's attention, his eyes closed. Light and feathery, her touch didn't hurt Jayden in the least. The crop being worked up his leg, then tapped against his balls a couple of times before going back down the inside of his opposite leg, tickled.

Her slaps became firmer when she reached his feet. A strong *whap* to each sole and then she was dragging the tool up his leg again, letting the rough stitching on the edge scratch him with a pleasant sting . . . then laying it flat and smoothing the crop up his ribs and over his chest. A brief wince escaped his control when the leather jarred against his nipples in rapid succession, but pride swelled inside the prostrate man at her murmured praise. "Lovely."

He was proud of himself for submitting to and pleasing his jewel, of course, but even more so of Erin and how well she was doing thus far. There was a faint awareness of the crop tapping back down along his left side. Leather connecting with his balls again, harder that time, yanked Jayden's focus back, while more liquid seeped from the slit at the end of his cock.

Jayden groaned into the gag when she first licked then sucked his cock into her mouth, cleaning off what had leaked from him. A tiny click, followed by a wet, gloppy sound prefaced her palm wrapping around his shaft to slip up and down with ease.

It felt so goddamned good he wanted to cry.

Soon, a familiar coil began to tighten low in his stomach, building an ache in his balls that would only be relieved one way. Knowing he was getting close to shooting jizz all over her hand forced him to start thrusting into her movements. Desperate and horny, Jayden was sure he would explode into her hand at any moment . . . when she stopped.

Oh, the irony of payback!

He wanted to beg her to keep going, ask her to give him a couple more pumps so he'd find relief, but he couldn't speak.

Because of the gag.

Because he was forbidden.

Dropping his head back against the wood, Jayden squeezed his eyes shut. Harsh breaths whooshed out of him while he fought to level the raspy air. That moment of ecstasy was still so close—he wondered if he could concentrate and orgasm without her touch.

No.

That would be very bad. She might've been new to dominating, but she was practiced enough at submitting to know she'd have every right to punish him if he came without her permission.

Fuck!

His eyes flew open when white hot heat seared his cock. Daring to peek down, he saw her holding a tilted candle over him, wax dripping from it while the small flame flickered and danced in the draft of the central air. A loud, unmanly whimper betrayed his neediness when she used the crop to push his cock against his stomach, then drizzled more wax on the underside of his shaft and balls.

Up righting the candle, she asked, "Are we green, *peata*?"

Eyes wide, and he hoped pleading, Jayden nodded with fervor. Drool dripped from the ball gag. He could feel the thick, warm paraffin trickling toward his ass and found himself wishing she'd shoved something, anything, in it because the fullness would feel so good right then.

"Do you like being bound and exposed for my pleasure?" Madame queried then let his cock fall away from his stomach to drizzle more wax along the top.

His nod was aggressive and emphatic.

"I like seeing your skin flushed while your muscles strain." She emphasized her point by dragging the crop over his tightened abs, up toward his chest. "Mmm." With a quick snap, the crop bit each of his nipples. "Should I wax these, too, my naughty boy?" His Domme rubbed the crop in a circular pattern over them, soothing the sting out.

Jayden didn't reply, hoping he was conveying that it was her choice.

The leather smacked against his nipples again followed by the searing drops of wax. He hissed around the gag while the burn faded into a pleasant tingling warmth.

A rapid staccato thrummed in his chest while Jayden's mind raced. He was trying to take mental notes because he wanted to do this again . . . with *her* bound to the cross and *His* hand wielding the candle and crop. Thinking about reversing the scene on her served to heighten the intensity of what they were doing and soon Jayden's mouth betrayed him again. "...-ore!" He tried to beg for more, not caring about the consequences of speaking out of turn, but he was muffled by the gag.

She quirked her eyebrow at him. "Did you get permission to speak?"

Jayden wiggled, trying to spread his legs and open his ass to her the best he could within the confinement of his bindings.

Her heated stare burned into him. The crop returned to between his legs then moved up toward his puckered hole. A quick flick of her wrist and a sharp but wonderful sting crawled up his insides. "Does my lad need this hole filled?" She'd reopened the oil and was coating his cock—what wasn't covered in wax, that was—with the liquid that ran down between his ass cheeks.

When she easily slid two fingers into his willing backside, his hips bucked, and a throaty groan escaped him. Jayden was awestruck when she emitted a soft moan, and he looked over as she dropped the crop. From his vantage point, he could tell she was using her free hand to stroke herself in sync with her slim fingers moving inside of him.

"...-et me see –ease." Drool gathered around the gag with his efforts to speak.

Taking her hands away from both of their bodies, Madame reached for the buckle on the gag and undid it. "What did you say?"

He stretched his jaw and licked his dry lips. "Your boy said, 'Let me see, please,'" he answered in a quiet but polite tone. Her resulting smile was beyond stunning.

Moving slowly, she raised a foot to place it on the cross, near his thigh and returned a hand to her pussy. Watching her ring and pointer fingers, Jayden's whole body clenched when she spread her pussy lips open, revealing a very swollen clit.

"Stroke it." Jayden choked out the order, forgetting his current place.

Her fingers shoved back into his ass, forcing a gasp from him in shock. "Uh-uh, lad. I'm in control right now. Don't make me put that gag back on you."

"Yes, Madame, your boy is sorry."

She used her middle finger to rub her clit in rhythm to the fingers pumping in his ass. His woman was a sex goddess, of that he was certain. Pulling and tugging at the cuffs, Jayden's basic nature wanted so badly to get his hands on her body, to play her the way she was playing him. Instead, he had to settle for being at her mercy while grinding against her hand like a depraved dog.

Jayden's orgasm began building again, and there was no doubt it would be intense. The closer his release pressed down on him, the more he panted.

Erin pulled her fingers from him and stepped back, leaving him teetering on that edge.

"Please, Madame," he whimpered, not above begging by that point. "Please let your boy come."

"Not until I say. You will hold it." With an air of aloof cruelty she commanded, and he had no choice but to obey while traitorous tears formed in his eyes.

The crop was back in her hand, and with no warning, she brought it down over his nipples several times, breaking off the wax.

"Fuck! More please," he begged.

Acquiescing, the crop hit his ball sack, and there was a moment of coolness when the hardened wax broke away before the next strike warmed the tender skin of his scrotum. She was hitting the sack from side-to-side and it was quickly becoming too much.

Jayden was on the brink of safe wording when the tool moved away from his balls, up to his straining cock.

"Oh, fuck. Fuck. Fuck! Yes!"

Dragging his gaze to her fast moving fingers, Jayden's hunger grew at the sight of her rubbing her cunt with a manic degree of animal ferocity. Erin's eyes had grown wide and glassy, and she was flushed from her tits to her forehead. Her lips were parted, and she panted now, too. Knowing how to read her body as he did, he knew she was coming undone.

The Domme's strikes had shifted into haphazard attempts that resulted in bits of wax falling to his stomach and thighs in a random pattern. Writhing against the cross, he couldn't look away from her—from his soul mate and perfect partner. Each breathy word she whispered sent goose bumps racing over his flesh.

"Oh, god. Oh, fuck. Oh my . . . shit! Please come now, Jayden." The begged command was issued while she slapped her own clit and brought the crop down on the head of his cock at the same time.

Seconds later the room filled with the sounds of them exploding—grunts, curses, and gasps. The air was thick and reeked of animalistic sex. He wanted to watch her, but couldn't keep his eyes open while an unending orgasm erupted from his cock, sending jizz across his stomach, hot and thick.

When Jayden did open his eyes again, he had to scour the room, looking for his girl.

Erin was slumped in a ball on the floor. Her shoulders shook, and he could hear her soft crying. His reaction was immediate. Rotating his thumb, he was able to push the quick release button on the cuffs.

Shaking and somewhat numb, Jayden got down off the cross and hurried to her. Her body was light and limp when he scooped her into his lap. He sat there rocking her while he stroked damp red locks away from her face. Over and over he whispered to Erin, telling her it was ok, he had her.

Jayden wasn't surprised when she began to drop into the trancelike state of subspace. This scene had been crazy intense, and whether she'd run the show or not, it was her nature to crash hard when their scenes involved more. Pushing their limits was always a physical and mental challenge.

"Erin, sweet girl, are you okay?"

She turned her green eyes up to him and fluttered her wet lashes. "I'm sorry, Jayden. I feel like a failure right now, and I'm worried I hurt you. Did I hurt you, *A rúnsearc*?"

"No, you didn't hurt me at all." An amused chuckle rumbled out of him, and he leaned slightly away from her so he could look into her eyes. "Do you see how much come is drying on me? My god, woman." He smirked before adding, "There is never a dull moment with you, Ms. O'Chancey, soon to be Mrs. Masterson. Now, why do you think you failed me?"

Erin swallowed, her pink tongue flicking out to lick her lip. "Because, um, I'm supposed to be the one in charge right now. Yet for our second scene in a row, *you* are comforting *me*. Why can't I see a scene all the way through to do your aftercare?"

Jayden gathered her back into his arms and tucked her into his chest. It was time for a little lesson. "You're familiar with sub drop, right?"

She nodded once.

"I know you are because it happens to you—a lot. That's not a bad thing. It just means you're ruled by your emotions and your desire to please everyone around you." Kissing her nose, he continued with a grin, "It's a big part of what makes you such a fanfuckingtastic submissive. You give so much of yourself without expecting anything in return."

Her giggling against his chest made him smile. It was what he'd hoped for with his silly comment. While he'd talked, she'd been playing with the smattering of chest hair he had. Jayden realized she was picking pieces of wax out, and he let her carry on while his lesson resumed.

"Did you know the partner to sub drop is top drop?"

Her body stilled, and she looked up, meeting his gaze. *Good, he had her attention.*

"The same intense reactions can happen to those in charge as well. Trained dominants have learned to control the drop, postpone it if need be, until they've tended to the needs of their submissives. Then, and only then, do they allow themselves to unwind and experience the drop. Usually alone."

"But—" she started and he cut her off.

"No buts, Erin. We are, in essence, role playing this weekend—like I explained to you this morning. You've not been trained to dominate, and you have no reason to feel shame at your body's natural response system. You started this scene telling me you wanted to be able to 'show me off' to Landon tonight, have bragging rights over my stamina, right?" He waited for her answer.

"Aye, Master," She nodded.

He'd let her instinctive slip into submissive mode go since it was the proper state for them in light of their current conversation.

"Well, if anyone is going to have bragging rights, I think it will be me. Landon knows you're not trained and that this is your first attempt at full control. I honestly believe he's going to be amazed at how well you do tonight—as long as my feisty Madame joins us in the playroom, that is." He tickled her and let out a content sigh when she snickered and squirmed in his arms.

Becoming serious again, Jayden had to ask her, "Are you okay, sweet girl? If you don't want to do this anymore, we can switch back to our usual for the rest of the weekend, or we can call an end to the playtime altogether and take the weekend off, just be us."

She was quiet for a long moment while considering the offer. "No, Jayden. I *need* to see this through. I can do it." A flash of determination turned her eyes into green fire, and he laughed with a jovial, carefree sound.

"Of course you do, jewel. Always my high achiever, aren't you?"

At that, Erin stood up and reached out to help him up. "Damn straight!" she chirped. "Come on, *peata*. I need to rinse the sweat off my body, and you need to be scrubbed. Oh, and I still need to dress you for our evening . . ." Her grin was mischievous while her words trailed off.

One thought permeated Jayden's mind. *Oh, shit. Have I created a monster?*

෨෦ඣ
CHAPTER TWENTY-NINE
ෂ෦ඣ

G oing to the mini-fridge, Erin grabbed two
bottles of water and a square of chocolate
from the stash that was kept in there. When she
returned to Jayden, unwrapping his treat, she glanced
up and caught him trying not to grin.

"Something amusing you?"

He remained silent.

"Good lad. Kneel, and you may answer."

Dropping to his knees, he responded, "No,
Madame, not amused so much as pleased at the

attention Madame is lavishing on her boy." When he smiled, her heart melted a bit more. The man could be gorgeous and adorable at the same time.

"Open," Erin commanded, then laid the candy on his tongue. Easing his jaw closed, she gave him a kiss. She always appreciated when Master would feed her one of the sweet treats after an intense session, especially one on the cross. Often, a person didn't realize until later how tight their muscles had been strained in some of the positions. The chocolate was great for leveling out the endorphins and adrenaline in her system, easing her descent from subspace.

It was her turn to smirk—he was just too cute, humming in approval while the candy melted on his tongue.

The Domme passed a bottle of water to her sub. "I'm going to go prepare the bathroom for your cleanup. You have ten minutes to relax and drink all of that." She pointed to the bottle in his hand.

"Thank you, Madame." He untwisted the cap and took a long drink of the water, a single bead of sweat trickling along the curve of his brow.

Heading into the bathroom, she paused to set the wall timer. In nine minutes and forty-five seconds, it would signal that time was up. In the en suite, she switched on the towel warmer and added a couple of bath sheets to it. A quick look revealed nothing but her scented bath products in the shower, so she went to the supply closet in search of the all-natural soap she'd gotten him. When Erin noticed the enema supplies at the back of the cupboard, she wondered. *Do I dare?*

She held a silent debate with herself. Jayden seemed to be enjoying himself so far, so the possibility was there that this wouldn't be their last time to switch. At the same time, it could be the only time they ever did this. There was a part of her that wanted to give him a little taste of 'all things submissive.' For Catherine, humiliation scenes were a big part of being submissive. While she didn't care for public humiliation so much, in private she found it humbling. A little bit of humiliation acted as a reminder that she'd given herself over to her Master—to do anything he wished.

Her rambling thoughts along with the knowledge that Sir Landon—who had a taste for his subs being prepared such—would be joining them, clinched her decision. She gathered the supplies along with the soap.

Glancing at the clock startled her into motion. Five minutes remained on Jayden's break, with thirty minutes until Sir Landon was expected. Leaving the enema supplies next to the sink, Erin hurried to the shower, deposited the bar of soap, and turned on the water.

Moving into the playroom, Erin found him finishing the last of his water. At her arrival, Jayden redirected his attention to the ground then knelt.

She stepped up to him and ran her fingers through his hair, scratching at his scalp and gripping his hair for a heartbeat. "Such a good lad, aren't you?" *A whisper, to taunt.* Stretching her hand down, she smacked his ass and directed, "Crawl to the bathroom and bend over the counter."

The Domme followed her pet, enjoying the sway of his tight rear end in front her. With morbid curiosity, she paid close attention to his reflection when he began to move into position over the counter.

Jayden froze, brown eyes bulging.

"Is there a problem, *peata*?" she crooned. "You may answer."

The debate warring in his eyes was crystal clear when he shifted them from her eyes in the mirror to the supplies on the counter, and back to her. At last, he took a deep breath and answered with a quiet, "No, Madame." *Submitting.*

Respectful of how thorough Jayden always was with her whenever they did something new that she was unsure of, Erin explained her rationale for the procedure. He listened, still and patient, while she summarized her earlier thoughts on humiliation and Landon's preferences. By the time she'd finished, Jayden's countenance had grown serene. "What color are we?" she asked softly.

"Green, Madame, we are green."

"Good. Now spread your legs and bend over the counter. We need to do this quickly."

To his credit, though he tensed when the warm rinse first began filling his backside, he relaxed soon after, thereby making the process easier. Once she'd filled his colon, she gave him permission to use the toilet, then stepped into the shower to wait for him.

When he joined her several minutes later, his red face betrayed his embarrassment. Jayden stared at the tiles on the bottom of the shower.

"Come here." She guided him beneath the pelting spray. "You did very well, *A rúnsearc*. Let me wash you." Taking the lush soap in hand, Erin lathered him from head to toe, rubbing in firm circles and letting her nails scrape to get all the wax off his sculpted form. The mild scent of saffron with a hint of sweet clover honey wafted up in the steam. She lifted the shower head down, and he kneeled without being asked so she could reach his hair.

Her man was luxuriating in her touch, and she understood. Erin lived for these sensual, loving moments with her Master. Jayden's eyes slipped shut, a soft purring sound coming from him soon after, when she set about washing his hair. By the time she was ready to rinse out the frothy lather, he'd dropped his forehead against her stomach and had resumed that content humming.

Did she make noises like this, unbeknownst to her, when He worshiped her?

"All done, *peata*. Please retrieve our towels from the warmer."

Erin stepped out of the shower after she finished rinsing off and found Jayden waiting, a towel around his waist, and holding the other one open for her. She raised her arms, and he came forward to engulf her in the warm, plush cotton. After tucking the top of the towel at her breast to lock it in place, she brushed past him with a quiet "Come" and returned to the playroom.

"Sir Landon will be here in about ten minutes. I'm going to dress you and then retire to my room to get ready." She gathered his evening wear while she talked. "Drop the towel." He complied, and Erin appreciated his lithe body before she approached him.

He stood still while she enclosed his neck in a leather play collar. Next was a set of beginner clamps connected by a chain, which she threaded through the D ring of his collar, before securing a claw to each of his nipples. Erin was unconcerned about leaving the clamps on him since their bite pressure was very low. She knew from experience that it would be nothing more than a tugging sensation.

Wetness gathered between her thighs when she stepped back to take in his appearance.

To place the next item, Erin had to kneel in front him. She chuckled when his semi-hard cock started to thicken in front of her face. "You're going to want to get a handle on that. Otherwise, the next part of your outfit is going to be difficult to get on," she stated and showed him the cock cage in her hand.

Jayden gulped, nodded, and then whispered, "Yes, Madame."

Erin gave him a moment to collect himself. The skill was one he'd perfected in his years as a Dominant, and her arousal heightened when his erection lessened. That amount of control was commendable to her. Once Jayden was flaccid again, Erin wasted no time putting the cage in place and tightening the lock.

The first breath he inhaled was deep and shaky.

With measured steps, Erin circled him, appraising her handiwork. "Aye. This will do fine." The tips of her fingers skimmed his caged flesh, and he hissed.

Jayden's cock was trying to swell under her touch but couldn't because of its confinement.

"I'm off to get ready for our dinner guest. You may go set the table and make any finishing touches on dinner. When he arrives, I expect you to answer the door on your knees." Erin took a deliberate pause to see if he would react. Other than a slight widening of his eyes, he remained focused, so she continued. "You're to remain on your knees from that point on until one of us tells you otherwise. Do you understand?"

"Your boy understands, Madame. May your boy ask one question?"

"Go ahead."

"Is your boy allowed to crawl to move around or must he stay only on his knees?"

She considered his request, and knowing from experience that it was easier to crawl than attempt to "walk" on your knees, she gave him the okay to crawl.

With that resolved, she departed, leaving Jayden to carry out her commands.

෮෬

I n a trance, Jayden stared after her towel-clad form while she left the room. Her hips had a gentle sway when she walked and, once again, his cock tried to stand up and take notice. Wondering which of the outfits she would choose to wear that night didn't help his situation either. The remaining costumes in her closet wouldn't cover near as much skin as the cat suit she'd worn the night before.

Fuck—this damn cage sucks balls.

Out of habit, Jayden went to shake his head in an effort to clear it, but the movement pulled at the chained clamps. Again, his stupid cock attempted an unsuccessful awakening. It was going to be a long night.

After spending a few minutes testing how much range of motion he had, he strode out, headed for the kitchen. With the oven set to preheat, he stirred the stew and added the quick-cooking ocean delicacies.

Gathering dishes and moving to the dining room, Jayden started to set three places, but remembered Madame's decree for him to be on his knees until further notice. Two place settings were laid instead.

Back in the kitchen, he broiled the garlic bread and then packed the slices in a basket. While the bread toasted, Jayden had ladled the stew into a serving dish and taken it to the table. Last to be set out was the wine, and he was in the middle of uncorking it when the doorbell rang. His hands shook, and he had to be careful when setting the bottle down. Suddenly Jayden's heart was racing, and he was starting to sweat.

Why the fuck am I nervous about this? Could it be because he'd arranged this whole evening, so anything that happened tonight was on him?

The chiming of the doorbell a second time spurred him into action. *Can't leave your guest waiting. That would be rude and punishable.* He smirked at the idea.

Jayden's hand was on the doorknob when he remembered he wasn't kneeling like she'd required. *I'm going to do this.* His body seemed to travel to the hard floor in slow motion, a myriad of revelations overtaking him while he peered down his torso to stare at his clamped nipples and caged cock. *I'm going to let Landon see me in this get-up, and it's going to be humiliating.*

There was a small click as the knob turned in his palm, and the door swung open. He backed up, dropping his eyes to the floor.

Boots tapped over the entryway while Sir Landon entered, then closed the door behind him.

Jayden waited for his friend's laughter, for the good-hearted mocking to begin. His days training beside Landon back at Rice had never included this.

"Evenin', Jayden. Thanks for having me." Landon's southern drawl was relaxed and sincere.

The submissive snapped his eyes up to look at Landon, expecting to catch a cocky grin while his friend tried to hold back laughter at Jayden's appearance. But Landon wore a friendly smile and his blue eyes were filled with softness.

He isn't going to laugh.

It clicked. After so many years of being a Dom, understanding and enlightenment slammed into Jayden with a vengeance.

We never laugh at our submissives. We find pleasure in them.

Any outlandish outfit or situation a Dom asked for wasn't done with the intent to embarrass. It was done to test the limits of their submissive's devotion. There was no greater gift to a Master than to have their submissive indulge any request with an eager *"Yes, Master."*

Or, in his case, an "Aye, Master."

Every time Catherine submitted to him, she found her pleasure in His pleasure. There was no awkwardness or shame in any of their activities, only pride and beauty. A certainty sank into Jayden's heart at that moment. Whatever was asked of him in the coming hours, he would do.

If she wanted him to sit in the corner and watch them fuck, he'd do it. If she asked them to take her at the same time, they'd do it. If she told Jayden to suck Landon's cock, he'd do it. Hell, if she wanted them to read bedtime stories and drink hot cocoa with her, then that's what he would do.

Anything she asked of him, he was going to do without hesitation. Because if this was the one time he could show her that he got it, that he understood down to his core what she gave Him every time she knelt at His feet, then he wouldn't waste the chance.

Catherine O'Chancey had agreed to be his wife *and* lifelong submissive. For that, he would give her anything she desired, aside from his heart and soul—she already owned those.

ကလ

CHAPTER THIRTY
Welcome, Sir Landon

ကလ

L andon grinned down at his yella rose, who was being rather exuberant with her clapping. He'd granted her permission to entertain herself in their playroom while he was out that evening. She could come as much as she wanted, but she had to document each orgasm in her journal— how achieved, what toys used, and level of intensity—so that they could discuss, and possibly recreate, them later.

"Thank you, Master!" Paige shrieked before jumping into his arms and kissing him brazenly. She pulled back to rest her cheek against his chest while letting her fingers play over his ribs.

The kiss had been deep and filled with their love for each other, leaving his heart racing as she often did.

"This color does amazing things to your eyes," she whispered. The Dom had donned a royal blue, soft cotton tee to pair with his black leather play pants.

Landon placed a finger under her chin, then lifted her face to his. "I love you, sugar. Be a good girl, and I'll be home before you know it." He gave her a chaste kiss on her lips, followed by a quick peck on her nose just as his phone alarm sounded, telling him it was time to go.

The drive to Jayden and Erin's took about twenty minutes. Parking in front of the house, he exited the car and headed up to the porch, intrigued to see how well the switch weekend had worked out for them so far. Landon's honest expectation was that Jayden was having a harder time of it than Erin. She would do what was asked of her. Jayden, not so much.

He snickered at the idea of how fun this was going to be to witness and rang the doorbell, taking a step back to wait. A few moments later, the door swung open and Landon walked in, enjoying the sound of his boots tapping on the marble with each measured step. After closing the door behind him, he took in the sight of Jayden kneeling to the right of the door.

His back was straight, though his head was bent, his dark hair falling forward. Connected to a leather collar around Jayden's neck was a chain attached to a set of nipple clamps. Landon was shocked to see his friend's dick encased in a cage.

Well, call me a cow and tip me over.

Jayden's form was perfect, like he'd been a submissive all his life. While Landon hadn't questioned if Erin was the woman for his friend, the vision before him now convinced beyond doubt. The mighty Jayden Masterson did not submit to anyone anymore, but apparently he did for this woman. Landon's amusement from moments earlier on the porch was replaced with distinct pride in his friend.

"Evenin', Jayden. Thanks for having me."

His eyes rose to meet Landon's. "Good evening, Sir. It's a pleasure to have you join us," Jayden welcomed him with sincerity.

"Hi, Landon, so nice of you to come over tonight." Erin's voice sounded behind him, and Jayden's mouth dropped open as his eyes opened wide.

Landon leaned down to whisper in Jayden's ear, "You might want to close that or risk catching flies." Straightening, he turned to face Erin and froze himself.

Erin stood on the second step, a slim hand clenching the banister, and in the other, a leash. Bronze armbands twisted around her upper arms, giving the impression of vines crawling over her skin. The green leather corset fit her torso like a glove. Her breasts were on display in the half-cup design, the J's he'd pierced her with glimmering and catching the fading rays of sunlight in the foyer. A matching skirt showed off her hips, accentuating her waist and brushing against the tops of her thighs. There was about an inch of her creamy skin visible before her legs disappeared beneath a pair of nude thigh highs with a pale green leaf pattern worked into the silk. Her wood nymph look was completed with bronze-colored heels on her feet.

The Dom opened his mouth to speak and closed it. Landon was speechless. After a few seconds, he was able to choke out a "Wow, Darlin'," resulting in her chest and face blooming a soft pink. From the corner of his eye, he could see Jayden nodding his agreement, and he chuckled. "Think I'm feeling a bit overdressed here."

Her soft giggle reverberated around the foyer and helped to ease some of the sexual tension that had risen to a crescendo at her appearance.

"My *peata* has prepared a lovely dinner for us. How about we enjoy that first, and then see what we can do about your state of dress?" Erin proposed with a smirk on her face. Jayden's quirks were rubbing off on her more every day.

"*Peata?*"

"Pet, of course." She winked and descended the last few steps, then sauntered over to Jayden with a sway in her hips.

Landon watched while she stroked her pet's hair then leaned over to whisper in his ear before she hooked the leash onto his collar.

"Come, lad."

Jayden fell forward onto his hands and began crawling behind her while she led him by the leash.

Until that moment, Landon would have willingly bet on the least favored horse to win at Lonestar before he would've believed there was a real dominant streak in Erin. He'd been positive she was submissive through and through. Watching her now, though, he could see that Jayden had been correct all along, and his dick throbbed in anticipation of what was to come.

Dinner was pleasant, the stew spicy enough to warm his mouth but not cause pain. He passed on the wine in favor of ice water. Given the circumstances of their meeting, Landon was the alpha Dominant for the night and took that responsibility to heart. He had the welfare of all three of them in his hands.

They ate in silence, each of them likely reflecting on the evening ahead. Jayden spent the time kneeling on a pillow beside Erin while she fed him from her own plate. While strange to witness, it served to increase his feelings of respect for his friend.

There was a serenity to Jayden's composure tonight which had Landon wondering what it would be like to go home and do this—switch—with Paige. Maybe. He'd been on top for so long that he wasn't sure he could do it.

When they finished their meal, Erin gave Jayden forty-five minutes to straighten up the dinner mess then get to the playroom, where he was to be in a waiting position. Seeing her blatantly stare at his naked ass when he left the room with a stack of plates made Landon laugh.

"Shall we move to the den while Jayden carries out his task?" she asked, rising from her seat.

With Jayden now gone, he noticed Erin couldn't quite bring herself to look him in the eye. Landon gripped her hand and squeezed it to reassure her. "Lead the way, Darlin'."

Once the pair was settled in a set of facing armchairs, Erin inhaled and melted into the chair, her confidence and strength visibly fading from her body. She raised her green eyes to Landon at last.

"I owe him a punishment!" Erin blurted.

He responded with an understanding smile. "Oh?"

People outside their Lifestyle tended to assume they were a group of fetish freaks who got off on inflicting punishment. In most cases, that wasn't true. The excitement came from administering pleasurable sensations, and for some, that happened through pain. Punishments were necessary at times to maintain the boundaries in their roles as Dominants and submissives, though. This was a structured Lifestyle, after all, and the rules had to be followed, and enforced—or it became something else.

"Start at the beginning, Erin. Tell me what y'all have done since switching roles last night." He wanted to encourage her to open up, choosing to use the informal address to remind her she was an equal at the moment.

Landon reclined into his seat and listened while she recounted the scenes they'd played out, and how

Jayden had needed to step back into Dom mode to handle her when she'd broken down. Even though it sounded like his friend had handled the situation, he could tell by Erin's words and the way she held herself while she spoke that the woman still felt like she'd let Jayden down, especially with regard to failing on aftercare.

"Yeah, so, there you have it," she mumbled, holding her hands open out in front of her for a moment before dropping them into her lap.

They sat in quiet solitude while he pondered everything. To say he was impressed was an understatement. Erin had attempted a lot in a small amount of time, and from the sounds of it, Jayden had enjoyed every minute of it. The biggest surprise she'd revealed was that Jayden had prepared his ass for her—and she'd used it. That tidbit caused another stirring in his lap, and he had to shift in his seat to adjust himself.

When she disclosed that Jayden had been prepared with an enema, for Landon's benefit no less, there was no hiding the prominent swelling between his thighs. Landon attempted to shift again, and she grinned at him.

Time was almost up. They would need to join Jayden, so he asked the most pressing question. "Have you thought about what you want tonight to entail?"

She shook her head then whispered, "No."

Okay, perhaps a more basic question is a better place to start, then. "Erin," Landon waited for her to meet his gaze. "Do you need me to be a sub or a Dom tonight?" Landon opted for 'need,' because if he'd said 'want,' he was pretty sure she'd choose to drop to her knees and have him dominate them both. While that sounded like fun, it wouldn't allow Erin and Jayden to get the most out of this experience.

She looked frustrated while working out her answer. "I—I don't want to disappoint him, Landon. I need you to help me dominate him."

"I know you don't, Darlin', and I have every confidence that you won't. That you haven't," he amended then leaned forward to take her small hand in his. "Okay," Landon stated, getting down to business, "I'm detecting your first concern is the punishment?"

"Aye." Her eyes brightened at him taking charge.

"Well, as I see it, what he did was a minor infraction, and you've had him in that cage for a couple of hours now . . ." he trailed off to give her a chance to pick up his drift.

"So, he's *already* been punished hasn't he?"

The Dom nodded, and Erin flew out of the chair, throwing her arms around him in a tight hug. "Thank you, Sir."

"No thanks necessary, Darlin'. Now, here's what I suggest."

Laying out a plan, Landon gave the highlights of a scene the three of them could do that kept Jayden as the submissive while he and Erin topped. It was pretty much what he and Jayden had discussed in prior planning for the evening. What he held back from Erin was that, depending on how the scene unfolded, Landon had every intention of rewarding her tenacity by taking full control at the end. He was certain he could help transition her back into her comfort zone as a submissive, thus ending the evening on a high note.

"Ready, Ma'am?"

She grinned, her eyes sparkling now, and nodded her head with vigor. After standing and offering his arm, they headed downstairs.

Upon entering the room, they found Jayden in a perfect waiting position. His dick bulged against the confines of the metal encasing him, while wetness leaked from the tip. Jayden kept his stance. He didn't flinch at the sound of their entry, and his breaths remained steady and slow. His friend wanted this.

Landon moved inside and to the right to slip off his boots and pull off his shirt while Erin went to retrieve the cane they'd talked about. He kept watchful eyes on her when she picked it up, ready to suggest something else if she showed *any* signs of panic.

With it gripped in her hand, she turned back to him and nodded her assurance. *Good girl.*

Coming from opposite sides of the room, they met in the middle in front of Jayden's kneeling form. Landon accepted the tool when Erin handed it to him before she lowered to a squat in front of Jayden. She placed her hands on his knees and ran them up his thighs. At his groin, she curved her touch inward until she came up underneath his sac.

Jayden's chest rose and fell, his dick deepening in color while trying, in vain, to swell.

"I think you've had this on long enough to learn your lesson, *peata*." Erin purred the words at him while unlocking the catches on the cage. "Next time you're given an order, you'll follow it to the letter. Won't you?" Leaving the last two clips in place, she lifted his chin to look at her. "You may answer."

His adoring eyes were full of gratitude when he looked upon her. "Yes, Madame." She undid the final clips then pulled the metal away. Jayden's dick grew to its full potential at once, and he let a relieved sigh.

"*Cailin buachaill.*" After standing back up, she patted him on the head then looked to Landon, giving a short nod to begin after answering the inquisitive look on his face. "Irish for 'good boy'."

He was humbled, like he'd just been let in on some secret ritual the two shared. "Stand up, Jayden." Landon held the cane in both hands against the front of his thighs, so that Jayden wouldn't miss it when he looked up. The submissive stood, his eyes widening before Jayden grinned. Landon's message that Erin was on board had been received.

"Would you like to see more of my skin, Jayden?" She inquired once he had been led over to his favorite observation chair and seated with his knees wide, ass perched on the edge. No leisure lounging for the submissive.

Jayden gulped, then nodded, and Landon wanted to laugh at the sophomoric look on his friend's face. Shaking his head, he went to the mounted control panel to choose a song from the sound system. Landon scanned the music selection, deciding on Jewel's "Serve the Ego." It seemed perfect for what they'd planned, and he pressed play.

Hypnotic pulsating notes, followed by a melody of chimes and drums, flowed into the room, and Erin's hips took up an amorous sway while she trailed her fingers up her front with seductive intent. In the song, Jewel's raspy voice took up coaxing the magic mirror.

Landon moved closer to the pair while Erin cupped her breasts, distracting her mesmerized man from Landon's actions. He did lay the cane against the bottom of Jayden's foot to remind the submissive of his presence, but Jayden's eyes were only for Erin and her strip tease.

While she bent her knees, dipping her body with the changing pitch, Landon drew back the cane to swat Jayden's foot with it. Bucking his hips in response, Jayden's eyes flickered shut. Erin's nimble fingers released the tie on her skirt, and it fell to the floor, revealing her bare, creamy skin. Another sharp tap to Jayden's other foot drew a groan from the man. In a rather dexterous move, Erin brought a svelte leg up and stretched it over her boy's lap, straddling him. The music continued on while she bent from the waist to dangle her breasts in Jayden's face.

Landon began a steady tapping up the inside of Jayden's legs with the tip of the cane while Erin shimmied her shoulders, forcing her round breasts to swing and her nipples to brush over Jayden's parted lips. The Dom could see the restraint his friend was displaying by not licking or trying to bite down under the taunting of Erin's hard peaks. Next, she pulled back to lower herself onto Jayden's lap, trapping his hard dick against her folds. She ground onto him to the rhythm of the music for several refrains. Dismounting from Jayden's lap, she took a few step backs.

Landon gave pause when she lowered onto her hands and knees, then crawled across the floor toward Jayden's waiting erection. In time with the lyrics, he watched her mouth close over Jayden, taking him all the way down her throat before coming back up and repeating the motion. Over and over she sucked him until, at the last moment, Erin pulled off to place a kiss over his slit while Jewel's voice crooned the virtues of turn-ons being surreal. Standing up again, Erin put her hand out, requesting the cane from Landon.

Jayden broke form then, whispering, "Oh, shit. Yes," while his glistening dick twitched and pulsed while Landon moved him from the chair to mount the wooden pony.

For the remainder of the song, Landon stood behind Jayden, holding the man's arms above his head and acting like a living rope.

She circled Jayden while Landon monitored them each time she swung out with the cane. Her hits were light and airy over Jayden's inner thighs and dick, but harder on the outside of his thighs where his taut muscles strained with his building arousal.

Small welts began appearing in the flesh, and Erin developed a light sheen of sweat. Landon's own dick was at full attention, trapped behind the leather of his pants. Jayden squirmed and writhed, but when he pulled against the restraint of Landon's arms, it was without much conviction. He was enjoying this too much to want to break away for real.

As the final chords of the song trailed off, Erin let out a breath and dropped the cane on the floor next to the pony. Her eyes were shocking green pools of liquid lust. The scent of her arousal permeated the air around them.

"Release him, Landon."

Landon let go and stepped back.

"Help me, please," she requested in a softer tone then leaned forward to wrap an arm around Jayden's waist. Together they helped him off the pony and to his knees so he could stabilize. Erin knelt before him so that she was face to face with him. "What color are we?" Tenderness threaded her words.

The force of his answer astounded Landon when Jayden growled, "We are so fucking green! I'm so proud of you right now, Erin."

She threw her head back and laughed. It was a carefree sound, and Landon had to concur with Jayden. He was proud of her, too. This had been a long time coming. She'd handled the cane without a meltdown. It was further proof how deep her trust and love for Jayden ran.

But now it was time to take things to the next level. She'd confessed to Landon her secret desire to see Jayden be intimate with a man from the receiving end. Since Jayden had given her free reign this weekend, Landon wanted to help her make it happen. The pair had agreed that by using her as a diversion, Jayden would be more open to Landon's rectal advances. Initial touches weren't going to be a problem since they knew Jayden had no problem receiving male affection . . . to a point. However, giving a blowjob and receiving one were two different experiences—the same went for anal sex.

The plan they'd concocted was to try and get Jayden so wild with need that, when the time came for Landon to "claim" him, he wouldn't be alarmed or feel the need to safe word. Landon had suggested the dance routine—whether she realized it or not—as a distraction for Erin to allow her to adjust to the sound of the cane hitting flesh until she was ready to take over.

ঋෲড়

CHAPTER THIRTY-ONE
Sir Landon's Games

ঋෲড়

Landon remained patient while he waited for Erin's initiation of the next phase. She stood and undid her corset, letting it fall to the floor and leaving her in the thigh highs and heels. There was no denying she was gorgeous to look at.

With a wistful sigh, Jayden reached out to stroke her thigh.

It was Landon's turn to try and hold back a laugh, which resulted in a strangled barking sound coming from him when Erin smacked Jayden's hand away and scolded him for touching without permission. Jayden shrugged and gave his Madame a cheeky grin.

"Put him on the pony, Landon, on his back. I want his head flat so I can sit on his face while I watch you." Her lustful intentions were clear the way she eyed Jayden while speaking.

Jayden's grin vanished, replaced by his own look of pure hunger at her declaration. He continued to stare at her with longing while Landon positioned him.

She swung her leg back over his head so that her feet were on either side, her pussy hovering above his mouth while she faced Landon. A single drop of thick arousal fell from her, landing on Jayden's quivering lip. A soft moan slipped from Jayden while he dragged his tongue over his lips, capturing the droplet right before more dripped down onto him.

Remembering how sweet she'd tasted when he'd pierced her back in October, Landon grew envious that Jayden was about to feast on her. Until the submissive's dick twitched and Landon remembered what he was about to dine on, that was. Landon retrieved the cuffs and fastened the leather around

Jayden's ankles, then snapped the clips to the O-rings attached to the legs of the pony.

A nod from Landon indicated he was ready, and Erin lowered herself until her pussy was against Jayden's mouth. By the way her eyes rolled back and the soft "Oh, yes," that fell from her lips, he knew the man below her hadn't wasted any time plunging his tongue in.

Moving between the submissive's spread knees, Landon let himself finally take a good look at Jayden's dick. His mouth watered at the sight of it, swollen, long and thick, the head shining from the pre-come that had leaked out. For the first time since he'd parted ways with Sir Tom years before, Landon found himself longing for the feel and taste of a dick in his mouth.

Jayden's balls were heavy where they lay against the seat, and Landon decided to start there, running his tongue across first one nut, then taking his time to move to the other one. On instinct, Jayden tried to close his legs, and his hips thrust up at the air, but he was unable to do any more than that, thanks to the cuffs. Landon laughed with his mouth against Jayden's sac, sending vibrations shooting up into his friend.

Jayden's moan came out muffled by Erin's flesh, but her loud cry was erotic when she reacted to the vibrations he'd likely caused her.

With every teasing tongue lap, Jayden grunted, moaned, or shivered beneath Landon. Like before, it was a domino effect, with Erin the last domino to fall, again and again. Jayden's arms had encased her thighs, wrapping around her so that his large hands clenched tight the flesh of her ass while he pulled her even closer to his mouth.

She responded by rocking her hips within his grasp.

Landon didn't want to wait any more and pressed his body against Jayden's thighs, leaning forward to put a hand on the flat surface of the pony on either side of his waist. Erin's half-lidded eyes watched Landon's every move while he grabbed Jayden's dick, angling it away from his stomach and toward Landon's mouth. She reached up and started tugging and rolling her nipples between her fingers.

"Come when you want, Jayden," Landon allowed before his mouth descended. Jayden was large, and he had to stretch his lips and jaw to close over him. Halfway down the shaft was as far as Landon could get before he had to pull back up with a light scraping of teeth. He was out of practice. Landon's mind boggled over the fact that Erin, with her tiny little mouth, could take all of that dick in—but if she could do it, then so could he.

Landon retracted and licked his lips to wet them for another pass. After wrapping his lips around the head, he stopped to savor the taste and feel of Jayden. When he ran his tongue around and under the rim, some pre-come seeped onto his tongue, and Landon wandered. No longer was he aware of the discomfort in his jaw. All Landon knew was the tasty dick, and he plunged down until it hit the back of his throat. He halted to adjust his breathing, making sure he was using his nose to move air in and out, then relaxed his throat and went further.

Nice and slow, Landon crept downward, feeling his throat relax, bit-by-bit, as Jayden's dick pushed past the tonsils, deeper into his throat, until at last, his nose hit Jayden's pubic bone. Landon rolled his eyes up to look at Erin, and he gulped when he found them both looking back, watching him. Jayden had released his hold on Erin so she could lift up, giving him room to raise his head.

Seeing his friend staring back at him, his parted lips glazed with Erin's juices and framed by her delicate skin, was almost too much for the Dom. Landon swallowed around Jayden again, forcing himself to focus on the thickness in his mouth in an effort to fight off his own building need to come.

"Oh, fuck," Jayden murmured, throwing his head back, ass rising from the chair, and pushing even deeper into Landon's mouth before his come spilled.

Landon waited for the deluge to end, then pulled up halfway. He continued to work up and down the dick, encouraging every last drop of come out of Jayden and ensuring that his friend stayed hard. When he was satisfied the man wasn't going to lose his erection, he released Jayden's dick and stood up, offering his hand to Erin to help her stand, too. The scene, thus far, had gone better than he could've hoped.

He was going to offer Catherine her submissive role.

Landon undid the button of his pants and lowered the zipper. His dick fell away from his stomach, desperate for the freedom and fresh air.

"Tell me, Darlin', do ya want to keep topping or are ya ready to trust me to make this very good for the both of you?" While he spoke, he ran his fingers along his dick, gripping and releasing it, teasing himself almost as much as he teased his small audience.

She looked to Jayden, asking his opinion with her silent gaze. He gave her a smile then assured her, "Whatever you want, sweet girl, there will be no punishment for your decisions during this scene. I'll be anything you need me to be, do anything you want me to do, and I promise I will thoroughly enjoy every minute of it."

Erin returned Jayden's tender smile, extending her hand to caress his cheek. Reading the truth of his words that they could both see in his eyes, she nodded. She looked back to Landon, then down, and sank to her knees, her hands going to their natural position behind her back. "This girl trusts in you, Sir."

They were simple words, but the meaning behind them was so much more. Her whole body seemed to relax with their recitation, and just like that, she'd shifted back into the submissive role where she thrived.

Landon shrugged out of his leather pants and tossed them toward the door before approaching her. Stroking her head, he centered his intentions into full dominant mode.

"Good girl. On behalf of your Master, greet my dick." Jayden had claimed he would do 'anything,' but Landon didn't believe he'd really be comfortable taking a dick in his mouth. Landon's eyes stayed on his friend to make sure Catherine performing in his stead wasn't going to flip a switch either.

Jayden seemed calm, and rather fascinated, while she leaned forward to kiss the head of Landon's dick, flicking her tiny tongue out to clean it of leakage.

A throaty plea for "More," and she parted her lips to allow Landon room for gentle thrusting. Soon, his balls were seated against her lips, and he had to stop or risk blowing his load on the next pass. He withdrew until the tip rested on her mouth. She kissed it again, and he stepped back.

"Perfectly done, sugar," he praised. "Now, go choose a vibrator, then meet us at the bed." Landon unhooked the cuffs from the pony legs and steadied Jayden while he stood. Moving him to the bed, he directed the submissive to lie on his back with his ass at the end of the mattress.

Catherine, having followed her order, joined them with a toy he recognized from his time with her that engagement weekend. Landon chuckled and shook his head. "I should have known."

She blushed and gave him a coy smile while fingering the replica of Jayden's dick with an excited sparkle in her eyes.

"Go stand between Jayden's legs and shove that dildo in your pussy for me, Darlin'." While she did that, Landon went to the cupboards to find the lube and some bondage rope.

Setting his supplies on the floor next to the bed, Landon reached out, grabbed the bit of dildo that stuck out of Catherine, and pulled it out a little further. Getting a better grip, he then pumped it in and out of her a few times until she started mewling and he was satisfied with the sloppy wet sounds accompanying the toy's movement. He pushed it all the way back in and gave it a tap to make sure it was deep-seated.

Next, Landon grabbed Catherine's hands, helping her bend forward to place them on either side of Jayden's head. The new position placed her tits over his face so he gave Jayden the order to suck her nipples nonstop.

With both of them distracted by the sucking task, he went about removing the cuffs from Jayden's ankles, giving them a quick massage to stimulate blood flow. Lifting his feet up on the bed forced Jayden's knees to bend, leaving his ass open and exposed. Landon picked up the rope and crawled onto the bed so he could grab Jayden's wrists and pull his hands above his head where he placed them by

Erin's, who was busy whimpering under her lover's attentions.

"Enough, Jayden. Stop sucking." At once, the submissive released the bud he was suckling and Landon's hand darted out to pluck each of her nipples, ensuring they were good and hard. "Good. I think Jayden's had the clamps on long enough, but I like how they're threaded through his collar, so I'm going to leave them like that. Now it's your turn, Catherine."

He made quick work of moving the clamps from Jayden's to Erin's nipples, ensuring her range of motion would be limited since she'd be tethered to him. Continuing with deft movements, he took up the rope and wrapped it around Erin's right wrist, then Jayden's, before threading the rope through an eyebolt on the headboard and bringing it back to bind their left wrists together. He stepped back to admire his handiwork. *Perfect.*

He got off the bed to pace around it. On his return pass, he retrieved the discarded cane from earlier. Because of the way he'd tied them together, neither one could move their head around to see him. Landon stepped up to the side of the bed and extended the tool to let Catherine see what was in his hands.

"What color are we, Catherine?" The question was posed with utmost calm. Landon couldn't have her panic now, not when they were so close.

Her honeyed hue paled, and she swallowed hard but didn't say a word.

"What do you have, Landon?" Jayden asked when he registered the change in her as well.

All pretenses of him playing sub were gone. This was Jayden the Dominant, and he was ready to protect what was his—no matter what.

ഏഝ൯
CHAPTER THIRTY-TWO
Tearing Down the Wall
ഏഝ൯

Taking a gamble with his impromptu decision, Landon let the weight of the cane settle on top of their bound hands, then began rolling it up her arms while her stare tracked the wood. When he reached her elbows, the tool entered Jayden's line of vision, and his brown eyes widened.

"Landon . . ." he started through clenched teeth.

"Shh, Jayden, trust me," Landon replied in a low, firm voice and continued rolling the cane over

417

Catherine's flesh. When he reached her shoulders, he slowly pulled it across her chest, letting the far end dig into her with the slightest of pressure, and she shuddered as her eyes drifted closed.

The cane dropped off the edge of her body, and he slid it back under her arms, resting it flat against the tops of her breasts. In the same controlled rolling motion, he brought it down until it hit the clamps. Again he pulled it away, repositioned it under the chain, and then rolled it along the underswell of her tits, down over her ribs and stomach. Slow. Steady. Mindful.

At that point, he reached her hips and, holding the right side of the cane with one hand, he moved behind her. Stepping in close enough to trap his dick between her ass and his stomach, Landon reached for the left side of the cane then pulled it toward him, bracing the rod tight against her mons.

Jayden was breathing hard, his lips a tight line while his eyes stalked every one of Landon's actions.

The Dom massaged the cane over Catherine's pussy, not letting it go further than a few inches up or down, getting her to accept the texture, opening her trust to the experience. Placing his mouth against her neck, just behind her ear, he asked again, "What color are we, Catherine?"

She *still* didn't answer him; couldn't, it seemed, so Landon carried on, moving the cane down the tops of her thighs until it hit Jayden's lower stomach. Stretching forward allowed him to roll the cane up Jayden's torso while he pressed his own chest into Catherine's back. In doing so, Jayden got to experience what Catherine had, and it gave the girl a moment to collect herself without the cane's touch.

With his retreat, the cane came back down Jayden's chest and stomach until stopping at her knees, at which point Landon dropped one side and stepped away from the pair, taking the cane with him. He then used the bamboo to lift and push Catherine's hair to the side, over her shoulder.

She gave a delightful shudder when the tip brushed her cheek.

Landon put the cane against her shoulder blades then rolled it along her spine, not stopping until he'd run it over the swell of her ass and it was resting below the curve of her cheeks. Flexing his wrists, Landon lifted and lowered the length of wood, forcing her ass to move with it. That little bit of movement would affect the dildo inside her.

"Color, Catherine? And if you do not answer me this time, we will end the scene now and call it a night. It is your choice, Darlin'." There was no harshness in his voice. It was level and smooth, to let her know that she held the power this time. The cane would go away if she didn't want it.

Catherine looked at him, like she was really seeing him, then together they turned their gazes down to Jayden. The tight line of his lips had softened. Landon could see the trust he'd asked for in Jayden's countenance.

Jayden lifted his head to place a gentle kiss on her, lips followed by a whispered, "It is your choice, sweet girl. You never have to feel the cane again if you don't want, but Landon is not going to hurt you." He shrugged his shoulders the best he could within his confinement and looked at Landon while raising his voice. "I'll kill him if he does."

Landon tipped his head in silent acknowledgment. *Warning heard loud and clear, and she will not be hurt.*

Catherine gave a tentative laugh, looked from her lover to Landon, and then nodded her head.

"Say it, Catherine," Landon demanded. No way was he going to proceed without a verbal affirmation on her part.

"Green, Sir. This girl is green."

Now confident to proceed, Landon shifted the cane from her ass to rest against the inside of her right knee. "Excellent, Darlin'," was all he gave her before he started flicking his wrist in a swishing motion. The cane tapped from side-to-side while he moved it up her thigh with enough force to leave a pink tint to her skin. By the time he reached her upper thighs, Catherine had started whimpering and her hips were flexing. Landon tapped the exposed dildo with the tip of the cane and she squealed, then hurried to apologize for her outburst.

"No worries, Darlin'. Please be as vocal as you want." He tapped the toy one more time and moved the bamboo over her outer hip, working it in much the same fashion her thighs had received.

She moaned and surprised him with a whispered, "Harder." Not sure he'd heard her clearly, Landon asked her to repeat herself.

"Harder please, Sir. This girl would like to feel more of the sting."

Well, fuck me. Landon tightened his grip and put more force behind the next swing. There was a *swish* when it cut through the air, followed by a *thwack* when it hit her hip.

"Mm. Thank you, Sir." The words came out with a purr.

By the time Landon had caned both sides of her outer thighs, her hips, and her ass, her skin was bright red, and there were a few welts—nothing that wouldn't have faded by morning with some arnica cream. The insides of her thighs were slick and shiny from the amount of nectar that had seeped out of her while he worked her over. Landon's dick also had been leaking profusely and had dripped on the floor several times. At last, he threw the cane down.

"Catherine, put your chest against Jayden's and bring your knees up against his ribs."

Once she'd complied, having to climb on the bed to do so, both were open and on display for him. Landon grabbed the lube and drizzled a large amount over Catherine's ass until it ran down and coated Jayden's dick. Lifting Jayden's balls out of the way, Landon ensured the lube coated his asshole, too.

They both groaned when Landon began massaging the lube, with two fingers, into each of their puckered holes. By scissoring his digits, he pried them open to prepare the couple in tandem. In sync, both flexed their hips with wantonness, clearly enjoying the sensations Landon was bestowing upon them. When he felt they were ready, he removed his fingers from their backsides and poured some lube on his own aching dick after slapping a condom on.

It didn't take Landon much to get between Jayden's legs and hook his arms under the man's knees, then lift him enough to line his dick up with Jayden's hole. He took his time pushing in, relishing the tightness of Jayden's ass while the muscles grasped and flexed against his dick, pulling Landon deeper in. Once his balls were resting against skin, Landon stopped to let Jayden adjust.

Reaching down, Landon palmed Jayden's cock and held it rigid. "Catherine, I need you to back up nice and slow," Landon instructed through gritted teeth when Jayden flexed around his dick again. "Fuck, Jayden! Control yourself or this is going to be over before we get started." He was having a hard time controlling his panting.

"Sorry . . . shit . . . can't help it," Jayden choked out even as his ass clenched again.

"Catherine, now," Landon said with more sternness, and she shifted backward, barely stopping when the head of Jayden's cock breached her stretched opening. Once the head was inside her, Landon moved his hand to her hip, to help guide her down until all of Jayden's dick had disappeared into her.

"Oh, dear god," the redhead whimpered when the absolute fullness from the fake dildo in her pussy and now, Jayden's cock in her ass, settled in.

Shifting his hand from her hip and locking it around her waist, Landon wedged his arm against Catherine's stomach then drew her body upward until her clamped nipples were pulled by the chain still latched through Jayden's collar.

"Don't let yourself fall forward any more than this, Catherine." Landon took hold of her hips before shifting his own back to slip out of Jayden a tad. When thrusting back into Jayden's ass, his grip on Catherine's hips ensured she rocked up and off Jayden's dick a bit. Again Landon pulled out of Jayden, emptying his friend while she slid back down over his swollen dick with the force of Landon's pull.

Thus their rhythm was set. Landon slid into Jayden's ass, and Catherine slid off Jayden's cock. When she ground back down onto the thick shaft, Landon pulled out of the tight passage. It was tricky, but it worked.

Landon fucked Jayden's ass while using Catherine's body to "fuck" his friend's dick. She kept mumbling something along the lines of, "So full, so good," meanwhile trying to decipher Jayden's words

425

was a lost cause. His friend had been reduced to a series of caveman-like grunts and sounds.

He was close, so goddamn close. Landon had been fucking the pair relentlessly for a good ten minutes at least, and after all the foreplay, he'd reached his limit. With a final smack to Catherine's ass, Landon gave the command to come.

Jayden's pelvis shot upward, driving deep into his woman's ass, causing her to be flung back against Landon's chest. Under the abrupt force of the movement, the clamps were ripped from her nipples. The rope binding their hands had enough slack in it that they came up also. Landon noted they'd threaded their fingers together and were gripping each other so tight that their knuckles were white.

Catching Catherine around the waist again, Landon rested his chin on her shoulder, and she dropped her head back against his sweaty chest. It gave him the perfect view down the front of her body and of Jayden's torso, rippling and contracting from the intensity of his dying orgasm. When she then started squirting, coating Jayden with hot come all the way up to his face, Landon gave up the fight.

His dick pulsed while what felt like gallons of come burst forth from his body, filling Jayden's ass.

No one spoke.

They were all trying to regulate their breathing and clear the white spots from their vision. Landon was doing his best to stay upright, supporting Catherine's weight instead of collapsing on top of the pile.

After a few minutes, Jayden's strained voice announced, "Scene Over."

Snickering into Erin's neck, Landon nodded and replied, "And what a scene it was!"

He couldn't be prouder of how well she'd done and was sure that she'd turned a corner in her healing. Her mental cage built of canes was coming down.

❧❧❧
CHAPTER THIRTY-THREE
❧❧❧

"Oh, did she? I see, okay . . . I guess that'll be fine. Aye, aye, well, thank you for calling. Aye, of course I'll let her know, no more changes. Thanks again, bye." Erin huffed and dropped her head into her hands after ending the call and propping her elbows on the table. "Argh!" Her scalp tightened and began tingling when she tugged at her hair in frustration. A sandwich sat next to her, untouched.

It was Wednesday evening and, yet again, they'd had to forego their "kinky date night" because she needed to do wedding things. When she'd helped Paige out, all this stuff had seemed fun. Now, it was just becoming a serious pain in her ass . . . and not the kind she liked.

"What is it, sweet girl?" Looking up from the report he'd brought home to review, Jayden cocked his head to the side, a confused look on his handsome face.

The love of her life was pulling longer hours at work, preparing to be gone the last week of July and most of August. Her boss had also changed Erin's hours to cover the ten-to-six shift at the dental practice, but by the time the last patient was checked out, the front desk shut down, and she'd made the trek home, it was often pushing seven-thirty in the evening. She couldn't complain, though. They were letting her take a month off for the wedding and honeymoon *and* holding her job while she was gone.

However, between trying to maintain her submissive requirements for regular exercise and at least six hours of sleep a night, work, seeing to

Natalie's prenatal care and attending Lamaze classes with her, and wedding planning, there wasn't much time left for extracurricular activities. Scratch that, there was no time at all. Erin had to be grateful her Master hadn't cut weekend play, too. She doubted very much that she'd be sane if he had. But even their last scheduled session had been interrupted because she'd had some spotting and cramping. Dr. Ellison had warned her that might happen with the cessation of her quarterly *Depo* injection—not a heavy price for the chance at a baby, in her opinion.

"What has Mom done this time?" Jayden asked with a chuckle.

If he weren't so damn gorgeous, she might have felt the urge to punch him. "That was Gavin, the event coordinator at Boi na Braza. He got a call from Jillian earlier today . . ."

"Oh?" Her fiancé was smart and didn't say anything else, simply raised an eyebrow.

"Apparently we now need seating for another seventy-five guests. On top of the three hundred already planned for."

"Three hundred? I thought it was two hundred. Do we know that many people?"

"Exactly!" Erin threw her hands up and stood from the table to begin pacing back and forth. She was gathering steam. "Last time I talked to her, the number was two-fifty, a week before *that* it was two. Jesus Christ, Jayden. We're seven weeks away from doing this, and she keeps adding to the guest list behind our backs."

"She means—"

"If you defend her and tell me she means well, I may very well start screaming," Erin spat out, cutting him off in the process. "They don't have room for any more people in the private event area. If she does this again, we're going to have to find a new place for the reception. Just how easy do you think that'll be at this point in the game?"

The sharp sound of Jayden's fingers snapping drew her attention, and she froze mid-step.

"Come here, please, Erin." He set the report down and pushed his chair back.

At his invitation, she shuffled over to him, crawled into his lap, and leaned into him. She welcomed the security of his arms coming around her waist, and the lone finger slipping under the hem of her shirt to rest on the soft skin of her belly was bliss.

"I didn't think this would be so hard. Paige's preparations all seemed to go so smooth . . . It isn't fair." She sucked in a breath when a second finger joined the first. "Her wedding was quaint, simple, and so beautiful. I don't know even a fraction of the people that are being invited, but your mother expects this to be some elaborate society event. Why can't we just get married without all the other shit?"

┏┓┗┛

Jayden felt bad for his jewel. Having grown up around his mother's society life, he was used to Jillian Masterson's large soirees, but could see how it would all be unnerving for Erin. His hand splayed over her belly, and he was alarmed to notice it was smaller beneath his palm.

How long had it been since he'd explored and touched her? he considered with some distress, then counted back in his head to realize almost two weeks had elapsed since their last intimate encounter of any kind. Not acceptable.

"Have you been eating properly?" He got his answer when her frame stiffened in his lap. In reaction, his hand closed on her flesh, tightening until her breath caught and a tiny whimper formed in her throat. "Answer me, pet," he ground out through clenched teeth. Jayden was not pleased.

"No, this girl has not, Master." Though shame threaded her tone, she straightened further in his lap, her form adopting a submissive posture. "With all that's been going on, your girl has been using her lunch hour for wedding appointments."

"And breakfast?" With the change in her hours, Jayden left for the office before she did now. The thought never crossed his mind that she would skip a meal if he wasn't there to eat with her.

"That's when your girl gets her exercise in, Master."

"I see." Unfortunately, he didn't like what he saw. Of those three things, a proper diet should have been her top priority, especially given their talk about trying to have a baby. Also, he'd be damned if a marriage ceremony was going to affect her health in a negative way.

"Catherine, I do believe you've taken on way too much, and I don't approve. Tomorrow, Samantha will be tasked as your personal assistant for any and all things wedding related. I can get by without her at the office until after we've said our vows. I'll also call Mom and have a talk with her. In the meantime, what else is on your list for tonight?"

She'd twisted in his lap to look at him and now gave him an adoring grin before ticking off items on her fingers. "Call Silver Spurs and schedule the bridal party in for hair and make-up the morning of the wedding, Sir Shawn had some ideas for our photo setups and wanted to set a time to meet. Your mom is handling the invitations, and it's a good thing, too, but I still need to—"

"So all things that Samantha can handle?" Jayden spoke over her, stopping her running list.

"Aye, this girl supposes so . . ."

"Then it turns out you are free this evening, Catherine. And we're both hungry. Eat your sandwich, use the bathroom, and join me downstairs in thirty minutes." It wasn't a request.

He tapped her thigh, signaling her to get off his lap. Once he'd stood, Jayden leaned in to kiss the top of her head then pinched her hip before pivoting on his heel and taking his exit. A scene had begun forming in his mind, and he would need the full thirty minutes to prepare for it.

෨෧

When Catherine joined him in the playroom—with a few minutes to spare—the charge in the atmosphere was palpable. She entered without a word, the clack of her heels matching his heartbeat while she hung her robe then assumed her waiting position in the center of the room. He stood by, a wide stance bracing his legs and his hands clasped behind his back, holding a surprise. For this scene, the Dominant had chosen to remain dressed, knowing how much more possessive he felt when she was totally bare in his clothed presence—and vice versa for his pet.

Her thick scarlet hair was pulled back and twisted into a tight bun atop her head, leaving her neck and shoulders open to him. Dropping his gaze awarded him the sight of her puckered nipples displaying his mark. He smiled when the gold and gems flickered under the nearby candlelight. Jayden hadn't decided if he would use the wax or not. It would depend on how well she handled the pins.

Tonight, the Dom was prepared to spend the entire evening showing his submissive, reminding her, how he treasured her. However, he also expected his rules to be followed, and she clearly needed a lesson in prioritizing. When he was done, they'd both be a mess.

Satisfied she'd settled as much as she was going to for the time being, he stepped up and circled her, letting her feel his stare while he inspected every inch of her exposed skin. *Feet neatly tucked, tits out, palms up, cunt visible . . .* he checked each point off in his mind.

"Exquisite. Stand up." His voice was low and steady. In one fluid motion, she obeyed, and he brought his hand forward to show her what he held— a thong. "Lift your left foot." While squatting down to slip the garment over her heel, he murmured, "Again." Moments later he slid the material up her legs, stopping to lick at her cunt for a few minutes before hiding her bare sex behind the sheer black fabric.

A quiet groan slipped from her when he tucked the thong strap into place between her plump buttocks, letting his fingers brush over her back hole. Where the strap formed a 'T' just above her ass crack, two spring clips dangled from the garment, waiting to be connected to the matching cuffs he'd be placing on her wrists soon.

Jayden took his time moving around her. He caressed her silky skin with his fingers and knuckles, nipped at her flesh with his lips, and kept up a barrage of whispered praise for how beautiful she was in her submission to him. The deepening of her breaths, each one causing her chest to rise and fall more noticeably than the last, told him how much she was enjoying the attention. Had there been any doubt, it would've been silenced at the creamy discovery inside her cunt when he teased a finger below the fabric to check.

Time for phase two.

"You've broken an outlined rule of mine, haven't you, Catherine?" Her admission came in quiet tones once she'd kneeled and he'd permitted her to answer. "I need to be sure you're getting an adequate amount of nutrients for *your* health, not *my* own shits and giggles. If you aren't in top form, then I can't enjoy your body on my whim. Nor will I begin to consider allowing you to risk your own life to grow another if you can't take care of yourself first. When I run my palm over your hips, I want to feel the soft swell of a healthy curve, not the sharp edge of a bone."

He paused to let the words sink in. Jayden hated this. Administering pain in seeking pleasure was euphoric, but doing it for punishment never did anything for him. However, the rules had to be adhered to. If he didn't follow through on his promises of punishment for her misconduct, then how could she trust that he'd follow up promises of reward? This was for her own good. "Tonight we're going to work on your concentration."

$$\text{🙰🙰}$$

CHAPTER THIRTY-FOUR

$$\text{🙰🙰}$$

Master's announcement didn't surprise
Catherine. She'd been letting her
mounting task list get the better of her—she knew
this. The last place her thoughts should be while
scening with Master was on entrée selections for the
wedding menu or reviewing the dental codes she was
learning at work. *What was fluoride again, 1204 or
1206?*

"Ouch!" Her nipple exploded with heat, compliments of the crop in Master's hand, which she'd failed to notice before.

"Where were you just now?"

She looked down and mumbled, "Not here, Master."

"Precisely," he scolded.

"Your girl is sorry." Catherine lowered herself, bending at the waist to kiss the top of his bare foot. She remained bowed, offering herself and awaiting His instruction.

"I'm going to give you the chance to prove that. Get up and get to the shackles."

She rose and hurried over to where the hoist and rig system resided. For the next few minutes, the submissive kept her eyes closed and enjoyed His strong hands on her body. With great care, he fastened cuffs to her wrists and ankles, another wider one wrapped around her waist before he attached the harness rigging to her bindings. Catherine squirmed with the realization that she wasn't going to be allowed to close her legs when he placed a spreader bar to the ankle cuffs. Her arms were pulled behind her back and the links on the cuffs were clipped to their waiting counterparts on her thong strap.

Master guided her back down onto her knees then took a step back. He unzipped his jeans, working his thick cock free of its denim prison, and came close again to tap the hard flesh against her lips. "Suck me, slut. You're going to swallow a serving of protein, for your health, and to see to my needs. And then, well, my pet, we'll see . . ." His words became garbled when his length disappeared into the warm depths of her throat as she opened and he slid in.

Locked behind his back, his hands mimicked hers while she worked his cock until tears escaped the corners of her eyes. While sheer willpower kept his hands in place, hers were cuffed, making her do all the work with her mouth.

Skilled and determined, Catherine soon sucked Master's orgasm from him, gagging and swallowing around him. He slipped from her mouth, a dribble of come spilling on her lip, and she rested back on her heels, eyes lowered while she caught her breath. It was then that she noticed their newest toy—a wand—was plugged into one of the numerous floor outlets in the room.

The submissive also knew the toy as her "guaranteed O-stick." Pure magic, she melted under its intense vibrations anytime Master used it on her. Spread legs. Wand. *Oh, yeah, I'm in trouble.*

Catherine must've made a noise because Master let out an evil chuckle and reached between her legs to pinch her clit. It happened too fast, was over too soon, and she just managed a strangled plea for "More."

"Oh, you're going to get more, slut. So much more you'll be begging me to stop. And I won't . . . unless, of course, you safeword. Now, up you go." He helped her get to her feet and freed her hands from the thong. Master re-clipped them to another spreader bar that hung down from above, stretching her into an X.

Soft clicks and whirs sounded while the hoist came to life. She began to lift up onto her toes, and a few moments later, swing freely in the air.

Master's hands remained on her, steadying and guiding her body into the position he wanted before panic could take root in her mind. Like the other flashback-inducing activities they'd tackled together, this one—bound suspension—had been an act of patience and love on his part until she'd grown comfortable with it. With his reassuring touch came soothing words of praise. Whispers of "Good girl," "I've got you," and "Almost set," eased her sense of well-being.

Once he brought her to a stop, Catherine was upside down. She doubted it was a coincidence that her mouth was level with his crotch, or that her pussy was displayed at the perfect height for him to play with at his leisure.

Squatting down after digging something from his pocket, Master kissed her. Distracting her with his mouth, he fingered her nipples, twisting them until she cried out against his mouth and quickly clamping them. Through her glazed vision, she noted his hand wrapping around the wand before he stood.

She grinned, and then stopped almost as fast. The look on His face wasn't a happy one.

"Color, Catherine?"

"Green, Master."

The toy came to life. For a few seconds, a high frequency buzz filled the room, but it was soon replaced by a wanton groan falling her lips when he pressed the head against her fleshy mons—so very close to her swelling clitoris yet not quite there—and held it. Pressing his hips forward, his reawakening cock bumped her lips, and she obediently parted them.

When she began to suck around his length, he rewarded her by moving the vibrator along her pussy. It felt amazing, and her mouth fell open, releasing him. At the cessation of activity on Master's cock, he took the toy away.

With a longing whimper, she snapped her lips closed and resumed her ministrations. The delicious vibration returned. Catherine increased the tempo of her sucking, and in return, he teased the wand over her sex. She soon became lightheaded and paused for breath.

Contact was broken again, but she could her feel her clit continue to pulse like it would pull the toy back if it only had hands. "Please . . ."

Cool air tickled her hot flesh when he shifted the fabric of her thong to the side and pried her labia apart. "Suck me, Catherine, and you may come when you like." Something in the way he said it made her believe it wasn't going to be that easy.

His cock pressed forward again, her mouth clamped down on him, and shock waves overtook her when he positioned the wand against the underside of her exposed clit. Highly sensitive, her orgasm started to crest and once again, the submissive forgot her task.

Just when she would've come, the toy was taken away, and he slapped her breast. The action jostled her adorned nipple hard enough for the clamp to shift so that it dangled from her peak. She stared down at the biting item with wide eyes, then screamed around his cock when he smacked her breast a second time to knock the clamp clean off. A wonderful, searing fire shot into her freed nipple when the blood rushed back into it, purple giving way to darkened rose-colored flesh.

"Again, slut. Suck me and come—if you can."

Around they went.

Master maneuvered her about, not leaving her upside down for more than a few minutes at a time. Each position he chose allowed him to fuck her face and throat, and, of course, tease her pussy into a throbbing mound of need.

So many times the submissive found herself on the verge of release, just to have it snatched away because her mutinous body got lost in its own pleasure. Having her throat filled with His cock, the constant pressure and vibration on her groin, and the lingering pain in her nipples—he'd knocked the other clamp free at some point, too—was all encompassing and intoxicating.

I'm sex drunk. The thought made her start giggling, and in a flood, Master was suddenly coming down her throat.

The intensity of the orgasm forced from her while she swallowed his spunk and he ground the wand against her pussy sucked the air from her lungs. Tiny sparks of white light flitted across her vision, and she exploded in the heat. Her heartbeat thundered in her skull. Cool air rushed into her lungs, and the buzzing in her ears lessened when Master turned her upright.

Catherine was only half-aware, and still giggling, while he removed her bindings and guided her to the armchair. There were items sat atop the end table next to the chair, but she couldn't be bothered to try and identify them. More titters escaped her. She was tingling all over and effervescent—downright bubbly.

Master's fingers dug into her arms. "Down, pet, let's get you stable before you fall over."

Her legs folded beneath her, her bottom met the cold hardwood floor, and she sobered a bit. The hushed whisper of fabric shifting met her ears, and his shirt landed on the floor beside her. She sighed with contentment when he slid into the chair behind her, placing his feet near her hips and leaning her back into his hold.

Craving Master's touch, Catherine let her body mold against his while placing her trust in him to support her. Her body buzzed under his whispered affections and barely-there touches. With each hushed compliment, she felt her resolve weakening, all fight leaving. *Why was she so stressed again?*

Drowsy, dopey, and somehow still burning with the need between her thighs, Catherine was unprepared when a plastic clothespin bit into the flesh over her lower ribs, and she gasped. She pushed the air out and sucked in fresh as a second and a third pin were attached to her with lightning-quick precision.

"Did you enjoy your orgasm, slut? Answer freely for the rest of the night, please."

"Aye, Master. This girl did, thank you."

"You worked hard for it. You deserved the reward." More clothespins found their way onto the opposite side of her torso, pinching her skin. The clamps weren't secure, more like he was placing them so they held a tiny amount of skin in a painful bite on purpose. "Is this comfortable?" he asked and flicked his finger over one of the pins so that it wavered, pulling at her skin. It was just beneath her right breast, where loose flesh had been lacking.

She hissed. "Not really, Master."

"Shame. If you'd been eating and fleshier, the pins could've had something more substantial to hold onto and you might be enjoying this instead. But you chose sloth through nonchalance, and that does not deserve a reward. Such detrimental behavior must be corrected . . . with punishment, if necessary."

Catherine literally felt the color drain out of her. He was going to use pain to punish her. Master had never done that before—meaning *this was serious.* The severity of her infraction crashed down on her and shame tightened her chest worse than the clothespins digging into her clammy skin.

He continued to fasten pins to her—inner arms, hips, across the top of her pussy, and even her breasts got a circle of them around her nipples—all areas that had become thinner, but none of it hurt. Not the way she now hurt on the inside. She'd disappointed the man who, to her, meant everything.

Because she hadn't put enough importance on taking care of what meant everything to Him—*her.*

When he tipped the candle over her torso, letting hot wax spill down and coat her pinched skin, she welcomed it. Whimpering "sorry" over and over,

Catherine kept her breasts thrust out in acceptance, but she couldn't stop the salty rivers flowing down her cheeks. By the time he moved from behind her, taking up the crop when he passed, she was desperate to be exonerated. She knew once this was over, she'd be forgiven, with the expectation that her habits would be rectified.

Never would she show such disregard for her well-being again.

Drawing her wet lashes upward, the submissive fixed her eyes on her Master. He stood a few feet back, the riding crop held firmly in both hands before him. Catherine sucked in a jagged breath. "Do it, Master. Absolve your girl."

His face was pained when he drew his arm back. "This is for you, *A rúnsearc.*"

Knowing with unwavering certainty that she was His beloved secured her inner peace. The submissive held his words around her heart while her body exploded with cathartic pain as he used the crop to knock every last clothespin free.

Later that night, in the warmth of their plush bed, Jayden pulled Erin even closer than normal. He'd not stopped touching her since they'd left the playroom. In the shower, reverent touches had guided his fingers to remove the wax and sweat from her body. After, she'd almost wept at the tenderness of his caress while he worked arnica cream into the numerous red marks that would likely still cover her come morning. In the silent darkness, his mouth sought hers even as his cock found purchase between her eager thighs. No words were spoken.

None were needed.

Their love was secure.

ಐಎಲಿ
CHAPTER THIRTY-FIVE
ಐಎಲಿ

"Erin."

A whispered breath tickled the shell of her ear, and she groaned. Jayden's arm tightened over her waist, coaxing the sleepy woman back into her slumber.

"Erin, please." A mangled grunt followed the cold touch upon her shoulder.

Erin opened her eyes, and Jayden sat up behind her with an alarmed, "What's going on?" She reached for the lamp switch, yanking the sheet up to cover her bare breasts when the light flooded the room to reveal a sweaty, ashen-faced Natalie at their bedside. The clock read 3:18 a.m.

"I think we need Dr. Ellison. I'm so sorry—"

"Stop that before you get started, lass. You're having a babe, there's not a thing to be sorry for. Give Jayden and me a couple of minutes, and we'll be on our way."

Behind her, Jayden was already talking to Holly on the phone, his voice still slurred a bit by sleep.

"Okay, thank you. I—I'll go wait by the door. My bag is—" Natalie's words were cut off when she grabbed her abdomen and cussed through what had to be one hell of a contraction.

Erin glanced over her shoulder at Jayden in concern. Covering the phone, he mouthed at her to go. Not caring that she was bare-assed naked, Erin threw the covers back and hurried past the younger woman—who was leaning against the bed, hands gripping the duvet while she made funny noises and shapes with her mouth. Erin rushed to the closet and pulled on some panties, skipped a bra, then grabbed a pair of capris and an oversized T-shirt.

Jayden was still sitting in the bed, covers over his lap, when she came back out tugging the shirt down into place; Erin showing her bits to Natalie was cool, but Jayden wasn't big on flashing his willy just for the sake of it. She needed to get Natty out of the room.

"Come on, sweetie. Let's start making our way down." Erin put her hands on Natalie's arms to help her stand back up. When she was sure the girl was okay to move, she turned to Jayden, "See you downstairs in a few?"

He nodded, and Erin led Natalie away. Five minutes later, they were throwing open the front door and heading out into the cool early morning. "Alright, lass. Let's go have a babe!" Erin chirped when Jayden pulled around in the Towne Car.

Natalie's skin took on a strange greenish hue right before she curled forward to throw up in one of the potted palms.

ഌരു

Jayden cringed while the car screeched to a stop harder than he'd intended. He really hoped his eyes were deceiving him, that the girl hadn't just deposited copious amounts of stomach acid on his expensive tree.

With a frustrated huff, he climbed out and came around the car to help the girls get in. Taking in Natalie's sweaty brow and pained expression, he at once felt remorse for his attitude. It was a fucking porch decoration—not a living, breathing human.

Make that two humans. *Oh, god.* The ground wavered in front of him, and out of nowhere Jayden felt nauseous. Soon, a tiny miniature person would be taking its first breath of fluid-free air. A crushing absolute certainty descended on him in that moment.

He wanted this with Erin.

Jayden burned with the urgent longing to spill his seed deep inside of her, leaving it to create that ultimate representation of their love. To see their child draw its first breath would be . . . he couldn't even describe what it would mean.

"Jayden. Yoo-hoo . . ." Erin's hand touched his forearm. "It's not the time for daydreaming. We need to get Natalie over to Baylor. Now."

Her voice was tinged with alarm, but it took him a few seconds to realize it. By then, Micah had come out of his apartment to see what the racket was. The next thing he knew, Jayden was in the backseat with the girls, Micah having relieved him of driving duties.

Sitting next to the girls, he felt helpless. Natalie's usual bouncy curls had become limp with sweat, and she looked miserable. Beside her, Erin looked the picture of calm. He marveled over his fiancée's grip on the situation while she gathered Natalie's hair up into a messy ponytail and began rubbing the girl's back with her free hand.

A contraction must have hit, because Natalie let out an ear-piercing scream that sent chills racing up his spine. Darting his eyes to Erin, he got what he needed when she lifted her emerald eyes to meet him—and smiled.

"Remember to breathe, Natty, just like we practiced in class." Erin slipped into coach mode, transforming into the powerful woman he'd glimpsed back in April, when she'd held the crop.

Jayden relaxed, and soon enough Micah was dropping their small party off at the doors of Baylor University Medical Center. Once they'd gotten the girl admitted and were waiting for the nurse to take her back to labor and delivery, he grabbed Erin and kissed her.

"What was that for?" She giggled.

"Because you amaze me every fucking day, Erin. And you're beautiful . . . so I couldn't resist." He hugged her to his chest after she asked if he was okay. "I've never seen a woman in labor firsthand, and it's a bit alarming, honestly. But at the same time, realizing that in the next few hours there is going to be this new little person is making me want to get going on *our* baby plan."

Her eyes misted over, and he worried that right then had been the wrong time to bring it up, but all around them activity buzzed. Before he could say anything else, her fingertips were slipping from his as she backed away from him, waiting to turn and follow the nurse to Natalie's room until she'd reached the threshold. God, she was perfect, and he was oh, so lucky.

For the first few minutes after the doors closed, Jayden stood there with his hands in his pockets, unsure what to do. He had no idea how long this was supposed to take. Trying to be subtle, he looked around the waiting area for some kind of chart to offer an estimate. All he saw were pictures of babies and cross-section diagrams of pregnant bellies. On a whim, he pulled out his phone to call his mom and ask, but noticed the time. Four a.m. was way too early to call.

"Sir."

Jayden turned around. In all the hustle of check-in, he'd forgotten about Micah.

"This could take a while. Do you want to sit or maybe go get some coffee?" Amusement twinkled in Micah's blue eyes.

"Yeah, coffee sounds great. Let me tell the nurses' station in case Erin comes looking for me."

One of the nurses gave Jayden a beeper and told him they'd page if he was needed. Feeling better about leaving after that, he and Micah headed out to find coffee. They eventually located the cafeteria after getting lost twice. Damn hospital was like a labyrinth—he couldn't fathom how sick and medicated people didn't end up in supply closets while trying to navigate the place.

For the next couple of hours, they sipped on the less-than-stellar coffee while catching up. Shawn and Micah were working out well, and that pleased Jayden to no end. They were both good people and deserved happiness in their lives. Especially Micah. Jayden was proud of the man his young assistant was becoming and gave himself a mental pat on the back for getting Micah out of the boys' home. An errant thought crossed his mind—before too long, Micah would be moving on, and it would be time to give a new kid a chance to make something of his life. However, for the first time in all the years he'd been helping out the orphans, he had to think about Erin and what it could mean bringing a stranger into the fold. Which led to him realizing he also had to think about Natalie and the baby she was about to deliver, since he was hoping they were going to stay on at the

Villa. It was unconventional, but he had a family to think of now. *Maybe Natalie could take Micah's place in a year or so, when the baby was older?*

The ancient beeper went off, rattling on the table top and making Jayden jump and spill the coffee he'd just topped off for the fifth time. His heart started thundering in his chest with the unceremonious adrenaline dump into his system.

"Shit, Micah. I gotta go. I'll call you—"

"Go, Mr. Masterson. I'm fine. Can you find your way back?"

Jayden was already retreating when Micah's question gave him pause. He ran the maze of halls and turns through his head, and once confident he could do it, nodded and left. Wanting to run but satisfying himself with a vigorous walk, he reached the maternity ward and marched up to the counter. The nurse manning the station was on the phone and held up her finger, indicating it'd be just a minute.

He couldn't stand still, shifting from one foot to the other and wiping his sweaty palms down the front of his jeans. The ridiculousness of the situation didn't escape him. He was acting like he was about to be a first-time dad and it was Erin was beyond those doors. Fuck that . . . when, *if*, they were able to have one of their own, Jayden was going to be by her side for every second of it.

Right before he felt her, he sensed her. Her shorter form pressed into his back, hugging him tight. Erin let go, and he turned around. The exhaustion in her eyes worried him until his gaze dropped to her vibrant smile.

"How is she? Is the baby here? What—" Erin's light laughter cut him off.

"Natalie is resting. They've taken the baby down to the nursery for cleanup and observation since his APGARs were a tad low. Oh, Jayden, he is so beautiful." She kissed him and pulled back with a giggle that ended with a snort, "The wee lad has red tufts of hair. I guess Dominick wasn't a natural blue head, after all."

Jayden didn't understand everything she'd just said, but her demeanor was a hundred percent positive so he smiled with her. "Can we see him?"

"Aye, we can." She took his hand and led him through the mysterious doors, down a hall, and around a corner before they stopped in front of a large picture window. On the other side were rows of small cribs, most of which were empty, but there were a few with tiny bundles. "He's right over there."

Jayden followed her finger to find the crib holding Natalie's son. One of the attending nursery workers noticed where Erin was pointing and went over to pick up the boy and bring him closer to the window. However, he was only half paying attention to them because he'd been distracted by the placard on the crib identifying the baby.

NAME: Matthew Aaron Brown
DOB: 2014 JUL 09
SEX: M
HT/WT: 21 in / 8 lbs 7 oz

Natalie had named her child after them, and he had no idea how to process the emotions the gesture was bringing to the surface. Honored didn't even begin to cover it. He looked over to Erin, who was watching him, her own tears threatening to fall. There was no reason not to embrace her in that moment, so he did. Jayden put her in front of him so he could lean over and hold her from behind, their fingers clasped over her belly while the pair of them watched the yawning little boy on the other side of the glass.

Cঞৎ৯

Half asleep, Jayden rolled over to wrap around Erin, except she wasn't there. He blinked and rubbed his eyes, trying to see in the dark room. Her pillow was still indented, and her scent lingered. She hadn't been gone long.

With an accepting sigh, he got up to pull on some pants. He was pretty sure he knew where he was going to find her. The same place she'd gone practically every night since Natty and Matthew had come home from the hospital two weeks prior. After a quick stop in the bathroom, Jayden made his way to the kitchen to fix some hot cocoa for the girls, then headed to Natalie's room.

As he passed the den, Erin's soft whispers stopped him. Peeking in, he watched her. The soft moonlight from the bay windows silhouetted her small frame in the over-sized glider chair. One leg was tucked beneath her, the other stretching to the floor where she used her foot to push off and create a gentle swaying motion. Her attention was on the blanketed bundle in her arms.

Though he didn't understand the words, he recognized her Irish brogue and assumed she was singing a childhood lullaby to Matthew. Jayden soaked in the vision for a few more moments before approaching the pair. He couldn't ignore what a great mother she would be, if given the chance.

Jayden leaned over to give her a kiss and hand her one of the hot cocoas. "Why are you in here, sweet girl?" he asked in a quiet tone so as not to wake Matthew. "Shouldn't you be letting Natalie do the mom thing and bond with her little champ?"

She sipped the drink and gave him a tired smile. "I couldn't sleep anyways, too excited about marrying you tomorrow. So I offered to take him and let her rest."

"Erin, I know you adore him, I think he's pretty awesome myself, but tomorrow is *your* big day. You should be resting. Besides, you've taken the night shift every night, it seems." He nudged her leg, asking her to scoot over and make room so he could slide in next to her, then put his arms out to take the baby in exchange for the cocoa.

Bending forward, she tucked the edge of the blanket back from Matthew's face. "But look at him, Jayden. I might not be sleeping, but there's something so relaxing about just holding him." She ran a finger down his cheek. "I know it's probably not healthy, but I really am enjoying spending the time with him."

"My concern is that we aren't giving Natalie enough room to do what she needs to do. I don't know what that is exactly. It just feels like she's withdrawing more rather than getting involved with this whole mommy thing."

Erin sighed and leaned back, taking another sip. "Her body has just gone through a huge ordeal, it's only natural she's tired, right? We told her we'd help.

Besides, having the little guy around has been a great distraction from all the wedding nonsense." She gave a light laugh. "Thank you so much for bringing in Samantha to help and getting your mom to back off. It made all the difference in the world in these last weeks."

Jayden made a *pfft* sound at that. "At the end of the day, it's our wedding, not hers. She gets that. At least, now she does." He winked. In his arms, Matthew stirred and his face scrunched up seconds before his bum warmed against Jayden's arm. "Did he just shit his diaper?"

Rolling her eyes, Erin stood with a laugh. "Here, let me get him cleaned up and put him back down in his bassinet. I'll be along shortly." That time she bent down, kissing Jayden on the top of the head for once, then scooped up the boy and disappeared down the hallway, the soothing lullaby coming from her lips once again.

Jayden finished off her cocoa, took Natalie's untouched cup back to the kitchen, and headed back upstairs to wait for Erin.

ॐ

CHAPTER THIRTY-SIX

ॐ

Erin stared, awestruck, at the woman before her. What she saw conjured images of expensive, French porcelain dolls—the kind of dolls that were crafted from the finest materials and assembled with the most skilled fingers.

Champagne-colored chiffon clung to the woman's torso, almost hiding the swell of her breasts, and cascaded down to her ankles in a flowing skirt. The copious amount of her crimson hair had been fashioned into three converging French braids, with the tails arranged into a pretty knot at the base of her neck below her left ear. Miniature red silk orchids and black pearl-tipped pins were nestled in the knot. Her makeup had been applied with an artistic flair to enhance her flawless skin, her green eyes were accented by purple and silver shadows that gave a smoky effect, and her full lips were painted a deep, glossy crimson. A matching set of champagne, bronze, and black pearls with diamond accents hung from her neck, ears, and wrist—a gift from Jayden for her 'something new.' The overall look was, in a word, stunning.

Erin was finding it hard to believe it was her reflection staring back at her from the glass. She was afraid to move, worried that the vision would fade and she'd wake up. A soft cough pulled her from her self-perusal. Using the mirror in front of her, Erin looked over her shoulder.

"Hi, Da," she whispered, afraid she'd start crying if she tried to speak aloud, and turned around.

"Hello, *iníon*." He seemed to be choking on his words as well. "My goodness, but you look like a princess, Cat. I feel like I missed watching you grow up. When did you become a woman?"

Heat crawled up into her cheeks at his compliment. "Thankya, Da. And you're here now, so don't think about the sad times of the past. We have a great future ahead of us, full of happiness. I just know it."

Woody nodded his head. "Aye, I think ye might be right about that. I have to say, while I haven't known Jayden long, and he is more than a bit older than you—"

"Da!"

"Let me finish, Cat." He chuckled. "That man has been nothing but upstanding. He's come through on more than one occasion, and I couldn't imagine someone with better intentions in their heart than Jayden has toward you. So, um, are you ready to do this?" The old man's nerves were showing more than the young bride's.

Before Erin could reply to her father's question, Paige bounded into the small dressing room. "Of course she's ready!" chirped her Matron of Honor extraordinaire. Her crimson chiffon dress was done in a similar Grecian style to Erin's, but with less fabric so the skirt wasn't as full as the bridal gown.

"Except for her 'something old.'" She shot a wink over at Erin's dad. "Which I believe you are taking care of, Mr. O'Chancey?"

"Paige, I've told ye to just call me Woody."

"Fine, Mr. Woody, then. Erin's all set for new, borrowed, and blue. She just needs her old from you, though you're anything but." Her friend's tinkle of laughter was chased with one of her trademark winks.

To Erin's surprise, her father's sunburned cheeks turned a deeper shade of red, and he toed the ground. Paige had made the old man blush.

"Aye, of course." Woody reached into his inner pocket to pull out a velvet rectangular box. Inside was a silver chain. "This was your *maimeo's.* It was given to her on her wedding day as her 'something new' by my da. Just before she passed, she told me I was to make sure you got it on your wedding day."

Erin felt like she was in a haze while he reached for her unadorned wrist and fastened the bracelet around it. It was an interlocking series of Celtic heart knots, and she recognized it at once because she'd never seen her *maimeo* without it. The surprised bride had thought her grandmother had been buried with it.

With Jayden's gift set, the borrowed pearl pins in her hair, and a deep blue satin garter adorning her thigh, the tradition was complete.

"There," Woody declared and placed a soft kiss on her cheek. "You're beautiful, Catherine, and I know she is here with you, proud as ever. She would've been so touched by your choosing today to do this."

"Oh, Da." Erin sniffled, the first tear on the brink of falling.

"Now, now . . . none of that! You'll ruin your makeup, Erin," screeched Paige. "Oh, and it's show time, sweetie," she added in a calmer voice, handing Erin the bouquet of deep red orchids. The flowers were an homage to those with which Jayden had courted her.

Taking a deep breath, Erin slipped her arm around her father's. "Shall we?"

Woody harrumphed and Paige giggled, then the three of them moved from the anteroom to the main doors of the chapel. Paige poked her head through the door to signal the organist. While the first notes of the wedding march began, Micah and Warren—their ushers—pulled open the chapel doors, and the assembled guests rose to their feet.

Samantha's little sister Meredith was standing in as their flower girl. Joon wasn't walking well enough yet to manage the task, and they didn't know anyone else with a young girl. Meredith's dress was cream-colored satin and tulle, finished with an intricate sash about her waist that had been hand-beaded with seed pearls and rhinestones. Erin had choked when Jayden insisted that all the pearls be real.

A naughty grin crept onto her face at the memory of the argument she'd gotten into with him because of the cost. He hadn't appreciated her tone. The disagreement had ended with her over her Master's lap, receiving a thoroughly satisfying spanking, which had been followed by an even more satisfying fucking.

Meredith pranced down the aisle, sprinkling petals from a basket while she went. *Adorable.* Paige, followed by Ronnie in a matching crimson bridesmaid dress, went next. While Erin and her da waited for the girls to work their way down and take their places at the front, she took in the room from her vantage point.

Shawn was just inside and to the left, already snapping pictures. The assembled crowd was intimidating to her, but everyone looked amazing. Dressed in their finest clothes, they'd all turned to face the incoming bride, making her the center of attention. Her pulse began racing, and her eyes darted down, away from their beaming faces.

This is happening. I'm about to become Mrs. Jayden Masterson. Her heartbeat gained momentum, thrumming in her ears.

Everywhere she looked, crimson orchids and pearly white roses graced the available surfaces. Steel gray bunting brought it all together, matching the gray runner down the center of the aisle—now littered with Meredith's white rose petals. Jillian and Steph sat at the front with Benny and Joon, and next to them was Natalie, with Matthew asleep in her arms.

Erin's gaze went back to her bridesmaids. They'd almost reached the front, so she allowed herself to look at the men on the right side of the aisle. Malcolm Masterson and Sir Landon had their hands clasped in front of them, looking impeccable in their dark gray tuxedos with cream silk shirts. Like her da, they had a single red orchid pinned to their lapels. Gray Stetsons were perched on their heads—Malcolm had insisted.

Next to her, her father tugged on her arm to begin the walk down the aisle, and her gaze drifted to Jayden.

Unlike his comrades, Jayden's tuxedo and hat were black in color. His cream-colored shirt, patterned necktie, and crimson vest were breathtaking and complimented Erin's gown. Her eyes met his warm, brown ones, and she lost her breath. He was beyond handsome. In the locking of their stares, the entire room disappeared.

All she was aware of was Him—her friend, her lover, her Master.

It wasn't until her da responded in a boisterous voice to the pastor's question of, "Who gives this woman to be married?" that Erin became aware of her surroundings again and realized they'd made the walk up the aisle. With painstaking effort, she pulled her eyes away from Jayden's to pay attention to their pastor, but not before she caught Jayden's enamored grin.

"Beloved family and friends, we are gathered here today . . ." began the minister.

Erin listened to the greeting and then his recitation of Corinthians with a fluttering heart. She was getting her happily ever after. Never had she felt more like a princess than at that moment, with her Prince Charming standing next to her, holding her hand while the pastor spoke.

The couple had decided to recite a poem to each other before their actual "I do's." Though the poem each had chosen was a surprise, they'd worked on the vows together. Some of their guests were aware, and even part, of the Lifestyle, but most were not, so

Jayden and Erin had to be subtle with the inclusion of that side of their lives into their vows.

She had to steady her breathing when they turned to face each other. Taking Jayden's hands in her own, Erin looked into his eyes and began repeating an Anne Bradstreet poem from the 1600s. Her lips trembled while she formed the words of "To My Dear and Loving Husband." When a tear rolled down her cheek, Erin gave Jayden a soft smile.

His warm thumb brushed it away.

She took another deep breath, and another tear escaped while the lines fell from her lips. That time, he leaned in and kissed the tear away. His intoxicating scent, a mix of being freshly showered and the underlying hint of male, crashed into her senses and befuddled her for a moment.

Pivoting, Erin collected the inlaid gold and platinum band from Paige. Turning back to Jayden, she lifted his left hand and positioned the ring at the tip of his fourth finger.

"*Mo anam cara*, my soul mate, for the remaining days of my life, I promise to love and cherish you, to comfort and honor you, and to serve and obey you. For richer or poorer, in sickness and in health, for better or for worse as long as we both shall live, I promise to be a faithful wife and keep my body for you—it is yours to do with as you wish. I, Catherine Eilene O'Chancey, take you, Jayden Matthew Masterson, to be my lawfully wedded Husband, the Master of my heart, soul, and body. With this ring, I submit to you, and I thee wed." She bowed her head and lowered her gaze while sliding the ring onto his finger.

He lifted her chin with a gentle touch. "Thank you, Catherine," her Master whispered then cleared his throat and took her hands in his. "Eyes on me, my jewel," he commanded before raising his voice again so that everyone could hear.

"How do I love thee? Let me count the ways."

Erin beamed, recognizing the opening to Browning's well-known text. Jayden's voice was strong and sure as he continued. When he'd recited the poem, her heart melting with every word, he collected her band from Sir Landon. Clasping her left hand in his, Jayden positioned the ring at the tip of her fourth finger and began his vows.

"My jewel, I promise to be a faithful husband and to keep my body for you, and you alone. I promise to love you and cherish you, to comfort and honor you, to guide you—and push your limits."

A quiet laugh rippled through their guests. While those in the know found humor in his promise of ecstasy, those who were not still found humor in the idea of a husband pushing his wife's buttons.

Jayden winked at her and continued over the interruption. "For all the days of my life. For richer or poorer, in sickness and in health, for better or for worse as long as we both shall live. I, Jayden Matthew Masterson, Master of your heart, soul, and body, take you, Catherine Eilene O'Chancey, to be my lawfully wedded wife. With this ring, I humbly accept your submission, and I thee wed." Their eyes were fixed on each other while he pushed the platinum and gold *Claddagh* band that matched his own onto her finger.

Lowering his voice so only she could hear, he said the most beautiful words Erin had ever heard. "I love you, Mrs. Masterson."

Smiling like fools, the couple turned back toward the reverend, waiting for him to finish and present them. "By the power vested in me by the State of Texas, and before these witnesses, I now pronounce you man and wife. Jayden, you may kiss your beautiful bride if you so choose."

Her husband threw his head back and laughed. "Hell yeah, I so choose. Come here, Catherine!" he ordered and pulled her into his arms to capture her waiting lips. His tongue pushed into her mouth, and they kissed deeply to the sounds of applause and catcalls from friends and family.

When they broke the kiss, the pastor spoke again. "Ladies and gentleman, may I have the honor of presenting to you, Mr. and Mrs. Jayden Masterson."

ಬಂಡ
CHAPTER THIRTY-SEVEN
ಬಂಡ

A bout an hour later, they arrived at the restaurant for the reception. While the guests had left after the ceremony, those in the wedding party had stayed behind for a full photo session. Erin couldn't wait to see the shots Shawn had gotten. It would be nice to display his work in their house where it could be admired by others, unlike the private shots he'd done for their playroom.

Several of the photographs Shawn had taken of Erin the year before in the garden at the spa had been reproduced as poster-size black and white prints. They adorned the walls of their playroom. Jayden's favorite was the one Shawn had captured of her spread out in the hammock with her hand on a breast, the other between her legs, and her head thrown back in ecstasy while her whole body blushed from the force of an orgasm. That one he had left in color and had blown up to life size. It was the centerpiece of the collection.

The happy couple stood together while the guests came by to congratulate them with hugs and whispered words. They laughed when the embarrassing toasts were made before the meal was served. Jayden and Erin shared their entrees, delicately feeding each other bites.

Erin was brought to tears when it came time for their first dance. Unbeknownst to her, Jayden had made arrangements for Woody to serenade them with a song from her childhood. In his deep baritone, his Irish lilt shining through, he belted out the words of "You Raise Me Up." Afterward, Woody shuffled Erin around in a small circle while Jayden and Jillian glided around the floor.

She'd never been happier.

When it was time to throw the bouquet, Paige called all the single women to gather around and slipped a silk blindfold over Erin's eyes. She laughed, a light tinkling sound, when the bride glared at her. Her friend hadn't forgotten her whiny tendencies where blindfolds were concerned. "Oh, Erin, it has to be fair . . . no peeking!" she chirped.

With a toss, the flowers went over her shoulder, and she hoped she was at least getting it in the vicinity of the waiting women. Erin heard a shuffle, followed by squealing and laughter, and she slipped off the blindfold to see who'd caught it.

Samantha was holding it up with an exuberant smile as she made eye contact with Sir Ryan across the room.

One Ryan Bishop had an adorable, but panicked, look on his face.

Jayden's arms slipped around her from behind, and he nuzzled into her neck, teasing her with discreet bites and soft kisses that caused a dull throb to spark between her legs. She rested her head against his shoulder for a moment before Sir Landon's drawl commanded the attention of the room.

"Alright, y'all. Erin and the ladies have had their fun. It's Jayden's turn now. I need all the eligible menfolk to step on up if y'all are interested in a piece of the bride's lingerie."

She gasped at his announcement, and Jayden chuckled in her ear, sending another pulse of desire shooting between her legs.

"Paige, I need ya to grab a chair and put it in the center of the room," Landon instructed. Walking over to us, he took Erin's hand but looked at Jayden, "May I borrow your bride for a moment, Jay?"

Jayden released her to be led over to the waiting chair while he followed behind. With Paige's help, Erin got her gown arranged and then sat down in the chair, crossing her ankles in demure fashion. While Jayden knelt in front of her, Sir Landon leaned over and whispered in Erin's ear, "Uh-uh, Darlin'. Assume a proper position. Now." He winked at her then stood back up.

Erin straightened her back, uncrossed her ankles, and placed her feet on the floor by the legs of the chair in obedience. For good measure, she placed her palms flat on her thighs, just above her knees.

Jayden lifted her left foot, bringing the ankle to his mouth for a kiss. "Good girl," he whispered and the crowd *ooh'd* him on. Lowering her foot back to the ground, further out from where she'd first set it, his fingers started to trail up her leg, under her dress.

Her heart raced. Landon was turning an innocent tradition into something sexual in front of all their guests, in front of her da. She knew she had to be bright red while glancing around at the men who had gathered to watch and wait for their chance to catch her garter. All of a sudden, Erin was apprehensive about Jayden's reaction if, *when*, he discovered the surprise waiting beneath her gown.

Why had she listened to Paige again?

She must have tensed up, because her attention was pulled back to Jayden by the soft-spoken tone of his words. "Catherine, eyes on me, sweet girl. You're doing great." He smiled, his fingers stroking the back of her knee.

Jayden's words and touch coaxed her into relaxing. *Maybe this won't turn out too embarrassing?* He would reach the blue garter on her thigh and pull it down. With a few inches to spare between the satin and her pussy, he wouldn't notice. No harm.

Suddenly Landon spoke up again. "Steady there, Jayden. I think you're movin' a bit too quick." He winked at Jayden before addressing the group. "So, should Jayden be a gentleman and continue on his polite journey to round up that garter or," he turned his smug grin on Erin, watching her reaction to his next words, "should he duck under that gown and go after it like a real man, with his teeth?"

Her groan was loud when their audience started chanting "teeth" over and over. She looked to Jayden, pleading with her eyes to please ignore them and get this over with so they could be on their way. Erin was beyond ready to get their honeymoon started.

By her Master's orders and her lover's request, she'd not orgasmed in two weeks, nor had she felt his cock in her, or even seen it for that matter, in four. He'd explained he wanted her "virgin tight" on their wedding night and had spent the next two weeks after his announcement teasing her, stroking her to release, but with no deep penetration. With two weeks to go to their wedding, he'd then declared her orgasms would be denied so that he could bathe in her come when he forced her to a squirting orgasm . . . on their wedding night. His reason for keeping it in his pants and hiding it for a month? In his words, because she was, "Too damn tempting."

Erin knew her begging was pointless when all she got for her silent pleading was a sexy, but smug, grin.

He leaned over and kissed her ankle again before lifting her dress enough to crawl under it. She squeezed her eyes shut and tried to block out everything else. Those two jackasses had decided to turn this into a scene, and she needed to focus and go with it. She'd told Master that she wanted to explore the exhibitionism side of herself more, and they'd been working on it. Catherine just never expected to be pushed at her own wedding.

Jayden was kissing up her leg when Landon moved behind her chair. He leaned down and whispered in her ear, "Relax, Catherine, we're just havin' a bit of fun with you."

Jayden bit her calf, and she yelped, it wasn't heard over the chanting the crowd was still doing.

Landon straightened up and laughed. "Atta boy, Jayden!" he shouted, encouraging the cat calls.

"Landon," Erin hissed. If those two were in cahoots, then she was sure he also knew it'd been two weeks since she'd come and that she was walking a very fine line on her control. What he didn't know was that Paige had encouraged her to do a bit of naughtiness, too. She needed to warn him that their 'bit of fun' could have embarrassing results.

He cocked a brow at her before leaning back down so she could speak for his hearing only. "Yes'm, Darlin', what is it?"

"We might have a problem." She whimpered when Jayden's tongue dragged along the edge of her knee.

Landon snickered. "Oh? What would that be?"

"Two fucking weeks, Landon," she growled at him, and his blue eyes enlarged at her boldness. "Two weeks, no release, and I'm not wearing any panties."

Erin panted while Jayden's tongue licked her thigh, tracing the bottom of the garter. *And cue the waterworks.* The thought was valid, considering her lack of undergarment left it blatantly obvious that her lower lips were no longer dry.

"Not even a thong?"

With as little movement as possible, she shook her head. He grasped the situation with an impressive quickness and on a low whistle, let out an "Oh, shit."

She snorted. "Aye, my thoughts exactly!"

Jayden's nose skimmed over the top of the garter, again tasting her skin, moving his tongue up her thigh. She knew he'd discovered her little surprise when he stopped moving and exhaled against her with enough force to ruffle the gown. Her body clenched at the heat from his breath tickling the edge of her pussy.

"Landon, help me." Erin's whisper was frantic.

At once, his hands went to her shoulders and began a harsh squeezing, digging his thumbs in deep. It hurt, but helped her concentrate. "Deep breaths, Darlin'."

Under her dress, Jayden shifted so that his head, and mouth, were now in front of her moistening slit. *Oh, god . . . oh, god . . . oh, please . . . Jayden, don't do it*, she begged in silence.

His tongue brushed her pussy lips. Wide and flat, he dragged it up toward the nerve bundle he'd find swollen and yearning for him.

"Red!"

The encouraging chanting came to an abrupt halt, the room going silent as all eyes in the room focused on the screaming bride—like she'd lost her mind.

Though he began to back away at once, Erin clamped her legs together around his head, halting his retreat. She needed a second . . . or sixty.

"Uh," Erin stuttered, "Orchids. Aye, the red orchids are beautiful. They were the perfect choice," she offered in a lame distraction. She felt Jayden's mirthful shaking beneath her dress.

He gave one last kiss to her thigh, then closed his teeth around the garter and pulled.

Thank god.

Within moments, he was kneeling next to her, her dress sorted, and her garter dangling from his mouth. Landon gave her shoulders a final squeeze before patting them with an appraising touch.

"Well now, it seems Jayden's a man after all!" he bellowed.

Everyone laughed, and she couldn't have been more appreciative of the diversion. Taking a breath, Erin risked a look in Jayden's direction. He was staring straight at her, his eyes dark with lust . . . and something else, something good. She granted him a shy smile, and he stood up, removing the ring of blue satin from his mouth.

He bent forward under the pretense of kissing her cheek and whispered against Erin's ear, "I'm very proud of you, Catherine. You will be rewarded very soon."

She remained frozen, sitting in the chair and gathering her mental faculties, while Jayden threw the garter. In an ironic twist of fate, Ryan caught it.

Samantha's resultant squeal was ear-piercing and caused another round of laughter from the guests.

Cake was next—two elaborate works of art—one chocolate, one Italian crème, and both decorated with orchids. The reception began winding down soon after. Jayden and Erin got in a couple more slow dances, the bride rejoicing in the feeling of her husband's arms holding her close and secure.

Before she knew it, Paige had grabbed the microphone and was announcing their departure. "The lovebirds need to be on their way, or they'll miss their plane."

There was no time for her to change into her traveling outfit. She'd be flying in her wedding dress. They headed outside with the remaining guests while Landon went to get the car.

Erin was in a tight hug with her da when she heard Jayden yell, "Oh, fuck no!" Startled, she spun around and then was overcome with a bout of hysteria.

ଋଔଔଷ

CHAPTER THIRTY-EIGHT

ଋଔଔଷ

L andon leaned casually against Jayden's Wraith, a wide, arrogant grin on his face. Micah, Shawn, and even Malcolm came out of the crowd to stand next to him—and admit their part in it. The car, once sleek and sexy, now looked like an overpriced clown transport. *Just Married* was soaped over the back window, while strands of designer shoes and soda cans trailed from the back. If that weren't enough, they'd even decorated the car with inflated condoms in all shapes, sizes, and colors.

A flash of anger hit Jayden at the sight of his expensive baby, and an expletive bolted from his mouth. But then he heard Erin's angelic laughter, and a calmness overcame him. He turned away from the joke that his Rolls Royce now was to take in the love of his life.

Her hand was clasped over her mouth while she tried to stifle her guffaws, but her eyes were wide, sparkling emeralds. She'd never been more beautiful.

"Oh, Jayden, sweetie, I'm sorry." She tried to say the words without giggling, but failed. However, she also directed such an intense look of happiness at him that he didn't resist the urge to lean down and brush a soft kiss across her full lips.

Grinning, Jayden relaxed and shrugged. "Oh, well. I guess it's only fair after what I did to his Porsche when they got married." He'd made sure his friend came back from his honeymoon to decked-out wheels of his own, knowing he'd be safely out of the country when Landon made the discovery.

"Okay, Mrs. Masterson," Jayden declared, taking her hand in his own. "I'm ready to get this honeymoon started—if you know what I mean." He wiggled his eyebrows at her.

She batted her eyelashes. "Me too, Mr. Masterson."

Jayden helped his wife into the car, then made his way around to the driver's side. Giving a final wave to their few remaining guests, he ducked inside the car, and they were on their way. When they reached the airport, he continued through the second security gate, which led to the private airfield.

"What are we doing, Jayden?"

"We're borrowing the company plane, sweet girl. It's going to take about twelve hours to reach Shannon International Airport, then we have to get the car and drive over to Bunratty. I intend to consummate this marriage while it's still our wedding day, but what with time changes, it will no longer be July twenty-fourth when we reach our hotel. Can't very well consummate on public transport, now can we?" Somehow Jayden deadpanned through his spiel. It was commendable, considering he was using a lot of words to say that he simply needed to get her alone to fuck her as soon as possible.

"No, I guess we can't." Erin's grin turned naughty, her eyes filling with a primal hunger.

He wondered what she was thinking, and his cock twitched at the possibilities of what could be going through her head. Jayden knew his girl was eager because of the restrictions she'd been under. What he'd found, or *not* found, under her dress had enlightened him to her adventurous mood. Remembering the incident caused his lips to twitch, too.

Landon had been acting like a clown and egging on the crowd, having assured Jayden that he'd handle Erin while Jayden fetched the garter. Neither one of them had counted on her providing Jayden with an irresistible temptation.

In hindsight, he should've known better, but truth be told, Jayden had been surprised to discover her bare and glistening. The shock had drawn a rough exhalation from him that had resulted in her clit twitching and swelling right before his eyes. *How was a guy supposed to pass up that kind of invitation?*

He hadn't. Instead, though he knew it would take little to ignite her into a burning inferno, he'd had to have a taste. A small one, over the outside of her pussy lips so it teased but didn't induce orgasm.

Once again, she caught him off guard when she'd yelled red. At the time, she hadn't known his intention to leave her clit alone—and her response caused his heart to swell with pride. Erin had been willing to admit she couldn't control herself, and she ended the scene. As promised, he'd backed off the moment she used the safe word, but he couldn't stop from shaking with laughter while she tried to explain away her outburst.

Red orchids indeed.

Bringing his thoughts back to the present, Jayden found a space and parked the car, then helped Erin out. An airfield attendant appeared and grabbed their bags from the car while the couple boarded the small luxury craft. After the formalities of pre-flight checks and safety reviews were done, their flight attendant—who introduced herself as Kristine— brought the couple a fruit and cheese plate, along with an ice bucket holding a bottle of ice wine and two glasses.

He had to chuckle when the crew woman spared a brief glance at him, but let her eyes really roam over Erin. Attempting to be polite in his dismissal, he told her that would be all, and she disappeared through the door to the front cabin, leaving Erin and Jayden alone in the main cabin.

Finally.

Jayden poured them both a glass of the sweet, crisp beverage—a very *small* glass. Erin passing out on him was not part of his immediate plans. Not from the wine, anyway. He'd gladly allow her to slip into a satiated, well-spent slumber later when he was done with her.

While the plane taxied out to the runway, Jayden doted on Erin, feeding her berries and cheese as they sipped their wine and reminisced about the wedding. However, the moment the pilot turned off the seatbelt sign, letting them know they'd reached cruising altitude and leveled off, the eager man undid his belt and had his wife do the same.

He stood and extended his hand to her with a small bow. "I believe it's time to get you out of this dress, Mrs. Masterson. If you'll accompany me to the bedroom, please?"

His bride blushed, and Jayden groaned. That she could still act like an innocent maiden after all the times—and ways—he'd had her, amazed him.

"Turn around, Erin." One by one, he removed the pins from her hair, followed by the tiny silk buds. Then he worked his long fingers through her braids, undoing the intricate red weaves. Gathering the silky tresses, he moved them over her shoulder, granting him access to her neck. Her response—an involuntary shiver—to the light kiss he planted between her shoulder blades, incensed his arousal. "You've made me the happiest man alive today."

There was a quiet rustle while he began loosening the laces on her dress. "Breathtaking doesn't begin to describe how enchanting you look, *A rúnsearc*—like a goddess." He ran the tip of his tongue along the back of her neck and up to her earlobe. Timid giggles and sighs slipped from her, and he sucked the tender flesh of her ear between his teeth, hypnotized by her light scent and taste.

With the back laces of her gown undone, the thin straps slipped from her shoulders and down her arms, and the dress fell and pooled at her feet. Stepping from behind her, Jayden positioned himself where he could view all of her and sucked in a sharp breath. He would never tire of seeing all of her natural beauty on display for him.

Careful to not touch her skin, Jayden reached out with both hands and clasped the J's dangling from her nipples. "Mine," he said in a low growl, then moved to capture her mouth in a passionate kiss. Taking her hand, he continued to kiss her while guiding her over the pile of chiffon. He picked up the pricey garment and hung it in the small closet.

When Jayden turned back around, Erin had moved to the bed and was reclining on her elbows in the center, one knee bent.

"So beautiful," he murmured, more to himself than anything.

His cock was now at full attention and straining against his pants. If it wasn't released from its confines soon, the pain would become intolerable. *Would she like his surprise, the real reason he'd kept his cock hidden from her for a month?* He'd find out soon enough whether the bothersome pajamas and lonely showers had been worth it.

"Please, Jayden. I need you," she begged without shame.

Like he would say no. Jayden unbuttoned his shirt, prowling forward a step as each tiny fastener slipped free of its hole. He let the shirt fall open and undid his pants. Erin was watching his every move with passion in her eyes.

"Are you going to behave?"

"Only if you want this girl to, Master," she purred, letting her knee fall out to the side so that he had a perfect view down the inside of her thigh.

He chuckled at his insatiable partner. "We'll play soon enough, sweet girl. Right now, though, I want to worship and make love to my wife." Lowering his pants and boxers, Jayden bent forward, then stayed doubled over to crawl onto the bed and position himself between her legs.

Leaning down, he placed a kiss at the top of her mons. On instinct, she lifted her hips, a silent plea for more. Jayden followed through, alternating with open mouthed kisses and tiny nips to each of her lingering burn scars. She'd been so ashamed the first time he saw them, but now she looked forward to his loving attention on them.

"I just love when you get this worked up. So responsive to my every touch," he kissed her hip, "and each caress." His light, glancing touches across her breasts made her back arch, and he stopped until she settled back. With a deep breath, he resumed his vexing strokes. "The room fills with the heady aroma of your sex," he pinched one of her pierced buds, "and your delicious nipples get so hard."

"God, Jayden," she moaned, "you're killing me, baby. Please stop teasing. I need you so bad . . . please."

Jayden stretched his body over hers, holding his weight above her while placing a hand at either side of her head. His cock rested against her warm folds, her erect nipples scratching lightly at his chest, while the sides of his shirt hung down, enclosing them in a private cocoon.

She snaked her arms up and around his neck, then drew him closer to run her tongue over his lips. Jayden willingly parted them, letting her in to enjoy the fruity taste of her mouth while she lifted her hips and started rubbing herself against his erection.

Moaning, he untangled from the kiss and pulled his crotch away from her enthusiastic grinding. Jayden choked a bit while shaking his head. "No, Erin. That feels too good. You'll have both of us blowing before we're ready. I know I said I wanted to bathe in your come, but I intend to drink down as much of you as I can first, not have you soak my thighs. That will come later."

She mewled, and it nearly undid him.

A quick peck to her belly then he moved to get comfortable near her pussy, where he could see the moisture pooling beneath her. *Fuck, she's so wet.* His tongue nudged between her folds and sought out her clit, then swirled around the hardened nub before he gave it a small tug with his teeth. When he pulled back, her body jerked.

Crawling back off the bed, Jayden sank to his knees at the edge, grabbing Erin and pulling her toward him. She squealed at the unexpected change in position. Once he had her positioned just right, ass at the edge of the mattress and knees bent, he dove in.

With gentle licks all over the outside of her sex, he started flicking his tongue over the tip of her clit. "Erin, my jewel, this isn't a scene, and I do want you to come when ready, but try to hold it as long as you can."

Her whimper was followed by a breathy, "Okay."

That's my girl, he thought. Using his left hand, Jayden pried open her swollen lips and resumed licking. Her juices were free-flowing when he lowered his mouth to her opening, where he sucked and lapped with greed at the nectar that escaped her. She was pumping her hips against the bed, and him, and Jayden realized he was making the same motion against the bedspread, his cock seeking any kind of friction it could find.

"Fuck, Erin. Your taste is so good, so sweet . . . so divine," he mumbled into her quivering sex. Knowing she wouldn't be able to withstand his next move, he prepared by taking a deep breath. Easing two fingers into her, he breached her over and over, slow and coaxing. She was tight, and they both groaned at the sensation.

He lifted himself onto his knees, forcing her legs up and back while tilting her pussy up toward the ceiling and bracing his bare chest against her ass. Still holding her labia apart, he wrapped his lips around her clit and sucked at the same time he withdrew his fingers, just to plunge the digits back into her. Hard and fast, repeatedly. *Three, two, one . . .*

"Oh, shit! Jayden, I'm . . . oh, god, I'm coming!"

Her proclamation was unnecessary, though. He felt the hot blast of her orgasm against his tongue. Squeezing his eyes shut and opening his mouth, he kept pumping his fingers in and out of her. Swallowing when his mouth was full, he opened to catch more of her spray. She continued riding her orgasm for about two minutes.

When she stilled and he slipped his fingers out of her, Jayden's face and chest were soaked. Drawing the back of his hand across his eyes, he opened them to find his jewel flushed and panting heavily.

"Wow. Oh, wow. That was . . . oh, god, that was amazing, baby," she croaked and threw her arms above her head.

Happy sounds bubbled out of him, and she lifted her head to look down her torso at him. "Oh, my. Looks like you need some cleaning up." She giggled and curled her body into an upright position, kissing his lips before she started licking his face to clean it.

Jayden reveled in it, tilting his head back while the temptress snaked her tongue down his jaw and along his neck. Erin bit down on the column of his throat, and he groaned, thrusting his hips at the bedspread again. She reached down and wrapped her tiny hand around the base of his engorged shaft, stroking it with a light, barely there, pressure.

Moving back to his lips, she kissed and nibbled. "Your turn, baby," Erin murmured against his mouth. "I need to taste your cock. Now," she growled the word and tightened her grip.

Jayden needed her to taste him, too. It was time to share his surprise. He drew back from her kiss and stood up. As he rose, he watched her eyes trail down his chest, toward his cock.

The moment she clocked the changes, Erin's eyes widened, and her breath hitched.

ಬಂಬ
CHAPTER THIRTY-NINE
ಬಂಬ

E rin was still shaking from the mind-blowing orgasm her lover—her *husband*—had just provided. That didn't stop her gaze from devouring his muscular chest, then slipping down to his chiseled abs when he stood. She was desperate to feel him inside her, but she also wanted to taste him. It had been too damn long since she'd had her lips wrapped around his thick cock.

Trailing her eyes down the natural V of his abdomen, she froze when color entered her line of sight—*ink*.

Cautiously, Erin lifted her hand to feather her fingertips across the script that matched hers. Same colors, same style. The inked words: "Property Of," a stark contrast on his otherwise unblemished skin.

"Um?" Erin shifted her eyes back up to Jayden's face where she found him biting his lip, waiting for her reaction. "Where's the rest of it?" she squeaked out, not knowing if he needed to turn around to show her, or if it just wasn't finished yet . . . or what.

He groaned, then panted out, "C-cock."

Erin had tightened her grip on him in her hand without realizing it. "Oh, shit, sorry!" The words rushed out and she released him, but he was shaking his head.

"No, you're fine. The rest of the tattoo is on my cock," he amended, and Erin looked down.

Inscribed down the length of his shaft was her name: Erin. If that weren't enough to shock her, there was also a Celtic heart knot. The symbol was positioned just below the head of his cock—her man had inked his cock with a heart for her.

Her breath wavered when she released it. The warm air rushed over his cock, and it jerked so that she caught a flash of something shiny. Reluctant to look away from the beautiful ink, Erin did anyway and found silver metal piercing the head. A barbell penetrated his cock from side-to-side, a ball fastener on each end at either side of the head.

Oh, damn. That is going to feel so good.

"Do you like it?" His whisper was uncertain.

The insecurity she heard in his tone drew her eyes up to his face. This man had made modifications, painful ones at that, to his manhood to show Erin he was hers forever. She was having a hard time wrapping her brain around what he'd endured on her behalf, but she knew she needed to acknowledge his sacrifice.

"Oh, Jayden, do I ever." Erin kissed the head before standing and throwing her arms around his neck. She pressed her breasts into his chest, and he wrapped his arms around her waist. They kissed.

Erin pulled away to stare into his soulful brown eyes. "It's grand, *A rúnsearc*. I can't believe you did this, though. How? When?" She was flustered and couldn't form coherent questions.

"Shawn and Landon helped me. I didn't trust anyone else, and I figured you'd be okay with them touching my junk," he joked.

"Yes, much better that they did it instead of some strange whore who probably would've offered to suck you off anytime you started, uh, lagging." She giggled. "Hey, how did you get around that?"

He would've had to have maintained a hard-on to get the ink done, and Erin couldn't figure out how that was possible while a needle pounded away at him. He didn't enjoy pain the way she did.

"Well, I, kinda asked Holly for some help."

"*What*?"

"No, Erin, not like that! That would've been, just, wrong. Holly supplied me with a dose of Viagra so that I'd stay hard through the procedure."

"Does she know why you needed it?"

Jayden chuckled. "Yes. I had to explain what I wanted to do before she would give me the pills. She'd have refused otherwise, seeing as I'm 'too young' to need that kind of assistance yet. Believe it or not, Holly made me come in for a full physical to be sure I was healthy enough so it wouldn't have any damaging side effects."

"Wow. I can't believe you did all this for me."

He shivered when her fingers traced the pattern.

"Erin, don't you understand yet? I would do anything for you." A chaste kiss was pressed to her lips. "The piercing wasn't part of my original plan, though. Shawn convinced me. He said something along the lines of, 'Since you're torturing your dick anyways, why not have Landon pierce it? Erin will love the way it feels'." He shrugged his shoulders. "So what do you say, sweet girl? Ready to take the new me out for a spin?"

Instead of a verbal reply, Erin leaned forward and took him into her mouth all at once.

"Fuck," he ground out. "Give a guy some warning." He didn't ask her to stop, though. Instead, Jayden panted while she worked her mouth up and down, applying light but firm suction to his cock.

Jayden's hands wove into her curls, gripping with a controlled tension while he guided her mouth along his cock a few times then held her still. Her wet moan was audible in the tiny airplane room when he started pumping his hips, giving her an oral fucking.

"Jesus Christ, Erin. Your mouth . . . I can't . . . always feels so . . . *ungh* . . . fucking . . . oh, yeah, like that, sweet girl . . ."

His thrusts picked up speed, and she prepared for him to come down her throat. Suddenly he pulled out, his hands still tangled in her hair, and huffed, gasping for air. "Feels too good—I'm going to come."

"Jayden."

"Yes, jewel?"

"Fuck me."

A big grin spread across his face. "It would be my pleasure," he said then grabbed Erin's waist and hoisted her up.

She wrapped her legs around his waist and could feel his erection bobbing beneath her ass, his new metal chilly on her skin. Holding her close to him, her husband crept to the middle of the bed and lowered her body to the mattress. Rolling her hips and ass up again, he sank into her in one satisfying thrust, and stopped.

"So tight, pet. You're always so tight . . ."

And then the fucking began, just like she'd asked for. Jayden pounded into her. Deep inside her pussy, the balls of his piercing rubbed against her, and it felt oh, so good.

Erin braced her ankles on top of his shoulders, then curled her body up and rested her palms behind her. This resulted in her being nearly folded in half, an upright V. She lifted her breasts towards him, begging for him to pay attention to her hard nipples.

He got the hint, latching onto first one, and then the other. Working back and forth between them, her lover suckled and bit, never losing his rhythm while he pummeled her needy pussy.

Jayden manipulated her body for what seemed like hours. Every time she thought they would fall into orgasmic bliss, he slowed down to almost no movement, lingering with his lips on hers until they'd retreated from that proverbial cliff. In control again, he would resume the hard thrusting, taking them back to that place of sexual limbo, again and again.

Feeling the tight coiling in her belly for the seventh or eighth time, Erin knew she couldn't hold it again. "Please, Jayden. I need to come. Let go . . ."

Her voice faded at the sensation of his lips wrapping around a nipple and drawing it in. He reached a hand between their slick bodies, and then increased his pace from a languid roll of his hips to a near violent colliding of flesh. Erin let her knees drop toward her chest and head, opening herself wider, allowing him to sink deeper. His long fingers found her clit and pinched at the same time his teeth closed on her nipple.

Erin cried out the next time his cock slammed into her.

They fell.

Hard.

It took a few minutes, but eventually he pulled out and dropped to lie by her side. Erin was shaking, her body still being hit by aftershocks, but she managed to roll onto her side and snuggle into his chest. "Thank you, baby. I needed that." She grinned peppering his chest with light kisses.

Protective arms engulfed her, giving her a squeeze. "Are you sure you're not mad at me, you know, for denying you my cock for a month?"

"Not at all. That was worth the wait, for sure." She stretched her neck, seeking out his lips. Their tongues teased each other, slowly stoking the fire that burned within them.

After several minutes of heated kissing, Jayden pulled away. "Mrs. Masterson, if we continue, I won't have the control not to have my wicked way with you again." He rocked his pelvis at her with a smirk, making sure she was aware he'd recovered and was ready to go again.

Tender from the round they'd just gone, after a month without, she wasn't sure she could handle another go at the moment. To placate him, she reached down and wrapped her hand around his stiff cock. Squeezing, she slid her palm over his satiny flesh.

Jayden placed a hand over hers, stopping her motions. He leaned in and kissed her, letting her feel all the love he held for her, until they couldn't breathe. With a contented sigh they parted, letting their heavy heads fall against the covers.

Erin giggled, then her whole body shook as she gave in to laughter.

"Care to share with me?" His nose teased along her neck, tucking behind her ear.

"That has got to go down as one of the best consummations in history!"

Jayden's laugh barked out, letting her unfettered happiness match his own. "I'd have to agree with you, Mrs. Masterson." His arms came around her waist, hands resting on the curve of her ass for a second before he scooped her up and headed toward the bathroom.

"How about a quick shower and then we can take a nap before landing?"

"Sounds perfect, baby," she murmured and nuzzled into his salty neck. Her feet landed on the floor, and she leaned on the counter while the water warmed up. They rinsed off and made their way back to the bed. Folding back the covers, they crawled in naked. Erin backed into Jayden's waiting arms, and he pulled her snug against him.

"Jayden?"

"Hmm?"

"I love you."

He smiled and kissed the back of her head. "Lucky me."

ೲ
CHAPTER FORTY
ೲ

"**C**ead mile failte romhat!"

Erin smiled at the little old man who greeted them on the tarmac at Shannon. His hair was white with a hint of red still visible on the tips when the sun hit it right, and his eyes had a sparkle to them that just made her feel. . . happy. Or it could've been the sincerity of the traditional greeting she'd almost forgotten.

Jayden dipped his head so his question for her ears alone. "Can you translate, sweet girl?"

With a giggle she explained it meant "a hundred thousand welcomes" then proceeded to help him return the sentiment, slowly sounding out and enunciating each syllable for him to repeat while the bright-eyed man looked on with amusement. "Kade meela," she began.

"*Cead mile.*" His tongue rolled around the words with a smooth cadence.

"Fall-cheh."

"*Failte.*" Now he licked his lips.

The final word slipped from her mouth on a whisper: "Row-itt."

"*Romhat.*" She nodded, and his smile grew. "*Cead mile failte romhat!*" Jayden reiterated with enthusiasm, the accent and words flowing seamlessly from his mouth and cocooning her for some strange reason. Perhaps because to get the accent right, he'd had to adjust his tenor, and the lyrical language was being delivered with an undercurrent of her Master's presence.

"Aye, sir, well done," praised the man who now stepped forward and extended his hand. "Seamus McInerney at your service. Welcome to the Emerald Isle. I've got your car waiting just over there." He nodded over his shoulder, and Erin assumed the lone car that was running idle a few feet away was the one he referred to.

Jayden shook Seamus' hand and reached around her to place his palm against the small of her back to guide her toward the waiting car. Mr. McInerney acted as their tour guide, pointing out and talking about the sights while the miles disappeared behind them en route to their destination, Bunratty Meadows Bed and Breakfast.

☙❧

"What are you up to, you little minx?" Jayden asked and cocked his eyebrow at her.

She'd woken before him and had taken a quick shower to wake up more. They'd consummated their marital vows on the plane then crashed when they reached the bed and breakfast. Now that they'd rested and had a chance to freshen up, *Catherine* wanted to consummate their D/s vows, too.

"Please, this girl needs more. She needs to be punished," the redhead said, lowering her eyes to watch where her hand stroked him, hoping he'd catch on.

He said nothing at first and made no move to stop her hand from palming his decorated cock. At last, he broke the silence. "And why do you think you need to be punished, Catherine?" he crooned in the sultry Dom voice that always sent her pulse off on a gallop.

Her girly parts did a mini dance at his acknowledgement of her desire to play. Catherine racked her brain, trying to come up with some indiscretion that she could admit to. *Dammit, why did I have to be so good all the time?*

"Catherine, answer me," he ordered.

She swallowed and went for honesty. "Your girl has not actually done anything wrong, Master. She just misses the feel of her Master's hand on her ass."

"I see."

She could've sworn she'd heard a hint of amusement in his voice, but she kept her eyes lowered instead of looking up to gauge his reaction.

"Very well, *slut*," he purred, and her pussy purred back, "on your knees."

Catherine gave his cock one last tug before letting go to get on her knees. His strong fingers pressed against her back, indicating she should lean forward, while he whispered in her ear. "On your elbows as well. Spread your knees wide. I want to be able to see the excitement in your cunt dripping out and running down your thighs."

Shit. How she loved it when he talked dirty to her. Without any hesitancy, Catherine leaned forward and spread her legs as wide as she could.

"I'm going to blindfold you, Catherine, so that you can focus on the attention your ass is about to get," he said then covered her eyes with her silk robe.

The submissive's body trembled and tingled at his words while his fingertips brushed over her back in slow, lazy circles. With her sense of sight gone, she was able to zero in on the sensation of his touch, shooting fire across her skin. With no warning, his hand came down on her right ass cheek. She exhaled sharply while the sting faded into a dull throb.

"What do you say, Catherine?"

"Thank you, Master. Please, may this girl have another?" *Smack.* He connected with the left cheek, and she followed with a "Thank you," then asked for yet another.

The next two came in rapid succession, landing an inch apart. "Thank you!"

"Fuck, slut! The sight of your ass turning pink under my hand makes my cock throb." Master moaned and rubbed the head of his cock across her ass.

With a grunt, she pushed back against him, which earned her two more slaps.

"Be still."

"Aye, Master. Your girl is sorry, Sir. May she have another?" Catherine's skin sizzled as her whole body reacted, becoming almost painfully aroused under his ministrations while she panted through her breathing.

Another slap landed on her gaping pussy and she let out a feral sound. Master's finger circled her opening before pushing inside at an agonizing pace. He pulled it out, then pushed it back in, adding a second finger.

"My, my, Catherine. You have a very messy cunt." The bed shifted when he knelt beside her head to push the sloppy fingers into her mouth. Her eagerness in sucking them clean was commendable.

"Do you like the taste of your cunt, slut?"

"Aye, Master," she ground out.

Master shifted his body again, moving his hand between her legs to stroke her puffy outer labia. With a possessive hold, he cupped her pussy, holding it tight for several seconds before dragging his hand upward to spread her arousal up into the crack of her ass. She laid there, trying to be still and control her breathing while he repeated the action several times. The rhythmic stroke was broken when his hand came down on her at the same moment he slid a stealth finger into her asshole.

"Shit!" She gasped in surprise. "Th-thank you, Master." The submissive was willing herself not to come, trying to think of something to distract herself, finding that she was unable to do anything but ... feel. His next words were her undoing.

"I wonder," he mused. "The desk clerk was cute. Should I call down and invite her to come clean up this sloppy cunt of yours?" He worked a second finger into her ass then and began scissoring them, stretching her. "I saw the way she was looking at you when we checked in. She looked even hornier than the flight attendant who was eye-fucking you. Do you think the clerk would lay under you and suck all of your come out while I fuck your ass?" He emphasized his question by adding a third finger into her ass and letting his thumb enter her pussy.

Her orgasm sprayed out of her unexpectedly, leaving her sure she'd soaked the bedspread. "Oh, god. I'm sorry, Master. I tried not to come, but your touch . . . your words . . ." Catherine rambled until a sharp smack on her ass quieted her.

"Oh, Catherine, if only we were at home in the playroom right now. The things I could do." His chuckle was dark. "First you forget yourself and address me in the first person, and then you come without permission. Tsk, tsk."

Strong fingers were still working in and out of her, and his free hand had taken up rubbing her stinging bottom.

"But seeing as we're not, and I, therefore, do not have the proper instruments to punish you with, I'll have to settle for fucking your tight little ass instead." Master grabbed her hair, pulling her up till her back was flush with his chest. Catherine groaned when he grabbed her hips, lifted her, and held her over his cock. As he thrust up into her, he grunted in her ear, "Do not come again, slut."

₧₨

Once he'd rammed his cock into her, Jayden stilled to let them both adjust. He absolutely loved fucking her pussy, but taking her ass was pure heaven, a special kind of amazing. To put it in shallow terms, he loved how tight her channel was, and now, with the barbell in place, it was even more constrictive.

Her responsive whimpers translated into shivers that leapt from her body to his and back again. Jayden wrapped his left arm around her chest, pressing his forearm into the tops of her tits and holding her tight. "What color are we, Catherine?" It came out as a grunt.

"G-green, Master," she panted.

That's my girl. Jayden's little slut loved having her ass fucked as much as he loved fucking it.

He pulled out then pushed back into her, and they both emitted deep groans. After a few more thrusts, he reached around with his right arm and started pinching her rock-hard nipples. She could've cut glass with those things, they were so puckered and tight right then.

The Dom continued to fuck his jewel, treating both her nipples to the roughness she loved, pulling and twisting them, pinching them while her breaths came harder and faster. Releasing her peak, he slid his hand down her stomach to her cunt. Jayden had thought his slut was a mess before, but he'd been wrong. Catherine was positively creamy and slick now, potent arousal flowing out of her. With light, firm taps

Jayden slapped her, sending her into a frenzy that had his girl writhing and grinding down onto him—as much as she could in her restrained position.

That familiar tightening began in his balls. Jayden was on the edge, his release seconds away, and all he could think was how immensely proud he was that she'd fought her need to do so as well. By the way she was moaning and thrashing, he knew she needed to come.

"Yellow."

It wasn't more than a whimper, but he stilled all motions. "What is it, Catherine?" Jayden asked the question, although he was pretty sure he knew what she would say.

"Your girl is about to come, Master. She doesn't know how long," her body twitched and ground against his cock, "she can hold it." The pleading in her voice was beautiful.

"Then ask me." He thrust into her again.

"God!" Catherine gasped. "Please, Master, may your girl come?"

"Only if you play with your pussy for me, slut. Don't stop until I've filled your ass with my spunk."

Ever obedient, her hands dropped to her pussy. Once she'd spread her lips and started rubbing fast and furious on her swollen clit, he took up pounding in her ass while she screamed through her orgasm. Like the good girl she was, his pet didn't stop rubbing while he pumped in and out of her ass. When he roared out with the vicious orgasm erupting from him, Catherine followed him into the abyss with another release of her own. Jayden managed to pump into her a couple more times before he had to stop, his cock spent.

"Think this girl is going to need another shower before we go anywhere today," Catherine teased, and Jayden had to agree.

He also agreed that their honeymoon was off to a fantastic start.

෨෬ᲒᲔ
CHAPTER FORTY-ONE
෨෬ᲒᲔ

By the time Erin and Jayden got back to the room after their busy day of sightseeing, she was too tired for much else. She hadn't wanted to get dressed up and go back out again as they'd done every night of their stay thus far. Instead, she puppy-dog-eyed Jayden into running down to the local pub to pick up some dinner for them. After all, wasn't that what a honeymoon was all about? Getting to set their own schedule. Choosing what they wanted to do, not based on whether it was the correct time of day for the activity, but because their hearts—or stomachs— said it was.

Eating and relaxing in the room had been just what she needed, and she thought that, after she grabbed a shower, maybe they'd get a little frisky. The average daily temperatures weren't reaching seventy degrees, but the day's vigorous activity had kept her extra warm and sweaty. Even with the nice breeze they'd had while hiking around Bunratty Castle, the constant movement had worn her out, and now she had to peel out of her damp clothes. Humming to herself, Erin got the shower going while her thoughts drifted.

Despite the physical strains of the day's adventure, the trip overall had been surreal. Visiting her *maimeo's* grave a few days ago and introducing Jayden—in spirit—to the special woman, the local cuisine, the rounds of marathon sex, being old enough to do some of the touristy things she'd never been allowed to do on her visit as a child . . . all of it had been just amazing. Never in a million years had she expected these things to happen, but once again, Jayden was making her dreams come true.

In a bedraggled trance, Erin puttered around, getting ready for bed with a sense that something special was going to happen—an unseen force trickled through her veins, while hope for a drama-free future bloomed. She leaned down to spit her toothpaste into the sink, and when she stood up, she jumped. Jayden had snuck in, so his reflection from behind her was startling.

She let out a half-laugh when he stepped into the small bathroom and pressed his chest to her back. His arms found their way around her, nice and snug and comforting. "Hello, beautiful. Are you going to hide in here all night, or can I get my wife fed and then tucked in all nice and cozy?"

"Mm." Erin closed her eyes and reclined into his warmth. "I can't think of anywhere I'd rather be. Just let me finish up, and I'll be right there, baby."

Giving her a final squeeze, he moved away. "Don't take too long, Missus. This old man needs his beauty sleep after chasing your young ass around today.

That castle terrain was killer. Even you slipped." He lifted her hand to kiss the jagged cut on her palm.

"Aw, poor baby," Erin cooed back. "Thank you for humoring me and hiking all over the place. I thought the fertility stone would've been, I don't know, something more than it was after all the buildup from the tour guides. I really expected something like the Blarney Stone, not a small chunk of rock in an alcove. And I don't know what I tripped on. I was a step away and just wanted to take a closer look, but when I leaned over, it was almost like I got pushed. Guess I just lost my balance." She shrugged.

"The scenery was almost as pretty as the company. Trust me, the pleasure was all mine, *A rúnsearc*."

Tears welled in her eyes while she made a sound between a laugh and a cough. "Sorry." Erin wiped at the wetness then cringed when the salty liquid burned the wound on her hand. "Silly hormones."

"Shh, sweet girl. You don't have to apologize. Holly warned us you might be . . . unstable, while the Depo works out of your system. Another month or two, and your cycles should be smoother."

Cocking her head to the side, Erin was amazed at how lucky she was. "I know it shouldn't anymore, but it still surprises me at how cool you are with . . . girl things. It squicks most guys out, yet you take it in stride."

He chuckled. "I wouldn't be much of a kinky freak if a little bit of menstrual blood got to me, now would I?"

Scrunching her nose in playful disgust, she pushed at his chest. "Go on with your freaky self, then. Golden showers are still a hard limit for me."

With a boisterous laugh, Jayden raised his hands in surrender. "I'm going. Just hurry up because I don't know how much longer I can keep the big guy awake." He popped his hips forward, and her stomach clenched at the prominent bulge that now defined his crotch.

"Aye, sir, now get out of here before I wee myself."

"You sure I can't stay and watch?"

Erin laughed. "Jayden!"

"Okay, okay, I'm going. I'll find us a movie to watch while we eat our apple chicken and tomato tartlets, but then I'm eating you."

Christ on a cracker, the way he manipulated her when she least expected it. She was a lucky girl, indeed.

☙☙☙

"Goodness, but I'm stuffed."

"Not yet, but you will be," Jayden retorted without missing a beat.

He was in quite the amorous mood tonight, she'd noticed. Everything out of his mouth was suggestive, and he was managing to take anything she said as an innuendo. While her cheeks hurt from laughing so much, despite having just watched *Braveheart*, Erin was having trouble keeping her eyes open now that her belly was full.

Jayden leapt from the bed in an exaggerated movement and puffed his bare chest out. "You can't take my freedom to be horny!"

"Oh, my god, will you stop?" She tried not to grin at him, but as usual, failed.

He jumped back up on the bed, landing so that he had her pinned beneath him. "Never, my jewel," he whispered and lowered his head to nuzzle at her neck.

It felt wonderful, so she didn't fight the moan that crawled up her throat when he began suckling the skin below her ear, but turned her head to give him access. His hand moved up her thigh, gathering the edge of her cotton shift to drag it up with the motion. Large and warm, his hand found her breast and took up a gentle kneading that she felt throughout her whole body.

"Mm, Jayden, feels good . . ." she murmured, hoping to encourage him.

"Yes, you do." Jayden's lips had moved from her neck to tease her mouth, his breath hot and humid on her tongue.

Over the next several minutes, they worked to divest each other of the few clothes they'd worn to bed on the pretense of behaving. With each bit of skin he uncovered, he pressed his lips to the spot and kissed or bit gently, until she was naked and covered in goose bumps.

Sitting back on his heels, Jayden stared down at her lying below him. The look of pure wonder on his face made her feel like she was the most beautiful thing in his world. Under his intense look, all playfulness vanished from the atmosphere.

"Thank you, Erin."

"Why are you thanking me?"

"I don't know that I can put into words what having you come into my life has meant. Before meeting you, I never would've opened my home to a homeless pregnant woman. Written a check to set her up, yes, but invited her into my personal space? I don't think so. I never would have thought myself capable of caring about someone other than, well, me. Not on that level."

Erin scoffed, stunned. *Did he not realize what an amazing, caring, gracious man he was?*

"*A rúnsearc*, you are anything but selfish. I'm here today because of you, Jayden. You helped me find myself again. You brought my da back into my life and made his life better, too, by doing so. For the first time since *maimeo* Caroline died, I have a real family again because yours accepted me, no questions asked. And that's just the surface, baby. You are a good man, Jayden Masterson, and I'm the most fortunate woman alive to be able to call you mine."

When he lowered his body to wedge himself between her parted legs, she welcomed him. Tears of pure joy trickled from the corners of her eyes while he drove forward, filling her, showing her, in the best way he knew, how much she meant to him. She could feel the totality of their union in the tense line of his back, the tight press of his cock stretching her and hitting deep within. His arms shook with the effort to hold his weight off her, but she reached up and pulled him down, whispering encouragement through words of love and devotion in the meager space between them. Lips biting, licking, kissing. Hands roaming, gripping, and squeezing. Hips grinding. Lost in ecstasy, the couple reached the pinnacle together, then jumped over into the abyss one after the other.

Trembling, he stopped the luscious roll of his pelvis against hers. Muscles rigid and tendons protruding, Jayden barely held his body off hers while the unmistakable heat of his come spilling inside drew a gasp from her as Erin cried out his name in blissful abandon.

"I love you, Erin."

"Lucky me."

ഇരൻ
CHAPTER FORTY-TWO
ഇരൻ

"Erin, wake up, sweet girl. We'll be landing soon." Jayden kissed her nose and inhaled her scent, a feeling of contentment swelling inside. He was relaxed, refreshed, and on cloud nine. His life was damn near perfect.

She blinked, and the green of her eyes still took his breath away when they were turned on him.

"Want to share what you're thinking, baby?" Her voice was soft and sleepy, and her smile warm.

"That I can't wait to get home with my wife by my side to start the rest of our forever."

"Home." Erin's lips brushed his. "I like the sound of that. I'll never forget this trip, Jayden. It was more than anything I could've dreamed, but I'm ready for our own bed."

Jayden laughed. She had him there. "You, naked in our bed, does sound good."

Erin rolled her eyes but laughed while she straightened and stretched as best she could. "I also miss Matthew and Natalie, of course. How big do you think he's gotten in the three weeks we've been gone?"

He shrugged, not having a clue. "It'll be good to see the little guy."

Overhead, the pilot's voice crackled out the usual spiel, welcoming them to Dallas, where the weather was sunny and mild with a chance of showers later that night. Jayden had sent the company jet back, so they were flying commercial home.

The next hour passed without event. They landed, got their luggage, and made their way out to the curb. Jayden had arranged for a hired car since they were returning on Micah's day off, so when they found Landon and Paige waiting for them, he went on high alert. Erin didn't seem alarmed, just excited as she rushed forward to hug her friend.

"Landon." Jayden reached out to accept his friend's extended hand. "What's up?"

His friend chuckled. "Why would anything be up?"

Checking that Erin was wrapped up in eager chatter with Paige, he led Landon around the back end of the car to the trunk. In a lowered voice, he laid it out. "I know we're close and all, but I doubt you missed us so much you had to see us the second we were back on Texas soil. So spill. What's going on?"

"You always were too smart for your own good. Alright," Landon drew in a breath, "Natalie—"

"Is Matthew okay?" A sensation like he'd been punched in the gut surged through Jayden. He recognized it, because it was always present where Erin was concerned: worry . . . and love.

Landon's hands came up in a time-out gesture. "Matthew is fine. Jillian's with him."

"My mom? She was supposed to go home two weeks ago. Where's Natalie?"

Now Landon's gaze shifted down to where he toed at the asphalt with the point of his worn cowboy boot.

"Dammit, Landon. You're freaking me out. What the fuck, dude?" Jayden's stomach lurched up into his throat when his friend's melancholy blue eyes looked up.

"She left, Jay."

ᏣᏛ

"What's the matter, Mom? Out of practice?" Jayden teased. He couldn't remember having ever seen her so frazzled. Usually she was the perfect Southern lady, coiffed and ready to host.

"Shut it, son. Keeping up with a baby is a lot harder at sixty-three than it was in my twenties. You should be thanking me for not interrupting y'all's honeymoon."

Matthew squawked then began fussing, gaining volume with each second.

"Here, Jillian, let me." Erin took the little boy and brought his tiny body in against her chest. The crying stopped the moment he'd nuzzled into her.

An involuntary grin tugged at Jayden's lips seeing Matthew's chubby hand splayed possessively over Erin's round breast. He could relate—her boobs were a very happy place. A few minutes later, the baby was asleep, and Erin took him upstairs to put him down in the bassinet.

Sparing a thought for it, he realized they would need to get a nursery set up pronto. *Maybe if they'd done that earlier, Natalie wouldn't have left.* He didn't know what to think of the situation. He'd thought that they'd made it clear over the past months that she and the baby were welcome to stay on at the Villa.

When Erin returned, baby monitor in hand, the small group moved to the living room. Paige joined them moments later with the tea and coffee service she'd prepared while Erin was seeing to Matthew.

"Okay, Mom. Start at the beginning. We left for Ireland, then what?"

"Everything seemed normal—for the first few days. Natalie came across as tired but attentive, like most new moms."

"That's understandable. Her delivery was more than she'd expected, even with the birth classes," Erin said.

Jillian nodded. "So I did what any grandmother worth her salt would do. I told her I'd stay and help until you guys returned. Call it a gut feeling, but I sensed she shouldn't be left alone, even though Dr. Ellison had given her the all-clear to resume regular physical activity. The look of relief on her face told me I'd done the right thing." She paused to sip her coffee.

"Over the next few days she withdrew, almost like—"

"She was distancing herself," Landon interjected.

Erin shook her head and huffed. "I get being tired, but how could she abandon her son? Matthew is innocent!"

She'd slid to the edge of the couch, her body language suggesting she would be up and pacing next. Jayden laid his palm on her thigh to calm her. Of course this was unfathomable to his jewel. "Let's hear them out, sweet girl."

"That's just it, Erin. Matthew is innocent in all of this, and Natalie understood that. I really believe it was her good heart that made her leave," Jillian consoled in a soft, motherly tone. "Like I said, she pulled back once she knew I was staying. She went from keeping us company during bath time or feeding time to not showing up. If I went looking for her, I found her asleep in her room or just staring out the window. After two days of her refusing to use Matthew's name, I called Landon. I didn't know what else to do."

"You did well, Mom. While I'm sorry you had to step up and handle this, I'm so very grateful that you were here to do so."

"Of course, son. You know how much I love babies." Jillian smiled. "Paige has been a godsend, too, helping me with Matthew while Landon sorted Natalie out." She paused then grimaced. "Gosh, that sounds awful."

A collective chuckle traveled the room.

"We get what you're saying, Jillian. No worries." Erin settled back into the couch, leaning against Jayden's side. "Were you able to learn anything from her?"

"Short answer?" Landon looked around the room.

"For starters," Jayden replied.

"Even though it kills her inside, she can't bring herself to love that little boy."

Erin's hand went to her mouth, and she made a small choking noise. Jayden squeezed her thigh, a silent *I've got you*. "Okay, Landon, maybe a little more than the short answer."

Landon stood, his hand rubbing his chin while he prepared to speak. "I'll try to sum up what she shared in combination with what I determined from my visits with her."

"Sounds good."

"Natalie's young. Who knows where she'd be right now if you hadn't helped her that day outside the club," Landon started.

Jillian shot him an inquisitive look, and Jayden explained. "It's a place downtown where we sometimes go for an evening out, Mom. I happened to notice her hiding in the shade of the awning one day, looking rather distraught. Since I know the club owner, I brought Natalie inside. Ended up getting her a job."

"Oh, Jayden. You make your momma proud."

"He is pretty great," Erin piped up.

"Enough, you two. Let Landon speak." Jayden didn't like all this attention on him. He'd just done what anyone would have if they'd been able. *What was the big deal?*

"Anyway," Landon resumed, "Her life wasn't exactly stable. Meeting Poles was unfortunate for her but not anyone's fault. We went over all this last year when we found out. Yes, he was a pig and an ass, but other than what you walked in on, he never broke any rules. All protocol was followed. That being said, Natalie still felt responsible. In her mind, she led him on and asked for what happened. She resents him, has nightmares about what he did to her, and deep down she believes she'll always hold that against Matthew, in particular if he ends up looking anything like Dominick, which that red hair is suggesting he will."

In a small whisper, Erin interrupted. "But he's half of her, too."

Jayden spoke up next. "And that's why she left. I get it."

"I guess. I just can't imagine leaving a child of mine if I were able to have one someday."

The room grew quiet while Jayden pulled Erin in for a hug.

"About that . . ." Landon cleared his throat. "Natalie didn't just vanish in the night. She asked for my help in getting some things put in place before she left."

Jayden glanced up. "Oh?"

"Everything is set for you guys to adopt Matthew. The paperwork just needs your signatures."

CHAPTER FORTY-THREE

Late September found the international side of his business booming, so it'd been necessary for Jayden to travel to China. He'd been there for two weeks, handling account matters that needed his personal, face-to-face attention, while Erin stayed home, holding down the fort.

In his absence, she was going to work during the day then trying to distract herself in the evenings once Matthew was down. They'd hired Kaitlyn,

Katarina Svenson's submissive, to come babysit Matthew while Erin was at work. She was lucky to have Paige swinging by to check on her and helping get a nursery sorted out for the boy. More than once, Erin had taken her friend's offer to lay down for an early evening nap. Jillian hadn't been kidding about a baby being draining, in particular on top of working a full-time schedule. However, she wouldn't trade it for anything. Besides, between adopting Matthew and their decision to go forward with attempting to get pregnant, Jayden had convinced her to stop being stubborn and turn her notice in at work. They didn't *need* her paycheck, but they did need her not to be exhausted.

With the time difference, she hadn't been able to talk to her lover every day. Jayden wanted her resting and storing up her energy for their reunion, not staying up until the middle of the night for a phone call.

"Hello!" Her answer was breathless, since she'd run to the phone from the porch, where she'd been reading and enjoying a smoothie for dinner. Another hour and the temperature would begin descending, but it was a balmy seventy-three right then. A perfect fall evening.

"Good evening, Catherine." The firmness of his voice seeped through the phone like molasses and coated her skin, suggestive and arousing.

She shuddered before replying, "Good evening, Master."

"How was your last day at work, sweet girl?" he inquired, becoming less formal.

So he wants to chit-chat. Oh-kay. She rolled her eyes. Playtime sounded more fun.

"Bittersweet, I guess."

"How so?"

"I'd—" she started, but was cut off by his throat clearing. "Sorry," Catherine whispered. "This girl had made some friends she'll miss. But she is quite excited to be starting the next leg of our journey, Master."

"As am I, my jewel." She heard his smile through the phone.

Today had been the end of her two-week notice at work. Though she loved the job, she and Jayden wanted to focus on their family. The short time they'd shared with Matthew in the picture had solidified that decision. The baby's addition had also taken all pressure off the couple. They wanted siblings for him, but knew if they weren't able to have any of their own, they'd always have Matthew to love, and that would be enough.

Dr. Ellison had discovered damage to Erin's cervix early on in her relationship with Jayden. In all likelihood, the scarring was from Spencer's improper use of the cane on her. Her doctor was concerned how far into term Erin would be able to carry a child before her cervix collapsed, triggering a premature delivery.

Erin had an appointment in the morning so Holly could collect all the baseline information needed before they began the active attempt to conceive a baby. They'd left for Ireland under the assumption they'd be coming back to work on a first baby, not a sibling, but no matter. The road ahead was likely to be a long one, and the sooner they got started on it, the sooner there might be a brother or sister for Matthew. Once she got pregnant, cervical cerclage would be used to keep her cervix closed for the duration of the pregnancy. The good doctor had also hinted at extensive bed rest being a high probability. *Oh, joy.* Jillian had promised to be on hand if that happened though. They would need the help with Matthew.

They'd scheduled the physical so Erin would have her test results and instructions by the time Jayden returned home from his business trip. Their collaring anniversary was coming up, too, meaning some special time with her Master was long overdue. Three weeks would've passed before they were reunited.

"Just the thought of you all round, curvy, and glowing has my cock hard," Jayden's husky voice drew her from her wandering thoughts.

"Oh, my." She rubbed her thighs together, moaning softly so he'd hear what he was doing to her.

"Have you missed your Master's cock, my sweet slut?"

"Aye, Master." A tiny whimper slipped out.

"Have you been a *good girl* and followed your Master's orders, Catherine?"

"Aye, Master. Your *cailin maith* has used the mock-cock each night you've been away to reach the edge of orgasm and then stop. She has not come." *She's been too tired to*, Catherine thought with wry amusement.

"Very good, pet. You've earned a reward, then, I think."

The grin splitting her face was wide, but she kept her voice calm, "Thank you, Master." How he'd arranged a reward for her from the other side of the world, she didn't know. It was not her place to question, only to accept and enjoy.

"In a moment, we're going to hang up. You'll use the bathroom, then go to the playroom and remove your clothes. I've left a laptop in there that I want you to boot up. Do not touch anything that is laid out without further instructions from me. I will see you on Skype in ten minutes."

"Aye, Master." Her finger hovered over the 'end' button on the phone, eager as she was to begin, when he continued.

"Oh, and Catherine?"

"Aye?"

"I love you. Don't forget the baby monitor." After some kissing noises, he disconnected the call before she could respond, and she smiled.

Seven minutes later, Catherine crossed the threshold into the playroom clad in nothing but her satin robe. The submissive's pulse picked up just being in the room. The dark colors, the strong smell of leather, images from her garden photo shoot on the wall—all reminders of the many times Master had awakened her senses and brought her to new heights.

She placed her garment on the hook next to the door, set the monitor down on the entry table, and turned to the interior of the room. A table was set up at the foot of the king-sized bed with a laptop and a covered tray. Across the foot of the bed lay a polished board with a notched, plastic ring mounted in its center.

Catherine fingered the edge of the cloth lying over the tray, wanting to lift the corner and take a peek before she turned on the computer. She knew better, though. Instead, she slipped between the table and the bed and flipped the on switch for the laptop.

While it booted, she leaned against the mysterious board and noticed that if she sat on it, she'd be in direct view of the webcam.

Before her mind could conjure images of what Master might've planned, Catherine shut it down. She was too keyed up from having been away from him for so long. Her nightly task had served to magnify that longing and need for him, and to say she hadn't been sleeping well was an understatement. The sexual creature she was, she was too needy to lift that cloth and risk turning whatever he'd planned into a punishment, rather than the pleasure that was sure to be waiting for her. All she had to do was trust him and give her full submission to him.

Taking her ritualistic deep breath, Catherine clicked the accept button on the webcam. It had been her full intention to lower her eyes to greet her Master when he came on the screen. However, she didn't do it fast enough. The moment his brown eyes came into focus, Catherine was trapped in them.

She stared for a few moments before his left eyebrow quirked up and the hint of a smile pulled at the corner of his mouth. "Feeling bold, Catherine?"

Heat washed over her body from the sound of his voice, and her eyes widened at her own carelessness. She lowered her gaze to the floor. "Sorry, Master," she mumbled, "your girl has missed you and couldn't help herself."

His soft chuckle allowed her to relax. "I understand. I'll let it slide this time, my jewel. Are you ready to play, Catherine? Look at me and answer."

A soft smile curled her mouth when she raised her eyes. In brief glances, she took in his chiseled features from his bare chest up to his strong jaw line, then she settled her gaze once again upon his eyes.

"Aye, Master. Your girl is more than ready."

"You have no idea how much that pleases me," he confessed while his eyes roamed over her body. "I've missed our time together. I'm sorry that I can't be there in the physical sense for this, but we'll take what we can until next week. What I've planned will have to be satisfactory for now. I assure you this will be all about pleasure, nothing too strenuous since I can't have you dropping without me there to care for you."

Her smile grew wider at his words. "Thank you, that is very thoughtful of you."

A slight nod was his acknowledgment. "First things first, Catherine. I want you to pull back the left corner of the fabric on the tray next to the laptop. About three inches should do. Retrieve the item you find and present it to me."

Following his instructions, her breath hitched when she unveiled her leather "slut" collar which he'd presented to her two years prior, on that fateful weekend when he'd proposed. Master reserved this collar for attending play parties or for when he had an extra kinky scene planned. Catherine's nipples hardened at the thought.

She picked up the adornment and allowed it to rest in her upturned palms that she held out in front of her while coming back into view of the camera. At his instruction, she fastened the collar around her bare neck. Her black pearls had been put away for the time being to spare them Matthew's death grip.

"Your servitude is always surreal, Catherine," he whispered, beginning their ritual.

"To serve you will always be divine, Master."

The familiar comfortable tightness around her neck freed her mind to get to where it needed to be. From there on out, the submissive would not try to guess what her Master's next move would be.

He would command.

She would obey.

৪৩)(৫৪

CHAPTER FORTY-FOUR

৪৩)(৫৪

"That is a lovely sight, Catherine. It'll be lovelier when you spread your feet to the markers I left on the floor." He paused while she made the adjustment. "Now, lift your chin high and bend forward from your waist, I want those tits dangling in front of the screen."

His voice was deepening in reaction to their exchange. The knowledge that she was affecting him, even though they were not in the same room, encouraged the wetness to gather at Catherine's core.

"Run a finger through your folds without stroking your clit, and show me."

Obedient, she presented the damp finger for his inspection.

"I know your body is capable of more than that, slut. Your nipples aren't hard enough, and that cunt isn't wet enough for my liking . . . yet. Let's see what we can do about that, shall we?"

Her body rocked at the implication of what was to come.

"You may straighten and return to the tray. This time, fold back the bottom right corner, then collect the items. Be sure to return your feet to the markers when you come back. Unless I say otherwise, your feet will be on those markers—when they're on the floor—for the duration of our scene. Do you understand?"

"This girl understands, Master." Moving the cloth back, she revealed two teardrop-shaped weights with hooks at their pinnacles. Catherine lifted one in each hand and returned to the markers, again presenting her find out in front of her body.

"Very good. You know what they are. Attach them to your nipple rings, but do not release the weights yet."

With careful dexterity, she was able to pinch open the hooks and connect the weights to her nipple rings so that they were attached next to her J's.

"Same as before, bend forward at the waist."

Palms cupping the teardrop weights, she leaned forward until her breasts hung away from her body. Catherine could hear her Master's heavy breathing coming through the mic while he left her standing. The anticipation was building in her body. Her legs were spread by the position of the markers, causing her pussy lips to part enough to feel the cool air conditioning on her inner labia. She itched to apply pressure to her breasts, to squeeze them and pinch her nipples. Instead, Catherine waited patiently.

"Look at me, slut," Master ordered after several minutes.

Her gaze traveled up to the screen, where his arm moved up and down in a slow tempo, his camera positioned so that his lap was just off the screen— hidden from her till he chose to reveal his secrets.

"Drop them."

At the command, the submissive pulled her hands away, releasing the weights. When gravity took over and she felt the delicious yank, Catherine breathed out in a whoosh. The violent stinging burn was immediate.

"Fuck, Catherine. Look at your nipples. Do you feel the weights pulling and elongating them?" His breathing was getting heavier, making his words almost incomprehensible.

Her answering, "Aye, Master," had to be deciphered through a groan of her own.

"How's that pussy doing now, my sweet slut? Has it gotten wetter for me?"

Nodding was all she could manage with her nipples still adjusting to the heavy pull. Each breath she took caused a searing flash of pain that disappeared as fast as it came, delighting her even as it tortured her.

"Stand up and use your finger to show me again."

This time Master hadn't said to avoid her clit, so with purposeful intent, the submissive pressed against the tiny nub when dragging her fingers through her wetness. She trembled at the contact, her breasts shivered, and the weights shifted. With her eyes down, she presented her finger.

"Mm, that's much better, Catherine. Rub that juice on your nipple until it's coated, then repeat the process on the other one."

Holy hell, he was going to kill her with all the drawn-out teasing.

Obedient, she used her own lubrication to coat her stretched nipples until they glistened under the dim lights of the playroom. Out of habit, she clasped her hands behind her back when she'd completed his instructions and awaited his next command.

"Catherine, look at me." Master spoke the words with a gentle lilt, coaxing her eyes up. "I appreciate your respect. However, for the remainder of our session, I want you to keep your eyes on me—unless I request otherwise. I won't tell you again tonight. If you look down or close those eyes, there will be a punishment with the aerated paddle when we are together again. Now, would you like to see what your voluptuous body and pussy-covered nipples are doing to me?"

He smiled, devilish and distracting. Her voice would not cooperate, so she had to nod again.

"I'm sorry. I didn't hear you, Catherine. Perhaps you need to beg to see your cock?"

Fuck! If she'd not been wet before, there was no question she was now. "Please, Master. Allow this girl to see her cock all long and thick and aching to be in her pussy," the submissive begged with no shame.

"Whose pussy, slut?"

She was quick to correct herself. "Master's pussy. It's your pussy, Sir!"

"Very well. Shake those tits while I readjust my position. Don't stop until I tell you. Focus on those weights and feel the pain in your nipples. That should help remind you who they, and that cunt, belong to." His terse words finished with a growl.

At once, she started to shimmy her chest. Catherine's nipples began to burn, and she started to squeeze her eyes shut but remembered his instructions and snapped them open. They filled with tears, not so much from the pain, but from knowing she'd slipped up over something so simple that

Master felt she needed correction. Even now, she wasn't doing what she'd been told—to focus on nothing but the pain. With determination, she shut her mind down and put more force into her shimmy. The weights shifted side-to-side, taking her hard nipples with them, yanking them to and fro until they started to numb. Catherine's breasts ached from the motion. With tears falling free and trailing down her cheeks, she heard his voice.

"Shh, good girl. You may stop now. You always take your punishments so well, Catherine. Look upon your cock."

His dulcet tones coming from the laptop speakers stroked Catherine's mind, calming her. Inhaling deeply through her nose and then letting it out through her mouth helped her take the final steps to clear her head and ready herself to continue their play.

When she lifted her eyes, the submissive was met by her Master's deep chocolate ones watching her carefully. She trailed her gaze down his chest, to his lap, and watched his large hand stroke his engorged flesh. A single drop of milky fluid oozed out, and

Catherine licked her lips, wishing she could capture the droplet.

"Do you like what you see, slut? Is longing to feel this cock, in any way I might allow, making your cunt throb?" His deepened voice increased the desire coursing through her.

"Aye, Master. Your slut would like nothing more than to be able to wrap her mouth, or any other orifice that would please you, around it." She taunted him back by letting a small purr caress her words.

He tightened his grip on the upstroke and let out a cacophonous groan. "Fuck, Catherine! I suggest you be careful with your teasing. It is my intention to allow you a release. However, I can and will change my mind if you aren't cautious." Master's threat was emphasized with a raised eyebrow.

Catherine whimpered in response and nodded, while keeping her eyes on the motion of his hand. She ached to squeeze her thighs together, but she couldn't in her current position. The warmth of her arousal burned trails down the inside of her thighs.

"How are the weights, Catherine? I know they're heavier than anything you've experienced before, so you may remove them if you wish."

The submissive didn't contemplate his offer for long. "If it pleases you, Master, your girl would like to keep them on. They are painful, but not unbearable, and they are assisting this girl in controlling her urges." He smiled, and so did she. She liked pleasing him.

"As you wish. Let's proceed. Step over to the tray and fold the cloth back another three inches. Present me with your findings."

Eager to see what awaited her next, Catherine was barely able to control herself while she followed his instructions to a tee. When she revealed a flesh colored dildo, she gasped, the moisture in her mouth evaporating. Catherine would recognize the shape anywhere since she knew it quite intimately. The dildo was lying inside what looked like a hospital basin, except near each end, a clamp had been attached, and one side was higher and curved inward—like a wave. At the base of the dildo there was a circular plastic cap with L-shaped notches on it.

She returned to her position, feet on the markers, and held the basin out in front of herself on upraised palms. Her confidence was high while she awaited Master's next instructions.

"Since I am unable to fuck you with the real thing," he punctuated his point by squeezing and shaking his swollen cock at her from the other side of the screen, "I hope this will suffice. Set the container on the board behind you, then get on the bed and position yourself on your knees, just behind the board. Go."

The basin placed, she withdrew, walking backward to get into the position he'd requested. Once Catherine was kneeling, Master continued.

"Show me you are ready, slut. Pinch those pussy lips and spread yourself open. Let me see that clit. Show me how creamy you are."

Catherine melted into the eroticism of the task, and her movements slowed.

"Wider," he barked out.

Her eyes were heavy, and she had to concentrate on keeping him in her sight. She pulled harder on her lower lips until her entrance was stretched open. He made Catherine hold herself like that until the evidence of her arousal dripped onto the bed.

"Perfect." Master licked his lower lip. "You can release yourself now. Remove the dildo from the tub and attach it to the ring mount on the board."

So that explains the odd shapes around the base. She lowered the dildo, lining up the notches, and then twisted it to the right. With it locked it in place, she looked back to him.

"The clamps on the tub are designed to attach to the board. Be sure to center it in front of the dildo," his instructions continued. "Move onto the board and kneel over the cock so that it's lined up with your cunt."

She shivered at the impact his words had on her. How she loved it when he talked dirty and called her filthy names during their playtime—the dirtier, the better. This was her time to give in to her baser side and embrace her carnal cravings. Catherine never felt more beautiful or more alive than she did in these moments.

The submissive shuffled forward on her knees until she felt the press of the toy against her outer lips. Surprised at first by the contact, she thrust her hips against it and moaned.

"Knees more forward, let the toy slide through until it's lined up with your fuck hole," he ordered.

Her moan was loud when she shifted forward. The dildo pressed against her clit for an all-too-brief moment before slipping through her arousal. Catherine rolled her hips forward until the toy was positioned as Master had requested. It took all the control she had not to plunge down on it and fill herself.

"I can tell by the way your tits are rising and falling that it's getting harder for you to breathe, you naughty slut. You can't wait to feel that cock filling and stretching your tight little snatch, can you, cock whore?" His tone was almost playful.

Her answer was nonverbal while her body trembled.

"Sometime in the near future, I will be mounting your pussy to that board while I use the real thing on your ass. I know how you love to have both your passages fucked at the same time," he crooned, drawing out and emphasizing the word 'fucked' so that she felt it through her whole body. "Perhaps I'll even gag you with a dildo so that you are, as they say, airtight."

Oh, God, he was going to kill her. He was certainly upping his game with the dirty talk. She supposed he was using the tools at his immediate disposal, his voice and words, since he couldn't use his touch or scent to work her into a lusty frenzy.

"Slide your hand under the edge of the board to your right, and pull out what you find."

She complied but had to lean to the right until the tip of the dildo pulled away from her, and she immediately missed it. At last, her fingertips felt something, and she tugged on it. It was a Ziploc bag with a black cloth inside. Curious, she uprighted herself until she was once again hovering over the dildo.

"As much as I would love to deprive you of your visual sense right now Catherine, you will need your vision soon, so you will not be tying the blindfold around your eyes, but your neck. Make a pretty bow for me."

The moment she opened the bag, the scent of his cologne wafted up into her face, filling the air around Catherine. "Oh, shit." She groaned wantonly and pulled the cloth from the bag, winding it around her neck. Another wave of lust rippled through her then, and she allowed her hips to lower, taking the dildo inside just a tad more.

Catherine was pretty sure Master was about to have her fuck herself with the dildo for his amusement, and she worried that she wouldn't be able to hold off her orgasm for long. The weights felt heavy on her nipples. Her sex dripped and throbbed. She had the erotic view of him still stroking his engorged cock. And now? Now, Catherine was surrounded by *Him*.

"Please," she begged in a soft whisper.

He stilled his hand and smirked at her. "Please what, slut? Tell your Master what you want."

"Oh, god. Master, please. Please give your girl, your slut, permission to move. Permission to come . . ."

"Soon, pet," he teased. "First, I want you to use one hand to open your cunt, then the other to pinch yourself. I want to see that clit pulled taut."

Catherine's hands dropped to her center and orchestrated the moves he'd just dictated.

"*Ungh* . . .fuck . . . need more please," she begged again.

"Tsk tsk, you naughty slut. Lower yourself onto the dildo about an inch, then stop." He waited for her to shift down before continuing with his verbal torture. "I should let you just hold this position and watch me jerk off for trying to tell me what you need."

Her eyes widened in shock. *He wouldn't, would he?* Not after having her tease herself with no satisfaction, no release, for the last two weeks.

She watched while his hand stroked up, twisted over the top, and then stroked back down. Twice more he went up, around, and down. When her breath caught, she was assaulted by his delicious scent.

Surreal

Again he made the slow circuit while she exhaled roughly, causing her breasts to sway. At least the weights served to help ground her, sort of.

By his fifth stroke, her thighs were beginning to shake from holding the precarious position. For the first time in a while, the word 'yellow' whispered through her mind. Catherine's eyes drifted closed, and she prepared to utter the word while the burn in her legs flared bright.

Her lips parted. "Yell—"

His forceful growl cut her off. "Open your eyes and drop that slick cunt all the way down right fucking now!"

At once, and with copious gratitude, she complied. "Aye," she cried out, delighting in the feel of every ridge rubbing along her inner walls. The submissive's eyes locked with her Master's in a heated stare.

"Watch me, Catherine," he demanded, and he opened a bottle of lube and drizzled a generous amount all over his cock. "Pace yourself with my hand. Let me imagine it's your hot heat working my

577

cock instead of my hand while I watch you ride that dildo."

"Aye, Master." Catherine's breaths came fast and hard while her gaze dropped to his lap, and she waited for his hand to resume stroking his thick cock. She knew he needed to release as bad as she did. His cock was swollen and dark purple, the tip leaking profusely.

His hand moved up his shaft, and she lifted her body until the head of the dildo was resting just inside of her. The submissive watched her Master squeeze his tip and she clenched her walls to mimic him. His hand slid back down, and her body followed.

By the fourth pass of her body over the dildo, she knew she wasn't going to be able to hold her orgasm off much longer. It had been too long, and she ached for release. The impact of the scene he'd set up for them was assaulting all of her senses, physical and mental, and it turned the desire burning through her into a raging inferno. It was time to beg.

"Oh, god. Please, Master! Please let this girl come. She needs it so bad."

Her pussy slid down the dildo, and he stroked down to the base of his cock, then back up again before he answered. "You may come, Catherine. Try to hold it off as long as possible, until you can't anymore. Only then are you to pull off that dildo and fill the basin with your squirt."

That was too much, her undoing.

Just as his hand squeezed his cock, forcing more liquid to ooze from the tip, she pulled off the dildo and leaned back on her heels while a geyser of come sprayed out of her. Catherine threw her head back, screaming her pleasure while her pussy pulsated and convulsed. The sound of her come splattering against the hard plastic of the basin was obvious, slowing to a pitter-pattering like raindrops on a window while she rode through her euphoria.

She wilted. Her shoulders slumped, her hands fell to her sides, and her head rolled forward. Catherine reopened her eyes to find her Master still squeezing his very rigid cock.

"You are fucking exquisite when you fall apart, Catherine," he purred at her.

She smiled and felt her body blush. *Really*? She could maintain her cool while she was ravaged and he uttered deliciously filthy nasty things to her, yet she blushed when he complimented her. It was laughable.

They held eye contact while he gave her a minute to calm down. "Are you ready to continue, my sweet slut?"

She nodded. "Aye, Master."

"Good, because I have a very large problem here that needs to be addressed. Retrieve the buckwheat pillow from the head of the bed and set it next to you, then detach the dildo from the board. You'll find that the bottom screws off. Remove the pressure ball just inside, then carefully remove the basin and pour that sweet nectar you've collected *into* the dildo, replace the pressure ball, and screw the base back on." His instructions were methodical, and he waited patiently while she followed them.

Once she'd done all he'd asked, Catherine looked to him, awaiting his next command. She wasn't sure how this set up was going to help get him off, but it wasn't her place to question.

"Now it's your turn to set the pace, pet. I want you to lie back and let your head hang off the end of the bed. Place the pillow over your chest; the weight should feel like my weight resting on you. Then you are going to give that dildo a blowjob. It is designed to 'come' with suction. I will stroke in time with you, but I won't have that sweet honey be wasted. You are going to suck it out of that cock and swallow it all."

Oh, fuck.

"And Catherine?"

"Aye, Master?"

"If you can make me come by the time you empty the toy, you'll be rewarded with another orgasm." He winked at her, and she laughed. "So glad you find me funny, Catherine. However, now is not the time for giggles. Suck that cock."

With the dense weight of the buckwheat pressed against her breasts, she dropped her head back, elongated her throat, and slipped the cock between her lips. It was still slick from being inside of her, and she spent a couple of minutes licking it clean while she hummed, trying to work the display for all she was worth. Catherine wanted to earn the right to come again. She wrapped her lips around the head and pushed the dildo into her mouth, then down her throat.

Master let out a deep groan. "That's my *cailin maith*. Such a good little cock whore, aren't you?"

Catherine nodded and took the toy from her mouth, pulling it all the way out while she extended her tongue to flick at the drops of liquid seeping from the tip, before plunging it back in. She kept her eyes open while she worked the dildo in and out of her mouth, making sure to hollow her cheeks for maximum suction each time she withdrew it. Master kept his word and stroked his cock in time with her sucking. If she pulled it out and licked the dildo, he'd release his cock and trail his fingers over the taut flesh to mimic her tongue.

The submissive's come was escaping the dildo, filling her mouth, and she moaned for Master's benefit each time she swallowed some of it. While she sucked, licked, and swallowed, he encouraged her with erotic whispered words. She knew he was getting closer by the rapid rise and fall of his chest and the desperate way he'd begun gripping and stroking.

"Just a little more, slut, I'm so goddamned close. Suck that cock. Make me come, Catherine," he cried out with an edge of heavy need.

Catherine made a split decision, not sure if it would work but hoping like hell that it did. She pulled the dildo out and stretched her neck back further while opening wide. With the dildo held just over her mouth, she used her free hand to apply pressure at the bottom, squeezing while sliding her hand upward. Just as the last of her juices burst from the head of the dildo into her waiting mouth, Master exploded. The submissive watched his come spray out of his cock, angling up toward his sweaty chest and stomach, in several thick spurts.

"Fuck fuck fuck fuck!" he hissed while his cock continued to convulse and then began to dry shoot. His balls were completely empty, but he was still coming.

It was his turn to collapse. His head lolled against the back of his chair, and his arms hung limp at his side. Though his brown eyes were hidden behind his closed lids, he had a lazy, satisfied grin curling his lush mouth. It matched the grin Catherine felt stretching her own face.

She waited patiently for him to recover and compose himself enough to acknowledge her again. At last, he opened first one eye then the other before he managed to sit upright again. "Dammit, woman, are you trying to kill me?" Jayden groaned. "That was, just, fuck. I should threaten your ass for that little stunt at the end, but I won't because I can't remember the last time I came so hard that my cock dry heaved." He laughed.

She gave him a coquettish smile. "Your girl is happy to have served your needs, Master."

"That you have, Catherine. Without a doubt. If you can stand, I'd like you to get some water to rehydrate yourself." Her heart thrummed at his need to take care of her.

On shaky legs, the submissive wobbled over to the mini fridge and retrieved a bottle of water, then made her way back to the markers and positioned herself. He had gotten a bottle of water and a towel by the time she returned. While she watched, he ran the towel over his tight abs, wiping away his spunk. She sipped on her water.

While he finished off the last of his water, his eyes looked over at something off the screen. "Jewel, my time is up. I need to get ready for a meeting. Before I go, you'll find a blanket at the head of the bed. After we disconnect, you have my permission to use that dildo to fuck yourself until you come, as many times as you want—or as many times as you can manage before Matthew wakes up for a feeding." He paused to look at her with hungry desire. "When you feel you can handle no more, I want you to just cover up with the blanket and give in to the sleep I know you'll want. After you've rested, clean the playroom and then I want you to journal, in detail, what you did with your time tonight. Write down how that dildo felt, how you worked it in and out of your pussy and mouth, how many times you came. All of it, Catherine."

Though she'd just come hard, she could feel the need building again, knowing he was giving her free reign for the rest of the evening. Catherine intended to take advantage of it. When he read this journal entry, he would be so aroused, he'd be unable to resist giving her the fucking of her life—she hoped.

"Aye, Master. Thank you."

"I've set the alarm in the room, you just need to turn it on. You have an important appointment in the morning, and I don't want you to be late. My schedule for the next week is all over the place, so I don't know if we'll be able to do much more than text until I can get out of here. A courier will be by the house tomorrow afternoon with instructions for our reunion next week."

His words were making her heart ache. It was going to be a very long week if she couldn't even hear his voice.

"Do I need to tell you to keep your hands off yourself after tonight, Catherine?"

"No, Sir. This girl is aware Dr. Ellison said there could be no sexual activity for a week after the stitches go in." Her lip trembled a bit, the nerves kicking in.

Sensing her mood change, he softened his voice, "I'm sorry I can't be there for this appointment. I promise I will be for all future appointments, though. We are going to do this together."

"Thank you, Master."

He chuckled. "Hmm, as much as I like the way that rolls from your tongue, I do believe this scene is over. I want to say goodnight to my wife. Remove your collar, Catherine." The command was filled with a reverence, an unmistakable love.

First, she removed the cloth from about her neck, still heavy with his scent, and laid it on the bed. She was going to be putting it on her pillow while she slept. Then she undid the collar and held it in front of her while beginning their ritual closing, "To serve you has been divine, Master."

"Your servitude, as always, has been surreal, my sweet Catherine. Thank you."

She leaned forward, setting the collar back on the tray before kneeling in front of the table so she could get closer to the screen. His virtual fingers met hers, their fingertips appearing to touch, though neither one of them could feel it.

"I love you, Erin, with all of my heart and soul," he whispered.

"And I love you, Jayden. I miss you so bad, baby." She sniffled under the threat of tears.

"Shh, sweet girl. Go on now, enjoy the rest of your evening. I'll have you in my arms in a week. Text me when you get home from your appointment, after you get the package from the courier service."

He blew a kiss into the camera, and with a click, his image disappeared.

She slipped the weights off her nipples and laid them on the tray, then finished her water and checked the baby monitor. Content she still had time to play since soft snores were the only sound, she picked up the dildo and the scented cloth and then crawled to the head of the bed, where she leaned against the headboard and draped the cloth over her eyes. The extra length of the soft silk hung down over her aching nipples, caressing them while they pulled up tight. With a smile, she spread her legs. Replaying their scene over in her head, she managed three more orgasms before she gave in to her exhaustion and pulled the blanket over herself.

C38O

Jayden's instructions from the courier when they arrived the next afternoon had included a plane ticket. Jillian came up to look after Matthew for the weekend so Erin could fly to Vancouver to spend their two-year collaring anniversary at the Wickaninnish Inn. According to the brochure, the inn was a hotel on the ocean that boasted amazing storm watching opportunities since the sea came right up to the picture windows. The place sounded amazing, and she couldn't wait to get there. What was a week? Nothing.

ഇൗരു

CHAPTER FORTY-FIVE

ഇൗരു

I t wasn't until Erin turned the shower off that she noticed the change from when she'd arrived an hour before. That amazing roar of the waves outside their room remained. However, now the symphony had grown—the distinct rumble of thunder chased the crashing water. The sound was hypnotic, and a tired grin tugged at her mouth.

Erin toweled off and worked a comb through her fiery tresses. After switching off the bathroom light, she stepped into their suite, hoping she'd be able to sleep. Jayden was due to join her in the morning, and after not having seen him for weeks, her excitement levels were through the roof. Her appointment with Holly had gone well, though she'd had some mild cramping in the days following the procedure. At least she felt as good as could be expected now, given the circumstances.

Crawling naked into bed, Dr. Ellison's words flitted through her mind. *"Please have a seat, Erin. We'll get to your exam and stitches momentarily. First, I've got the results of your lab work here. We need to talk."*

Despite her excitement, the surrounding ambiance soon lulled her into a fitful slumber. She didn't resist, happy to escape some of the hours before she could see and touch her man again.

���

While Jayden didn't like to flaunt his wealth, there were times when he appreciated being able to pull a few strings simply because of what he had accomplished with his life. Erin wasn't expecting him for another ten hours, but he'd wrapped things up and had managed to catch an earlier flight out of China. Arriving at the Inn in the pre-dawn hours, he'd collected a room key. Now he found himself standing just outside the door, debating over whether he should enter and wake her up, or go elsewhere until he was *supposed* to show up.

With a shake of his head, he slid the card into the lock. Two years ago, he never would've hesitated. Beyond that door was what he would've considered his property, to be fucked and used to his satisfaction, then cared for and returned to her pretty box until he needed her again. Now, though . . . Jayden was adamant in his belief that even if he and Erin were never capable of being physically intimate again, he would still live out the rest of his life as the happiest man on the planet.

The moment the door swung open with a soft *whoosh*, he could smell her. The fruity scent of her bath products lingered in the air, and he knew he'd find her clean and fresh in the luxurious bed. Jayden slipped into the room, his heart catching in his throat when he spotted her on the bed. The fluffy white bedding might've hidden her if it hadn't been for the halo of scarlet around her head. How he wanted to close the distance and scoop Erin up in his arms, but instead he pivoted and crossed to the bathroom after setting his bag down.

Jayden refused to touch her with half a day's travel grime on him. Peeling out of his clothes, he hopped into the shower for a quick rinse. He gave himself a brisk toweling off, then he stepped back into the main suite, his erection pointing the way. The man had been away from his lover too long, and now had every intention of ravaging her. He would be lying if he denied wanting to take her hard over the nearest flat surface. They could slow down and be gentle with each other afterward. First, there were carnal desires that needed to be worked out of their systems.

"Hi, baby."

Her sleep-tinged whisper pulled him up short, his head snapping up even as a smile burst forth, hurting his cheeks. There she was, his jewel, beautiful and radiant when she rose to a sitting position and the sheet slinked down, baring her torso. Frozen in his spot, Jayden took her in, soaked in the rosy creaminess of her skin while letting his eyes rake over her frame. His brow furrowed in confusion when he noticed extra fullness in her breasts. Then he looked closer, thinking back to their Skype session and remembering how he'd thought she had looked rounder then. He had written it off as a distortion of the camera. Seeing her now, in the flesh, he could still see the . . . extra. Jayden sighed in resignation.

Indecision warred in his mind. He could let it go, or he could start their reunion with a punishment. It was now apparent to him that, yet again, she had not been eating properly, except this time instead of not eating enough, it would appear she had taken the lazy route and grazed on easy-to-grab prepared foods. She likely had slacked off on her exercise routine, too. With her slight stature, it didn't take much for a change in her weight to show.

With purpose, the Dom took control and strode across the room, stopping when he reached the foot of the bed. Erin had begun to crawl toward him before he'd moved, but now she held perfectly still, like she sensed his displeasure. That didn't surprise him. Being the excellent submissive that she was, Catherine was adept at reading his emotions.

Could he let her infractions slide this time? No, he couldn't. They'd worked too hard in the last two years to get where they were. He could be 'just' Jayden later, able to tell her that she was beautiful to him no matter what. However, as her Master, Jayden had to correct her for the unhealthy eating. Her well-being had to be his top priority, even if it crushed her feelings.

"Get out of the bed, Catherine." The order was harsh. He didn't want to start this way, dammit.

Catherine kept her eyes down while she stood up, but he could tell she was chewing her lip, nervous. Without the protection of the bedding, her new curves were even more apparent while she stood there.

Shit. Best to just get this over and behind them. The painful tightness of his hard-on was gone when he stepped closer to her. "Would you care to explain your negligence, Catherine? Did you completely disregard my rules for proper eating in my absence? Have you allowed yourself to plump up so much you can't even fit in your clothes?" Waving his hand at her naked body, he barked the words at her, rude and hateful, and at once felt sick.

Jayden braced his resolve, expecting to hear her whimper or sniffle, or even beg his forgiveness. He was not prepared for her to start giggling. *She fucking giggled.*

What the hell? Had she been hitting the mini-bottles while she waited for him to get there? Anger started to replace the guilt that clenched his heart at having to be so harsh upon their reuniting.

With a confident boldness that quite frankly made his cock hard again, she raised her eyes to his. Jayden was taken aback by the elation he saw in them, liquid emeralds sparkling with amusement.

"Catherine?"

"Aye?" Her gaze now roamed his torso, searing his skin where it landed.

Where the hell was her submission? Why was she toying with him like this?

Confusion kept Jayden fixed to his spot when her hand came up to his face. Soft fingers brushed the hair from his forehead before trailing down his cheek, over his chin, and then down his chest. Jayden's skin was hot where she'd touched it, and he didn't stop her when she gripped his cock. He didn't want to stop her. He gasped at the feel of her tiny fingers closing around it.

She dropped to her knees and began stroking him, taking all control away from Jayden while he thickened and lengthened in her hand. Some part of his brain was telling him to put a stop to this immediately, but then her mouth closed over the head of his cock and he didn't care anymore. He wrapped his hand in her silken tresses and guided his cock into her mouth.

Erin swallowed around the head when it bumped the back of her throat. No more was said for the next several minutes while he took his time pumping in and out of her mouth. Seeing her on her knees with her lips around his length while her tits bounced as she bobbed up and down on him was all it took.

"Going to…" was all he got out before Erin took him all the way down again, burying her nose in his pubes, and began swallowing while he emptied down her throat. She pulled off, licking and cleaning him the whole way. Jayden collapsed to his knees in front of her.

"I've missed you." She giggled again.

"Come here, Erin." Jayden gathered her in his arms and hugged her to his chest. "I've missed you, too, sweet girl. Thank you. That was magnificent." He kissed the top of her head. "Can you answer my question now? I want to get that out of the way so we can just enjoy our vacation." He pulled away from her, his hands on her shoulders while he looked down at her, serious once more.

Erin's answering smile was nothing short of glorious. "Well, I haven't changed anything. I've followed my allowed diet and exercise program."

"Then how? I mean, you look beautiful, Erin. Honest, sweet girl. But if we are going to have any chance of getting you knocked up, you can't be too careful with your health right now."

She tapped her finger against her chin seemingly lost in thought. "I guess you could say there might have been an abundance of a certain . . . protein, responsible for the new weight . . ." she trailed off with a sly grin.

His jewel was trying to tell him something, but his travel-weary brain wasn't catching it and he shook his head. This was the strangest conversation he'd had in a while.

Her eyes darted over his face, willing him to figure out what she was trying to say. At last, she grabbed his hands and placed them on her stomach, then leaned in to share a soft kiss with him. The words she whispered against his lips would forever alter their life—for the better.

"Happy Anniversary, Daddy."

Jayden blinked several times, his mouth hanging open. Her words played on repeat. *Had he heard that right?*

"Daddy?" He choked out. "Erin, are you? Are we . . . shit!" *When had he lost the ability to form a complete sentence?*

Erin's hand cradled his face. "Shh, baby, take a deep breath." She laughed, and the sound was soft and comforting. "I know it's shocking, and that we weren't expecting it this soon. According to Dr. Ellison, I'm about two and half months along right now. A pregnancy screening was part of the routine lab work before we could start the course of treatment she recommended. We found out when I went in last week. It's been killing me not to say anything, but I really wanted to be able to tell you in person." She kissed him again, a brush of her lips on his.

"We're having a baby?" Jayden asked, still trying to wrap his head around it. While he knew they were ready to try, he'd been so sure it would take some time, and that it would be months before they maybe got the news that she'd conceived.

She smiled and nodded. "Looks like that silly Irish rock made a difference after all."

"We're having a baby!" Jayden whooped and threw his head back, laughing before picking her up off her feet and twirling her around.

"Whoa, easy there, tiger." She squealed. "Spinning, rapid movement . . . not good for my nausea." Her color paled a little.

"Oh, shit . . . I mean shoot. Sorry, *A rúnsearc*," he stammered and set her back down with care. Wow. They'd been pregnant for nearly three months already, a month of which he'd been gone. No matter what, he would not be missing another minute of this adventure. "How are you feeling? Did we go too far with the scene last week? If I'd known, I never—" Jayden began rambling, panic hitting him over the intensity of their Skype session.

"Jayden, stop." Her fingers touched his lips to shush him. "I've had a little bit of morning sickness this week, but not too bad. Our play last week didn't hurt anything. Dr. Ellison does want to meet with both of us when we get back so she can go over what we can and can't do, though. I think we made the right choice choosing a doctor from the club who understands and is aware of our Lifestyle. Oh, and I've already had my first craving!" she said happily.

He couldn't control the grin on his face. "Oh, yeah? What is my baby momma craving?" He waggled his eyebrows at her.

She rolled her eyes and smacked his arm. "Don't you ever call me that again, Jayden. I am not your baby momma. I'm your wife, and in about six months, will be the mother of your child," she scolded. "And my craving, Mr. Pervert, has been peanut butter. I can't seem to get enough of the stuff!"

Lunging for her, Jayden took her back to the bed, tickling her as they went. His heart was soaring at the sound of her laughter and the knowledge that he held not just his wife at that moment, but his child, too.

"Happy Anniversary, sweet girl," Jayden murmured against her mouth, then captured her lips in a searing kiss. He would make sure they both knew how much he loved them by showering them with attention and pampering them every chance he got.

ᔑᗢᘓᔑ
CHAPTER FORTY-SIX
ᔑᗢᘓᔑ

"**A**re you sure you guys don't want to know?" Dr. Ellison asked for the second time while moving the paddle over Erin's huge belly at their weekly appointment. Seven months had elapsed since their honeymoon. So many changes in such a short amount of time. Matthew was taking his first steps and cutting teeth. Meanwhile, Erin's body had swollen up like a balloon as it stretched to accommodate her growing angels.

She loved that Holly kept the gel in a warmer. The first couple of times, it'd been so cold the mommy-to-be had been a shivering mess. Catching Jayden's eye, Erin smiled, and they answered together: "We're sure."

He gave Erin's hand a light squeeze, encouraging her to stay focused on him instead of their babies on the screen by her head. "Matthew would probably appreciate it if at least one of them is a boy, though. Come to think of it, I might, too. Otherwise, we men are going to be outnumbered."

Erin smacked his arm, and he kissed her in retaliation.

Holly gave a soft laugh while she slid the paddle around, stopping to click and record measurements. She soon finished, and Jayden took up the task of cleaning the goo off Erin's stomach.

"Well, kids, everything looks good. Great, in fact," she said, giving Erin a smile. "The babies, while still small, are a respectable size for seven months in. I'd still like to see you get to that thirty-eight week mark, but if you go into labor at this point, I'm sure they'll be fine. Just to be sure, though, we're going to hook you up to the monitors for a stress test today. All you need to do, Erin, is relax, close your eyes, and rest for the next twenty minutes," the doctor instructed and went about wrapping the straps that would hold the sensors in place around Erin. "Comfy, dear?"

She nodded.

"Okay then. Jayden, you had some questions for me? We can go into my office while your wife takes a little nap." Dr. Ellison patted Erin's leg, and Jayden leaned down to place the gentlest of kisses upon the patient's lips. She hummed at her husband's contact.

"I'll be in the next room if you need me, sweet girl." He gave her one more peck for good measure.

She nodded and whispered, "Aye, Master," and a longing stabbed her when his eyes darkened. *Jesus, she was beyond horny.*

They left, and Erin shook her head with a sigh. Jayden had been nothing but kind, loving, and supportive while her pregnancy had progressed—a perfect gentleman. But she missed her Master. *God, how she missed Him.*

For the safety of the twins and Erin, Dr. Ellison had advised the couple refrain from all things sexual. Even a small orgasm had the potential to send Erin into early labor in her high risk state, so all activity had ceased once they returned from Vancouver. The last few months had been trying, to say the least.

Erin couldn't deny it had been difficult—the ultimate test in orgasm control—in particular when Jayden would slip from their bed in the middle of the night to take care of his urges in the bathroom. She understood, though. He was a man.

A very sexual man . . . with needs that she couldn't tend to right then because of her 'condition.'

Though the sounds coming from the bathroom had disappointed Erin because she felt it should be her providing Him release, they'd excited her too. The steady rhythmic *fwaps*, which always ended with a grunt or hiss when Jayden spilled his seed, never failed to leave her flushed and damp between her thighs.

Over the months, she'd offered the service of her mouth every chance she got. A pained look always crossed his face when he would decline, explaining that he knew what servicing Him did to her. He didn't think it fair to get her worked up into such a state when they could do nothing about it.

With a mischievous smile, Erin rested back into the mattress. Her spirits were high, knowing that her Master was in the next room trying to get permission for them to play from Dr. Ellison, and dare she think it, the prospect made her pussy wet.

⁋∞⁋

T he moment his naughty girl whispered the endearment against his lips, his cock had sprung to life. He knew Catherine wanted to play as much as he did, but her health and the health of their children came first.

Twins. With two babies and Matthew, they were going to have *three* kids running around. Who would've thought? It was a concept that had taken him some time to accept. What shocked him more, was that he was looking forward to having a full house. That first ultrasound appointment had been quite the shocker, and Erin had gloated all the more because of it. She wasn't letting him live down his initial tantrum over her weight gain. Jillian, not surprisingly, had been downright ecstatic when they'd told her the twin gene had surfaced again.

Once again, his wife had amazed him with her dedication over the last months. Erin had been so much stronger than him, not a single orgasm erupting from her body since their anniversary weekend so long ago.

Jayden, on the other hand, had been nothing but a weak male who'd resorted to hiding in the bathroom at night while she slept and he stroked. His releases were mere shadows of what he experienced with his jewel, his wife, but they were better than what she was getting—nothing.

Following along behind Dr. Ellison, Jayden was anxious to have this talk and get the all clear to play again. At the very least, he wanted to be able to take his wife in his arms and stroke her until she doused his hand with her fluids. *Fuck, I sound crass. Like playtime is the most important thing*. It wasn't; ever observant, Jayden knew Erin's mind and heart. The Dom understood that her need to submit was part of who she was the same as his need to dominate shaped who he was.

He was also pretty sure she'd caught on to his nocturnal escapades. Always so conscientious, the knowledge that he was seeking release without her had to be making Erin mental. Jayden wouldn't put it past her to have started questioning her own worthiness to Him. More than once, he'd tried to reassure his jewel and help her to see he wasn't, in *any* way, disappointed with her. Yet he still worried it hadn't been enough.

Jayden's always-present concern over the issue settled the bulge between his legs while he took a seat in the chair across from Dr. Ellison's desk.

"I got your message yesterday, so I kept your questions in mind while doing Erin's assessment. As of right now, I can give you the okay for some *light* playing. My final answer won't come until after her stress test is complete, however."

He let out the breath he'd been holding. "Thank you. Thank you so much, Holly. You must think I'm a horndog," Jayden professed with exasperation. It was how he viewed himself of late.

"Not at all, Jayden." She laughed. "Remember, I've watched you two interact in and out of the Lifestyle. I understand that Erin is a submissive and your life partner. Besides the physical limitations I placed on you guys, she's also had the mental limitation of not being able to escape to her happy place. That place that can only be found by a submissive when they submit to their Master . . . or Mistress."

He was pretty sure Holly added the last to remind him she also held the dominant position in her playtime.

"I get that you guys need this time together before the babies arrive, that's all I'm saying. Do you have any more questions for me?" she prodded.

Jayden took a moment to gather his thoughts. "I'm nervous, Holly. About pushing her too far. About hurting the babies. If anything were to happen to any of them because I allowed us to play a sexual game, I . . . I wouldn't recover from that," he choked on the final words.

"Jayden, look at me," she demanded in what had to be her Domme voice, because he didn't hesitate to react and his head popped up. "You are an excellent Dom, and you know how to read her body, what physical signs to watch for. There is no doubt in my mind that the woman in the other room," she pointed at the door that led to Erin, "wants to come. A lot. But I guarantee you that what she wants more is to get into her submissive headspace and please *You*."

"But her needs are more important than mine," he tried to protest, and Holly began chuckling.

"You two are a right pair." She came around her desk and leaned against it. "First, as your doctor, I will not give you carte blanche permission to string her up and whip her orgasms from her. I *am* giving you permission to play in a sensual, controlled scene that is mindful of any deep vaginal penetration. That would be unwise with her cervix."

Jayden wished he'd brought something to take notes.

"Now, as a sister in the Lifestyle, I suggest you think along the lines of teasing, shallow-depth toys, and the knowledge that every part of her is extra sensitive right now. Not just the normal erogenous zones, but her scalp and skin are so sensitive that a simple breath brushing over her will make her flush. Erin's breasts will also be different from the last time you did anything like this."

He felt like he was in some alternate world while having this conversation. "But—"

"No buts, Jayden. They'll be larger, her nipples and areola will be darker, and if you haven't removed those piercings yet, you should go ahead and do that. Her milk will be coming in when those babies get here, and neither she nor the infants will enjoy the metal being in the way."

A grown man pouting in public was never a good thing.

Laughing, Holly offered her help. "Tell you what. I have an assignment for you when you get home tonight. I want you to plan out a scene based on sensations and demanding your own pleasure. Plan it out down to the last detail, from how you'll let her know you'll be playing, all the way through to what you plan to do for her aftercare at the end. Full detail,

Jayden." She looked at her calendar. "I have an opening in three days, at ten a.m. on Thursday, March thirteenth. I'm putting you in that time slot. Come see me with your written plan, and we'll go over it together. If any part of it gives me concerns, we'll work it out."

A weight lifted from Jayden's shoulders. "That would be fantastic. Three days. Ten o'clock. Got it!"

"Okay, before I have to see the thing that knocked that girl up trying to escape from your pants, let's get back in there and check on Erin," Holly joked then lead the way back.

His jewel was snoring softly, a smile teasing her lips while their babies' heartbeats beeped through the monitors.

ℬℴℭ
CHAPTER FORTY-SEVEN
ℬℴℭ

The appointment with Dr. Ellison the day before had gone well. Jayden had even arrived early, eager to show her what he'd come up with. She'd been impressed, but she still made a few notes for adjustments to the scene and suggested a couple of different toys that he didn't have in his arsenal. After the appointment he'd called Landon, and then with his friend's permission, Paige, prior to going shopping. He wasn't going just for what Holly had recommended, but for some additional items

Jayden would need to bring his plan to fruition. After visiting the lingerie store Thursday night, he'd stopped at the florist on his way home from work Friday to pick up the last few items.

Erin had been napping when he got home, so he was able to sneak everything into the playroom and get it set up. It was safe to assume she wouldn't go in there, given she didn't expect to step foot in the room before the babies came. She had been adorable, and pouty, since Dr. Ellison had played her part and told Erin a little white lie—that it was in Erin's best interests to ride the pregnancy out and resume intimacy with Jayden *after* the delivery and post-partum recovery.

Her poutiness reached the point at which he was itching to put his naughty girl in the corner and flog her, tease her into oblivion . . . then fuck her senseless. Of course, the last he would have to wait for. He had every intention of heeding Dr. Ellison's warnings to the letter. His sexual satisfaction would not come before the safety of his family.

With an audible groan, he adjusted the growing bulge in his pants and looked around one last time. Satisfied he'd done all he could for the time being, Jayden grabbed the bag with his lingerie purchases and a red rose, then he exited the playroom. Next, he stopped by the submissive bedroom and arranged her outfit on the bed. The final touch was to put a couple of fluffy towels onto the warmer in the bathroom for later and text Landon that it was okay for him and Paige to head over.

Though excited to get this long-awaited evening underway, he left Erin to her nap. She would need to be well-rested for their session. He might also have been convincing himself to go forward with this.

After checking in with Kaitlyn—Katarina's girl, who'd continue to help out with Matthew during the day so Erin could stay in bed—and letting her know that Landon would arrive soon to take over with Matthew for the night, Jayden retired to the kitchen to prepare their dinner. Holly's final warning blared in his head. *"If you follow through with this, Jay, be ready to start being a dad. I can't promise this isn't going to put her into labor. Know this as well. My staff is the best, and your babies are strong and healthy. Remember, the odds of survival if delivered now are considerably high—in their favor."*

But did he want to take that gamble?

Waking and feeling quite refreshed, Erin was shocked when she looked at the clock and realized she'd been out about four hours. She'd needed it, though. All morning she'd felt anxious and achy . . . and exhausted. By the time the lunch hour had crept around, she'd managed to eat the grilled cheese Kaitlyn had fixed her before giving in and crawling into her big, luxurious bed.

Wait! Four hours? Jayden should be home, and I haven't even planned dinner, let alone started it!

Erin wriggled off the bed and waddled to the bathroom to relieve her bladder, which was threatening to burst. She washed up while deciding that tonight would be soup and sandwiches. She'd make it up to him tomorrow with a big country breakfast. Landon had given her his momma's recipes for sausage gravy with buttermilk and honey biscuits, and she'd been looking for a reason to try them out.

She'd throw dinner together and then go see how Matthew was doing. Feeling like a tortoise, Erin waddled downstairs and toward the kitchen, continuing to plan breakfast in her head.

It'd be an excuse to use the new juicer to make a fresh pitcher of orange and pineapple juice, and of course a pot of French-pressed coffee for Jayden is a must. Scrambled eggs with a sauté of green pepper, mushrooms, and onions folded into them would be delicious. Oh, and pears poached in their favorite chocolate port since the alcohol would cook off . . . her stomach growled, and she snickered at how hungry thinking about all that food had made her.

"Hello, sweet girl. Did you have a nice nap?"

Distracted by her mental menu, she'd made it to the kitchen without realizing it, but now she gave her husband a stupid grin and nodded. Her gut instinct began screaming at her. There was a gleam in his coffee-colored eyes, like he was up to something.

Jayden strolled toward her, then kneeled and placed his hands on her humongous stomach. "Hi, babies. Have you been good for your mommy today?" His lips pressed against her belly while he mumbled the words, and the babes started kicking and squirming in response.

Her stomach growled again, making Jayden laugh and rise to his full height of over six feet. He wrapped his long arms around her girth until his hands rested on her lower back, just above her ass, and began kneading. She groaned.

"Are you hungry, Erin?" They both knew the question was rhetorical while he applied pressure to her back, pulling her in against him. *When hadn't she been hungry in the last few months?*

Erin moaned once more under the onslaught of squeezy goodness, and her tummy let out yet another rumble that made both of them laugh. He kissed her nose and led her over to the table, where several covered dishes sat.

"What's all this, and why are you home early? Where are Kaitlyn and Matthew?"

"So many questions." He laughed. "Can't a man come home early to his wife without needing a reason? You, my beautiful lady, looked so peaceful upstairs that I decided to fix dinner and let you rest. Matthew has a babysitter for the night, so you and I can enjoy a quiet evening." Lifting the first cover, he went on, "These are just some light finger foods. However, the way your belly keeps going off, I'm now wondering if I fixed enough."

"Hey! I'm eating for three . . . I can't help it!" A pretend pout turned her lips down.

"Well, far be it from me to keep my family waiting. Let's eat, and then I have a . . . request to make of you," he said with a mysterious air, pulling out her chair.

Hungry and curious, she got settled into her seat and watched while he removed the remaining covers and served up their plates—avocado slices drizzled with olive oil, lemon juice, and black pepper, followed by bruschetta and shrimp cocktail. As if that weren't enough, there were also fruit kabobs made up of grapes, melon, pineapple, and banana slices, all speared together on sugar cane. The food had been meticulously prepared and presented with class. Erin couldn't wait to dig in, and she licked her lips while rubbing her belly.

It was while he poured sparkling water into their crystal goblets that she noticed the vase with a single red rose in full bloom sitting in the center of the table. In the soft light, the petals reminded her of crushed velvet. An involuntary tremor hit her when an image came to mind of being teased by those soft petals while they circled her nipples, then trailed down over her stomach and pussy.

"That blush tells me you're thinking dirty thoughts. Or are you just cold, sweet girl?" he asked in a deepening voice.

Jayden's words refocused her, while her skin warmed at being caught in her mental wanderings. She tried to play it off and act cool. "Maybe. Not that it matters right now, Mr. Masterson. Can we please eat? I really am starving," she declared, and her stomach rumbled once again in agreement.

"By all means, Mrs. Masterson." He gestured for her to begin, and she dug in with gusto.

They made pleasant conversation while snacking on the small feast he'd prepared for them. Their discussion meandered from how his workday had gone to the separate phone calls they'd gotten from their parents regarding coming to Dallas to help with Matthew and the twins after they were born. Jillian wanted to get there beforehand, if possible, so that Erin would stay off her feet and rest up for motherhood, while Woody would have to arrange time off to be away from the Flying M Ranch. Malcolm had promoted him from a ranch hand to one of his managers.

Once she'd thanked him for the meal and pushed back from the table, groaning while her head fell back, Jayden replied, "So glad you enjoyed it, because it was my pleasure doing it for you, *A rúnsearc*. Now, stay put while I get the table cleared."

It sounded good to her. With her hunger sated, she was more than happy to chill. He bustled back and forth for the next ten minutes, clearing the plates and putting away the leftovers, while she sipped her water. When he came back to the dining room after starting the dishwasher, his stance had changed. His posture was straighter, and his eyes had darkened.

If she didn't know better, Erin would have sworn her Master had entered the room. *A girl could dream, couldn't she?*

He moved to stand by her and took the rose from the vase. Erin held her breath when the tips of the petals touched the top of her hand that rested on her swollen belly. With an agonizing slowness, he moved the flower up her arm, dipping it along the front edge of her top and then back down the opposite arm. She was ready to start panting, and anger toward him began to simmer for the teasing—for starting something they couldn't finish.

"Catherine, I'd like you to go to your submissive room and prepare yourself to be in the playroom in one hour. Your outfit for the evening is on the bed."

The woman found herself speechless when He leaned down and gave her the kiss to beat all kisses—deep, hot, and breath hindering—and then strode out of the room.

Did he say playroom?

❦

CHAPTER FORTY-EIGHT

❦

The second Jayden cleared the kitchen doorway, he let out the breath he'd been holding. Part of him, the part that was Erin's husband, had wanted to stay and gauge her reaction to his instructions, except if he'd done that, it would've broken the mood he'd set out to create. Staying would've been akin to calling a time-out on the ever-present mind games that were so crucial in a D/s relationship, so he'd played his part and left. *Maybe the kiss had been overkill.*

In the end, he'd given in to the temptation for two reasons—one, to give her a taste of what to expect tonight, and two, to convey his love to her one more time before assuming their Master and submissive roles.

He should've known letting down the wall they'd put into place these last months, even just a little bit, was going to send him into overdrive. The man now sported the hard-on to beat all hard-ons, and they hadn't even started. Knowing it would be an hour before she'd join him and that he would need complete, total control to avoid giving in and ravaging her like a nefarious sex fiend, Jayden headed upstairs to shower and relieve himself. Perhaps knocking one out before they started would help him keep the beast at bay.

Positioning his body under the hot spray, he squirted a dollop of body wash into his hand, wasting no time wrapping it around his cock and going to town. Considering he'd become an expert at the quick wank in his efforts to get back to Erin's side each night, all he needed were a couple minutes of tight, steady strokes, and another batch of his spunk was washing down the drain.

With that out of the way, blood flow returned to the rest of his body while he washed. In his head, he went over his plans for the night one last time. When it was time to get out of the shower, his erection had returned in full force. *Fuck*. It was going to be a hard night—pun intended.

Though ready to get out, Jayden stood under the spray for a few more minutes, willing his cock to deflate. He refused to give in and stroke out another one, not when he was so close to stepping into the playroom with his jewel. With a sigh of relief, he felt the swelling relent at last, and his cock began softening.

It took him moments to get dried off and go to his closet. Jayden opted for Catherine's favorite Dom outfit for him—a pair of low-rise black jeans, a fitted black tee, bare feet, and commando underneath it all. Tonight was about appealing to her senses—all of them. Taste already had been handled with the dinner he'd prepared.

He intended to fill her sight with his image before putting the blindfold on her. Once Jayden took away her vision, he'd then begin easing her into the proper headspace, encouraging her to place all of her trust in Him, thereby bringing her total submission forward.

After a final look in the mirror, the Dom headed downstairs, pausing outside Catherine's room to listen at her door. A moment of wistfulness came over him when it dawned on him this was the first time in months that they'd not been attached at the hip when in the house at the same time. Sighing, he rested his forehead against the door and tried to picture her on the other side. That's when he heard it, a faint *"Jayden . . ."*

The Dom in him raced to the surface, and he grappled with his uncertainty. *Surely she isn't in there pleasuring herself? Taking what was His before they even got in the playroom?*

Like you just did, Jayden? A smug, small voice whispered in his mind, making him step back.

"Master," she cried out, louder that time, and without a hint of pleasure in her voice. There was plenty of panic, however.

Jayden threw open the bedroom door and rushed into the room. Her outfit still lay on the bed, untouched. Spinning around, he noticed the closed door to the en suite and hurried over to it to push it open, scared of what he might find on the other side. He relaxed at the sight of her grinning in the tub with her abundant red hair atop her head in a messy pile.

"Erin? Sweet girl, are you okay? What's wrong?" When she started giggling, Jayden's jaw dropped and he gaped at her.

"I'm so . . . sorry, Jay–Master," she stammered out while trying to regain control of her adorable giggles. Her green eyes glazed over while they roamed his body.

"Catherine?" The surprise of his appearance was now blown, but he'd be damned if he wouldn't keep up the Dom façade. "Why did you call me in here when you are supposed to be in the playroom in," he looked to the clock on the wall to verify, "fifteen minutes?"

At his question, she had the grace to lower her eyes. Her lip started quivering, and the smile vanished. "Well, your girl wanted to shave and, um, that was a fail because she can't even reach the lower part of her legs." Her lip trembled while she waved at her feet.

Jayden let his gaze follow her hand to see that her ankles sported a set of stubble cuffs. Suppressing a sympathetic grin, he asked in a soft tone, "So you called me in here to help you finish?"

"Well, that would be lovely, Master, but this girl thought you would be understanding and wouldn't hold it against her. This girl actually called for you because . . ." she trailed off, and looked away in a coy manner, causing his cock to react.

"Because?" He quirked an eyebrow at her to continue.

Her smile was sheepish. "Because I realized I can't get out of the tub," Erin whispered.

Jayden wanted to smack himself for not thinking of that possibility when he'd been so meticulous in planning everything else for this evening. He should've known that when he instructed her to prepare for the playroom, she would include shaving. *Way to be attentive*, Jayden, he chastised himself in silence, then he knelt beside the tub.

With a gentle shushing to allay her embarrassment, he picked up the razor and finished for her. Once he'd rinsed the area clean of small hairs and soap, he stood. She accepted his arms under hers, and he helped her rise out of the water and step over the edge of the tub. When he had her firmly on her feet, he released her and turned to grab one of the warm towels.

"I love you," she whispered near his ear while Jayden dried her swollen body, caressing every one of her curves with the soft, warm cotton.

He couldn't contain his smile when he swiped the towel over her belly and a small foot stretched the skin outward. Moving quickly, he kissed the little appendage before it retreated, then looked up to find Erin gazing down at him with a look of complete adoration on her face.

"As I do you, *A rúnsearc*." He stood to kiss her plump lips, which were turned up in a smile.

Their tender moment over and knowing she was okay, Jayden moved behind her to guide her out to the bedroom. He gave her ass a quick swat, earning him a small squeak followed by a low moan while she wiggled her derriere at him.

"Get dressed, Catherine. I will see you in the playroom shortly," the Dom instructed, reclaiming the mood with his departing words.

Jayden let his guests in when he passed the front door. Landon went to relieve Kaitlyn, while Paige accompanied Jayden to the playroom, where he lit the candles before they retreated to the shadows to await his jewel's arrival. He couldn't wait to see Catherine's reaction.

𝕭𝕮𝕭

*N*o one but me. Only I could get stuck in a bathtub. I feel like a cow, and I can't believe Jayden finds anything remotely attractive, let alone sexy, about me right now.

On instinct, Erin had called out for Jayden when she realized she wouldn't be getting out of the tub by herself. She'd been so excited that he was taking her into the playroom that she hadn't thought ahead before lowering herself into the warm water.

The look on his face when he'd barged into the bathroom had been priceless and endearing. In response, the giggles had poured out of her until she really looked at him and saw what she'd been missing for so long—her Master.

But it was her husband who helped her, making her believe with his simple touch that he found her beyond beautiful. He'd been so tender while finishing her hack shaving job, and then getting her out and dried off. However, *His* final reminder of what was to come—his hand smacking her ass—had left her standing there with a throbbing pussy.

Let's not keep the Dominant waiting, Erin.

She went to the bed to see what he'd chosen for her. White and lacy, Erin first picked up a scrap of material meant to pass for panties and slipped them on. They sat just beneath her belly, and when the material confined her, a sexy awareness began taking over her. Next, she lifted the matching gown from the bed and slipped it on like a coat, since it was open in the front. The wide straps were lacy, as was the rest of the top. She drew the sides together and tied the satin ribbons in a pretty bow to keep her engorged breasts from being bared. Beneath the ties, the top flared open, framing her swollen belly in virginal lace. The satin-finished hemline swished over her calves and sent goose bumps skittering over her sensitive flesh. The final item had been hidden beneath the gown—Catherine's play collar.

It had been too long since her throat had been enclosed. Their Skype session about four months ago had been the last time. Matthew's tendency to latch his chubby fingers onto anything he could these days was still keeping her black pearls stored until the boy had outgrown the grab-and-yank phase, whenever that would be. With a content sigh, she buckled the leather around her neck. *To serve is divine*, the words echoed in her head with her actions.

Her reflection in the mirror amazed her. Like a seductress, Erin looked bewitching, and she felt incredible. The messy up-do didn't detract from the ensemble but rather added to it, so she left her scarlet locks alone. With a deep breath, a feeling of excitement, and an air of confidence long absent, *Catherine* descended the stairs to meet her Master.

Stepping into the playroom, the submissive inhaled deeply and was overcome by the smell of leather, fire, and wax. She shivered and glanced around, discovering a white rosebud sitting under a low light near the door, like it was spotlighted for her. Low music pulsed through the speakers, not loud enough to demand her focus, but enough to add an erotic heartbeat to the dim room. Shadows from the candles danced along the wall.

Catherine picked up the rose, pausing with the thorny stem half out of the vase to see if there would be a reprimand. When none came, she brought the pearly bud closer to her chest and turned to face the center of the room. There was a single bright light over her kneeling area.

However, instead of bare floor or even a pillow waiting for her, centered under the light was a Z-shaped chair. She recognized it as one of those ergonomic office chairs that let a person kneel, but with support. Her eyes grew misty at the sentiment.

Master had found a way for her to safely be on her knees.

Next to the chair stood another table, housing a small collection of items—flickering candles, a length of chain, and a square of white satin. She'd just walked to the chair and was preparing to settle into it when first His voice, and then her Master, came from the shadows.

"Good evening, my jewel." In his fingers, he held the velvety rose from upstairs.

"Hey, sweetie. Aren't you looking gorgeous tonight?"

Catherine startled—open palm landing on her chest—at the appearance of her friend at Jayden's heels. "Oh, my goodness. Thank you, Paige, but . . ." her confusion stalled her words.

"Paige is here tonight to act as witness for us."

"Witness?" Her gaze dropped to her hands, then moved to the table, Paige, and finally, back to him while she put the pieces together. Everything was set up for a private ritual of some kind.

With a gentle smile, he extended the rose in his hand, "Catherine, will you partake in the Ceremony of the Roses with me?"

She glanced down to the white bud in her own trembling fingers and began blubbering. "Aye, Master Jayden." It was the first time she'd ever reconciled his two halves as one, and she knew they'd both felt something shift inside.

⊗⊙⊗

She was breathtaking.

He wanted to run to her, gather her in his arms, and get lost in her, but he refrained from such overzealous actions. In an almost enchanted state, Jayden stepped forward, and placing a modest kiss upon her lips, he murmured a reverent, "Thank you." Before pulling back, he reached behind her neck to unfasten the collar and begin.

Pivoting toward the table, he ran the leather choker through the candle flames, then returned it to her neck, buckling it. Jayden choked on his emotions when trying to speak, but he pressed forward, needing to get the words out. "By fire, this is my promise to you, Catherine. For now and for always, it will be my greatest honor and duty to protect and guide you. Like fire untethered, my desire for you rages on, burning away the negative influences of your past." He stole another kiss, then took one of her hands in his and turned her palm up.

Before she could think about it, he'd pricked her middle finger with one of the thorns on his red bloom. Catherine let him move her bleeding finger over the rose bud in her other hand, and they both held their breath while two crimson drops splattered onto the white landscape, symbolizing the giving of herself—her pure self.

The tears trailed down her cheek, unbidden yet welcome while she wordlessly proffered the bloodied flower to Jayden. He turned a thorn on himself and hovered his finger above the bud, letting his own life force drip and blend with Catherine's. Pressing their fingers, and thereby their open wounds, together, their union extended, making them flesh and blood— making them one.

At that point, Paige lifted the length of chain, and like Jayden had done with the collar, she ran it through the flames. "Each of these links represent different parts of your separate lives, coming together until the chain was formed. Passing it through the flame removes the bad and leaves the good. By accepting the binding, you both promise to be bound in heart and soul for the rest of eternity."

Catherine and Jayden nodded their acceptance and raised their arms, each holding their respective rose. Paige wrapped the length around their forearms and then the lovers tipped their flowers together in a 'kiss' before exchanging them. He moved to kiss Catherine's salty lips right after.

Next, Paige removed the chain and wrapped it in the silk cloth. She then took their roses and returned them to the vase. With a polite curtsy, the blonde wished them both well and good blessings, and then backed from the room, leaving them to finish their scene in private.

ಐಲಿ
CHAPTER FORTY-NINE
ಐಲಿ

Keeping her under his intent stare, the Dom waited, watching while Catherine's breathing settled after she returned to the z-chair until he could barely make out the movement. Only then did he approach her from behind. With head bowed and hair up, her exposed neck beckoned him, and he leaned forward to kiss her once, twice, and then he nipped her with his teeth.

She shivered but stayed quiet like the good girl she was.

"Good evening, Catherine," he murmured into the flesh of her neck, testing her.

Again, she remained silent.

His cock was already fighting to break free of his jeans when he hooked his fingers under her lingerie straps and slid them up to her shoulders. Rotating his hands outward, he slipped the straps off her shoulders.

"Beautiful," he whispered with a kiss to her left shoulder, then her right. Her breath stuttered, and his cock pulsed.

"Is my naughty girl excited to be on her knees before her Master again?" When she didn't respond, he gave her permission to speak.

"Aye, Master, but Dr. Ellison said that it was not safe to play."

He nearly smacked himself, realizing that she couldn't know that he'd coordinated this evening with Dr. Ellison. "Holly has assured me that everything I want to do with you is safe," he paused to swallow, "and that if you go into labor because of it, our babies are healthy enough to make their appearance."

"Oh." There was a brief flash of alarm in her eyes.

"Jewel, if you want to stop, we can. I don't want to do anything you don't." The decision was hers. Jayden would never pressure her to keep going, particularly if she was worried about their children.

She studied him for several moments before taking a deep breath and nodding. "Aye, Master, your girl wants to proceed."

The man circled round to the front of her, squatting to kiss the big baby belly with a wink. He stood back up and pushed her knees further apart, until they were on the edges of the chair. Jayden caressed her pussy before pressing his fingers into the warmth of her folds where he found her already *so* wet. He approved.

Standing back up, Jayden pulled his tee up and over his head tortuously slow. She was watching his every move, soaking it all in while her tongue darted out to wet her lips. He unfastened the button on his jeans and teased the zipper down. The flaps of material fell open, and he knew when she realized he was bare underneath, because she gasped.

"Have you missed your cock, my pet?" The Dom slid his hand into his jeans to grip himself, pulling his cock out of its confines. Her lips parted like she was going to answer, but she caught herself just in time.

Jayden went to retrieve the step stool he'd hidden earlier. Returning, he set it on the floor in front of her and mounted it. Not exactly 'sexy,' but it was the best he could come up with to reach her mouth since she was higher in the z-chair. She must've sensed that he felt a little ashamed of the setup, because she sniggered.

"Catherine, I can think of a better use for your mouth than laughing at my attempts to accommodate you. Now, why don't you open and show me how much you've missed this?" He pushed his jeans down over his ass, allowing his cock to stand proudly at attention mere inches from her face.

The submissive nodded and licked her lips again, leaning forward. She ran her tongue over his piercing, catching it with her teeth and tugging on it until Jayden moaned. Her tongue trailed along the underside, all the way down to his balls, which she took great care in giving a thorough laving.

"Fuck! Are you teasing me, you naughty thing?" Through clenched teeth, Jayden fought to remember to use sensual, dirty talk to tantalize her sense of hearing. It would've been all too easy to close his eyes and give over to the sensations.

With a nod, Catherine abandoned his balls, dragging her lips and tongue around to the top of his cock, right where the inked *E* was. She licked at the symbol then shifted down to the *R*, followed by the *I*, and finally, the *N* that branded his cock as *hers*. Her nibbling and licking teased him the whole time.

As soon as she freed him from the torture and wrapped her lips around him, sliding her mouth back down his length while relaxing her throat to get all of him in, Jayden grunted and shot his load down her throat like a sixteen-year-old getting his first head.

It was amazing.

Earth shattering.

Mind fucking blowing.

Jayden withdrew, his spent cock slipping from her lips while she looked up at him with a content smile. "Well done, my pet. I think you've earned a reward for that." He wriggled the rest of the way out of his jeans, leaving them on the floor. He took Catherine's hand, helping her to stand, and then led her across the room to the St. Andrew's Cross.

Leaving her there, the Dom went to get the things he needed for the next step. Jayden returned with the items in hand and set them on the floor before he returned his attention to his jewel. In quiet tones, he started telling her the things he wanted to do her, her flushed and heaving chest letting him know that he was affecting her.

Jayden moved in close, and taking her hands, he turned her so that her back was to the Cross. Slow and easy, he lifted each of her hands and latched her wrists into the waiting cuffs while continuing to whisper naughty nothings to her. She squirmed, trying to rub her thighs together for friction.

The Dom used his feet to get her to spread her legs a little, and then he gave the insides of her thighs a soft smack. "Knock it off, Catherine. You know that your orgasms belong to me, and you will come only when I allow it."

"Aye, Master," she whispered.

Jayden cocked an eyebrow at her for speaking, then with a small sigh realized he should probably lift that ban. "Catherine, as what I have planned next will be a bit . . . intense, I want to hear you while we progress. I need to be able to assess how you're doing. I won't do anything that pushes your regular limits, but it is of utmost importance, now more than any other time we've played, that you use your safe words because of the babies. Do you understand?"

"Aye, Master, your girl understands, and she trusts you implicitly."

God, she is perfect.

"*Cailin maith*," he crooned at her while running his hands up her thighs, curving in so that both hands brushed over her pussy where he could feel her arousal already seeping out. Jayden proceeded to move his hands up over her belly, seeking the ties to her top. With a firm tug, he released the neat bow she'd tied, and he was delighted when her enlarged tits held the top in place, the fabric pulling apart just enough to expose the valley between them, teasing him.

Stretching his arms out along hers, Jayden threaded their fingers together and leaned in to run his tongue from the top of her swollen belly, all the way up through that delicious valley to her neck, where Jayden sucked her skin into his mouth.

She tilted her head to the side and let out a soft mewling noise, driving Jayden to attack her neck with more fervor. When her mewls turned into whimpers, he abandoned the tasty spot on her neck, which was now marked, and trailed his tongue back down to her cleavage. Using his nose to nudge the fabric off her right breast, he then dragged his tongue across her skin, not quite touching the flesh, until he reached her hardened peak. He swirled his tongue around it, working from the outer edge of her areolae inward until he could suck her nipple, drawing it out and feeling it grow and harden further in his mouth, until at last he moved his lips from her flesh to the metal rings he was about to remove. Jayden captured one with his teeth and tugged on it.

Catherine cried out in pleasure.

Moving to her left breast, Jayden treated it to the same attentions the right had received until he pulled another cry from her. Satisfied that she was thoroughly worked up, he freed their hands from each other, using one to push the top back away from her chest as much as he could within the constraints of the Cross, while the other he slipped into her pussy, delighting in the way his hand became soaked while he stroked her.

Jayden knelt on the ground before her then looked up the length of her body to where she watched him with an intense gaze. "I'm thirsty, Catherine, and I want to drink from you." He bestowed on her a wicked grin before bringing his tongue to her dampened folds. "Let me hear you, jewel." Being gentle, he pushed two fingers just inside of her, to the second knuckle, and ran his tongue through her honeyed goodness in search of her clit.

Catherine did not disappoint. As he pumped his fingers in and out of her with shallow thrusts timed with his tongue flicking over her clit, she whimpered and moaned with abandon. Jayden teased her slick flesh, alternating the tiny laps of his tongue with the gentle grazing of his teeth until he could sense she was on the edge.

Easing his coated fingers from her pussy, Jayden trailed them back toward her waiting rosebud. He kept licking and teasing her clit and pushed one finger into her backside, working up to getting two fingers inside of her . . . stretching her, preparing her for what was coming.

Her moans turned into a high pitched keening interlaced with heavy pants while her orgasm built within, surging towards a crescendo that Jayden knew was going to be epic.

Once both fingers were seated in her, he took his mouth away. Pumping his fingers in and out, the Dom commanded her. "Let it go, Catherine. Squirt for your Master and quench my thirst."

Jayden opened his mouth, hovering above her pussy waiting for the rush of hot liquid that spurted out of her in pulses moments later. He drank down all she gave him like a parched man in the desert who has found an oasis. Reveling in the flavor of the tangy elixir, his cock awoke again.

When she was done, he slipped his fingers from her ass then grinned up at her. "Mm, thank you, Catherine. That was delicious, pet." He stood and went to retrieve a bottle of water from the small refrigerator. Jayden opened it and took a few swallows, then brought it to her lips, encouraging her to drink. He'd also grabbed a clean cloth, which he now poured a little water into before swiping it across her forehead and across the back of her neck. "How are you doing, sweet girl?"

Her body shuddered, an aftershock rocking it. "Your girl is so fucking green, Master," she almost growled at him.

"You would like to continue, then?" Under normal circumstances, he would've been satisfied with her saying it once, but he needed to be sure without a shadow of a doubt that she was not feeling any negative side effects from what they had done thus far. "Our time has been amazing and satisfying for both of us. I will not be upset or disappointed if we need to stop now," he added.

"No, Sir, please don't stop yet. Your girl promises she is green and she would like to continue," Catherine reiterated with resolve.

Would she ever cease to amaze him? He didn't think she ever could.

"Very well, my pet." He set the water and cloth down, then moved his hands to her breasts. "I'm going to remove your piercings, Catherine. We know they have to come out soon anyway, and I'm sure your nipples are extra-sensitive at this point. I don't want to push you too much with our new toy tonight."

While Jayden worked the metal free, taking care to roll her nipples between his fingers once the piercings were out, Catherine closed her eyes and sighed. Knowing her fondness for bondage, he then retrieved the black silk rope he'd brought over earlier and showed it to her, quirking his eyebrow to silently ask if she wanted it.

She bit her lower lip and nodded enthusiastically, causing Jayden to laugh at the innocence of her gesture. "Always so eager to please, aren't you, my naughty girl?" He began looping the rope around her.

The bondage started with a loose loop around her neck, so the knot settled between her breasts with no chance of choking her. With practiced skill, he wove the rope around her. When he finished, her breasts were bound at the base, her beautiful belly was framed on the sides, and the rope was threaded between her legs where it would provide friction to her now extra-sensitive pussy, before wrapping down around each of her legs.

Jayden knelt down and retrieved the other two items he had waiting. "Before I blindfold you, Catherine, I want to show you the special impact toy I purchased for tonight." He showed her the flogger with its red leather-wrapped handle. Plenty of black leather tassels bloomed out from the handle, each one tipped with a red satin rose bud.

"Oh, Master." She gulped in a deep breath. "It's beautiful, but . . . yellow."

"But what, Catherine? Please tell me what concerns you."

"The babies, Master. Because of the babies your girl is unsure about the use of a flogger at this time," she explained.

"Oh, my precious pet. Do you think I would do anything to hurt them?"

She shook her head.

"Trust, Catherine. It is crucial in this aspect of our relationship, remember?"

Nodding, she answered, "Aye, Master. Your girl just wanted to be sure."

"Good girl. Just to ease your mind, I do not plan on striking your stomach area. Your thighs and your breasts will be my playground."

"Thank you, Master."

"Now, close your eyes for me, pet. I am taking away your sight so that you may feel."

She did as instructed, and he wrapped the black satin sash around her eyes, placing a kiss upon her lips when he tied it off. Settling his grip on the handle, he swatted the flogger against his own thighs a couple of times to get a feel for how it landed and to let her hear it.

Then he started low on her calves. Jayden let her get used to the sensation before he moved up to her thighs, working them until the skin that peeked out between the cords of rope turned a rosy pink. A light sheen of sweat had broken out on Jayden, and his cock was leaking. He had missed this.

Taunting, he dragged the rosebuds over the swell of her stomach, letting them tickle her. Jayden continued the light teasing over her breasts and nipples before pulling his arm back to work them over like he'd done her thighs. He used controlled swings, each one landing exactly where he wanted it to, with just the right amount of force.

After about fifteen lashes, Jayden stopped to assess her skin. Catherine's nipples could have cut glass they'd gotten so hard, and her breasts matched her thighs with their rosy hue. Her lips were parted while she breathed in heavy pants, and Jayden was done with the flogging and ready to move on.

Wrapping his thumb and forefingers around each of her nipples, he pinched and rolled them while he spoke to her. "Did you enjoy that, Catherine?"

"Very much, Master. Your girl had forgotten how good you were at bringing her body to life. Thank you."

"Thank you for being so perfect for me, my jewel. Are we still green? Can you handle more?"

"Aye, Master."

"That's my girl," he whispered against her mouth and moved to release her from the cuffs after taking off her blindfold. He massaged her wrists where the cuffs had rubbed, easing the ache from them. "Are you ready to get off of your feet now?"

She nodded, still blinking while her eyes adjusted. Jayden took her hand and led her to the corner of the playroom he'd kept in the dark until he was ready to reveal the other surprise he'd purchased. Keeping the light for the area off for the moment, he guided her onto the tantric chair. Though Catherine was on her back, because of the chair's contours she was not flat, and therefore pressure was alleviated.

The Dom retrieved another of the velvety roses and an egg vibrator. In the dark, he teased her with the rose, similar to how he had upstairs at the dinner table, only this time he let the petals caress *all* of her.

Catherine's cheeks, her shoulders, breasts and nipples, and then down her arms—he spared no part of her. When he swirled it over her belly, one the babies kicked, making the rose bounce up off her stomach. She let out a soft giggle that he could never reprimand her for.

Jayden even lavished the skin of her legs with the rose, ensuring he had covered every exposed inch of her. Knowing she would still be dripping, he pushed the egg into her with no warning, earning a throaty moan from her at the intrusion. He switched it on low and set to work, starting with turning a low light on above her.

Catherine emitted the sweetest whimper of alarm when he pulled the straps up around her, making sure she was secure before activating the pulley system. At first her mouth popped open in a surprised O, but it then she got a hungry look on her face when she realized she'd been mounted into a swing.

At Dr. Ellison's suggestion, Jayden had gotten one with additional support straps, testing it for weight by hopping into it himself when he first rigged it up. At seven months pregnant, his jewel still weighed less than he did. If the swing could hold him, then it would hold her.

Once he'd elevated her, Jayden nudged the tantric chair to the side and gave the swing a gentle push, allowing her to adjust to the floaty swaying sensation for a minute before wrapping his hands under her thighs and guiding her back to him. With the vibrator humming away inside her pussy, Jayden lined his cock up with her asshole and began inching his way inside her tight passage. Lube was not an issue due to the copious amount of her juices dripping out of her and running down her crack—they had plenty of natural lubrication.

If there was a part of their playtime that they both always enjoyed more than anything, it was anal sex. Tonight was no different. As he pushed and pulled her body with the aid of the swing, the room filled with the sounds of their low curses, rough grunts, and heavy panting.

"Please, Master." The longing seeped out with her pleading and ignited things inside him—dark, lustful things.

"Please what, Catherine? Tell me what you need." He snarled and pushed into her again, just to lose the feeling of the warm constriction when the momentum of the swing slid her back off of his cock. Again, he buried into her.

"Please may your girl come, Sir . . . please!" she cried out while her legs began to shake in his hold.

It was too much, and as Jayden's balls drew up tight, his lower belly started tingling with his approaching release. He held off answering her for two more passes up and down his cock before he granted permission.

"Come with me. Now, Catherine."

For the second time that night, she erupted in a fountain of hot spray, that time coating his torso while he emptied everything he had deep within her backside.

When he could stand up straight and breathe in a normal fashion again, he extracted his softened cock from her depths, then lowered her back down. Using a tender touch, he removed the egg and got her out of the swing. With extreme care, Jayden took to unwrapping the rope from her limbs, but he became annoyed with himself when he saw the deep impressions left on her waterlogged skin.

He needed to get her circulation moving again, so he had her get back on the tantric chair while he ran to the supply cupboard for some massage oil. Taking his time, he started at her feet and worked up the front of her body. When her front side was done, he then guided her onto first her right side, then her left, so he could get her back. By the time he had massaged all of her, his jewel had dozed off.

Jayden hated to wake her, but he couldn't leave her there. "Catherine," he murmured and gave her a sympathetic shake. It took saying her name three times before her green eyes blinked open and she yawned while glancing around.

"Mm . . . It wasn't a dream." A lazy smile matched her words, bringing a chuckle from Jayden while he offered her his hand.

"No, sweet girl, it was not. Let's get you washed and into bed. You've certainly earned a good rest." He sighed deep, knowing their scene had ended and it would be months again before they could return to this room. But he knew that when they did return, their parental status would be behind the delay, and that made it alright.

Sliding his hands behind her neck, Jayden freed the clasp on her collar. "Your servitude has been surreal, Catherine."

She looked at him with grateful appreciation. "To serve you has been divine, Master."

Jayden slipped the leather from her neck, laying it on the chair. He would come back and clean up tomorrow—Erin was his priority now.

ೞಀಀ
CHAPTER FIFTY
ೞಀಀ

A puddle of goo.

Shaking. Weak all over. *Completely* satiated.

Erin's lower back ached while Jayden walked her upstairs toward their bedroom and the shower. After the two intense orgasms he'd drawn from her, factored with the time on her feet at the Cross, she wasn't surprised, but no way would she dream of complaining. Erin didn't want her husband regretting any of what they'd just shared.

The hot water felt incredible. His hands were pure heaven while he soaped her body with his loving caress. She started to turn and wrap her arms around him for a little shower snuggle, when a sharp pain shot through her belly and she winced, hunching over.

"Erin?" Concern laced his voice.

"It's nothing, baby. I think I just turned too sharp, too fast." Erin brushed it off as the pain receded.

They soon finished, and he helped her out. Erin stood there, sleepy and still a little delirious from their scene, while he tried to dry her off. He kept wiping at her legs and between her thighs, and she began thinking he was trying to get frisky, wanting another go.

"Jayden," she laughed, "what are you doing? I don't think I can handle any more right now." The smile on her face disappeared when she looked down and took in his grave countenance while he swiped the towel between her legs again. "Jayden?"

"Erin, I can't get your legs dry. I think you might still be coming?"

"Huh? What do you mean? Is the towel too wet to dry me off?" She *knew* she wasn't coming.

"I don't think that's it, sweet girl. You just experienced two orgasms that would've been major for a non-pregnant woman. I think your body is still producing fluids." Again, his uncertainty was clear.

In that moment, another sharp pain gripped Erin, causing her stomach to tighten and her lower back to feel like it was being pinched. She sucked in a breath, then let it out slow for a count of five, exhaling through her open mouth. Sensing her discomfort, Jayden spoke to Erin with a calm resonance while he convinced her to try going to bed.

"Maybe it's just Braxton Hicks. Holly did warn us about those. Let's go lie down for a while and see if things settle down."

She swooned, feeling the extent of his love, while Jayden dressed her in a soft cotton nightgown, then pulled back the covers for her to crawl into bed. Erin got settled on her left side and managed to doze lightly over the next several hours. However, as the time went on, the pains got sharper—and stronger.

Erin gave up on sleep eventually, in particular as her need to pee grew. Nudging Jayden awake so he could help her, she got into an upright position. When the cool air of the room hit her warm body, her nightgown clung to her, cold. They both looked down at the same time to see that Erin was soaked.

"Did I pee the bed?"

He looked from her, to the bed, and back again before his eyes widened. "Erin, I don't think you peed the bed, and I don't think you're having false contractions . . . I think it's time."

♋

"Oh, good god fucking shit!" Erin screamed when the sharp pain tore through her back and wrapped around her enormous belly. How her stomach could tighten harder than a rock while the latest contraction held her in its grip was still confounding her. It wasn't natural.

Erin had been at this for about six hours by then, and she was past ready to be done. The contractions had been sporadic but were getting more intense with each hour that passed since Jayden had driven her to the hospital in the early hours of Saturday morning.

In mad man fashion, of course—it seemed a rite of passage for new dads to get to make the maniacal drive. He'd been lucky she'd been too busy writhing in pain to smack him.

Minutes after they'd arrived, Erin had been set up in an observation room to determine if she was in labor for real, since her due date was still almost two months away. When all indications pointed to yes, Dr. Ellison had been called, and now they were waiting on her arrival.

As the pain subsided, Jayden stepped away to pick up his worn copy of *What to Expect When You're Expecting* and started reading the chapter on labor and delivery—yet again—out loud. His dedication to learning all things 'pregnancy' had been endearing, but right then Erin wanted him to hold her hand and feed her ice chips. She was fucking thirsty, and the hospital sadists weren't letting her gulp down anything.

Erin was also coming to the conclusion that she would be removing a part of her husband's anatomy with her bare hands before this ordeal ended. For her to accomplish that, he needed to be within reach.

Once again, her belly started to tighten seconds before the agonizing heat ripped through her.

"Jayden, put that damn book down and get the fuck over here, right the fuck now!" she hissed between rapid breaths through clenched teeth.

He dropped the book and was at her side in an instant, brushing her sweaty hair back from her forehead. Common sense told the frantic woman that he was trying to appear calm and controlled, but his eyes revealed the truth. He was just as panicked as she was.

"It's too soon," Erin began crying into Jayden's shoulder. "I'm supposed to have another two months. Something's wrong, Jayden. I'm scared—" Another wave of pain jolted her, and she bit down on his shoulder . . . hard.

He yelped and pushed her off. "It's okay, sweet girl. Dr. Ellison said this could happen, remember?" His eyes were pleading with her to calm down.

Erin could see the reason in it, she really could. But how was a woman supposed to remain calm when it felt like her body was being ripped open a little bit at a time? She was mid-curse into the next contraction when the door to the room opened and Dr. Ellison strolled in, looking like she was out for a walk in the park.

"Hey kids! How are we doing? Ready to do this?" The delight in her tone sickened Erin—*bitch was too chipper.*

Holly needed to be stabbed.

With a dull spoon.

"Um, well, we are a little concerned that it's a bit early," hedged Jayden.

Erin screamed through another contraction.

"And Erin is experiencing a tad bit of discomfort," he added.

"A tad bit? A tad fucking bit, Jayden! Ya think?" she shrieked in his direction. Dr. Ellison had a cheesy grin on her face while she watched them, amused by their exchange. *Maybe that spoon would work on her eyes, too.*

"Ah, come on, Erin, I thought you were into pain?" teased Dr. Ellison. "This should be a piece of cake for you. Hell, you might even enjoy it if you relax." Holly laughed and slapped her hand against her thigh.

Lovely, I've got a fucking comedian for a doctor.

Jayden, always able to read her, must have sensed that Holly was walking a fine line with Erin's nerves. "So, Dr. Ellison, is it going to be okay to let the labor continue?"

Bless him for trying to redirect the good doctor back on topic.

She squeezed his hand, hoping her momentary gratitude showed. Perhaps she'd gripped a little harder than she should have, given that he extracted his hand from hers and rubbed it.

At least Holly took the hint and got serious for a moment. "Alrighty, you two, here's the deal. We've been monitoring Erin's health closely, as you know. The babies are doing great according to the ultrasound and monitors, and they are looking to be about five pounds each right now. I dare say it's going to be easier to let them go ahead and make their appearances sooner rather than later. They're already larger than normal for twins at seven and a half month's gestation. Frankly, I don't think Erin's tiny frame can handle them going to full term, so this could be a blessing in disguise." She beamed at them.

Jayden and Erin sighed with relief at the same time.

"But . . ." Holly continued.

Oh, of course there's a 'but'. Erin might have growled, she wasn't sure. *It had been awhile since she'd played Domme. Maybe Holly would like to be her sub?* The image of the doctor under Erin's flogger made her giggle, and Jayden stroked her head.

"The pediatric team is on standby and will be in the room during the delivery, ready to act if there are any problems. Understand that there is a high probability the babies will have to stay here for a week or two before you'll be able to take them home. A precautionary measure, of course."

Erin was taking a deep breath while she neared the end of her latest contraction.

"Ready for the good news?" Dr. Ellison paused, like she was waiting for them to get excited.

Not happening right now, bitch.

"Their size is manageable enough that unless their heart rates drop and we have to do an emergency C-section, you should have no trouble delivering these two by the end of the night, tomorrow morning at the latest . . . naturally!" Dr. Ellison clapped her hands, and one would've thought she'd just told them they were going to Disney World.

Oh. Fucking. Joy.

I get to push a watermelon out of my hooha . . . twice.

Yipp-fucking-ee.

R.E. Hargrave

𝕊𝕆𝕔𝕊
CHAPTER FIFTY-ONE
𝕊𝕆𝕔𝕣

*T*welve hours later . . .

Erin was past all points of modesty or decorum. She had given over to begging for drugs. Her new alter-ego had ripped a fresh, new asshole out of every person who had come into her room, and Jayden was covering his crotch at every opportunity.

Smart move, asshole. I will be taking your cock if you ever try to come near me with it again!

Thirty-six hours into labor . . .

Erin was on her back, her legs spread wide by the stirrups while Dr. Ellison sat between them on her little rolling swivel stool. Jayden had his arm around Erin's upper back, helping her roll forward so she could push—and push some more. Members of the NICU staff were standing off to the side with two bassinets, waiting to get to work.

"Give us one more good one, Erin. You're doing beautiful, kiddo! The head is almost through, and once we get this one out, the next one will be a breeze!" While Dr. Ellison's routine was appreciated, sort of, it was no longer working. Erin was beyond exhausted and had no idea how she was going to finish this.

"I can't! I just can't anymore." The woman sobbed into her husband's chest, wanting to quit, to be done with it all. She hurt everywhere, felt slimy and gross, and was so very tired.

"Yes, you can, Catherine," Jayden whispered into her ear suddenly. "You can, and you will," he continued, his tone low and calm. "It's almost here . .

. come on, Catherine, show me our baby," her Dom commanded, and just like that, a mental switch was thrown.

Catherine *had* to serve her Master. She had to do what he asked because servicing him was what she lived for. She took a deep breath and bore down, channeling all her focus into her laboring body. Searing pain unlike any she'd ever felt before shot through her, sending little colored dots skittering across her vision, but Catherine kept pushing.

"We have a gorgeous baby girl!" called Dr. Ellison, and Catherine exhaled, then burst into tears. "Daddy, would you like to cut the cord?"

She managed to lift her weary eyes up to his face and watched him nod, silent while he stared down at the wiggling bundle in the doctor's hands.

"Well, get over here. We've only got a minute or two before Baby B will be ready."

His lips pressed against hers all at once, and then they were gone while he hurried to join the doctor between her legs.

The tears free-flowed down the new mother's cheeks at the sounds of tiny squeals and cries. She hadn't seen her daughter yet, but Erin knew she would be beautiful and perfect. Baby A was whisked away for her APGAR assessment, and Jayden made it back to Catherine's side as the next excruciating contraction overtook her. Falling limp into his arms, Erin shook her head. "Please, just get it out," she whimpered, the exhaustion catching up to her.

"Catherine."

Her reply was automatic. "Aye, Master?"

"I know you're ready to crash, jewel. We just need a little more from you. *I* need you to do this."

With a slow nod, the laboring woman willed herself to curl forward. Pain ripped through her abdomen, and she lapsed into a series of heavy pants and exhalations. *Oh, god. Did I just poop on Holly?*

"*Cailin maith.*" His hot breath whispered across her neck, distracting her, and then his mouth was on hers, breathing new life—new energy—into Catherine. When he pulled back, his eyes were dark and shiny. "You *can* do this."

Catherine locked onto his stare . . . and pushed.

"There ya go, Erin!" Dr. Ellison cheered the patient on while the pressure built to an almost intolerable level, then released on a wave of searing hot pain seconds before everything went numb.

"And we have another baby girl!"

With an exaggerated sigh, Erin started laughing. "We did it!"

Jayden stroked her cheek, "Yes, sweet girl, you did. You are so very amazing." Wetness collected in the brim of his eyes.

"Are you two lovebirds ready to meet your daughters?" Holly's voice was muffled while she snipped the second cord, then cleaned and sutured Erin.

Our daughters. We did this together. No other thought mattered.

While he wiped her forehead with a cool cloth and helped her get some water, the nurses cleaned up the babies then brought them over to the bed. Jayden rested his hip against Erin's when Baby A was placed in his arms and Baby B was placed in hers. The teeny thing immediately started rooting against her chest and she tugged down her gown, thankful that she'd been there when Natalie's lactation specialist had shown her what to do after Matthew was born. Little B latched onto her nipple and started sucking like a champ.

Amused, Erin could tell Jayden was torn between watching Little B nurse and looking down at the bundle in his own arms. His attention was demanded by the little female when a tiny squawk came from the blanket.

He laughed softly. "I think this one's hungry, too. Are you up to serving more than one, sweet girl?" he asked with a tenderness that made her tear up again.

Stupid hormones. "Can you help me?"

"Of course," her husband replied and walked around the bed to the opposite side. He slipped the other side of her gown down, then helped angle their daughter in against Erin's chest. Jayden perched himself on the bed again so that he could support the babe's head while she found the nipple and latched on.

The sensation from both of them nursing in tandem was hypnotic. The new mother was at peace while she looked down at the tiny red faces of her children.

Once the placentas were delivered, Dr. Ellison finished up between Erin's legs and pulled her gloves off. "You did fantastic, kiddo. Not only with the delivery, but with the cooking of those two. I can't remember the last time I saw such pretty babies," she said with sincerity. "Do you have names picked out?"

"Yeah, some of us have been wondering the same thing." Woody came into the room with Matthew planted on his hip and Jillian at his heel, and in spite of her delirium, Erin felt her energy renew. A huge smile broke out on her face. Paige must've called them after she and Jayden had rushed out of the house all those hours ago. How fortunate that she and Sir Landon had been on hand to keep Matthew while they went to the hospital.

"Hi, Da, Jillian. Come meet your granddaughters."

"About time you enlighten an old man. And did you say granddaughters? Two girls, then?"

Erin looked up at Jayden to find a proud smile transforming his face. They'd been waiting for this chance. He reached over and stroked the top of each of their daughters' heads in turn.

As their hair dried, the baby on her right was proving to have dark brown. The miniscule girl blinked her eyes open, and they were a dark blue.

Dr. Ellison leaned over for a gander before looking at each of Erin and Jayden's faces. "Eyes like that usually end up green," she commented with a wink at the Irish lass.

The baby on Erin's left had blue-brown eyes, however, and a crazy shock of red hair on top of her head. With a nod to Jayden, Erin let him know it was his call to make. They had picked four names in preparation of this—two boys and two girls.

His fingertip caressed the cheek of their redheaded baby. "I think this little beauty is Brianna Eilene Masterson," he said before bestowing the same loving gesture on their brown-headed baby. "And this lovely lady is Bryce Jillian Masterson."

Erin piped up, "Brie and Jill for short."

Dr. Ellison smiled. "I love them, great choices. Good work, kids, both of you. Alas, I need to get out of here and get your chart written up. The nurse will be in and out to check on you, but don't hesitate to use the call button if you need anything."

As she turned to leave, Erin called out to her: "Dr. Ellison . . ."

Holly looked back. "Yes, dear?"

"Thank you . . . for everything. We couldn't have had this moment without you."

She smiled, her eyes lighting up. "It's been a delight, Erin."

Jayden snuggled deeper into her side. Somehow, they all fit on the twin-sized hospital bed—their happy family. Matthew had his head on Woody's chest, a quiet awe in his expression while he sucked on his fingers and stared down at Erin and the suckling babes.

Heads touching, Jayden and Erin looked down at their beautiful little girls. Brianna and Bryce were the unsubstantiated proof that they could live a balanced life—one with vanilla *and* kink. Conceived when Jayden and Erin gave their love freely to one another, but born because he'd had the strength to be her

Master and call forth Erin's submission when she needed it. These children were their future.

She gave him a tired but content smile while the babes nursed and whispered, "Divine."

Knowing just what his jewel would always need, his calming, warm breath teased Erin's earlobe when he whispered into it, "Surreal."

೮೦೧೮

FIN

೮೦೧೪

Thank you for reading. If you enjoyed this book, the best compliment you can pay the author is to leave a spoiler free review on Amazon or tell a friend about it!

Now an excerpt from
a future companion novella to
The Divine Trilogy for the Micah Sanders' story

ଷଧଔ
Divine Salvation
ଷଧଔ

About a week passed after Micah's forced performance before Chase came to him again. It had been several days of pure hell for the confused teen. *Why had he enjoyed the way they'd treated him? How had it been possible for him to masturbate like that? Were any of them going to tell Mr. Salazar?*

The questions raced through his mind on repeat, sometimes shifting slightly, but all coming down to one bottom line. Micah was gay, and there was . . . *something* he needed, though he could not quite put his finger on what it was.

When Chase found Micah again, it was in the library—or what passed for the library at the home.

It was a small room, about eight by ten feet, with three mismatched assemble-at-home book cases, a round table with two chairs, and a loveseat. The loveseat had seen better days and sagged deeply in the middle.

When the doorknob turned, Micah hurried to shove the book he'd been reading under his butt. He'd just calmed himself and hoped he appeared normal, when Chase crossed over the threshold, closing the door behind him and locking it. Micah gulped.

"H-hello, Chase. Can I help you with something?" As much as he hated it, Micah's heart was pounding, trying to escape its physical confines knowing he was trapped in there with the older boy. For the first time, Chase said nothing, just stared Micah down. So Micah did the same, taking in what a physically appealing person Chase was, he found his body reacting.

Chase Hamilton had come to the home at the age of eight after being taken away from his parents. Micah never learned why. He'd been bigger than the other kids, even back then. Now, Chase stood just under six feet and had a shoulder span of about two. Tall and broad, shadowy stubble indicative of inky hair, piercing green eyes, and exotic dark skin, Chase caused Micah's pulse to race.

"Show me the book."

Spoken just above a whisper, the words oozed with authority, and Micah felt compelled to obey them. Sliding his hand beneath him, he found the tattered book and withdrew it to proffer to Chase.

Chase moved forward without a sound, eyes fixed on Micah. Without breaking their gaze, he reached down and took the book from Micah's outstretched hand. Not until the last second did he look away, to glance at the cover for a moment before tossing it down and looking back to Micah.

"Why do you read those?"

"They're exciting," Micah answered with honesty.

"How?"

Bewildered, the teen tipped his head to the side. "Have you not read a story that sucks you in and makes you forget about the troubles around you? Gives you a chance to be someone else, somewhere else?"

"My reading's not so good. I don't do it unless I hafta."

"Oh."

What could Micah say to that? He wasn't going to laugh at Chase, for there was nothing funny about illiteracy. A damn shame is what it was. Had Chase been adopted and cared about, somebody would've noticed his problem early on and helped him with it. An idea came to him.

"I could help you."

Chase's head snapped Micah's direction, and his cherry red lips parted to say something, but he stopped. "Why would you do that? I've been mean to you for years, and then, well, the other day—"

"Was exciting," blurted Micah before slapping his hand over his mouth in shock. He had no clue what had prompted him to reveal that bit of information.

Those red lips parted again, and Chase's tongue snuck out to lick them. "Why? Weren't you afraid?"

Ever so slowly, Micah nodded his head. "That was part of the excitement, though. And I want to help because I don't blame you ... for being, you know, the way you are. We're all stuck in this shit together."

At that, Chase laughed, the tension in his shoulders relaxing while he took a seat next to Micah on the loveseat. "Yeah, not like we got much of a choice in the matter, did we?"

Chase wasn't such a bad guy away from the others. Micah leaned over and nudged him with his shoulder. "Want to start now?"

"You're serious?"

Micah freed his lanky form from the couch by rocking forward and falling onto the floor. On his hands and knees, he retrieved the book. When he turned around, he found Chase staring at him again.

"Do you like dick?"

That caught Micah off guard. "Um, honestly?" he hedged, and Chase nodded. "I don't know for sure, but I think so."

"Oh." Chase's eyes darted to the book in Micah's lap.

Micah gulped, not believing he was about to ask the same. "Do you?"

"What? No! I'm not some freaky fag . . ." Chase trailed off at the pointed look Micah was blasting at him.

"I'm . . . I'm sorry, man. Truth is, like you, I don't know. Spent too many years having to shower amongst swinging dicks. I don't fucking know!" He threw his body against the back the couch, and it squealed as the legs dragged over the wood floor from the force.

"What about the girls I always see you talking to at school?"

"They always shoot me down. Nobody wants to date the orphan."

Micah felt a spot inside him softening for Chase. "Wow."

"Yeah, anyways. I don't wanna talk about it anymore. Tell me what that book's about. What kind of title is *Enslaved at Sunset*?"

Feeling his cheeks warm, Micah felt shy all of a sudden. "Um, well, maybe I could read a bit of it to you?" At Chase's nod, Micah wet his lips, then cleared his throat to begin after opening to a random page.

The gilded sheik stood from his jeweled throne and moved to stand next to her trembling husband. While the ropes dug into her skin, scratching her naked bosom, Sarah watched on with horrified fascination as the foreigner adjusted the fasteners on his billowing pants to reveal a long, limp penis. The tip looked nothing like her Henry's phallus, not until the sheik took himself in hand and began stroking it. To her amazement, as he thickened, he also lengthened, and the loose skin at the end stretched tight to reveal a glorious, bulbous head—

Chase started coughing, choking in shock. "Jesus, Micah! That's exciting to you, and you aren't sure if you like dick or not? I'd say it's pretty fucking clear you do."

Feeling berated by Chase's reaction made something inside Micah 'switch.' A sudden desire to make amends, to correct his discretion and earn Chase's approval came over him. He dropped his eyes to the floor and mumbled an apology before getting up from the floor. Micah had just reached the door when Chase called to him.

"You want to suck my dick, don't you?"

He froze with his hand on the knob, shame and arousal flaring to life within him at the same time. Why did this have to be so hard? He'd tried to be nice, but Chase was still making fun of him, teasing Micah for his own selfish gratification. Finding an inner strength, he decided to call Chase on his offer to scare a lesson into him.

Turning, Micah fixed a heated glare on Chase. "What if I do?" His heart managed to thump several times while he held his breath, awaiting the other teen's reaction. He wasn't prepared for what came, and it took him a moment to jump into action, but once he did, he didn't look back.

"Then I'd say get back on your knees and get my dick in your mouth, little boy."

ಐಯ

ಐ‍ಐ

About the Author

R.E. Hargrave is a fledgling author who has always been a lover of books and now looks forward to the chance to give something back to the literary community. She lives on the outskirts of Dallas, TX with her husband and three children.

ଞ୨ୠ

ଞ୨ୠ

Her works:

Sugar & Spice, a novella
Haunted Raine, a novella
Unchained Melody, a novella
The Food Critic, a novella
To Serve is Divine, Book 1 in The Divine Trilogy
A Divine Life, Book 2 in The Divine Trilogy
Surreal, Book 3 in The Divine Trilogy

www.rehargrave.com

Surreal

Made in the USA
Lexington, KY
24 January 2018